# Drifted

Renton Wolfe

# DEDICATION

To my family, filled with the strongest people I know—your support, love, and resilience have been my constant source of strength. This book is as much yours as it is mine. Thank you for always believing in me.

# CONTENTS

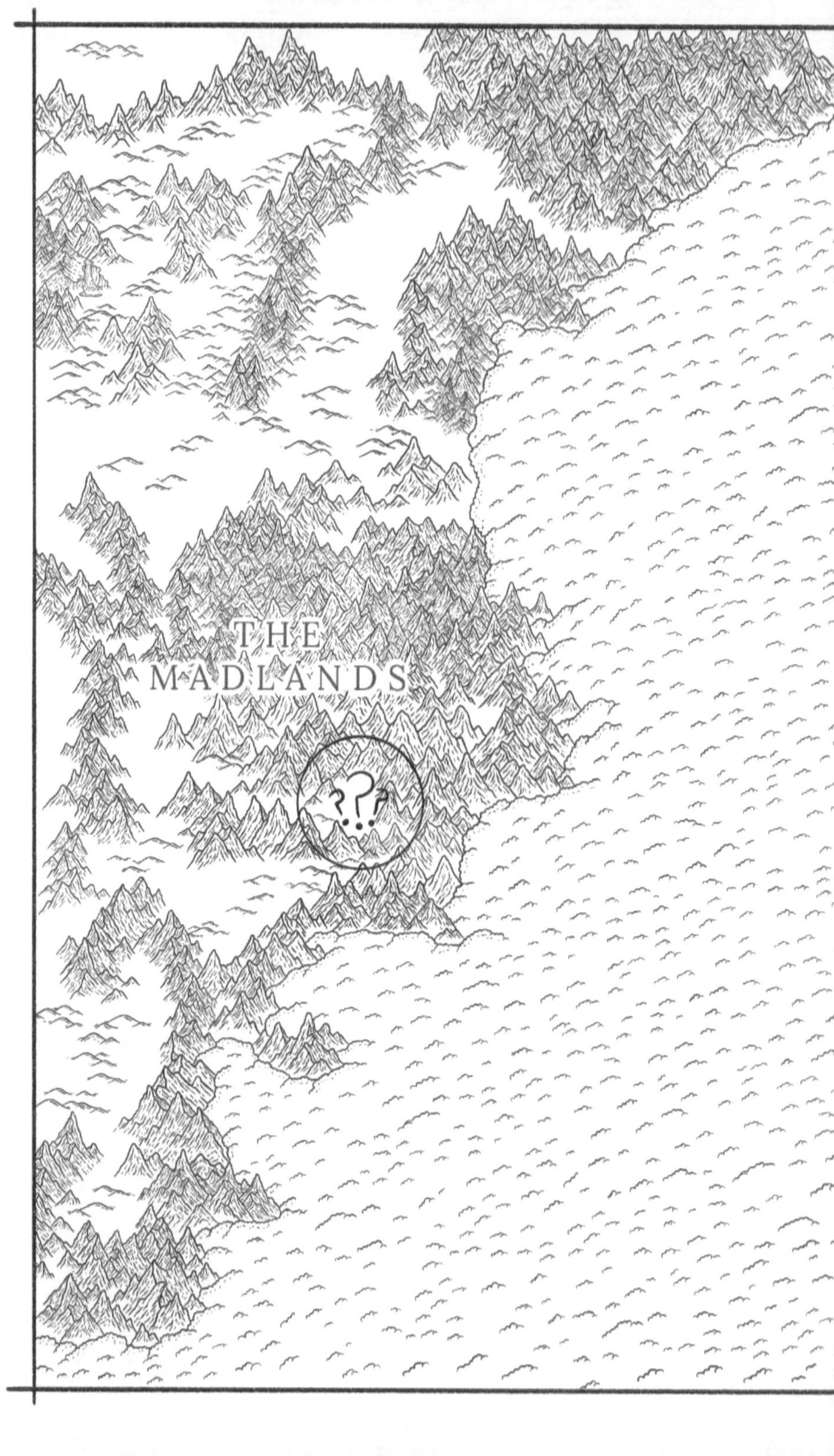

THE
MADLANDS

N
W    E
S
Nyxaris
Eclipsia
SELUNARIS
Noctiluna
Crescentia
Lunaria
MOONVEIL

CHAPTER 1

I jolted awake to the sound of loud, insistent banging on the door, each knock thumping against the inside of my skull. My eyes blinked open, cloudy and unfocused, as I groggily sat up, rubbing the sleep from my face. The surrounding room was dim, the early morning light barely filtering through the cracks in the wooden window coverings.

"I know you're in there, Isaac!" came the muffled voice from the other side of the door. "You're going to be late for class again!"

I groaned inwardly. It was my aunt, Silvia. She had a knack for showing up at the most inconvenient times, like when I was in the middle of trying to sleep. I really wish my parents hadn't given her a key before their passing.

"Isaac Thurston, get up this instant! Don't make me come in there!"

With a sigh, I swung my legs over the side of the bed and stood up, the wooden floor cold against my feet. My aunt wasn't someone you could easily ignore. She had a way of making sure you did exactly what she wanted, whether you liked it or not.

"I'm up, I'm up," I muttered, though I doubted she could hear me. I shuffled to the door and opened it a crack, peering out to see her standing there, hands on her hips, a stern look on her face.

She was a tiny woman, but she made up for her size with a commanding attitude. Her graying hair was pulled back into a tight bun, and her sharp eyes, the same shade of brown as my mother's, narrowed as they took in my disheveled appearance.

"You're going to be late again," she said, waving her finger in my face. "And don't you dare think about skipping. This class is important!"

"Yeah, yeah," I replied, trying to keep the annoyance out of my voice. "I'll be there."

She gave me a long, scrutinizing look before nodding. "Good. And don't forget you're coming to my house after class. We have things to discuss."

Before I could protest, she turned and walked away, leaving me still half-asleep and unsure of what had just happened.

"Things to discuss," I repeated under my breath, already dreading whatever conversation awaited me later. I wasn't in the mood for any serious discussions.

I glanced around my tiny room, trying to shake off the last remnants of sleep. The walls were lined with old books and trinkets my father had collected over the years, mementos of a quieter, simpler time when my biggest worry was our next trip.

After changing into fresh clothes, I reached for the gear that had been with me for as long as I could remember. First, I buckled on my sword belt, the worn leather familiar and comforting against my waist. Then, I strapped the shield to my back—a sturdy, reliable thing that had seen its share of practice but still held firm.

Lastly, my hand hovered over the sword, the one my father had left me. Its hilt was well-worn from years of use, the leather grip fitting perfectly in my hand like it had been made for me alone. The blade itself, though simple, gleamed with a faint, silvery shine in the dim light. It wasn't just a weapon; it was a reminder of everything he had taught me, of every lesson and expectation that now weighed on my shoulders.

With the sword secured at my side, I took one last glance around my room. It had been weeks since I'd attended an entire class, and I wasn't planning on starting now.

As I stepped outside, the crisp morning air hit me, waking me up the rest of the way. The town of Lunaria stretched out before me, bathed in the soft light of dawn. It was a small, ordinary place known more for its fertile fields and strong sense of community than anything else. The people here were close-knit, always looking out for one another, sometimes to the point of suffocation.

But even here, in this quiet town, there was an undercurrent of unease. The woods that surrounded Lunaria weren't as safe as they used to be, and whispers of fiends and strange occurrences had become more frequent with each passing year.

For as long as I could remember, we were strictly prohibited from venturing too far away from the town and the well-trodden paths surrounding it. Granted, the Kingsguard was rightfully concerned for the citizens. The woods weren't exactly the safest place to be. Fiends, and a lot of them started encroaching on the town. My father once told me that things haven't been this bad for a while, and apparently, it's been gradually getting worse since the day that I was born.

I made my way through the winding streets, dodging the early risers already out and about. The sights and sounds of the town greeted me: the distant clatter of a blacksmith's hammer, the smell of fresh bread wafting from the bakery, the chatter of townsfolk going about their morning routines. The streets were just starting to fill up with people, their voices blending into a low hum of activity.

"Happy birthday, Isaac!" a cheerful voice from a nearby fruit stand called out.

I turned, blinking in surprise. Mrs. Hargrove, the elderly woman who ran the stand, waved at me with a broad smile. Beside her, her husband nodded in agreement, his face lit up with a warm, albeit slightly toothless, grin.

"Uh, thanks," I said, giving them a distracted wave. My mind was still waking up, and the realization that today was my birthday had slipped my memory entirely.

As I continued down the street, birthday wishes seemed to follow me. It was as if the entire town had suddenly decided to remind me of the day. Children running past called out, "Happy birthday, Isaac!" and even the baker, who had just handed me a loaf of bread, gave me a wink as he told me to enjoy my special day.

"Yeah, I'll do that," I mumbled, feeling the warmth of embarrassment creeping up my neck. I hadn't planned on celebrating or even acknowledging my birthday, but it seemed the whole town had other ideas.

It wasn't hard to guess why everyone knew. My parents were practically legends in Lunaria. My father, a retired knight, a part of the Kingsguard, had a reputation that still carried weight. Then, my mother, a former guard nurse who tended to more wounded knights than I could count, was very well known. After leaving their old lives behind, they'd turned to trading, wandering from town to town with their wares. They were well-loved and respected, and people still spoke their names with admiration and fondness, even after their passing.

Trying to live up to my parents' image felt like a burden. While most kids grew up wanting to be just like their parents, I couldn't shake the feeling that I was just a shadow in their light. Maybe that's why I preferred the solitude of the woods, where it was just me and the trees, away from the eyes and expectations of the townsfolk.

I waved back at a group of old ladies who called out to me, their voices warm and recognizable. It wasn't that I didn't appreciate the kindness, but a part of me longed for the quiet and anonymity that the woods provided. Out there, I wasn't the son of Malikai and Alara. I was just Isaac.

I kept walking, the cheerful greetings fading behind me as I headed toward the town's edge. As I made my way toward the school, the crowd began to thin out, and the cobblestone streets were quieter now. The building loomed ahead, a modest structure made of stone and wood. Its purpose far removed from the swordplay my father drilled into me. Inside, they taught history, math, trading, and farming— the things that were supposed to prepare us for life in Lunaria. Lately, however, all that has felt distant and irrelevant as the world outside seems to grow more dangerous.

I paused at the school's gate, hand resting on the hilt of my sword. I knew I should go inside and sit through lessons about past wars, trade routes, and the intricacies of commerce. But none of that felt like it mattered.

My eyes drifted towards the town's eastern gate. It was just close enough that I could easily slip away and find a tree to hack at in the woods. I wanted to lose myself in the rhythm of training rather than the monotony of lessons.

I sighed deeply, realizing that Aunt Silvia would kill me if she found that I had skipped again. Begrudgingly, I made my way toward the school.

The building loomed ahead, a stone structure nestled in the heart of the town, filled with chatter and the unmistakable scent of parchment and ink. I stepped inside, greeted by a mixture of curious glances from the other students. They were already talking in their usual huddles, discussing yesterday's lecture on crops and market prices, or debating some minor town drama. I wasn't really listening.

I took my seat at the back of the room as Professor Rennard, the town's historian, cleared his throat at the front. His lessons always seemed to drag on, no matter the topic.

"We continue today with a brief history of our town's founding and its connection to the fiends that roam the woods,"

Rennard began, his voice a monotonous drone. He unfurled an old map, yellowed at the edges, and pointed at various locations with his pointer.

*This lesson again?* I thought to myself. Letting out a deep sigh as I lowered my head on my desk.

Professor Rennard continued, "As you know, Moonveil, the last bastion of human civilization, was founded by the first settlers who sought refuge from the fiends that terrorized the open plains. The dense forests surrounding us were both a barrier and a threat."

The lesson moved slowly, Rennard's voice blending with the murmur of bored students. "Fiends," he continued, "are an enigma, though many theorize that they are creatures born of the corruption in the land, first appearing long before our records. They were relentless, and it was through sheer will that the first settlers managed to carve out a town hidden beneath the moonlight."

I could feel my eyes glaze over. The others around me whispered between the pauses, trading notes and exchanging glances. It was the same lesson we had heard a hundred times before. Nothing ever changed in these stories—the fiends, the settlers, the old battles.

"The Dreadbeaks..." Rennard droned on, but I couldn't bother to listen anymore. Having heard the stories countless times before, I allowed his voice to fade into the background, a hum of words about the Kingsguard and their legendary defense against the creatures of the forest.

My fingers itched for a sword, for something more meaningful than sitting here listening to theories and old stories. I glanced out the window, where the woods called to me, the open air promising something more than just another dry lesson.

I let the professor's words flow through one ear and out the other, barely paying attention to the lecture. Soon enough, the first break in his lesson arrived, and he stepped out of the room.

The air in the room shifted. Students whispered amongst themselves, and others stretched, eager to leave their seats. A few kids walked over to me, trying to pull me into their conversation.

"Hey, Isaac, happy birthday!" one of them said with a grin.

"Yeah, hope it's a good one," another added, offering me a smile that I could barely muster a response to.

I forced a small, polite nod. "Thanks," I muttered, barely looking their way.

They kept talking and laughing among themselves, but I stayed silent, not really interested in their conversation. The words rolled over me, fading into the background. My mind was elsewhere—already halfway out of the classroom. This wasn't where I wanted to be.

When the chatter died down, and Professor Rennard still hadn't returned, I glanced around the room. It was the perfect chance to slip out. No one was paying much attention, and the woods were calling my name again, louder than ever.

But Aunt Silvia's stern voice echoed in my mind. *You'll regret it if you skip school again, Isaac. You know that, don't you?*

A cold shiver ran down my spine. Aunt Silvia finding out was a risk I wasn't sure I wanted to take. She'd be furious, maybe even worse than furious. She didn't tolerate me skipping school; if she found out, I knew there would be consequences. But... the woods, the training. The draw was too strong.

I glanced at the door and then at my classmates, who were still lost in their conversations. Professor Rennard wouldn't be back for at least a few more minutes.

I took a deep breath; the decision had already been made before I could convince myself otherwise. I quietly gathered my things, making sure not to draw attention to myself. My heart pounded as I slipped from my seat, careful not to make a sound.

The thought of Silvia finding out terrified me, but the urge to escape, to be out in the fresh air with a sword in my hand, outweighed the fear.

I was halfway to the eastern gate before I allowed myself a breath of relief.

Not too much longer, and I'd be gone.

I kept my pace steady, slipping through the streets. The gate came into view, the large wooden structure flanked by two guards. They were clad in armor, their expressions bored as they watched the world pass by. But as I approached, their eyes snapped to me, curious.

"Where're you headed, boy?" one of them asked, his tone gruff but not exactly unkind. He eyed the sword at my side, then glanced back up at me.

"Just going into the woods to practice," I replied, gesturing to the sword. I tried to keep my voice steady, though I couldn't help the slight edge of nervousness making its way through. The last thing I needed was trouble from the guards.

The guard raised an eyebrow and then chuckled. "Shouldn't you be in school, lad?"

Before I could answer, the second guard, older and with a few more scars than the first, clapped his comrade on the shoulder. "Leave the boy be. He's smart, this one. All that school mumbo jumbo is useless in the real world. At least he's spending his time doing something useful."

The first guard shrugged, seemingly convinced. "Alright, then. Just don't stray too far from the path."

I nodded, grateful that the conversation hadn't gone any further. With a small wave, I stepped past them, through the gate, and into the path that led toward the woods. The air grew cooler as I left the town behind, the trees ahead standing tall and silent, welcoming me back into their embrace.

The woods were quiet, save for the occasional rustle of leaves or the distant call of a bird. I followed a narrow trail, the path well-worn from years of my footsteps and traveling merchants alike. The scents of earth and pine filled the air, grounding me and pulling me deeper into my thoughts.

I walked until I found a tree that looked just right— a sturdy oak with a thick trunk, its bark rough and weathered. I drew my sword, feeling the hilt in my hand. This blade had been my father's once part of his life as a knight in the Kingsguard.

But even after he'd traded his armor for simpler clothes, he never abandoned the lessons of the sword. He'd drilled them into me with a quiet, relentless determination.

I wasn't sure why he was so insistent on it, why he'd made sure I could hold my own in a fight when we lived in a place where the biggest threat at the time seemed to be a bad harvest. But now, with each passing day and the growing unease around Lunaria, I was beginning to understand.

I adjusted my stance, gripping the hilt tightly, and swung the sword in a controlled arc. The blade cut through the air with a satisfying hiss before it struck the tree. The impact reverberated up my arm, but I maintained my balance, quickly following up with another strike and then another. Each swing came out exactly as my father had shown me.

I've never really admitted it to anyone, but I'm pretty good with a sword. Better than anyone in my age group, at least. It wasn't just the countless hours spent training with my father— it felt natural to me, like an extension of my body. I found a rhythm in the strikes, the movements coming almost instinctively.

As I continued, the bark of the tree began to chip away, revealing the pale wood beneath. My breath steadied, my mind focusing solely on the movement, precision, and power behind each swing.

Hours passed as I lost myself in the rhythm of practice. The sun had risen higher in the sky, its rays filtering through the canopy, casting shadows on the forest floor. My strikes became slower and more deliberate as fatigue began to set in. Finally, with one last swing, I drove my sword deep into the bark.

I leaned against the tree, sliding down to sit on the ground, the cool earth soothing against my back. The woods were peaceful, and for a moment, I closed my eyes, just listening to the sounds around me— the rustling of leaves, the distant chirp of insects. The training had taken its toll, but there was satisfaction in the ache of my muscles.

As I sat there, catching my breath, a sharp screech pierced the calm, echoing through the trees. My eyes snapped open, the sound unmistakable —Dreadbeaks.

I stood up quickly, straining my ears for any more noises, but the forest had fallen silent again. I knew what that sound meant— Dreadbeaks were fiends, vicious creatures. They weren't something to be taken lightly.

I froze as another screech echoed through the forest again. This time, it was slightly closer. My hand instinctively went to the hilt of my sword, tightening around the worn leather grip.

The underbrush rustled, and a group of guards appeared on the path nearby, jogging in formation. As they passed, one of the guards caught sight of me and slowed his pace, raising a hand to signal to the others.

"You there!" he called out. "It's not safe out here! Head back into town now!" His eyes flicked to the sword at my side, and his brow furrowed slightly. "Fiends have been spotted nearby. I'm sure you heard them."

"I will, thanks!" I replied with a nod.

With that, the guards continued their jog down the path, their figures quickly disappearing into the trees.

The logical part of me knew it was time to head back,

especially if fiends were prowling around. It wasn't wise to stick around and see how close they were. I wiped the sweat from my forehead and sheathed my sword. I enjoyed the time out here, away from the noise. But even I knew when it was time to go.

I remembered that Aunt Silvia wanted to speak about something important this morning. My class would have ended by now, and if I headed back to her house, I could pretend I'd been there the whole time. Silvia might be strict, but she shouldn't question me too hard if she thought I'd been doing what I was supposed to.

With one last look at the tree I'd been using for practice, I turned and began making my way back through the woods, keeping my ears open for any more sounds that might indicate I wasn't alone out here.

The walk back through the woods was quicker than I expected. The weight of the earlier encounter lingered in my mind, urging me to keep my pace brisk. I kept my eyes and ears open, but the forest had returned to its usual quiet. Still, I didn't let my guard down until I could see the rooftops of Lunaria through the trees.

The town's cobbled streets greeted me as I emerged from the woods. I could feel the tension in my shoulders easing slightly. It was late afternoon now, the sun begging to dip lower in the sky, casting a warm glow over the town. Most people were finishing up their work for the day, and the streets were a little quieter than they'd been earlier,

I made my way toward my aunt's house, which sat just next to mine. The small, cozy cottage had always been a second home to me. Aunt Silvia insisted on it, especially after my parents...well, after everything changed. Uncle Alfarr's sturdy figure was usually working outside, but today, the yard was empty. I figured he must be inside.

As I approached the front door, I took a deep breath. It was almost too quiet. Maybe I'd get away with this after all. My hand was on the doorknob when—

"Happy birthday!" The door swung open, and I was greeted by a chorus of voices.

I jumped, my heart skipping a beat. Inside, the small living room was decorated with colorful streamers, and a modest cake sat on the table, candles already lit. My aunt stood at the forefront, her stern face softened by a rare smile. Uncle Alfarr was behind her, grinning broadly, his thick arms crossed over his chest. And then there were the twins, Marcellus and Marciana, bouncing on their heels, clearly eager for cake.

"Come on in, Isaac! We've been waiting for you!" Aunt Silvia's voice was warm, but I could sense the underlying command. There was no way out of this.

I stepped inside, feeling the warmth of the room wrap around me, though my cheeks were red hot from embarrassment. "You... you really didn't have to do all this," I mumbled, rubbing the back of my neck.

"Nonsense!" Uncle Alfarr boomed, clapping a hand on my shoulder with enough force to nearly knock me over. "Seventeen's a big one! We couldn't let it pass by unnoticed."

"Yeah, Isaac! Blow out the candles!" Marcellus piped up, his twin sister echoing his words with equal enthusiasm.

Despite the awkwardness, there was something comforting about being here, surrounded by family. I'd never been one for celebrations, but I could see the effort they'd put into this.

With a resigned smile, I stepped up to the table. "Alright, alright," I said, leaning over the cake. "Thanks, everyone."

As I blew out the candles, the room erupted in cheers. I felt myself enjoying it, reminding myself to be grateful for the people who cared enough to make this day special.

As I stood there, trying to take in the moment, the twins

wasted no time descending on me. Marcellus and Marciana, both with identical mischievous grins, began their usual antics.

"Isaac! Bet you can't catch me!" Marcellus shouted, darting around the table, while Marciana tugged at my sleeve, pulling me towards the other side.

"No, no, no! You're supposed to chase me first!" Marciana protested, trying to drag me in the opposite direction.

I managed a half smile, trying to keep up with their energy. "I don't think I can chase either of you right now. How about we all just sit and eat?"

I turned to see Marcellus sniffing the air and wrinkling his nose. "Eww, you reek," he said, covering his nose with a dramatic gesture.

I blinked in surprise. "What?"

Before I could react, Marciana sidled up and took a deep sniff, mimicking her brother. "Eww, he's right," she confirmed, pulling a face. "You smell like you've been rolling around in the mud."

I laughed awkwardly, realizing my training session had left me sweaty. "I guess I got a bit carried away."

"Carried away? Carried away doing what, Isaac?" I looked up to see Aunt Silvia staring at me, her eyes narrowing as they met mine. "Isaac," she said, her tone suddenly more serious, "Did you really go to class this morning?"

I froze, realizing my mistake. "Uh... well... Of course I did."

"And you stayed the *whole* time? Right, Isaac?" Aunt Silvia replied.

"Is that so? Do you always have woodchips stuck in your hair after class?" Aunt Silvia asked as she ran her fingers through my hair, removing various-sized pieces of wood.

I'd been caught. I completely forgot to clean myself off before I walked in here. Caught, I fell silent.

"Ooh, he's in trouble!" I heard the twins mock simultaneously.

Aunt Silvia's eyebrow arched. "You know how important your education is. Life is not just about swinging swords and running through the woods!"

I swallowed, trying to come up with a convincing answer. "I... I meant to stay, but I got a headache. I thought I'd get some practice in to clear my mind."

Silvia sighed, crossing her arms. "Isaac, you can't just skip class whenever you feel like it. There are better things to do than sitting in the woods all day."

"Yeah," Alfarr chimed in, smirking. "Like arm wrestling. You could learn a thing or two from that. What do you say, Isaac? Fancy a round or two?"

I looked towards Uncle Alfarr, who was now flexing his arms and making a show of his muscles. "I think I'll pass, Uncle. I'm already worn out from training."

"Maybe if you spent less time swinging that paperweight around," he nodded toward my sword, "and more time working out, you might actually stand a chance of beating me one day."

I couldn't help but roll my eyes. "I think I'll just stick to the sword, Uncle."

"You'll have to face me sooner or later," Alfarr said, now curling the twins in his arms.

Aunt Silvia's eyes narrowed at me again, clearly unimpressed by my attempt to deflect the situation. "You're not off the hook for skipping, Isaac. We'll talk more about this later."

I nodded, feeling a mix of guilt and relief. Aunt Silvia wasn't one to let things slide easily, but I knew she wouldn't make a scene in front of everyone else. As she turned to adjust something, I finally had a chance to take in the spread she'd prepared.

The table was covered in an array of dishes, each more inviting than the last. Freshly baked bread still steaming from the oven, a platter of roasted vegetables, and a large pot of her famous stew. At the center of it all was a cake, simple but clearly made with care. It was decorated with what looked like freshly picked berries and a generous dusting of sugar.

"Sit down, Isaac," Aunt Silvia said, her voice softer now. "You should at least enjoy a proper meal before we discuss your little adventure today."

I nodded, moving toward the table, my stomach growling in response to the delicious smells. As I took my seat, Marcellus and Marciana immediately plopped down beside me, still buzzing with energy.

"Happy birthday, Isaac!" Marciana grinned, leaning on my shoulder. "Did you make a wish yet? I want cake!"

I smiled down at her, shaking my head. "Not yet."

"Well, could you hurry up?" Marcellus added, reaching for a piece of bread.

I watched as Aunt Silvia shot him a sharp look, and he quickly tried to backpedal. "Well, could you hurry up...please?" he added, trying his hardest to sound more polite, though the eagerness was still evident in his eyes.

I looked down at the cake, the candles flickering softly. Taking a moment, I closed my eyes and tried my hardest to think of a wish. After a small moment, nothing came to mind, so I decided to just blow the candles out, not wanting to waste any more time.

Cheers erupted around me, the twins clapping their hands and Uncle Alfarr letting out a hearty laugh. Aunt Silvia's stern expression softened momentarily, a small smile playing at her lips as she began cutting the cake.

The next few hours passed with heaps of laughter, food, and chaos. The twins alternated between shoveling food into their mouths and running around the room, their energy seemingly endless.

Uncle Alfarr was in his element, constantly challenging me to arm wrestle or trying to catch me off guard with a wrestling move. I dodged his playful advances as best I could, but there was no escaping his enthusiasm.

Aunt Silvia, ever the disciplinarian, was busy trying to keep order. She scolded the twins whenever they got too rowdy and reminded Uncle Alfarr not to knock anything over with his antics. Despite her efforts, the room was filled with the lively, chaotic energy that only a family gathering could bring.

As I sat back, watching the scene unfold, a feeling of contentment settled over me. It wasn't the quiet solitude of the woods, but it was something different, something comforting. For a moment, I allowed myself to simply enjoy it.

After the party finally wound down, I said my goodbyes and made my way back home. The night air was cool, and the moon was bright as I approached my front door. I stepped inside and got ready for bed, feeling the day's weariness settle into my bones.

Just as I was about to settle into bed, a soft knock came at the door. I paused, then called out, "Come in."

The door creaked open, and Aunt Silvia stepped inside with a small plate of leftovers. "I thought you might get hungry again later," she said, offering me a smile as she set the plate on my bedside table.

"Thanks, Aunt Silvia," I replied, sitting up in bed.

She sat on the edge of the bed, and a look of worry grew on her face. "It's been a rough year for you, Isaac, for all of us," she began. "I know that. Losing your parents...my sister... it's not something anyone should have to go through, especially at your age."

I looked down, a slight ache setting in my chest. "Yeah," I mumbled. "It hasn't been easy."

She reached out, placing a hand on my arm. "I'm proud of you, you know. You've managed to keep going, even when it's been hard. And I know I grill you about school, but it's only because it's what your mother would have wanted. She always wanted the best for you."

I nodded, understanding. "Yeah, I know."

Silvia gave a small chuckle, a wistful look in her eyes. "You were always one to sneak out into the woods, even when you were younger. Remember how you used to climb that big tree at the edge of the forest to watch the wolves from above?"

A small smile tugged at my lips. "Yeah, I remember. I used to think I was so clever, sneaking out without anyone noticing."

"Oh, we noticed," Silvia said with a smirk. "Especially that time you took a nasty spill from the tree and came back all banged up. You scared us half to death."

I winced, vaguely recalling the incident. "I don't remember much of that. Just... someone carrying me back to town."

Aunt Silvia nodded her head in agreement. "Aye, we never found out who helped you all these years later. We just opened the door to see you standing there, crying. Your father and I asked around the town, looking for someone to thank, but no one saw a thing."

I nodded slowly, still trying to understand the mystery. "Maybe it was just a passerby, someone who happened to be in the right place at the right time."

"Maybe," Silvia said, though her tone suggested she wasn't entirely convinced. The conversation left a lingering sense of unease, but Silvia didn't dwell on it. Instead, she offered me a reassuring smile. "Well, whoever it was, I thank the moon that they decided to do us all a huge favor that day."

"Me too," I said, returning her smile, though the memory continued to nag at me.

Silvia stood up, smoothing her skirt as she prepared to leave. "Get some rest, Isaac. Tomorrow's a new day."

"Goodnight, Aunt Silvia," I said, watching her as she walked to the door.

"Goodnight, Isaac," she replied, pausing momentarily to look back at me. "I hope you had a good 17th birthday."

I nodded, feeling a warmth in her words as she left, closing the door softly behind her. I laid down, staring up at the ceiling, and before long, I was asleep.

# CHAPTER 2

I woke up to the sound of the wind rustling outside my window. With a sigh, I dragged myself out of bed, forced down a quick breakfast of the food my aunt left me last night, and prepared for the day ahead. For the most part, my mornings had become a solitary routine: wake up, eat, and head towards the edge of town. It was how I managed to get through each day, finding solace in the woods.

As I exited the front door, I turned to see Aunt Silvia and Uncle Alfarr bustling around their wagon while the twins darted around, throwing various toys and snacks into the back.

"Are you sure we have everything?" Aunt Silvia asked, her voice carrying a note of impatience.

"Of course, Silvia," Uncle Alfarr replied, "We've got the supplies and the maps. We're all set for Crescentia."

Marcellus paused his frantic packing and turned to his father. "Father, where's Crescentia again? Is it far?"

"Yeah, where is it?" Marciana echoed, bouncing on her toes.

Uncle Alfarr chuckled and pulled out a worn map from his coat pocket. "Come here, I'll show you two again," he said, kneeling to their level. "This here is Selunaris, the capital of Moonveil. Everything starts here. From Selunaris, you've got paths branching out like spokes on a wagon wheel to each of the six towns."

He traced his finger along one of the paths. "Crescentia is right here." He pointed to a spot on the map, "We're here in Lunaria. And Crescentia is just northeast of us. See?"

The twins leaned in, their eyes following his finger as they tried to memorize the route. I watched them, a small smile tugging at my lips. They were always so full of questions, eager to learn about the world beyond our little town.

The region we're from is called Moonveil, a collective of six separate towns. Each one with its own distinct characteristics.

Selunaris, the main capital, sits right at the center of it all. It's an opulent city with grand palaces, sprawling gardens, and an air of sophistication. The King and the wealthiest citizens reside here, creating a stark contrast between the lavish lifestyle of the rich and the hardworking commoners.

Southwest of Selunaris is a town named Noctiluna. It's a lively place known for its vibrant nightlife and bustling marketplaces. The place never sleeps, with music, laughter, and the clinking of coins filling the air. It's a place where travelers and merchants from all over come to trade, entertain, and indulge.

Head on the path north from there, and you'll hit a town called Eclipsia. Admittedly, I don't know much about this town; almost no one does. It's heavily guarded, and many aren't allowed to travel there. Eclipsia is a mysterious town, often covered in mist—a place of secrets.

To the east of Eclipsia sits Nyxaris, a small town renowned for its observatory and star-gazing festivals. It sits atop a high plateau, offering clear skies and stunning views of the night sky.

South of Eclipsia is Crescentia, where my aunt and her family are headed now. It's a serene town nestled around a sizeable crescent-shaped lake that reflects the moon beautifully at night. The town is known for its tranquility, with residents who value peace and nature.

Lastly, southwest of Crescentia, directly south of Selunaris, is where I was born and raised, Lunaria.

I knew Moonveil pretty well, seeing as how my parents and I traveled constantly when I was younger. I spent most of my childhood riding alongside them throughout these woods in our horse-drawn covered wagon. I never really got to make friends my age, which probably explained why I enjoyed being alone so much.

As I finished adjusting the strap of my pack, Aunt Silvia approached me, her brow furrowed with concern. "Isaac, are you going to be alright on your own while we're gone?"

I gave her a reassuring nod. "I'll be fine. You know I prefer the quiet anyway."

She sighed, brushing a strand of graying hair back into her bun. "I know telling you to stay out of the woods is useless because you won't listen, but at least stay close to the path, alright? The forest isn't like it used to be."

"I will," I lied, knowing full well that my feet would lead me deep into the woods as soon as they were out of sight.

Aunt Silvia's words of caution reminded me of the many lectures about fiends that had been drilled into us in class. We learned that fiends had once ruled this land, their presence widespread about 2,000 years ago. Back then, they were at the top of the food chain, terrorizing humans and creatures alike. They ruled the lands for 500 years, and then, seemingly out of nowhere, they vanished. No one knows precisely what happened or where they went. But for whatever reason, about 16 years ago, the fiends started slowly reappearing, creeping back into the edges of our world.

I waved them off as they climbed onto the wagon, the twins already arguing over who got to sit in the front. Uncle Alfarr laughed, climbing up to take the reins, while Aunt Silvia gave me one last concerned glance. The wagon lurched forward, creaking as it began its journey toward Crescentia.

"Stay safe!" I called after them, knowing they wouldn't hear me over the noise. As the dust settled and their figures became distant blurs, the tranquil quiet returned, the one I sought most days.

Turning back toward town, I made my way toward the edge, where the wooden walls stood tall and weathered. It wasn't long before I noticed commotion up ahead— someone was frantically trying to enter the town, their cries growing louder as they neared the gates.

The figure stumbled closer, their clothes tattered and face wild with fear. They were screaming, their words garbled and incoherent, but sheer panic was unmistakable. The guards stationed at the gate exchanged uneasy glances, hesitant to approach the person now clawing at the walls in desperation.

"They're out there—watching, waiting! None of you know the truth!"

One of the guards, a burly man with a thick beard, stepped forward, raising his hand to calm the person down. "Easy now," he said, his voice firm but not unkind. "Who's out there? What did you see?"

The person looked up, their eyes wide with terror, darting between the guards as if expecting something to leap out of the shadows. "The eyes! The eyes! They won't let me go! They're coming closer!"

The second guard, a younger man who looked like he was barely out of training, swallowed nervously. "Maybe we should get the captain," he muttered to his companion.

"Get the captain for what?" the bearded guard replied, his tone irritated. "Another one of these lunatics ranting about things in the woods?"

I didn't need to be closer to understand the situation. The person was most likely affiliated with Hysteria, a strange disease that no one understood. It was rare but unmistakable when it occurred. The afflicted would return from the forest, eyes wide with terror, screaming nonsense. Some said it was the work of fiends, that those who ventured too far into the woods and got lost were never the same when they returned. Others dismissed it as mere madness, the result of isolation and fear playing tricks on the mind.

Whatever the cause, seeing someone in such a state was enough to send a chill through anyone who witnessed it. The guards were already on edge, probably deciding how they were going to take care of the person.

I slipped past the scene, careful not to draw attention to myself. My goal was the wooden wall further down towards the south of town. There was no gate there, and I knew this section of the wall wasn't as closely watched. Climbing it had become second nature to me over the years. It was an easy way to escape the confines of town and find solitude in the woods. Despite my aunt's warnings, I knew where I was headed, and it wasn't along any well-worn path. The deeper parts of the woods called to me, and as soon as I was sure no one was watching, I began to make my way toward them.

With a quick, silent climb, I pulled myself over and dropped down on the other side, landing softly in the underbrush.

I glanced back at the town one last time, its sights now distant and muted. The sound of the panicked person's cries and the guards' conversations faded into the background as I moved further away. The boundary between the town and the forest was a threshold I crossed often, but each time felt like stepping into a new world. The air was calm yet alive; the canopy above filtered the sunlight into a soft glow, and wildflowers carpeted the floor in a flurry of colors and vibrant hues.

I let out a deep breath, savoring the peace that surrounded me. The dense forest air was somehow smoother than that of the town's. As I ventured deeper, I felt the comforting embrace of the woods envelop me.

I made my way toward my favorite tree, a massive oak with

thick trunks and sprawling branches, a silent sentinel from my childhood. This was the same tree I used to climb when I was small, finding comfort and adventure in its size.

As I settled beneath the canopy, the shade of the oak providing a cool respite from the afternoon sun, a rare sense of peace came over me. Leaning back against the rough bark, I let out a long sigh and let the weight of the day slip away. The sounds of the forest—the rustling leaves, the chirping of distant birds—created a soothing backdrop. I closed my eyes, feeling the gentle breeze brush against my skin.

For a brief moment, the world around me faded into a quiet hum. I could feel my mind drifting, my body relaxing further as sleep beckoned. *Maybe just a few minutes...* I thought, sinking deeper into the soft earth beneath me.

But just as I began to surrender to sleep, a sudden, piercing screech shattered the tranquility. My eyes snapped open, my heart pounding as I instinctively scanned the sky.

High above, a flock of Dreadbeaks soared, their massive wings slicing through the air. These monstrous fiends, with wingspans easily stretching 15 to 20 feet, were covered in dense black feathers. Bone-like fragments jutted from their heads, giving them an eerie, skeletal appearance. Carnivorous to the core, they were known to swallow smaller prey whole.

I immediately froze, my gaze locked on the flock above. My breath hitched as one of them let out another scratch, loud and menacing. The sound echoed through the forest, sending smaller birds scattering for cover. I could feel the shift in the air, the sudden tension as though the forest itself was still with fear.

Another screech rang out, snapping me out of my fear. Instinct kicked in, and I dashed for cover under the tree, praying the flock would fly over. The massive trunk offered little cover from creatures like Dreadbeaks, but it was better than standing out in the open.

I pressed my back flat against the massive trunk, my pulse pounding in my ears. I tried to steady my breathing, but the air caught in my throat as I listened for the telltale screeches of the fiends above. The forest waited in silence with me. The usual sounds of rustling leaves and distant birds had vanished, swallowed up by the oppressive quiet.

*What are they doing here?* My thoughts raced, panic clawing at the edges of my mind. Dreadbeaks were supposed to stay deep in the woods—deeper than I was at least. So many of them shouldn't be circling so close. I clenched my jaw, a cold sweat beading on my forehead as I recalled the stories my father used to tell.

There was one in particular— a tale of a hunter who had strayed too far from the path. A Dreadbeak had picked him off like a vulture snatching a mouse, leaving nothing behind but splinters of bone. I'd always thought those stories were exaggerated, a warning meant to keep me from wandering too deep into the forest. Now, though, every horror he'd described seemed all too real.

I squeezed my eyes shut momentarily, willing my heart to slow its frantic pace. I was alone here, and there was no one coming to save me if those things spotted me.

For a few moments, everything seemed silent—too silent. I waited, still daring not to move, hoping the danger had passed. But then, just as I began to calm down, a sharp screech rang out, this one different — almost pained. It made the hairs on the back of my neck stand.

Suddenly, the air above me was filled with the sound of snapping branches. Something was crashing through the tree canopy above, hard and fast. Before I could react, a form tumbled through the foliage and landed directly in my lap. I flinched backward as the figure hit me, banging my head against the tree in the process. A soft thud followed by a dull, painful weight knocked the breath from my lungs.

I rubbed the back of my head, wincing as the pain forced my eyes shut. When I finally regained my composure and my vision cleared, disbelief washed over me. My eyes widened—lying in my lap was a girl.

I was frozen in surprise as she lay there unconscious. She was limp, unmoving— her face hidden beneath a hood. At a quick glance, I could tell she was still breathing, her chest rising and falling in a steady rhythm. There was blood on her hands and a fair amount of it on her lips. The crimson-red streaks stood out vividly against her skin. My mind raced—had she been attacked? No doubt by one of Dreadbeaks flying above.

I hesitated, my hand hovering just above her shoulder. "Hello?" I whispered, my voice barely a breath against the vast quiet of the forest. My brain yelled at me to keep quiet, scared of alerting the Dreadbeaks circling above. But I had to risk it. I had to make sure she was okay.

I felt a lump form in my throat when she didn't respond. I leaned in closer, gently gripping her shoulders. I gave her a slight shake. "Hey—can you hear me?" I contemplated trying to carry her back to town, but I didn't know if I was supposed to move someone in this condition. What if she was hurt badly?

Suddenly, her eyes fluttered open, startling me. They were unfocused and hazy as if she was still trapped somewhere between sleep and waking. For a second, her gaze drifted, passing over me as though I wasn't even there.

Then, in an instant, she gasped and jolted her body upright. The movement was so sudden that I barely had time to let go before she scrambled out of my lap, stumbling to her feet. Her breathing was heavy, and her eyes had a wild look—like an animal cornered, unsure whether to fight or flee.

I quickly rose to my feet, holding my hands out, palms up. "Hey, it's okay— I'm not going to hurt you," I said, trying to make my voice as calm as possible despite the pounding in my chest.

She blinked a few times, her expression still somewhat dazed. She swayed slightly, as if the ground beneath her wasn't quite stable, but steadied herself for a moment. She glanced down at her hands, stained with blood, and then back up at the canopy of trees from where she had fallen.

I couldn't help but steal a glance at her. She was of slender build, her form draped in a dark blue hooded cloak that billowed lightly in the wind. Beneath the cloak, she wore long black boots that hugged her legs snugly, with a scuffed appearance, no doubt from the countless journeys through the forest.

However, the feature that stood out the most was her hair—a cascade of orange-brown locks that slightly peeked out from beneath her hood. As she turned her head towards the sky to look at the clouds above us yet again, I caught a glimpse of her eyes—a deep shade of purple, not exactly a common eye color around these parts.

There was certainly an elegance to her, something graceful that didn't quite fit in with the ruggedness of the forest. Though at the same time something mysterious, as if her cloak was meant to conceal a secret. She had clearly been through something harrowing, and though I had a thousand questions swirling in my mind, I wasn't sure how to begin asking them.

"You probably shouldn't move around too much," I whispered harshly under my breath, my gaze flickering toward the sky. The Dreadbeaks were still above, waiting for any sign of movement.

She paid me no mind, her eyes fixated on the sky above us. Almost like she could hear something I couldn't. It was a bit unnerving, especially given the circumstances in which she had quite literally dropped into my life. I felt the tension gnawing at my gut. "Get down! I said again, a little louder this time. The Dreadbeaks could still be out there".

There was no reply.

"Hey, can you hear me?" I said, extending a hand toward her. "We need to get you back to town; we're not safe out here."

Finally, she turned her eyes towards me and away from the sky. Her deep purple eyes reflected none of the fear I felt. Her calm demeanor was almost infuriating, given the danger we were still in.

"We must traverse deeper into the woods." She said, her voice calm despite the urgency of the situation.

I furrowed my brow, still reeling from everything that had just happened. "Deeper into the woods? What are you talking about?" I shook my head, glancing around at the trees. "Lunaria is only a mile away. There's no reason to keep going. We can get help in town."

Her eyes fixed on me, steady. "You assume safety lies in proximity to your walls. But I tell you, it does not. The true danger is not what we see now but what lingers in the distance, hidden from your eyes. The town cannot protect us."

I blinked at her, trying to process what she was saying. Maybe she hit her head when she fell into my lap. I glanced up at the sky, making sure we were still safe from the Dreadbeaks. "Are you... sure you're alright?" I asked carefully. "Did you come from Crescentia? Or another nearby town? You might have gotten turned around in the chaos."

Her response was immediate, her tone unchanged. "I am not lost."

I studied her face, but she showed no sign of confusion. Still, something didn't sit right with me. I frowned, my thoughts swirling. *What the hell is with this girl?* I thought. Sure, the

Dreadbeaks could've driven her away from the main path, but why head deeper into the woods? Maybe she's disoriented… maybe she's scared.

But looking at her, calm and collected as she was, it didn't seem like fear. If anything, she seemed more composed than I felt.

"I think you're a bit confused," I replied with my hands in the air, trying to calm her down.

Her gaze hardened, not with anger but with a certainty that made my heart skip a beat. "It is you who is confused. The danger will come to your town and all of Moonveil if we do not act. Trust in what I say, or risk more than you know."

I stared at her in disbelief. Who was this woman? She falls into my lap, unconscious and bleeding, then gets up as if nothing happened and starts issuing orders without a single explanation. My frustration simmered beneath the surface. I wasn't the type who sought out danger; if anything, I did everything to avoid it. I spent my days hiking these woods, keeping to myself, and the only reason I even carried a sword was because my father had insisted I learn.

"Are you serious?" I retorted, "You fall out of the sky, tell me to follow you, and expect me to do it without question? Who even are you? Why would I just get up and go along with you willingly?"

She turned to face me fully, her deep purple eyes locking onto mine. "I am Celine," she said calmly, as if that explained everything. "That is all I know. It is… nice to make your acquaintance."

"Celine?" I repeated, my voice tinged with skepticism. She nodded her head.

"Well, Celine," I continued. "Do you have anything else you could give me? A backstory? Where are you from?"

She simply shook her head with a blank expression. Calm,

despite the blood-curdling screeches from the Dreadbeaks above. "I am but a drifter. My memories are like fragments of a shattered mirror, scattered across the winds of fate."

I frowned, trying to untangle the cryptic words as they bounced around my head. Was she being serious? It felt like she was holding back—hell, she had to be holding back. Who just loses their memory and carries on like this?

"Let me get this straight. You don't remember anything about your past or where you're from?" I pressed, my skepticism growing. "You're not giving me much to go off of here, Celine."

Her eyes narrowed slightly. "I understand your hesitation," she said. "But we do not have the luxury of time. You may choose to distrust me, but I am certain of one thing; staying here will not keep us safe."

Her words should have reassured me, but instead, they only made me feel more uneasy. I crossed my arms, still not convinced. "You're asking me to follow you deeper into the woods, into territory only the moon has seen, and all I've got to go on is your word? It sounds like a bad deal to me."

Celine's lips pressed into a thin line as she regarded me for a long moment. "You may think me strange," she said quietly. "Though I feel that you are the one I seek."

I frowned, confused. "The one you seek? What do you mean?"

She continued as if I hadn't spoken. "I sense there is a great plague that approaches these lands. I must head north ...though I cannot do it alone, you will aid in this journey."

"North? A plague?" I repeated, incredulous. It sounded like something out of a storybook told to scare children around the hearth. None of it made sense. I shifted uncomfortably on the ground, unsure how to answer her request.

"What kind of aid do you need?" I asked hesitantly. "I mean...

I'd like to help, but my aunt would kill me if she found me gone. Besides, how far north are we talking?"

Celine paused, her eyes reflecting the low light of the forest. She shook her head slightly as if searching for words that just weren't there.

"I... I do not know," she admitted, her voice soft. "I cannot say how far or how long the journey will be. Nor can I fully explain the danger we face. But what I do know is that I cannot make the journey alone."

I sat back, exhaling slowly. It wasn't the answer I was hoping for. Though admittedly, I wasn't sure of what answer I was looking to get back.

"Look, Celine, right?" I began, my voice very hesitant, "I don't know if I'm cut out for this whole travel the forest with a strange girl who fell out of the sky thing, and besides I- "

My words trailed off as I realized her eyes were now fixated on me, though her expression remained impassive. Her purple eyes bore into my own with such intensity it made the hairs on my arms prickle. It almost felt as if she could see straight through my thoughts.

I swallowed hard; the weight of her gaze almost felt tangible. "I mean, I have my own things to worry about," I continued, trying to sound firm. "I've spent a long time getting to the point where I could wander these woods without getting into trouble. I don't think I'm equipped to handle whatever this is…"

For a second, I expected her to insist again, maybe even frustrated with my reluctance, but instead, her gaze became less harsh. "Though you may not believe it," she said quietly, "it must be you. You don't see it yet, but you are Drifted," she said, her voice low and soothing.

I blinked at her, baffled. "I'm sorry? I'm what? Drifted?" The word sounded like it was supposed to mean something significant, but it made absolutely no sense to me. I opened my mouth to question further but was interrupted.

There was a sudden rustling above us, cutting our conversation short. We froze. The smell hit me next— rotting flesh, blood. My nose wrinkled, and my stomach churned as the smell hit my nose with ferocity.

My eyes snapped upward, and there it was.

Perched ominously in the branches above us sat a Dreadbeak, its bony frame blocking out the light. Its skeletal visage glared down with empty eye sockets that almost seemed to glow in the dim forest light. It shifted its wings, causing the branches to creak under its weight.

I stood stunned as the air grew still, thick with the threat of violence.

# CHAPTER 3

The morning sun was still low, casting long, dancing shadows through the dense canopy as Celine and I raced through the underbrush. Each step felt like a desperate gamble against the Dreadbeak's pursuit, its defining screech echoing through the forest, reverberating off trees as it closed in on us. Its ginormous form loomed above us, creating enormous shadows that swallowed the very sunlight itself. The massive bird moved with uncanny speed, wings beating furiously as it dipped and swerved through the sky, forcing the wind to bend to its will.

Each beat of its wings drew it closer. With every heartbeat, the fiend was gaining ground, relentlessly closing the distance between us.

It wasn't supposed to be like this. This was just supposed to be another simple hike, like the many before it. Yet somehow, my morning ritual of quiet solitude had turned into a fight for survival.

My legs ached with each step, burning with the effort of keeping up with Celine. I could feel the adrenaline coursing through my veins, fueling my tired muscles, but it wouldn't be enough. I knew we couldn't outrun this thing forever. With each breath, I felt the weight of the sword on my back, bouncing and jostling, reminding me that it might come to use very soon.

Beside me, Celine moved effortlessly with grace and agility, moving through the forest with an almost ethereal agility. It almost seemed otherworldly how easily she maneuvered through the trees. Where I stumbled over roots and ducked under branches, she flowed like water, slipping through gaps and stepping lightly across uneven ground. Her dark blue cloak billowed behind her, a blur of motions. Despite the danger we were in, Celine remained scarily calm, unreadable. It was as if she were detached from the peril altogether, her mind elsewhere, her body just going through the motions.

There was an obvious contrast between us. While I was breathing heavily, my heart pounding so loudly in my ears that it drowned out the sound of the Dreadbeak's screeches; she seemed entirely composed. It was unnerving.

I knew we couldn't outrun the Dreadbeak forever; I was getting tired, and fast.

"We need a plan," I muttered between breaths. "We can't just keep running."

Celine's gaze shifted toward me briefly, her eyes carrying that same calm certainty. "Fighting it is inevitable. Stand your ground when the time comes."

I blinked at her in disbelief. "Stand my ground?" I scoffed, frustration mixing with my fear. "Do you realize what that thing is? It's a Dreadbeak! We can't just—"

"Trust me," she cut in softly but firmly. "Your strength is needed here."

I wanted to argue, to demand a real plan—anything other than waiting to be torn apart—but before I could respond, the trees broke into a small clearing.

*Damn it.*

I skidded to a halt. I could feel the ground give slightly beneath my feet, leaves and dirt scattering as I spun to face the sky. Chest heaving, I drew my sword with one hand and planted my shield firmly in the other. Unfortunately, it was time to stop running. I couldn't help but think of how irksome of a position I was in as I got ready to defend myself.

The fiend circled high above us, its black wings blotting out the sun momentarily as it turned to position itself. The air around us was still, except for the ominous whoosh of its wings. My pulse quickened as I tightened my grip on my sword, and my breaths came out in short, rapid bursts. This was it.

Celine was to the right of me. Judging by her demeanor, you wouldn't guess we had just been running for our lives. With her arms at her side, it appeared as if she wasn't aware of the danger we were in at all.

"It shall descend upon us from above. Prepare yourself, for its attacks will be swift." Celine stated matter-of-factly.

As the creature circled above us. I shifted uncomfortably, struggling to compose myself. Any second, I was sure that the inevitable onslaught would occur. I could feel it in my bones. Every fiber of my being was tense.

"Now!" Celine let out, shattering the momentary silence.

Just then, the Dreadbeak let out a menacing squawk and began to nose-dive towards me. The air whistled around it as it plummeted, beak first, aiming directly for my chest. I raised my shield just in time; with a thunderous crash, the impact of the bird's talons against my shield reverberated through my arms as I struggled to hold my ground against the creature's strength.

I held firm, gritting my teeth against the clash. It was a test of endurance—its raw strength against my will. Before I could get the chance to counterattack, the creature disengaged, flapping its wings violently to gain altitude once more. I blinked against the sudden gust, keeping my eyes trained on the sky.

I turned my head right to look towards Celine; her eyes were fixed on the bird looming above us. Watching the creature's movements with great focus. I was glad that the fiend didn't go for her during its initial attack, not sure that she would be able to defend herself.

"Drifted!" Celine said calmly, "Stay vigilant!"

She was right; I couldn't afford to get distracted, not even for a moment. The Dreadbeak was circling again, its wings cutting through the air in wide arcs. It was sizing us up, testing our defenses.

It continued its test, swooping to peck at us ever so often. Seeing how quickly we could respond to its attacks. I evaded its persistent pecking easily enough, sidestepping and occasionally blocking with my shield.

The Dreadbeak's next dive came without warning. This time, its attack was far more aggressive. I sidestepped quickly, raising my shield just in time to block its vicious beak. I could feel the pressure of its jaws trying to snap shut around me, its sharp beak scraping across my shield. My heart thundered in my chest. How long could I keep this up?

With a deep breath, I steadied myself, focusing on the fiend's movements. Swiftly, the creature descended upon us with ferocious speed. I braced myself and waited for the perfect moment to strike. As soon as its talons collided with my shield, I lashed out with my sword and struck its left wing.

The bird let out a defining screech as my blade sliced through the bottom half of its wing. It recoiled in pain before taking a powerful peck at me. Luckily, I was able to block this attack, but its strength sent me flying back.

Pain shot through my shoulder as I hit the earth hard, my sword slipping from my grasp. For a moment, everything spun. My vision blurred, the world tilting as dizziness crashed over me. I could feel the cold earth beneath my back, but my body felt detached, numb from the impact. I tried to focus, blinking rapidly in an attempt to clear the fog from my mind. I had to get up. Celine... she was defenseless without me.

The world itself felt as if it were tilting and slipping around me. Celine, fading in and out of focus as dizziness clouded my vision. I tried my hardest to steady my breathing and fight off any panic that was threatening to engulf me. Through the haze and confusion, I saw her—a silhouette moving like liquid around the fiend's attacks. She danced around its strikes with an almost supernatural grace, ducking and weaving as though she could predict its every move. It was mesmerizing and terrifying at the same time. I was relieved knowing I didn't have to worry too much about her.

"Drifted!" Celine yelled through my throbbing headache, "On your feet! You cannot falter now!"

Her voice cut through the fog in my mind. She was right; who knew how long she could last dodging the onslaught on the Dreadbeak. Despite the protest of my body, I gritted my teeth and pushed myself up from the forest floor.

With my legs shaky, I stumbled back onto my feet, gripping my sword tightly as I retrieved it from the ground. The world still swayed, but my focus was fixed on the threat the Dreadbeak posed to Celine. I shook my head with Celine's words still bouncing around my brain. *This was all such a nuisance*, I thought to myself.

Celine was still dancing around the fiend, but I could tell she was getting tired. Her movements were still graceful, but there was a slight hesitation in her steps now. I had to get back into the fight, and quickly. The attack I landed on the Dreadbeak's wing earlier rendered it unable to fly. That was one less thing we had to worry about.

I rushed towards the beast, sure that I could land a fatal blow with Celine distracting it. I raised my sword in the air, prepared to take a heavy swing at the bird's neck.

"Duck Drifted!" Celine yelled.

"Duck?" I said, confused. At that instant, the bird swung quickly to the right, striking me with its wing. I flew back from the impact but was able to roll back onto my feet.

As I regained my footing, confusion surged through me. How

had Celine known that the Dreadbeak would attack at that exact moment? It was like she could read the future— No, it wasn't that; it was more like she was moving off instinct. A sixth sense that guided her every move. Something was innate about her intuition, something that I lacked entirely.

I didn't have time to dwell on this because the thought quickly disappeared into the chaos surrounding me. I readied myself again, and with the fiend still distracted by Celine, I rushed in again to deliver my next attack.

I drew in closer, ready to slash again. "Duck, once more!" I heard Celine yell. Without hesitation, I did just that, narrowly avoiding the swing of the Dreadbeak's wing. "Now! It will strike from the right!".

There wasn't enough time to analyze her instruction, only react. I raised my shield to the right side of my body just in time to block the Dreadbeak's beak as it slammed into me with full force.

"From above!" Celine shouted again. I shifted my stance seamlessly, dropping to one knee and raising my shield above my head. The fiend's heavy beak struck hard, but the blow bounced off.

Time seemed to slow for a moment as my mind tried to catch up with the chaos around me. *How does she know all this?* I thought, my muscles burning from the effort of holding the Dreadbeak back. Could it be that she's fought so many of these fiends before, learned their attack patterns? But that would be... impossible. No one survives more than a few encounters with Dreadbeaks. They were ruthless, unpredictable—yet here she was, directing me as if she knew their every move.

My thoughts raced as I blocked another strike, the Dreadbeak's talons screeching against my shield. *Just who was this girl?* I thought. None of this made sense. But there was no time to question it. Right now, all I could do was trust her instincts and hope that we'd somehow survive this.

"Roll right!" Celine's voice cut through my confusion. I obeyed without hesitation.

"It shall strike from above, yet again!" I instinctively dropped to one knee once more.

"From your left!" I spun on my heel, avoiding another attack.

Celine's commands were precise and accurate. Like a dance partner, her intuition guided my every move. Each movement flowed into the next as if I were performing a carefully choreographed dance, our coordination almost seamless. As beautiful as this must have been to any onlooker, I had to remind myself that this was a dance to the death.

I trusted every instruction Celine shouted at me; hell, I didn't really have much of a choice. The Dreadbeak was now directly in front of me, staring at me with beady eyes. Its gaze was determined, yet weary. The beast was tired, but so was I. I locked eyes right back with it. It was almost as if we silently agreed that our next attacks would be our last.

I could tell Celine could sense it too. Her demeanor was completely different; she almost seemed relaxed. There was a calmness in the air, as if time itself had stopped progressing. "Strike now, Drifted! With all your might!"

Her words snapped me back into action; I tensed my muscles as I prepared to deliver the final blow. With everything I had left, I lunged forward, letting out a primal roar as I drove my blade toward the Dreadbeak. The fiend lunged as well, screeching loud enough to pierce the sky. I was prepared and easily deflected its attack while my blade drove toward its neck, sinking into its thick plumage. The Dreadbeak let out a final, ear-splitting cry before collapsing to the ground in a motionless heap.

Breathless and exhausted, I lowered my sword, its weight suddenly feeling immense in my hand. The clearing around us was eerily quiet now, the echoes of battle fading into the distance. It was over. The Dreadbeak lay lifeless a few feet away, its once menacing figure now a crumpled mass of feathers and bone.

I turned to Celine, a weary smile tugging at the corners of my lips. She met my gaze with a nod of approval, her deep purple eyes softening ever so slightly, though the weariness was evident in the lines of her face.

"We did it," I breathed, feeling the words escape me in a mix of disbelief and relief. My chest ached with each breath, my body screaming from the strain of the fight. But we had survived. Against all odds, we had survived.

Celine tilted her head, her expression unreadable for a moment before she spoke. "Now, we rest, Drifted," she said, her voice calm as ever, though the strain was evident beneath the surface. Her eyes flickered toward the horizon, where the trees loomed like silent guardians. "There's a long trek awaiting us."

I quickly flicked the blood off my sword before sheathing it. A mix of emotions started flooding my mind. Sure, Celine helped me defeat that thing, but it was because of her I was in this position in the first place. Her calm demeanor got to me and grated against my frayed nerves.

"Rest?" I scoffed. "After everything that you just saw happen, you think that would make me want to go on any 'trek' with you?".

Celine's eyes remained steady; her expression almost unreadable. "Drifted, there are truths that you and I both have yet to uncover. Forces that elude our understanding are at play; our paths have been intertwined by fate itself."

I barked out a laugh, my throat still raw from the fight. "Excuse me?" "I don't care about fate or any of that nonsense! Whatever is happening isn't my mess to clean up; everything seemed fine before you showed up!"

Celine shook her head. "I cannot force you, Drifted. But know this— the path ahead for you is not one easily tread alone."

She looked towards the dead Dreadbeak on the ground. "This fiend is not the same you are used to seeing, am I correct?"

I glanced down at the dead creature, only now noticing the truth in Celine's words. This Dreadbeak was massive— larger than any I'd ever seen. Its talons were sharper, its beak thicker, and its eyes, even in death, held an unnatural gleam. Sure, I've encountered Dreadbeaks before, but never one of this size. And what's more, they never ventured this close to the town. A single fiend this close was terrible enough, but a whole flock was unheard of. It felt like the fiends truly were trying to reclaim the land, pushing further and further into areas they once avoided.

Celine's voice broke through my thoughts. "Without my aid, your survival is far from assured — just as mine is uncertain without yours." She paused, her eyes locking with mine, more intense now. "Think, Drifted. Your home is in danger. Do you truly believe the fiends will stop here? That they will spare Lunaria if we do nothing?"

Deep down, I knew she was right; without her instructing me through that fight, there was no way I would've been able to defeat the Dreadbeak alone, at least not without getting heavily wounded. Celine's instructions had been the difference between life and death.

I looked down, my grip tightening around my sword as my mind drifted back to Lunaria—the place I had always known as home. Aunt Silvia's stern voice warning me to be careful as I slipped out to the woods, Uncle Alfarr's infectious laughter as he challenged me to another arm-wrestling match. The twins, Marcellus and Marciana, always running around, pestering me with their endless energy, their teasing grins brightening even the darkest days.

What would happen to them if I did nothing? If these

fiends—stronger and more dangerous than anything I'd ever seen—started closing in on Lunaria, my family would be in their path. They wouldn't stand a chance. My aunt, my uncle...the twins. The thought of something happening to them twisted my insides in knots, leaving a hollow ache in my chest.

I couldn't lose them, too.

Celine stood before me, her gaze locked on, as if she could sense the turmoil inside me. She wasn't just talking about survival anymore—she was talking about protecting everything I cared about. If I walked away now, if I refused to follow her, there was a chance that I'd be dooming my family, my home, and everyone I'd ever known.

I glanced at her, studying her closely. Celine didn't seem like too much of a fighter. Throughout the entire encounter, I hadn't seen her lift a weapon or make a single offensive move. The only way to survive whatever was coming was to rely on each other's strengths. We were in this together, whether I liked it or not.

There was still a hint of doubt that rested within me. "What makes you think I should trust you to guide me through all this? How do I know you aren't just leading me straight to my death?"

Celine met my stare, her eyes holding a depth of knowledge. "Drifted," she replied softly, "whether you choose to believe it or not, our destinies are intertwined. Together, we may yet uncover the truth behind the chaos that threatens to consume us both."

Her words hung heavy in the air; I was torn between skepticism and curiosity. As much as I wanted to deny it, there was a nagging feeling deep down within me that wanted to trust her. Something bigger was happening, and only she would be able to lead me through it.

"What a nuisance." I let out with a heavy sigh. I had no other choice but to follow her lead into the unknown.

We began our journey.

# Chapter 4

Dappled shadows danced across the forest floor as Celine and I trudged through the seemingly endless woods. The air was thick with the scent of damp earth and pine, the kind of smell that clings to your clothes and lingers in your lungs. Every step felt like a test of physical and mental endurance as we navigated through the forest away from the well-beaten path.

"We've been walking forever! Are you sure you even know where we're going?" I let out, annoyed and unable to hold back any longer. The words came out harsher than I intended, but the fatigue and irritation had worn down my patience. I couldn't help but feel we were wandering in circles, no closer to our destination —if there even was one—than we were when we started.

It had to have been about three whole weeks of me aimlessly following Celine around the forest with no clear destination in sight. The days bled into one another, marked only by the constant need to find new paths free of the fiends that now seemed to inhabit every corner of the woods. The forest was dense and seemingly endless. We were on constant alert, knowing that fiends could suddenly appear from any shadow.

We'd spent days weaving through the woods, often doubling back when we encountered any sign of fiend activity. I learned enough about them to recognize the distinct marks they left on the landscape - trees with their bark stripped, claw marks gouged deep into the wood, and the occasional carcass of an unfortunate animal.

At times, we'd find a route that seemed clear, only to have it blocked by a fallen tree or a ravine too wide to cross. Each setback forced us to find new routes, often leading us deeper into the forest. The constant debtors were exhausting.

I was beginning to wonder if Celine even had a destination in mind. She glanced back at me, her expression as unreadable as ever. Admittedly, her calmness was starting to wear on me.

"Trust me, Drifted," she replied calmly. If I hadn't been so irritated, I might have noticed the tinge of amusement in her tone. "I may not recall but I feel as if I have walked these woods many a time before," she replied.

Despite my irritation, I had to admit that Celine wasn't the worst company to have. She was quiet, always on guard, and there was a certain solace in that. The woods, with all their hidden dangers, were still a place of beauty. The fresh air, the chirping of birds, the warmth of the sun on my skin—it was all a reminder of why I loved being out here. The sounds of nature slowly began to ease the tension in my shoulders, allowing me to focus on the present moment rather than the uncertainties that lay ahead.

As we walked, the worries and frustration I was feeling before seemed to fade away, now being replaced by the simple pleasure of being surrounded by nature's beauty. It truly was a great head clearer. Our path was uncertain, that was for sure, but Celine's calm demeanor was somewhat reassuring.

"So, can you tell me where we're headed now?". I asked Celine, probably for the millionth time, hoping that this time she might actually give me something to work with.

"North," she replied dryly, her tone giving nothing away.

"Yeah, you've told me that already. Can you give me anything else?" I sighed, exasperated. It was like pulling teeth trying to get information out of her.

"It is truly all that I know." She responded, her words leaving me with more questions than answers.

She hasn't been able to fill me in on anything about this trip. No duration, destination, or, more importantly, what the point of it all was. The most I gathered was that something was supposedly happening to the woods, and it would only get worse. And while I didn't doubt the danger, I just wished I understood my role in all of this. Celine's only answer was that our fate and destiny were 'intertwined,' whatever that meant.

"Well, okay, how about this trip we're going on then. How do you even know we need to do this?". I asked, my frustration mounting.

"It is but a feeling," she responded, soft but resolute.

"So, then at least give me more about who you are? Where did you come from?". I pressed, hoping to break through her wall of ambiguity.

"I do not know," she replied, her tone unchanged.

"Okay, well then, what about your parents and your family? Where are they?" I asked again, though I had a sinking feeling I already knew what her answer would be.

"I do not know," she replied yet again. However, this time, her words carried more weight, making me feel as if I was asking the wrong questions.

Celine remained frustratingly vague during my barrage of questions. I wanted to be angry, to demand more from her, but there was something in her voice, something in the way she spoke, that made me believe her. She was a mystery, wrapped in an enigma, and the more I tried to pry into her past, the more confusing and elusive it became. Who was she, really? How did she know so much about the dangers that lurked within the woods? And why couldn't she remember anything about herself?

I couldn't imagine not knowing anything about myself or my past. The thought of it made me feel a deep sense of pity for her.

Even if she didn't show it, whatever memory loss she was suffering from, it had to be a heavy burden to bear.

"Drifted! Do you smell that?". Celine proclaimed suddenly, snapping me out of my thoughts.

"Smell what?" I asked, sniffing the air but not picking up on anything out of the ordinary.

"You must follow me! And make haste!" she urged, her voice filled with a rare urgency as she darted off into the woods.

I didn't have time to think as my legs were already chasing after her on instinct. "Wait up a second!" I shouted to Celine.

Celine was quick and agile. Despite my best efforts, I struggled to keep pace with her, my legs yelling as I pushed myself to catch up. Whatever she sensed must have been important, and I had to trust she knew what she was doing. My heart began to pound with anticipation as I wondered what got her all riled up.

"Celine, seriously! Slow down!" I called out, my voice tinged with panic as I began to lose sight of her between the foliage. The dense undergrowth and towering trees seemed to swallow her up. Either she couldn't hear me, or just flat out wasn't listening. In fact, it seemed as if she was running faster.

Soon though, I lost her. Her figure disappeared into the dense woods ahead. I began to panic and frantically scanned the surrounding trees, trying to find any sign of her.

"Celine!" I shouted again, my voice echoing through the forest. There was no response, only the rustling of leaves and the distant calls of birds. My heart dropped a bit, fear creeping into my mind. Where had she gone? What had she smelled?

Once intimate and almost comforting, my surroundings now felt alien and menacing. The trees, which once felt protective, now seemed to twist and warp into strange shapes that played tricks on my eyes.

"Celine!" I called out again, but the forest swallowed my voice. The once rhythmic songs of the birds now felt dissonant, their melodies creating a uncanny symphony that permeated through the forest. My heartbeat quickened as I turned in every direction, desperately trying to catch a glimpse of her.

Nothing.

The underbrush grew thick, brambles and vines snaked around my legs, pulling at my clothes as if trying to hold me back. The ground was uneven, roots jutting out like claws, ready to trip me at any moment. I pushed forward, my breathing growing labored with each step. The deeper I ventured into the woods, the more I realized just how disoriented I was becoming.

"Where are you?" I muttered to myself, frustration and fear battling for dominance in my mind. It was as if the forest had swallowed her whole, leaving me alone in this vast, unforgiving wilderness. The sun, which had hung in the sky earlier, was now obscured by thick clouds, covering the world around me in a dim, oppressive light.

Each step seemed to lead me further into the unknown. The forest was no longer the peaceful place I once knew; it had transformed into a labyrinth of shadows and silence. My mind raced with possibilities—had she been taken by something? Was she in danger? Or was she just playing some twisted game?

The ground beneath me was damp, the earth soft and giving under my boots. I stumbled over a root, barely catching myself before I fell face-first into the dirt. A curse slipped from my lips as I righted myself, glancing around annoyedly. Every tree looked the same, their towering trunks blending into a maze of shadows, each one twisting into strange shapes. The branches above intertwined, creating a canopy so thick that it blotted out the sky, leaving only a few scattered beams of light to pierce through. Every shadow seemed to stretch endlessly into the darkness, moving with the faint rustle of the wind.

A chill ran down my spine as the unsettling thought crept in. I was lost.

Panic started to creep into my mind. My senses felt heightened; every noise and every flicker of movement in the corner of my vision made my heart pound. The forest was alive with sounds, but none of them were hers.

I looked around trying to find my bearings, but I couldn't make heads or tails of my location. The forest, once a place of solace for me, had turned into a nightmare, a living, breathing entity that seemed intent on keeping us apart.

As I began to get overwhelmed with fear, I heard it— A faint, distant sound that cut through my fear like a knife.

A scream.

A piercing scream.

Celine's scream.

My blood ran cold as I spun around, trying to pinpoint the direction it had come from. It was faint, almost too faint to hear, but there was no mistaking it. Without a second thought, I took off in the direction of the sound, crashing through the underbrush recklessly.

I didn't care about the branches that whipped my face or the roots that threatened to trip me with every step. All that mattered was getting to Celine before it was too late. The forest seemed to blur around me as I ran, my mind focused on one thing and one thing only—getting to Celine.

"Celine! Hold on, I'm coming!"

Just as I stumbled over an exposed root, nearly losing my balance, a sudden flicker of movement caught my eye through the dense foliage. My heart skipped a beat as I spotted Celine's hooded figure crouched low to the ground. She was partially hidden by the thick bushes and twisted undergrowth, her silhouette blending with the shadows around her.

For a moment, I just stood there, watching. Her posture was deliberate and controlled, and she seemed utterly absorbed in whatever lay before her. I couldn't make out exactly what it was, but her head was tilted slightly downward, her hands working meticulously at something out of sight. The quiet rustling of leaves and her faint movements were the only sounds that broke the heavy stillness of the woods.

"Celine?" I called out to her. The past few minutes' tension drained away as I hurried toward her. But as I drew nearer, I noticed something was off. She wasn't reacting to me at all—not a flinch, not a word. It was as if she hadn't heard me or was completely unaware of my presence.

The uneasy feeling that had been gnawing at me since she ran away flared up again. What could possibly have her so entranced that she didn't hear me? I approached cautiously, my hand trembling as I reached out to touch her shoulder, fearing what I might see when she finally turned around.

Before my fingers could make contact, she suddenly whipped around to face me, her eyes wide and startled. Her face was flushed, her lips stained red—not with blood as my anxious mind briefly imagined, but with the juices of the wild strawberries clutched in her hands.

"Drifted!" she exclaimed, her voice bursting with excitement. "I found them! I have located the berries!"

I froze, staring at her in confusion. She was sitting there, utterly absorbed in something so mundane, while I'd been fearing the worst. My heart was still thumping from the chase, and I couldn't comprehend how she could be so calm, so... blissfully unaware of the panic she'd just caused.

"Are you kidding me! You disappeared to pick some strawberries?" I snapped, my voice sharper than I intended. My annoyance was fueled by the leftover panic.

Celine didn't seem bothered by my tone. Instead, she let out a wistful sigh, her eyes shimmering with a kind of serene contentment I hadn't seen before. "Drifted," she spoke softly, "behold the humble strawberry, a marvel of nature's bounty. See the way its crimson hue glistens in the dappled light—they are a true testament to the richness of the earth from which it springs."

Her words took me by surprise. She spoke so passionately, so poetically, about something so simple. The anger I'd been feeling started to dissipate, replaced by a strange fascination. For the first time, she seemed almost...normal.

"Yea, that's great and all, but you were —.".She cut me off.

"Each berry," she continued, her voice now soft but assured, "is a symphony of flavors, a blend of sweetness and tartness that delights the senses and nourishes the soul. In fact, in the act of plucking them, one then becomes intimately connected to the rhythm of the land, a participant in the everlasting dance of life and renewal."

I found myself captivated by her words, unable to respond. Any anger I had left had all but melted away as I listened to her soliloquy. It was as if, for a moment, she had been transported somewhere else, to a place where the world was simpler, where the small pleasures of life could still bring joy. And as much as I wanted to be upset with her for worrying me, I couldn't deny the truth in her words. There was something magical about this forest, even with all its dangers.

It was clear to me that Celine had a connection with the woods and the simple pleasures that it offered. In a way, this connection to the land resonated with my own.

"Well," I said, exhaling deeply., "you might as well pack some to go. We need to get a move on".

Her gaze lingered on mine, a slight smile pulling at her lips. With a gentle motion, the cluster of berries she gathered disappeared into the folds of her cloak. Then, with another nod, we resumed our trek through the woods, the silence between us now less tense, more reflective.

Again, we began heading north through the woods. Just how I liked it, quiet. Though in the back of my mind, I couldn't help but keep playing out the scene of losing Celine through the thicket in the woods. I was sure something terrible had happened when I heard her scream my name.

"Those strawberries," Celine spoke up again, almost as if she could read my thoughts, "they hold the essence of the woods, a taste of its beauty."

I glanced at her, noticing the way her eyes softened as she spoke of the forest. There was something profoundly sad in her expression, something that hinted at a deep connection to this land that I still couldn't fully understand.

"And yet," she continued, her voice now tinged with a note of sorrow, "they are but a glimpse of the wonders that lie within these woods. Each tree, each stream, each creature, that all have a story to tell, a part to play in the intricate tapestry of life."

I listened intently. Daring not to interrupt her.

"Though, I can feel it, Drifted. The very woods themselves are changing. These strawberries, once abundant, are now but a fleeting memory."

I knew Celine was right. I hiked these woods plenty, so it was easy for me to notice the change. It was subtle; only someone who had spent most, if not all, of their time here would notice. The forest was different now—darker, more ominous. The typical wildlife and fauna that once littered the woods were slowly becoming scarce, pushed out by the ever-present threat of the fiends. It was as if the very essence of the woods was being slowly drained away, leaving behind a hollow shell of what it once was. As crazy as I thought Celine was, perhaps she was right. Maybe there was some encroaching darkness that was soon to be upon us, or perhaps it already was.

"What do you... what do you think is the reason behind all this?" I asked hesitantly, unsure if I really wanted to hear the answer.

Celine didn't reply immediately. She seemed lost in thought, her eyes distant as if peering into another world. When she finally spoke, her voice was soft, almost a whisper. "I fear... I fear that the darkness encroaching upon these woods is but a reflection of a greater darkness that is spreading across the land. And if we do not find a way to stop it, all that we hold dear will be lost."

Her words sent a chill down my spine, not just because of what she was saying but because of how much she seemed to believe it. This wasn't just a simple journey through the woods for her— this was a mission, one with stakes higher than I could have imagined.

I could tell she was afflicted with the whole situation; her expression was tinged with sadness and resignation. I didn't know how to respond. Comforting people had never been my strong suit, and right now, I was at a loss for words. Instead, I chose to let us continue in silence, each of us lost in our own thoughts.

As the day wore on, the forest began to change. The once vibrant green leaves turned darker, almost black, as the shadows lengthened and deepened. The cheerful sounds of birds and rustling leaves gave way to a subtle silence, broken only by the occasional call of some unknown creature.

"Perhaps we should make camp for the night," I suggested, breaking the tense silence that had settled between us. I didn't want to admit it, but the harsh atmosphere was starting to get to me.

Celine nodded in agreement, I'm sure she could've carried on, but I was grateful for the chance to rest and regroup.

We found a small clearing surrounded by tall trees that offered some protection from the wind. As we set up our makeshift campsite, I couldn't shake the feeling that we were being watched, that unseen eyes were tracking our every move from the shadows. Every rustle of leaves and every snap of a twig sent a jolt of anxiety through me. I kept glancing over my shoulder, half-expecting to see glowing eyes staring back at me from the darkness.

Celine, on the other hand, seemed calm, almost serene. She moved with a quiet grace, her every action deliberate and measured. Watching her, I couldn't help but feel a pang of envy. How could she remain so composed, so unaffected by the growing sense of dread that hung in the air?

The flames cast flickering shadows on the surrounding trees as we sat by the fire. I couldn't help but voice the question I had been asking Celine since we started this journey. "Celine...what are we really doing out here? What's the point of all this?"

She looked at me, her deep purple eyes reflecting the firelight. For a moment, I thought she might actually give me a straight answer, but then she simply shook her head. "I cannot say for certain, Drifted. I only know that we must continue. The answers we seek lie ahead, not behind."

Again, her response was frustratingly vague, but at the same time, it resonated with a part of me that I didn't fully understand. Maybe it was the way she spoke, or maybe it was the way she seemed so certain of our path, even if she didn't know where it would lead. Whatever it was, I found myself trusting her despite the lack of concrete answers.

As the fire crackled and the night deepened, we sat in silence, each of us lost in our thoughts. The atmosphere of the forest seemed to close in around us, the darkness pressing in on all sides. I could feel the weight of the unknown bearing down on me, a heavy burden that I wasn't sure I was strong enough to carry.

And yet, despite everything, I couldn't shake the feeling that this journey—whatever it was—was necessary. That there was something out there, waiting for us, that would change everything. Whatever that something was, I didn't know. But I had a feeling that, before this was over, I would find out.

And when I did, nothing would ever be the same again.

# CHAPTER 5

It was dark, really dark. Fireflies occasionally gave off faint enough light to briefly see into the woods around us. The darkness seemed to press in on us from all sides, and that nagging feeling that we were being watched persisted. I let the thought fade as I began to stoke the fire, adding a few more sticks to keep the flames alive.

Celine sat across from me; she was the only thing that I could consistently make out, her features illuminated by the flickering flames. The atmosphere was definitely eerie, but it wasn't as if I hadn't been in the woods in the dead of night before. Yet still, there was something different about this night—something I couldn't quite put my finger on.

We were silent. Celine wasn't much for conversation, and neither was I. Yet, the silence between us felt different this time—heavier somehow, almost oppressive. It wasn't just the absence of words; it was the weight of everything that had happened, everything that still loomed over us. My thoughts swirled in the stillness, restless and itching to fill the void with something, anything, to break the tension. I turned my head to look at Celine, wondering if she might want to talk about something, anything?

Her eyes met mine almost instantaneously, like she could sense me looking toward her. The deep purple hue of her eyes penetrated my very being, leaving me feeling exposed and vulnerable. My face grew warm as I quickly darted my gaze away from her and towards the fire.

Why did she always manage to make me feel like this? So

uneasy, like I was constantly on edge. Yet, there was something about her presence that also kept me rooted.

"It is a somber night, is it not, Drifted?" Her voice, soft as a whisper, cut through the awkward stillness that had been hanging between us. It was so gentle that, for a moment, I wasn't sure if I had imagined it. The crackling of the fire had filled the space between us for so long that hearing her speak again felt almost strange.

I nodded, unable to tear my gaze away from the flame. "Yes, it is," I replied, my voice barely above a whisper. "Though, it's kind of peaceful, don't you think?" I continued, trying to find something to fill the silence.

Celine inclined her head ever so slightly, her gaze never leaving mine. For the briefest second, I caught the faintest curve of a smile on her lips. "Indeed," she said, her voice like a soft breeze in the stillness. "Even in the darkest of nights, there is beauty to be found—if only one knows where to cast their gaze."

Her words caught me off guard, and suddenly, I felt heat rising to my face, a flush of warmth spreading through my skin. What did she mean by that? Was she talking about...me? I glanced at her, but her expression remained serene, unreadable. There was no way she meant it like that, right? I didn't take Celine for the type to flirt, yet her words hung in the air, making my heart beat just a little faster than it should have.

I swallowed, trying to shake off the confusion. "What do you mean?" I asked, my voice a little smaller, a little more sheepish than I intended. "Where do you think someone could find beauty in the darkness?"

Celine was silent for a moment before replying. "Turn your eyes towards here," she whispered, her voice barely audible above the cracking flames.

My cheeks were burning with warmth, and embarrassment

coursed through me like wildfire as I shifted uncomfortably on the forest floor. For a moment, I kept my eyes fixed on the mesmerizing dance of the flames, trying to build the courage to look in her direction. Slowly, I turned my head towards her. To my surprise, she was holding something in her slender fingers— the strawberries she had picked earlier.

I felt like an idiot; all my assumptions shattered in an instant. The small cluster of berries, their vibrant red hue catching the firelight, seemed almost mocking. "Behold the humble strawberry," she murmured, "a symbol of beauty that can be found even in the darkest of times."

Mortified, I abruptly got up from the forest floor. "I'm going to go collect some more firewood for the night," I said quickly, turning and walking briskly into the woods, away from the campsite.

My thoughts spiraled as I walked. I couldn't help but beat myself up over the misunderstanding; how in the world could I think that Celine was flirting with me? We hardly knew each other. I spent a few minutes wandering, picking up sticks, and trying to clear my head, letting the cool night air calm my racing mind. When I finally felt composed enough, I headed back to the camp.

"I left but a few," Celine said as I approached. I looked up to see her gesturing towards a small handful of strawberries on a few leaves she had left where I had been sitting.

"Thank you," I mumbled, still recovering from my earlier embarrassment. I sat down again, glancing at Celine. She simply nodded, her expression unreadable under the fire's dim light. I settled back down across from her and began snacking on the berries. They were amazingly sweet, and with each bite, the tension seemed to ease. I found myself lost in the simple pleasure of their flavor.

Celine watched me quietly, her eyes steady as if she could see right through me. I couldn't decipher what was on her mind as I ate the last of the berries. My best guess was that she was probably upset that she had to share.

"Drifted," Celine's voice cut through my munching, making me pause. "Tell me, what do you remember of your parents?"

Her question caught me off guard, and, for a moment, I was lost in memories that I had once forgotten. "My parents?" I repeated, buying myself a moment to think.

Celine nodded.

"Well, where do I start?" I said, more to myself than to her. "Once upon a time, my father was a knight in the Moonveil Kingsguard, and my mother was a medic who aided the knights."

Celine nodded; her eyes focused deeply on mine. "Yes, and what are your memories of them? What do you recall?

I was hesitant, unsure of how much to share. It had been so long since I'd thought about them in detail. Still, some memories remained vivid, like fragments of a life I'd once known.

"I remember my parents being good people," I began slowly. "They always got along with everyone in town, very well-liked, always willing to help others. They were probably the kindest people you would have ever met."

I paused, the weight of their absence settling over me. "My father was a stern but fair man with a strong sense of duty and honor. While my mother was probably the kindest soul you'd ever meet. She cared for the town's children like they were her own with so much compassion it was almost tangible."

After a slight pause, I continued, "When I was born, my parents decided instead that they wanted to travel between towns, peddling various spices. I think they wanted a change of scenery, even if just for a while. I couldn't blame them for that."

Celine continued listening quietly, her eyes never leaving mine.

"You know, it was my father who taught me how to wield this sword," I continued, pointing to my sword belt. "He was always so insistent that I learn. My mother... she was always there to patch me up whenever he pushed me too hard."

Λ pang of sadness hit me as I spoke. The reality of their loss, something I hadn't fully processed, hung heavy in the air.

Celine's gaze softened, a hint of sympathy in her eyes. "Loss is never easy to bear, Drifted, especially of those we hold dear."

I nodded, swallowing the lump in my throat. "You're right," I replied, my voice thick with emotion. "But enough of this. You should get some rest. I'll take the first watch; it's getting late". The truth was, I wasn't tired at all— I just didn't want to dwell on these emotions any longer. It would be easier to push them away and deal with them another time.

Celine nodded, understanding in her eyes. Her gaze lingered on me for a moment before she spoke.

"Rest sounds like a good idea," she agreed softly. "We have a long journey ahead of us, and our strength will be needed."

With a silent understanding, Celine prepared herself to sleep on the forest floor as I set up against a tree to keep watch. My mind was still buzzing with the memories of my parents that I shared earlier.

"As darkness falls, so too does the weight of the day," Celine's voice drifted through the air, her words a soothing balm to my restless thoughts.

I gave her a grateful nod, watching as she drifted off to sleep.

The night was quiet; the sound of the crackling fire pierced through the stillness of the forest. I sat against the rough bark of the tree, scanning the darkness beyond the reach of the firelight. My thoughts drifted back to my parents, their faces flickering in and out of my mind. Their faces, their voices, the warmth of their presence—they were all gone now, just memories I clung to.

I turned my eyes to Celine. Her gentle breaths filled the air, the rise and fall of her chest steady and rhythmic. Despite the darkness, I could make out a faint outline of her features, the soft curve of her cheek, the delicate line of her jaw. Even though her hood was constantly pulled up, covering most of her face, I couldn't deny her beauty.

At that moment, something occurred to me that hadn't before. Celine was always wearing her hood. I can't remember a time or moment in which she wasn't.

The thought nagged at me like an itch I couldn't scratch. Why did she always have her hood up? My mind raced with possibilities— was she hiding something?

I tried hard to distract myself from the thought. After all, there was no reason for me to try to pry on her privacy. Maybe she just liked having her hood up. Or, perhaps she was, in fact, trying to hide something. My imagination was full of endless possibilities.

Maybe she was hiding a scar or something extraordinary like horns or ears? Or maybe she was actually a fiend, attempting to guide me to a place where she could eat my innards with no one to stop her.

I shook my head. She had her reasons, and it wasn't my place to ask. But it was too late; the urge to see what was underneath her hood nagged t me relentlessly.

Before I knew it, I was on my feet, moving silently towards her. Each step felt like a drumbeat in the stillness, the anticipation building with every moment.

The closer I got, the quicker my heart pounded in my chest. A mixture of nerves and excitement was coursing through me.

Finally, I reached her side. I swallowed hard as I reached out towards her hood, my hand trembling.

As my fingers brushed against the fabric, a voice cut through the night, startling me and jolting me back into reality.

"Drifted," Celine's voice was stern.

I froze, my hand hovering mid-air as I met her gaze, my cheeks flushed red with embarrassment. Celine's eyes were wide, the dancing flames of the fire reflecting off of them.

"I... I'm," I stammered, unable to find the right words.

Celine shot up from rest; to my surprise, she wasn't paying any attention to me at all. Her head swiveled from left to right, her eyes scanning the darkness beyond the fire. I watched, confused, as her entire body grew tense.

"What is it?" I whispered.

"Something is approaching, fast," Celine replied, her voice barely audible.

I quickly scurried towards my sword and shield. Arming myself for the danger approaching. The air felt slightly different, but it was steady and quiet. I couldn't hear anything, but I trusted Celine's instincts.

Suddenly, a gust of wind quickly snuffed out the fire from our camp. It felt like someone, no, something, had blown it out intentionally.

It was dark, almost pitch black. I could just barely make out Celine's silhouette against the dim moonlight that filtered through the trees. I slowly made my way towards her, not wanting us to get separated.

As I reached her side, I felt it too—the eyes watching us, the presence lurking in the shadows. Someone or something was out there waiting.

"Drifted, your left!" Celine yelled out suddenly.

I was able to just barely raise my shield in time to deflect a blow aimed at my head. Something sharp clashed with it with a resounding thud.

I swung my sword in the same direction, but whatever it was that struck was already gone, vanished into the darkness. My eyes darted around, trying to pierce the gloom. Every shadow seemed to move, every rustle a threat. Celine stood beside me, her stance low, eyes sharp and focused. Whatever was out there, it was fast. I hadn't even heard it approach.

With lightning speed, something lunged towards Celine. She sprang out of harm's way just in time, narrowly avoiding the attack. The assailant disappeared back into the darkness quicker than I could blink. I felt a bead of sweat roll down my temple as I waited for the next attack.

I caught more movement to my right from the corner of my eye. Without hesitation, I pivoted, my body moving on instinct, narrowly avoiding a slash aimed at my flank. The blade whistled past me, missing by mere inches. Again, the assailant was gone as quickly as it had arrived, leaving only the unsettling sound of my heavy breathing.

Meanwhile, Celine was dealing with issues of her own, gracefully dodging and weaving between the numerous attacks thrown at her. But now, the assault was intensifying. No longer did the attackers strike one at a time; instead, they came at us in a chaotic flurry, their movements more frenzied, their strikes more aggressive.

"They're growing bolder," Celine said, her voice calm but focused as she slipped out of the way of another swift strike. "This is no mere ambush."

"What gave it away?" I called back, barely managing to deflect a blade aimed at my chest. My arms were aching from the constant movement, and every breath felt heavier than the last.

Celine sidestepped another flash of steel, her motions so smooth it was like she could predict every strike. "They're not just attacking. They're calculating."

I grunted, narrowly dodging another swing. "Calculating? Perfect. Because that's exactly what we need right now."

They seemed to emerge from every shadow, their presence multiplying as if the very darkness itself was birthing them. The once sporadic attacks had become a relentless onslaught.

A sudden snarl came from my right, and I turned just in time to meet a vicious blow. My sword met the attack with a clash, the impact sending vibrations up my arm. I pushed back with all my might, shoving the assailant away and swinging my sword in a wide arc to keep the others at bay.

"Hold your ground, Drifted!" Celine's voice rang out. She was commanding despite the chaos unfolding around us.

I nodded, trying to maintain confidence, but it was getting harder. The dark figures twisted and shifted around us, obscuring my vision and hardly providing us with any chance to breathe or recoup.

I caught another flash of movement approaching me. Another shadowy figure lunged at me with its blade. I managed to sidestep just in time, feeling the rush of air as the blade missed my throat.

I could feel the pressure mounting with every step we took. We were being corralled and pushed back into a tight circle with no room to maneuver. Every direction I turned, there was a blade, a claw, a shadowy figure lunging in from the tree line. With each passing moment, the odds seemed to stack against us.

"To your right, Drifted," Celine shouted.

I jumped back, but not fast enough. A searing pain shot through my brow as something sharp grazed my skin. I felt the warm trickle of blood run down my face, blurring my vision and stinging my eye. I blinked rapidly, trying to clear my sight, but the blood kept flowing, threatening to blind me.

My heart pounded in my chest, the reality of our situation sinking in fast. We were completely outnumbered, the attackers' movements so fast they were nothing but blurs in the darkness. Every time I raised my sword to block, another strike came from a different direction. Sweat poured down my face, and my arms began to feel like lead. We couldn't keep this up. It was only a matter of time before one of us slipped, and that would be the end.

The forest that had always felt so comforting now seemed like an endless maze of shadows and threats, each tree concealing another danger waiting to strike. The air was thick with the sound of rustling leaves, and the only thing keeping me from collapsing was sheer adrenaline.

Celine must have sensed my growing desperation. Her voice cut through the chaos like a lifeline in a storm: "Drifted, we must retreat. The woods are concealing their movements!"

She was right. Remaining here only invited further danger. We needed to put ourselves in a better position to fight, somewhere we could see our attackers coming.

With a nod of agreement, I quickly scanned our surroundings, searching for the safest route. Before I could formulate a plan, another barrage of attacks came crashing down on us.

The forest seemed to close in around us, the darkness growing thicker with each passing moment as if trying to suffocate us.

I struggled to keep my vision clear, the pounding in my head growing louder with each passing second. Blood from the wound above my brow flowed freely, running down my face in thick, warm streams. It clung to my skin, dripping off my chin and staining the front of my shirt. I wiped at it with the back of my hand, but it was no use—the flow was relentless. My right eye was completely useless now, and the world on that side was nothing but a crimson blur. I had no choice but to shut it, trying to focus on what little I could still see.

Every blink felt like fire, the sting of the wound mixing with the salt of my sweat. My left eye strained to take in my surroundings, but everything was a disorienting mess of shadows and movement. The woods around me seemed to swirl, the branches above dancing like twisted figures, mocking my weakness. My grip on the sword faltered as the pain sharpened with every heartbeat.

I didn't know how much more I could take.

"Drifted!" Celine's voice broke through the clamor again.

My eyes met hers, and in an instant, we understood each other. As one, we turned and sprinted into the darkness, my heart pounding in my ears as we raced through the tangled undergrowth of the forest.

The sounds of pursuit followed us, echoing through the trees—footsteps, the snap of twigs, the rustle of leaves. I didn't dare look back. Fear chewed at my insides. I didn't know what was chasing after us, and the vision on my right-hand side was still impaired, the blood now covering half of my face.

Celine ran beside me with her eyes focused forward; her presence was the only comforting anchor that I had in the chaos. However, there was something different in the air, a subtle shift in Celine's demeanor that I couldn't quite place.

Suddenly, without warning, Celine veered off course, darting into the underbrush with a fluid grace that left me momentarily stunned. "Celine!" I yelled out, my voice lost in the thick leaves of the trees around me.

She didn't turn back and disappeared into the darkness without so much as a glance back. I didn't have the chance to follow her; she was gone.

I wanted to follow, but I couldn't. Death was at my heels, and instincts took over. I didn't have much of a chance to process what just happened.

All I knew was that I was now alone, pursued by shadows through a forest that felt more like a living nightmare.

With each step, the weight of my solitude pressed down upon

me. Celine's abrupt departure left me reeling, grappling with the sense of abandonment. Though, I didn't have the luxury of dwelling on it. Not now.

I pushed the thoughts aside, focusing instead on my brain screaming at me to survive. The pursuit behind me grew closer; the sound of footsteps echoed louder now through the trees, like an ominous drumming of impending doom. I could feel the presence of blood lust looming just beyond the edge of my perception. My lungs burned with every breath, but I couldn't stop. I wouldn't

I was being driven by the desperate need to escape, but no matter how fast I ran, the darkness seemed to stretch out endlessly in front of me, swallowing me whole in its inky depths.

I kept running. Through the darkness, through the uncertainty, through the fear that threatened to consume me whole. Right now, there was only one thing that mattered:

Survival.

# CHAPTER 6

My breath came in ragged gasps, each inhale thick with the earthy scent of moss and damp leaves. I could feel my paranoia creeping up with every second, fueled by the shadows that danced at the edges of my vision. I pressed my hand against my brow, feeling the warm stickiness of my own blood trickling down, obscuring my vision. The wound throbbed with every frantic heartbeat, reminding me of the attack that had threatened to end my life.

I crouched under a dense underbrush, the thick vegetation large enough to conceal me. Celine was still nowhere to be found; not even a trace of her presence remained. Part of me wanted to believe that was a positive thing. *Good, things are better like this anyway*, I caught myself thinking. But as much as I tried to convince myself that was for the best, the truth was that the forest felt different without her now. Colder, lonelier, and somehow, even more dangerous.

I tried to push the thoughts aside; the immediate danger took precedence over my feelings of betrayal. The sounds of pursuit had faded, but I knew better than to let my guard down. My assailants were swift and relentless; one sight of me would prove detrimental. I shifted slightly, trying to find a more comfortable position without disturbing the underbrush too much. The branches and leaves provided good cover but restricted my movements. I needed to stay as still as possible.

I strained my ears, listening for any sign of movement. Every rustle of leaves or snap of twigs set my nerves on edge. The pain in my brow was a constant nudge of the attack, keeping me alert.

I didn't dare move, not even to wipe the dirt from my face, out of fear of being discovered. The pursuit seemed to have moved on, but I couldn't shake the feeling that eyes were still watching me.

I tried to focus on my surroundings, forcing my mind to stay sharp and present. My eyes traced the patterns of moonlight filtering through the canopy above, casting thin, web-like shadows that seemed to reach for me. The mist swirled around the base of the trees, thickening here and there, almost as if the ground itself was shifting beneath my feet. The gentle rustling of leaves felt distant, and the rhythmic pulse of my own heartbeat filled my ears.

Each detail seemed sharper than the last—the way the shadows danced, the subtle movements of the mist—yet my thoughts drifted. Everything blurred at the edges, the forest alive with a strange rhythm that pulled at my senses, coaxing me into a lull. It was as if the trees themselves were whispering, urging me to relax, to let go.

I blinked hard, trying to shake the weight pressing down on me, but the forest felt heavier now, slower. My limbs grew sluggish, my mind wandering in and out of clarity. The night stretched on, the world around me swaying, and for a brief moment, I wasn't sure if I was still standing or if the earth had shifted beneath me.

Suddenly, a twig snapped behind me. My heart lurched, and I froze, waiting for the inevitable attack. Instead, there was only silence. Then, from the corner of my eye, I saw a shadowy figure standing a few feet before me. It wasn't moving at all, just standing there. The figure was tall, slender, and cloaked in darkness, its features obscured by the night.

A sudden rustle to my left drew my attention, and when I glanced back, the figure was gone. I felt my heart rate quicken, and sweat began to drip from my forehead, stinging the cut above my brow. I couldn't stay here any longer.

I slowly began to inch my way from under the underbrush, trying to move with the utmost caution. Each movement was calculated, deliberate, and painfully slow. After what felt like an eternity, I was finally clear of my hiding spot.

The forest was eerily quiet as if it was holding its breath, waiting for something to happen. I needed to find higher ground or some form of cover where I could better defend myself. Scanning the area, I spotted a small rocky outcrop a short distance away. It wasn't much, but it would have to do.

I made my way slowly to the outcrop, nerves on edge. As I reached the base of the rocks, I paused to listen for any sign of pursuit. The forest remained quiet, but I knew better than to let my guard down. Climbing the rocks, I positioned myself with a clear view of the surrounding area. From here, I would at least be able to see any approach and perhaps spot Celine if she was still around.

I crouched low behind the rocks, pressing my back against the cool, rough surface of the outcrop. From this vantage point, I could see the forest stretching out before me—its dark canopy shifting slightly in the breeze.

Time passed slowly as I kept my wits about me. The adrenaline that had fueled my body began to wear off, leaving me exhausted but alert. My thoughts kept drifting back to Celine. Where was she? Why did she leave so suddenly during the chase? A part of me wanted to believe she had a good reason, but another part, a darker part, wondered if she had abandoned me.

Movement in the distance caught my eye, and I pushed myself below the rocks. A figure emerged from the trees, and my heart nearly jumped out of my chest when I recognized it was Celine. She was moving cautiously, eyes scanning the area as if searching for me.

"Celine," I whispered, just loud enough for her to hear. She glanced up and spotted me on the rocks, quickly closing the distance between us.

"Drifted!" she called out ecstatically.

She climbed up to my position and embraced me around the shoulders. The warmth of her touch surprised me, and for a moment, I forgot about everything else. I blushed hard, thinking it was strange to see Celine act this way. She was usually pretty cold; I'd never seen her behave so affectionately. I pushed the thought aside, figuring she was happy to have found me after we got separated.

"We must move," she said urgently, letting go of me. "They're still out there."

I nodded, and together, we descended from the outcrop and began to make our way through the forest again.

We walked in silence, the sound of our footsteps the only thing breaking the stillness of the forest. I could hear the wind rustling through the leaves and the distant chirp of crickets, but the quiet between us felt heavier than the night itself.

After what felt like an eternity, I decided to break the silence. "Hey, Celine," I called out, keeping my voice low but insistent. "What happened back there when we were getting chased? You just disappeared on me."

No answer. She kept walking, her pace steady, her figure barely visible in the shadows ahead. I frowned, picking up my stride to close the distance between us.

"Celine?" I tried again, a bit louder this time, my tone laced with concern.

Still nothing. She didn't even glance back. Her posture remained calm and composed, but something about her silence put me on edge. The question lingered in the air, unanswered, and the longer she ignored it, the more unsettled I became.

"Hey, can you hear me?" I called out, a touch of frustration creeping into my voice now. I reached out, placing a hand on her shoulder, hoping to pull her back into the present.

As soon as my hand made contact, she stopped abruptly. Slowly, almost mechanically, she began to turn around. The movement sent a shiver down my spine, and I instinctively took a step back.

Her face came into view, illuminated by the faint light filtering through the trees. The hairs on the back of my neck stood up. Her eyes were sunken and hollow, devoid of the purple that was once there. Her jaw hung open in a grotesque, unnatural grin.

"Celine?" I whispered, my voice trembling. This wasn't the Celine I knew. Something was terribly wrong.

Her mouth opened wider, revealing sharp, jagged teeth. "Drifted," she hissed, her voice a strange distortion of the one I remembered.

Maggots began crawling from her mouth, squirming as they fell to the floor. Disgusted and confused, I pressed my palm against my mouth, fighting the urge to vomit.

"Celine, what the he—" Before I could finish my sentence, her arms twitched and elongated, transforming into sharp, blade-like appendages. With a swift motion, she slashed at me. I barely managed to leap back, her blade missing me by inches.

"Celine, stop!" I yelled, though deep down, I knew the person I once knew was gone. She slashed at me again, her movements unnaturally fast. Panic gripped me as I realized I had to run.

I turned and bolted, my heart pounding in my chest. Behind me, I could hear the terrifying sound of her blades slicing through the foliage as she pursued me. My mind raced, trying to process what had happened. Was that why she disappeared into the woods? Had she been tricking me since the beginning?

Branches whipped at my face and arms as I tore through the underbrush, not daring to look back. I knew Celine was faster than me, and I couldn't outrun her for much longer.

Suddenly, my foot caught on a tree root, and I went crashing to the ground. Pain shot through my ankle, but there wasn't enough time to tend to it. I scrambled to my feet and pressed my back against a large tree, struggling to catch my breath. Celine wasn't far behind and came slicing through the greenery.

She emerged from the darkness, her twisted grin far more horrifying now that I could see it up close. My breath caught in my throat, heart pounding against my ribs as icy fear crept up my spine. I could feel the cold sweat on my brow, my hands trembling as I reached for my sword, though I knew it wouldn't help me. The air around us felt thick and suffocating. Each shallow breath I took felt like it wasn't enough.

Celine's eyes were gleaming with a terrifying malice. Her blades glinted in the pale light, and with each slight movement, I could hear the faint scrape of metal against the air. I could feel my pulse in my throat, my mouth dry as my mind raced for a way out, but there was none. She was too close, too fast. I had nowhere to go.

"Celine, don't!" I pleaded, my voice cracking with desperation. My throat felt tight, the words barely able to escape. But the creature before me—this twisted version of her—didn't even flinch. Her grin widened, mocking my fear. The person I thought I knew, the one I had fought beside, was nowhere to be found in those cold, empty eyes.

She lunged forward, her blade aimed directly at my chest. I squeezed my eyes shut and braced for the pain, my entire body tensing as the darkness seemed to close in around me, suffocating me in its grip.

And then... there was nothing.

I bolted upright, drenched in sweat, my heart pounding. I was lying on the hard ground of the forest, still underneath the underbrush where I had been hiding. I glanced around, half-expecting to see the twisted version of Celine lurking in the shadows. Instead, the forest was as quiet as I left it. Only the hoot of a distant owl broke the silence.

At some point during my hiding, I must've passed out from the blood loss and had a nightmare. I took a deep breath and tried to steady myself, but the image of Celine's distorted face and arms was seared into my memory.

I lay there for some time, listening to the soft sounds of the forest. The nightmare felt all too real, making sure to remind me of how worried I was about Celine. Where was she? Why did she leave so suddenly during that chase? I couldn't shake the feeling that something was terribly wrong. Was she in danger, or worse, had something already happened to her?

The more I thought about it, the more upset I became. I tried to force myself to calm down, knowing that panic would only get me killed. But this gnawing worry about Celine wouldn't leave me alone. Why should I waste my time worrying about someone who so easily abandoned me when we were in danger? Maybe she figured it would've been easier to save herself.

My thoughts churned as I tried to suppress the growing resentment. But that wasn't like her, was it? I'd seen her risk her life for me before. She'd been the one to drag me away from danger more than once.

My chest tightened with conflicting emotions. I had to find her, not just for my sake, but to make sure she was alright— or at least to confirm whether or not the twisted nightmare version of her was purely a figment of my imagination.

I gritted my teeth and pushed myself up from the damp ground., my body still aching from previous endeavors. I couldn't let my fear paralyze me. I was alone, and only I would be able to ensure my safety. The forest around me was quiet, the shadows even deeper now than before. Again, the feeling of being watched persisted.

With each step I took, the leaves beneath my boots crunched softly, the sound echoing throughout the otherwise silent trees. I tried to stay light on my feet, moving carefully between the roots.

The further I walked, the more I began to feel a growing sense of unease. The air was colder here, the mist thicker, clinging to my skin like a wet blanket. The trees loomed overhead, their branches twisting and gnarled. I'm sure my paranoia was playing tricks on my eyes, but I couldn't help but think that the trees themselves were whispering to me, taunting me.

A sudden rustling sound to my left made me freeze. I closed my eyes and strained my ears, trying to pinpoint the source. The rustling grew louder, moving closer, and I instinctively ducked behind a thick tree trunk, holding my breath.

A shadow moved through the trees, swift and silent. I caught a glimpse of something pale and humanoid, but it disappeared as quickly as it had appeared. Was it Celine? or something else entirely?

I peered around the tree, my eyes scanning the darkness. The figure was gone, but the sense of being watched hadn't left me. I forced myself to move forward, my muscles tense, ready to spring into action at any moment.

The path wound deeper into the forest, and the trees grew denser. The air grew colder still, and my breath came out in visible puffs. I kept moving, each step taking me deeper into the unknown.

Then I heard it —a soft, almost imperceptible sound. Footsteps, approaching fast. I pressed myself against a nearby tree, trying to blend into the shadows. The footsteps grew louder and closer.

Whatever it was, it was moving quickly. It would pause every so often and then move again as if searching for something. I held my breath as the footsteps stopped just a few feet away. I listened intently, trying to discern any other sounds, but there was nothing. Only silence.

Seconds stretched into what felt like an eternity. Though I couldn't see the figure, I could sense it standing there, unmoving. Was it Celine hiding from the same creatures that hunted us? Or was it one of those fiends, biding its time before it struck?

Before I could decide what to do, the footsteps moved on, fading into the distance. I let out a slow, shaky breath, my body trembling. I'd narrowly escaped detection. Or so I thought.

Suddenly, a low, lifeless breath resonated from the shadows, followed by the rustling of leaves. My blood ran cold as I realized I wasn't alone.

A shadowy figure lunged at me from the darkness. I barely managed to roll to the side, avoiding the sharp claws that slashed through where I had been hiding. The creature snarled, its eyes glowing menacingly.

I scrambled to my feet, drawing my sword just in time to parry another attack. This was undoubtedly one of the same creatures as before: fast and agile, with blurry movements.

"Celine!" I desperately shouted, hoping that she was nearby, that she could hear me.

But there was no response, only the deathly sound of heavy breathing surrounding me. The figures were still concealed by the shadows of the forest, and I had to find a better place to fight. Fighting here, surrounded, would only lead to my downfall. I needed an open area where I'd have a chance to see the next attack coming.

The creature lunged again, and I swung my sword in a desperate arc. The blade missed as I realized the monster was toying with me, testing my defenses.

My gaze flicked around desperately, searching for an escape.

Then I saw it—a faint path leading away from the thicker part of the woods. It was my best chance.

Taking a deep breath, I bolted for the path. The creatures screeched behind me, their guttural sounds echoing through the trees. They gave chase quickly, the sound of leaves rustling with their every move.

The path was narrow, but up ahead, I noticed a small clearing. I pushed myself harder, my sword gripped tightly in my hand. The clearing was only a few yards away. Making it there would give me a slight chance of defending myself more effectively.

I burst into the clearing, spinning around to face my pursuers. The creatures emerged from the shadows, their forms becoming clearer in the strong moonlight. They were a type of fiend I'd learned about in class many times—Grimroots. It has never been confirmed, but these fiends were rumored to come from the earth itself, a rumor that started because of the bark and mushroom spores that grew from their bodies.

I should've noticed what I was up against sooner. These specific fiends only attacked at night and usually in groups. They weren't exactly strong, but what they lacked in strength, they made up for with speed.

They were humanoid and twisted, their bodies a grotesque fusion of flesh and forest. Elongated limbs jutted out at unnatural angles, covered in patches of rough, bark-like skin. From their shoulders and down their arms, large, blade-like protrusions extended, sharp and menacing.

Their mouths were wide and twisted, with rows of jagged teeth that seemed to grin malevolently. Fungi sprouted from their joints and backs, emitting a faint glow. The smell of damp earth and decaying wood clung to them. But their eyes were the most horrifying. They glowed white, like the moon, with a feral intensity, filled with an insatiable hunger.

My body instinctively tensed as adrenaline began pumping through my veins. Each breath I took was now shallow, ready for the inevitable clash.

I steadied my breath and raised my sword defensively. The weight of it felt reassuring in my hands as my fingers tightened around the hilt. The memory of my father's teachings flashed through my mind, his voice calm and steady: "Always keep your guard up, Isaac. Stay light on your feet. Anticipate their moves."

I watched as the Grimroot's limbs bent in ways that defied logic, their twisted forms merging with the shadows as they circled me with deadly intent. Their glowing eyes never left me, tracking my every movement. I could hear their guttural growls, low and rumbling, vibrating through the air like a dark omen.

The fog seemed to thicken around us, a heavy, cloying presence that felt almost alive. It coiled around my legs, making each step feel sluggish and weighted. I forced my mind to stay focused, keeping my eyes darting from one Grimroot to the next, watching for any sign of an attack.

They were waiting, testing me, looking for a moment of weakness. I could feel their anticipation, the collective hunger that radiated from them.

One Grimroot let out a low, menacing hiss as it shifted to my right. I glanced at it from the corner of my eye, not daring to turn my head completely. They were trying to flank me, to overwhelm me with their numbers.

For a brief moment, doubt flickered in my mind. Was this how it all ended, alone in the dark, surrounded by these monstrosities? But then I shook my head, clearing the thought away. I wasn't about to give up now.

The Grimroots continued to circle, their eyes never leaving me. I could feel the sweat on my brow and the dampness of my clothes clinging to my skin. I knew the attacks would start soon. At some point, I would have to make a move; to strike and break their formation. But not yet. Not until I saw an opening.

For now, I would wait. I would watch. And I would be ready.

# CHAPTER 7

Five Grimroots surrounded me, each brandishing their own menacing blades. The glow of their eyes filled me with a deep sense of fear. I quickly counted them, trying to gauge their movements. Grimroots are cautious creatures, attacking only when they sense an advantage— typically when their prey is distracted or vulnerable.

The first Grimroot lunged forward, trying to make an opening for the rest of his comrades. I sidestepped, thrusting my sword quickly. My blade sunk deep into its bark-like skin, and the creature let out a guttural shriek. As I pulled out my sword, another Grimroot took advantage of the opening, darting in from the side. I barely managed to parry its attack, the impact almost causing me to drop my weapon.

A third Grimroot attacked from behind, forcing me to spin around and block again. The force of the blow reverberated up my arm, but I held firm, pushing back with all my might. The two remaining fiends hung back, their eyes gleaming with an burning light, waiting for the perfect moment to strike. I knew I couldn't let them all attack at once. I had to keep moving and had to prevent them from surrounding me completely.

With a surge of energy, I charged at the Grimroot I had wounded earlier, aiming for its legs. My blade cut deep, severing a limb and sending the creature toppling to the ground. It wouldn't kill it, but it would buy me some breathing room.

As the Grimroot crashed to the ground, its shrieks echoed through the forest. I wasted no time. I pivoted to face the next attacker, but before I could fully turn, another one darted toward me from the side. I reacted instinctively, unstrapping my shield from my back just in time to deflect its blade. The fiend's weapon became stuck in my shield as I pushed back, using all of my strength to keep the creature at bay. The Grimroot hissed in frustration, its features contorting in rage as it struggled against my defense.

The remaining Grimroots closed in, their blades poised to strike. I could feel their presence looming around me, their hunger hanging thick in the air. I knew I couldn't keep this up for long; I needed to find a way to turn the tide in my favor.

I kicked the Grimroot still tangled in my shield, creating a brief opening. Seizing the opportunity, I lunged forward, driving my sword into its chest with all my might. The blade pierced through its rough exterior, sinking deep into its core. The Grimroot howled in pain, its arms drooping to its sides as it staggered backward.

I withdrew my sword swiftly and turned to face the remaining attackers. They hesitated, their glowing eyes flickering with uncertainty as they assessed the situation. With one Grimroot dead, another disabled, and the others hesitating, I felt a rush of confidence swell within me. But I knew better than to let my guard down.

I squared my shoulders and kept my eyes darting between the three standing adversaries. The Grimroots mirrored my movements, their eyes fixated on me intently. I could sense their desire to tear me apart.

I lunged forward again, closing the distance between us with pinpoint movements. The nearest Grimroot raised its blade in defense, but I anticipated the move, angling my strike to bypass its guard. My sword cut through the air with a satisfying hiss aimed at the fiend's neck. The blade sliced through bark-ridden flesh with ease, sending the creature to its knees. A thick, sap-like liquid oozed from the wound, pooling on the forest floor.

As I withdrew my sword, I saw a flicker of movement from the corner of my eye. I turned to see two Grimroots advancing, their blades raised. My muscles tensed as I readied myself for their next attack.

Suddenly, a searing pain shot through my calf. In my focus on the advancing Grimroots, I had momentarily forgotten the one I left disabled. I looked down to see it licking blood off its blade. It had crawled up my blind side— the side impaired by the blood from the cut on my brow. Agony shot up my leg. I stumbled, nearly losing my balance. Panic set in as both pain and realization hit me simultaneously.

The remaining Grimroots sensed the opportunity and pressed their attack. I was forced into a defensive stance, my movements becoming frantic as my injured leg slowed me down. The situation was quickly slipping out of my control.

They lunged at me from opposite sides, their movements unnervingly coordinated, like they were one mind controlling two bodies. My instincts took over, and I managed to parry the first attack, my sword ringing out in the quiet forest night as it clashed with the Grimroot's blade. The impact jolted my entire arm, the force stronger than I anticipated. But while I deflected the first strike, the second Grimroot was faster. It saw the opening before I even knew it was there.

A sharp pain tore through my arm, its blade grazing my flesh, leaving a burning line of agony in its wake. I gasped, feeling the warmth of blood dripping down my arm, the sensation oddly cold against my sweat-soaked skin. My mind screamed at the pain, but I had no time to process it. Sweat and dirt mingled with the wound, sending a stinging ache through my nerves that made it hard to focus.

Instinctively, I tried to retreat, but the moment I shifted my weight, a searing pain shot up from my leg because of my earlier injury. My leg buckled beneath me, and I collapsed backward, my sword barely staying in my grasp as I hit the ground hard.

The Grimroot that had been crawling across the ground seized its moment. It moved with a horrifying speed, its body low to the ground, almost insect-like. I kicked out, trying to keep some distance between us, but my injured leg screamed in protest. The creature's blade slashed at my leg, the sharp edge grazing the skin but missing anything vital. Still, it was enough to make my entire body tense in agony.

Scrambling back, my hands dug into the dirt, feeling the rough earth beneath my fingers as I tried to pull myself away from the oncoming danger. My breath was ragged, each inhale a battle against the panic rising in my chest.

The standing fiends advanced, staring at me with delight. I was losing ground, both physically and mentally. Fear tightened its grip on my heart, and despair crept into my mind. *This could be the end*, I realized. The thought consumed me. I didn't want to die; I had barely begun to live.

"Stay away from me!" I screamed, my voice cracking with fear. I flailed my sword back and forth, trying to keep them at bay. The Grimroots paused, almost as if they were amused.

I continued to backpedal, nearly tripping over my own hands. Each beat of my heart was a frantic plea for survival. "I don't want to die," I whispered, my voice barely audible over the pounding in my ears. The Grimroots advanced slowly, savoring my fear.

Panic turned briefly to anger as I cursed myself for my lack of self-preservation. If only I had trusted my judgment and refused to follow Celine. I could be home right now, doing damn all. But no, I had trusted someone who abandoned me at the first sign of danger. I had only myself to blame.

"I don't want to die!" I shouted, my voice breaking. I swung my sword again, more a plea than a threat. The Grimroots encircled me, their movements methodical, almost mocking. Tears welled up in my eyes, further blurring my vision. I couldn't keep this up much longer; my strength was fading, and with it, my hope.

Just as the crawling Grimroot lunged at my legs again, a small glow zipped through the air from the tree line, leaving a trail of light in its wake. It struck the Grimroot, engulfing it in a blaze of fire. The creature let out a series of shrieks as its bark-like skin cracked and split. Within seconds, it was consumed by the flames.

It was a flaming arrow.

I turned my head to see countless glows through the forest. The flickering light revealed a group of figures emerging from the darkness. Leading them was Celine, her torch held hush as she guided the Kingsguard toward me.

I blinked, trying to shake the fog of pain and exhaustion clouding my vision, but the scene before me was unmistakable. The soft glow of torches illuminated the darkened forest, casting flickering shadows that danced against the trees like specters. For a moment, the weight of my injuries, the burning in my legs and arms, all seemed to dull as I realized help was finally within reach.

The soft rustle of boots against the forest floor reached my ears, and with it, the feeling of relief. But as the figures drew closer, something stirred within me—an unexpected mix of gratitude and apprehension. This was no ordinary rescue party. The Kingsguard were the elite protectors of the realm. Their presence alone seemed to change the very air around us, making it heavier with authority and power.

I could recognize their attire anywhere. The Kingsguard were a sight to behold, their presence imposing and majestic. Each guard was clad in meticulously crafted armor, a blend of practicality and artistry. Their helmets, forged from gleaming steel, bore a crescent moon emblem at the brow. Midnight blue cloaks flowed gracefully behind them, fastened with silver brooches bearing the moon's symbol.

Their weapons were as formidable as their armor—longswords with hilts embedded with moonstones, blades etched with runes believed to grant strength and protection. Some wielded rounded shields with the same moon symbol, while others carried bows, their quivers filled with silver-tipped arrows designed to pierce through even the thickest of hides.

Their armor was a marvel of craftsmanship. Each piece interlocked seamlessly to provide maximum protection while allowing agility. Upon their breastplates were intricate engravings of the lunar phases, denoting each knight's rank.

The first knight I noticed had a darkened, barely discernible new moon on his breastplate; he was young, an initiate just beginning his journey. The New Moon Knights were still training, eager and determined to prove their worth. They handled all of the basic duties and assisted the higher-ranked knights with their tasks.

Nearby was a knight that bore a slim crescent moon growing towards the right. This signified that he was a Crescent Moon Knight. These knights had progressed from their initial training and were not involved in patrols and minor skirmishes.

A third-quarter moon, split down the middle with the left side illuminated, caught my eye next. The Third Quarter Moon Knights were experienced defenders that proved who capability in combat and strategy. They often led small groups of lower-ranked knights and were crucial in the chain of command.

Lastly, my attention was drawn to a knight whose breastplate had the symbol of a fully illuminated moon. These were the Full Moon Knights, the commanders. They led the entire battalions and were responsible for crucial decisions during warfare. Their authority was unquestioned, and their wisdom was esteemed.

As they drew closer, I sensed their fierce determination, mirroring their loyalty and duty to the king and the land they swore to protect. The Kingsguard were not just soldiers; they embodied Moonveil's strength and honor.

Their torches blazed brightly, casting an intimidating glow that made the Grimroots hesitate. It was as if they could sense the resolve of the guards, a force to be reckoned with.

A guard notched another flaming arrow and fired, striking one of the remaining Grimroots. The fiend roared in agony as the fire spread rapidly across its body. The Kingsguard charged forward, their torches held high. The remaining Grimroot, noticing the flames, stepped back in fear.

"Drifted, on your feet!" Celine shouted, her voice cutting through the fog of my fear. She pressed toward the Grimroot, swinging her torch and forcing it to retreat.

I forced myself to my feet, ignoring the searing burn in my calf. The sight of the fire and Celine's presence bolstered my resolve. I was shocked to see her standing before me.

Celine moved closer, her torch illuminating the subtle purple glow in her eyes. Her expression was fierce, determined—a stark contrast to the fear I had felt only moments before.

"You are not alone, Drifted," she said softly. "The foul creatures exist no longer."

I nodded, adjusting my grip on my sword as I moved beside her. The weight of battle still clung to me, but her presence offered a strange sense of calm.

"Men, don't let that monster escape!" a guard shouted. Another flaming arrow soared through the air, striking the last retreating Grimroot. It let out a low, agonizing groan before collapsing to the ground, engulfed in flames.

"Form a perimeter!" The Full Moon Knight barked again. "Secure the tree line. Ensure there are no more lurking fiends."

The guards quickly formed a protective circle around us, their torches casting a warm glow that pushed the darkness away. Celine and I stood together, breaths ragged, hearts racing. As the last Grimroot smoldered to ash, the tension slowly faded.

Celine's gaze softened. "The danger has passed. Rest now and regain your strength."

I nodded again as exhaustion came crashing over me. The will-power that had kept me moving drained away, leaving my limbs heavy and sore. "Thank you, Celine," I murmured, my voice hoarse. "For a moment there, I thought… it was over."

One of the guards approached, his expression a mix of relief and admiration. "You fought well, lad," he said. "But if it weren't for this little lady here, you might not be standing."

The other guards nodded in agreement, a few clapping me on the back with relieved smiles. "Aye, you should've seen her! We lost sight of her five times. She was in such a hurry to reach you! You owe her a great debt," another guard chimed in, grinning.

Laughter echoed among the men—a strange sound in the aftermath of battle, yet it was welcome. A brief respite from the chaos.

Celine remained focused, keeping her expression steady. "We must return to town," she said. "Your wounds are grave. Rest and care are needed."

The guard leader nodded. "She's right, lad. Let's get you back to town. You can recover there, and we'll ensure your safety."

"Town? Where are we?" I asked, my mind still foggy from the ordeal.

"Not far from Noctiluna," the guard replied. "About a two-mile hike from here."

Noctiluna. I hadn't been there since I was young, always visiting with my parents. I remembered the bustling night markets, the street performers, and the scent of exotic foods in the air. The thrill of adventure always accompanied our trips there. Now, standing here, I realized how far I'd come with Celine by my side. We had traveled so far from Lunaria to here, covering a distance of nearly 220 miles. To now be only 2 miles from Noctiluna was a welcoming surprise.

We had trekked northwest through dense forests, infested rivers, and treacherous terrain. Despite all the obstacles, we have made it this far.

The guard's voice interrupted my thoughts. "No time to dally, lad. Let's move."

I took a step forward, but pain shot through my leg, sharp and searing. I winced, the rush of the battle no longer dulling the agony.

Celine noticed immediately. "You are more injured than I thought," she said, her calm voice laced with concern. "We must hurry, but tread carefully."

One of the guards stepped forward, offering an arm. "Let me help."

Reluctantly, I accepted, leaning on him as we started our trek toward Noctiluna. Each step was painful, but I gritted my teeth. I refused to show weakness in front of them.

The path was rough, covered with twisted roots and uneven ground. But the Kingsguard provided a sense of safety, their torches lighting the way. Every so often, I caught glimpses of Grimroot eyes glinting in the shadows. Yet none dared approach, repelled by the flames we carried.

Celine walked beside me, her expression unreadable. "You have shown courage," she said quietly.

I chuckled, though it was more out of surprise than amusement. Praise from her felt rare, almost misplaced. "Thank you," I said, appreciating her words more than I could express.

The night seemed less daunting with the Kingsguard by our side. The memory of the recent battle was still fresh in my mind, but with the guards encircling me, my fear was slowly replaced with a sense of determination.

As we finally neared Noctiluna, the town was as alive as I remembered. Even at this hour, the night markets bustled with energy, lanterns casting a mellow glow over the cobblestone streets. The air was rich with the aroma of spiced meats and sweet pastries. Vendors called out to passersby, and children darted through the crowds, laughing beneath the watchful eyes of their parents.

Colorful canopies were stretched over the market stalls, creating an assortment of vibrant hues against the night sky. Each stall was an invitation to explore, offering local crafts, homemade remedies, and various items unique to the surrounding towns. Artisans displayed their wares with pride; beautifully woven textiles, intricate poetry, and handcrafted tools.

Street performers added to the spectacle. Musicians played lively music on flutes and stringed instruments. Acrobats and fire-eaters drew crowds with their daring feats, and storytellers captivated listeners with tales of adventure.

Despite the late hour, children darted through the crowd, their laughter infectious as they chased each other under the watchful eye of their parents. The town felt alive, a place where the townsfolk never truly slept.

Noctiluna's architecture added to its charm. The buildings were adorned with ornate carvings and painted in rich, earthy tones. Balconies overflowed with flowering plants, their petals glistening in the lamplight. Narrow alleyways branched off from the main market, each covered in doors and art that led to various houses.

As we walked through the market, the Kingsgaurd's presence drew respectful nods and glances. Celine and I were a stark contrast to the atmosphere around us, but the townsfolk seemed to take our weary state in stride, offering smiles and warm greetings.

"We've arrived," the guard supporting me said, relief in his voice. "Let's get you to a medic."

Before I could respond, Celine stepped forward. "I shall tend to his wounds," she said, her tone leaving no room for argument.

The guard chuckled, glancing between us. "Ah, to be tended to by such a fine lady," he teased, a hint of jealousy in his eyes. "I envy you, lad."

Heat crept into my face; the embarrassment undeniable. I shifted under his gaze, unsure of how to respond. However, Celine remained composed, offering the guard a small, mysterious smile.

"Perhaps life will grant thee such fortune," she replied, her tone as cryptic as ever.

The guard chuckled again, nodding as he took his leave. "Aye, perhaps so. He's in good hands."

As he walked away, I tried to take a step, but the pain in my leg flared again, nearly toppling me. Celine moved swiftly to my side, steadying me with a firm grip.

"You cannot walk alone," she said softly. "Lean on me, Drifted. We shall find a place to rest."

I nodded, feeling a mix of gratitude and awkwardness as I leaned into her.

After what felt like an eternity, we reached an inn. The outside was modest, but it looked clean and welcoming.

"We shall rest here, Drifted," Celine said.

I nodded, the exhaustion creeping back as we made our way closer to the inn. The sign above the door read The Lunar Hearth. Celine guided me inside, where a plump woman with kind eyes greeted us.

"Welcome to The Lunar Hearth," she said, concern quickly

filling her gaze as she noticed my state. "Oh, dear, you've been through quite an ordeal. Do you need a medic?"

"A room," Celine replied before I could speak. "A room for us to recover."

My heart skipped a beat at her words. A room—just one? The thought made my mind race, but I kept silent.

The innkeeper nodded, fetching a key from behind the counter. "Room 3, up the stairs and to the left." She said, handing the key to Celine.

"And bandages, if you would," Celine added, her voice calm yet authoritative.

"Yes, of course, dear," the woman replied warmly. She ducked beneath the counter for a moment, rummaging through a few supplies before emerging with a set of bandages and a bucket.

"There you go," the innkeeper said with a wide smile as she handed over the items. Her gaze lingered on us briefly as if silently piecing together our story, but she didn't ask any questions. "If you need anything else, just let me know."

Celine gave her a polite nod before turning to me. "Come," she said softly, her voice gentle but firm. She slid one arm under mine and helped me move, guiding me toward a narrow staircase that led to the upper rooms.

Celine helped me up a narrow staircase, guiding me to the room. I tried to process the situation. Sharing a room with Celine felt comforting and unnerving.

As we reached the room, Celine unlocked the door and guided me inside. It was small but cozy—a single bed and a chair by the window. She lit a lantern, casting a soft glow over the space.

I glanced at a mirror on the wall. "Could you help me to the mirror?" I asked, my voice still weak.

She obliged, and as I gazed into the mirror, the sight was jarring. Dirt and blood smeared across my face, the cut on my brow still oozing slightly. I looked bruised and battered, but alive.

"You have endured much," Celine said, meeting my eyes in the reflection. "Rest now."

She guided me to the bed, and I sank into it, the softness a relief to my aching body.

I slowly removed my sword, sword belt, and shield, each movement sending a dull ache through my tired muscles. The sword's hilt felt heavier than ever as I placed it on the floor beside the bed. My shield followed, slipping from my grasp and landing with a soft thud.

Celine left the room with the bucket, coming back moments later with it filled to the brim with water. She sat beside me on the bed, dampening a cloth and gently cleaning the blood from my face. The coolness was soothing against my skin.

"Thank you, Celine," I murmured, embarrassed by her closeness, by her care. I knew there was no way to hide the embarrassment on my face now, Celine only a couple of inches away from me.

She didn't reply immediately; her eyes focused on my wounds.

"You need not thank me," she finally replied, her voice gentle. "Tending to you is...my duty." Her eyes flicked up in a blur of purple to meet mine for a brief moment. For a second, I thought I saw a hint of something more personal in her gaze.

I swallowed hard; my mouth suddenly dry. The cool cloth moved to the cut on my brow, and I winced as the water touched the wound.

Celine's touch was gentle, almost tender, as she applied a bandage with skilled hands. "You have a strong spirit, Drifted," she said, "but even the strong must rest and heal."

"You don't have to bother yourself though," I started, "I feel bad making you take care of me like this.". It was true; I rarely relied on anyone but myself ever since my parents died. Having someone suddenly take care of me like this felt foreign.

Celine's purple eyes focused intently on me, and I saw a depth in them that made me pause. "I have told you before," she said quietly, her voice almost a whisper, "our fates are intertwined. Your life is like my own. In helping you, I fulfill a part of my own destiny."

She continued, her voice steady, "This destiny has not yet been revealed to me, but I know that this is what is required of me. Being here with you is where my duty lies".

I was at a loss for words, caught between gratitude and the overwhelming sense of connection she spoke of. I couldn't think of any way to reply to such heavy words in a meaningful manner. The silence stretched, filled only by the faint sounds of the town below us and my own uneven breaths.

Celine finished bandaging me, her movements gently. Once she was done, she stood up, her eyes never leaving mine.

"Rest now, Drifted," she said, her tone soft but firm. "I will keep watch."

I wanted to protest, to offer some sense of duty in return, but the weight of fatigue was overwhelming. Through half-lidded eyes, I saw Celine move toward the window, her silhouette framed by the faint light of the moon outside. She sat in a chair by the window, her presence calming. "You have endured much, but the night offers solace to the weary soul.

With a nod, I settled into the bed and allowed the exhaustion to take over. The last thing I saw before closing my eyes was Celine staring out the window, watching the busy streets beneath us.

# CHAPTER 8

The morning sun came through the thin curtains of the Lunar Hearth, casting a warm glow over the modest room. I blinked against the light, my body aching from the previous night's battle. Each movement sent sharp pains because of injuries I'd sustained, though the worst of it had dulled to a manageable throb.

Glancing around the room, my eyes landed on Celine. She was still seated by the window, her posture relaxed but her gaze alert, scanning the streets below. She must have stayed there all night, watching over me.

"Celine," I called out, my voice hoarse. She turned toward me, her purple eyes softening.

"You're rested, Drifted?" she asked, rising from her chair and crossing the room to my side. "How do you fare?"

"Sore," I admitted, attempting to sit up. Celine quickly moved to help me stand. "But alive, nonetheless."

As I looked around the room further, I noticed a wooden crutch leaning against the wall beside the bed. "When did you find time to get this?" I asked, grabbing it.

"While you rested," she replied, her tone plain.

"Well, guess I'll need it," I muttered, testing my weight on the crutch. A sharp pain shot through my leg, but it was bearable.

Celine watched carefully as I gathered my items from the floor. Then, together, we made our way downstairs to the inn's common room, where the innkeeper greeted us with a warm smile.

"Up and about already, young man?" she asked, bustling over

to us.

"Better, thanks," I replied, leaning heavily on Celine.

"Good to hear. Breakfast is ready if you're hungry."

My stomach growled in response. "Breakfast sounds amazing!"

We sat near the hearth, where the fire's warmth added a comforting touch to the morning. The innkeeper brought plates of bread, cheese, fried eggs, fruit, ham, and steaming mugs of herbal tea. I dug in eagerly, savoring the fresh meal.

It's been a while since I got to eat a fresh meal like this. Celine and I spent most of our travels eating what we could from the land- foraging for wild mushrooms, picking berries, catching fish, and occasionally hunting rabbits. After days of foraging and hunting on the road, this simple spread felt like a feast.

Celine ate slowly, her movements graceful as always, though her eyes flicked toward me now and then, a mixture of curiosity and something deeper in her gaze. I couldn't quite place it.

As I sipped my tea, my attention was drawn to a painting on the wall—a regal man with a stern but kind face, his crown adorned with jewels. His eyes held a sense of benevolence.

"Well, if it isn't King Alden himself," I said absentmindedly.

Celine's eyes followed my gaze. For a moment, she studied the portrait in silence. "King Alden?" she asked.

I looked at her, slightly confused. "Everyone knows who the great King Alden was. Your memory loss must be really bad."

"Enlighten me, Drifted," she said, her focus on me sharpening.

"Well," I began, trying to recall my childhood lessons, "he was the one who built Noctiluna and the other cities in Moonveil. He united scattered tribes and settlements into a single kingdom."

Celine leaned in slightly, her interest piqued. "What made him such a visionary?"

I paused, searching my memory. "I think it was his belief in this land. Where others saw wilderness, he saw potential. He built this kingdom from the ground up and preserved it when humanity was on the brink, under siege from the fiends."

"A man of great stature, it seems," Celine replied, mused.

"Apparently so," I replied, nodding. "To the people of Moonveil, he's a symbol of hope, a show that even in the darkest times, unity can save us."

Celine's eyes flickered with interest as she asked, "Moonveil, such a peculiar name... Why pay homage to the moon?"

I shrugged. "King Alden was fond of the moon, though I don't know why. He built our traditions around it—our markets, festivals, even our architecture."

I took another sip of tea. "My parents used to say the moonstones in the Kingsguards' weapons were from the moon itself, a gift from King Alden. People believed the stones granted some form of strength and protection."

Celine nodded. "The moon possesses a certain energy," she said thoughtfully. "It is said that those who walk in its light are favored."

I raised one eyebrow in curiosity. "Is that so? You seem certain." I remarked.

"The moon has always guided me on my journeys, Drifted," she replied with a faint smile.

Curiosity stirred within me. "What sort of journeys have you been on?"

Her eyes grew distant. "Many, from a time before you. Some filled with wonder, others with danger. But the moon's light has always been my guide."

I grew even more confused by her mysterious answer. "Can you tell me more?" I asked.

"She took a deep breath, her gaze turning introspective. "I've alwa-"

Before Celine could finish, the innkeeper approached our table. "You two look like you've seen your share of adventures," she said with a friendly smile. "How did you travel here with things becoming so dangerous recently!"

I glanced at Celine, unsure how much to reveal. "We've had close calls," I said, glancing down at my leg.

"Yes, I recall the two of you shuffling last night," the innkeeper said, nodding knowingly. "You looked a sight, but your girlfriend here must be quite the nurse!"

My cheeks flushed. "Oh, no, she… We're…" My thoughts failed as I struggled to find the right response.

"Yes, I've been doing my best to tend to him," Celine interjected smoothly, her voice calm. She turned her gaze to me briefly before returning to the innkeeper. "He's been quite brave, considering."

I blinked in surprise. Confusion bubbling as I studied Celine's face, trying to find any hint of mischief or amusement. But her expression remained serene.

The innkeeper smiled, oblivious to my discomfort. "You're lucky to have such a caring, beautiful woman by your side! Not everyone finds someone who'll stick by them through thick and thin."

She offered me a friendly wink as I lowered my head in embarrassment.

I managed a weak smile, still trying to process. "Thank you," I mumbled.

Celine placed a hand on mine, grounding me. "We must take our leave," she said gently.

I nodded, eager to leave and gather my thoughts. As I reached for my pouch, the innkeeper stopped me.

"Oh no young man, your meal and stay are on the house,"

she said with a smile. "Consider it a token of my appreciation. It's been a while since I've had such a lovely couple share their company with me."

I opened my mouth to protest, but the innkeeper interjected before I could start.

"I will not be taking no for an answer," she said as she cleared our dishes from the table.

"Thank you," Celine said graciously. Her reply putting the innkeeper at ease. "Your kindness is truly appreciated."

The innkeeper nodded, her smile widening.

"It's the least I can do for such charming guests," she said as she continued clearing our table.

With a final nod of thanks, Celine and I rose from our seats and made our way towards the inn's exit. As I reached for the door, Celine's hand caught my other one.

I turned to see Celine standing there, her hand gently gripping mine. Surprise danced across my face as I saw her relaxed gaze.

"Celi—" I began, my voice trailing off.

"Come now, dear, we mustn't block the door," she said, gently nudging me forward.

As I closed the door behind us, I heard the innkeeper chuckle with glee. "Oh, young love always warms my heart!"

"What in the world…" I muttered, my face flushing as I stepped outside., the cool morning air soothing my burning cheeks.

Celine gave me a sympathetic look. "It seems she enjoys weaving tales," she said, her voice carrying a hint of mischief. "But we must not reveal too much of ourselves to anyone, Drifted. It may be safer to let them believe what they wish."

I listened quietly, taking in her warning. There was always something calculated about the way Celine spoke, as if she could see the path ahead long before I did.

"There may be those who seek to hinder our journey.

Continuing under the guise of two with romantic interest may be our safest option," she suggested, her tone carrying a weight of practicality and foresight.

I couldn't help but feel impressed as I digested her suggestion. Even then, as we had an innocent conversation with the innkeeper, Celine was anticipating a threat.

I understood her logic, currently, appearances would be our best defense, a shield that kept curious eyes at bay and prevented prying questions. For Celine, this wasn't personal, it was tactical.

I shifted awkwardly on my crutch, my thoughts jumbling together. "Right," I muttered, trying to sound nonchalant, though a hint of confusion bled through. "And besides, whatever people think, it's none of their business." The words came out harsher than I intended, a mix of annoyance and discomfort bristling under my skin.

Celine chuckled softly, her laughter lightening the mood slightly. "Indeed, Drifted. Let us leave them to their imaginings and focus on our journey ahead."

As we walked down the cobblestone path, I found myself wondering—had the innkeeper seen something between us that I hadn't? Were others assuming we were more than just companions? The thought weighed on me, and I stole a glance at Celine, who walked beside me, calm and composed. Could it be that there was something more?

I suppose we weren't too far off. Celine and I have gotten fairly close in a short amount of time. It wasn't hard to grow close to someone when you're together daily. It was possible that this was beginning to naturally portray itself in how we interacted.

With each step, I found myself becoming increasingly self-conscious. I stole looks at passersby, checking to see if they were watching us and if they, too, were making that assumption. My steps grew awkward, and I tried to put some distance between us, not wanting to give anyone the wrong idea.

Celine turned her head in my direction, noticing the gap I put between us. "Is something troubling you Drifted?" she asked calmly.

I hesitated, unsure how to explain the sudden feeling of unease. "It's nothing," I replied, forcing a half-hearted smile. "Just… thinking."

Her gaze lingered on me. "What of?" she prompted, her eyes now boring into mine.

I didn't respond immediately; instead, I focused on the road ahead. Celine let out a quiet breath, turning her attention back to the path before us. "People will see what they wish to see," she said, her voice soft yet steady. "It changes nothing. Their thoughts, their whispers, they do not alter our purpose. Let them think as they will."

She was right. The opinions of strangers shouldn't matter. Yet, despite knowing this, a small part of me couldn't help but wonder—what if there was something more between us? What if—

No. I pushed the thought away, feeling foolish. Celine was a partner on a journey of great importance, nothing more. That should be enough.

I matched my steps with hers again as we moved toward the main square of the city, where life had already begun to stir despite the early hour. The hum of conversation and the cries of merchants filled the air.

Stalls lined the streets, their vibrant canopies flapping in the breeze as vendors peddled their goods. Shoppers drifted from one stand to another, haggling over prices and inspecting produce. The scent of fresh bread mingled with the crisp morning air, and my stomach growled in response.

The city buzzed with activity, a constant stream of movement and sound, and everyone seemed to have a place to be. It was both energizing and overwhelming.

I kept close to Celine, wary of losing her in the bustling crowd. It was easy to get swallowed by the sea of people, and in that moment, I realized how vulnerable it made us.

Suddenly, Celine stopped. "Follow me, Drifted," she said, her voice carrying a quiet urgency.

Without hesitation, she slipped into the throng, moving with surprising grace and agility. I hurried after her, doing my best to keep up. Every few steps, I nearly lost sight of her as she wove effortlessly through the crowd. Meanwhile, I stumbled awkwardly behind, muttering apologies with each person I bumped into.

The crutch made it even harder to navigate, every step sending a dull ache through my leg. I gritted my teeth, determined not to fall too far behind.

Just as I feared I might lose her, I caught a glimpse of her turning a corner, heading toward the edge of the market square. I quickened my pace and rounded the bend to see her standing at a small, lively stall, her gaze fixed on something. A vendor was displaying baskets of strawberries, their vibrant red contrasting sharply against the worn wood of the counter.

By the time I reached her, Celine was already in conversation with the vendor, a warm-looking old man with twinkling eyes. He glanced at me as I approached.

"Good morning, lad," he greeted me with a smile. "Your friend here's got an eye for the finest produce. These strawberries are the best in all of Moonveil, I assure you."

Celine turned to me, her lips curling into a rare, full smile. In her hands, she held a small basket of strawberries. "I thought we could use a treat," she said.

*Right, us,* I thought to myself. I couldn't help but chuckle inwardly, knowing how this would play out—she'd devour most of them, leaving me just a few out of kindness.

The vendor chuckled along with me. "A fine choice, young lady. Nothing like fresh strawberries to start the day off right."

I returned his smile, feeling a sense of warmth and normalcy amidst the chaos of the town. I reached into my pouch to pay, but as I counted the Selens, my heart sank.

Looking up at the price, I realized how steep it was—far more than I had remembered from childhood. I'd say the berries cost almost triple what they did when I was younger.

"The price has really gone up, hasn't it?" I said, frowning at the coins in my hand.

The old man sighed, his cheerful demeanor dimming. "Aye, with the fiends growing bolder in the woods, gathering has become more dangerous. These are harder to come by now."

I stared at the small handful of coins and realized we couldn't afford them. This was all I had left from the morning I'd met Celine.

Her smile faded as she looked down at the basket. "It seems we'll have to go without," she said, her voice soft with disappointment.

Celine gently placed the basket back on the stall, her fingers lingering on the edge before she withdrew them. "Let's continue, Drifted," she murmured, turning to leave.

I gave the vendor a small nod and turned away from the stall.

As we began to walk away, the vendor suddenly called out.

"Wait a minute, you two!"

We turned back to see him watching us with a thoughtful expression. He glanced around before speaking in a lower tone. "You two look capable. I dropped something in the woods when I was foraging for these berries—something important. A fiend ambushed me, and I was barely able to get away. I can't go back there by myself."

He paused, his eyes earnest.

If you're willing to retrieve it for me, I'll not only give you the berries for free, but I'll pay you a bit of Selens for the trouble. What do you say?"

The opportunity sounded very appealing to me. Admittedly, I felt horrible seeing the look on Celine's face as she realized we couldn't afford the purchase.

I exchanged a glance with Celine. There was a spark of curiosity in her eyes.

"What did you lose?" I asked the vendor.

"A small leather satchel," he explained. "It's got personal items in it, but more importantly, my wedding ring. My wife... well, she won't be pleased if she found out I've lost it."

I turned to Celine. "What do you think? Up for a quick trip?" I tried to keep my tone light, attempting to hide the fact that my leg was throbbing as we stood here. I shifted my weight, leaning ever so slightly on my crutch in an attempt to hide the discomfort.

Her eyes flickered to my leg, her lips pressing into a thin line. Concern etched its way across her otherwise stoic expression, softening her sharp features. "You are injured, Drifted. It would be unwise to venture into the woods."

I straightened, ignoring the pain at my calf. I'd been through worse—at least, I told myself I had. "I'll manage," I replied, trying to sound more confident than I felt. "It's not far, right?" I asked the vendor for reassurance, hoping for something that would bolster my case.

"Not far," he confirmed. "A mile south, near a large oak. Though you must be careful, there was a large fiend there earlier this morning; I cannot guarantee you that it has moved on,"

"See, the fiend may not even be there anymore," I said to Celine, trying to puff my chest out.

Celine crossed her arms, her fingers tapping lightly against the leather of her cloak. She wasn't entirely convinced. I could see it in the subtle tightening of her jaw, in the way her eyes flicked briefly to the forest's edge beyond the town. The woods had become far more dangerous in recent months, and she knew it better than most.

Still, I gave her a reassuring smile, hoping to sway her. "We'll be careful. Stick together and move quietly. If we encounter the fiend, we retreat immediately. How's that sound?"

Celine hesitated, her gaze searching mine, weighing my words carefully. She was practical to a fault, and I knew she wouldn't agree to this lightly. For a moment, I thought she might refuse outright. But then, after what felt like an eternity, she nodded slowly.

"Very well. But we must be cautious. If we sense any unease— any at all—we must abandon our pursuit of the item."

I quickly turned back to the vendor, not wanting to give Celine a chance to change her mind. "That settles it then! We'll have that satchel back for you in no time."

The vendor's face lit up with relief, his shoulders sagging as if a great weight had been lifted from him. "Thank you," he said earnestly. "Just be cautious. Those woods are no longer as safe as they once were."

With those parting words of caution, Celine and I began to make our way out of the bustling marketplace. The sounds of the crowd gradually faded into the background as we walked.

As we reached the edge of town, the looming shadows of the forest beckoned us onward.

# CHAPTER 9

Celine and I stood between the marketplace and the southern gate. Steeling our nerves as we took a step forward in unison.

"Hold there!" A guard called out from the side, stepping forward with a stern expression. "Where do you two think you're going?"

"We're just taking a stroll in the woods, don't worry. We don't plan on heading too far," I explained, gesturing toward the dense foliage ahead.

The guard, weary, moved to block our path. I exchanged a puzzled glance with Celine, unsure of their sudden intervention. His eyes drifted to my leg and the crutch supporting me. "Look, we can't exactly stop you, but fiends have been encroaching on the town. I suggest you steer clear of the forest for now."

I stared at the guard, annoyed at his unwarranted concern.

"Listen, we appreciate your worry," I replied, my voice steady despite my annoyance. "But we have a task and can't afford any delay."

As we stood there, another guard approached from behind us, most likely drawn by the commotion we were now causing.

"What seems to be the problem?" He called out, making his way next to the guard blocking our path.

I rolled my eyes. Just our luck; another guard is coming to complicate things further.

"There's no problem. She and I need to enter the forest, but for some reason, we are being advised against doing so."

The guard squinted at us for a long while before his eyes widened. "Wait a minute," he said, stepping closer. "Aren't you two… the ones from last night?"

Celine and I shared a confused look.

"Yea. I'm sure of it!" he continued, admiration in his voice. "You're the one who led us to your friend here." He nodded toward Celine. "And you," he added, pointing at me, "fought off those fiends. I have to say, I'm surprised you're up and about so soon after that nasty wound you got."

I offered a grateful smile, admittedly touched by his recognition. "Takes more than a couple of scratches to keep me down," I said with determination.

The guard nodded, still impressed. "Well, just be careful. You know as well as anyone—those fiends are no joke."

He turned to his companion, who shot us a resigned look. "Fine," the other guard said with a sigh. "But if anything happens, I warned you. The forest is not a place for the faint of heart these days."

I nodded. "Thanks, we'll be cautious."

Celine stepped forward, her gaze focused on the two guards. "We appreciate your concern and shall heed your warning. We shall tread carefully and avoid unnecessary risks."

The guards stepped aside, allowing us to pass. As we entered the forest, the sounds of the noisy town faded, replaced by the rustling of leaves and distant bird calls. The air cooled as the canopy of the trees enveloped us, offering a welcome shade from the afternoon sun.

It felt good to be back in the woods, away from the hustle of town. I breathed deeply, savoring the crisp, earthy scent of damp soil and foliage. The tranquility here sharply contrasted the chaos we'd left behind, and a sense of peace began to wash over me.

Celine walked beside me, her eyes scanning our surroundings, alert in a way that made me feel like I should be too, "The forest breathes with a quiet life of its own, does it not, Drifted?" she murmured, her voice blending with the soft hum of nature around us.

"Yeah," I replied, smiling. It was nice to share this love of the forest with her.

The path ahead narrowed, winding through thick underbrush. I maneuvered carefully with my crutch, each step requiring focus. My leg throbbed with a dull ache, but I gritted my teeth and kept moving. Still, a renewed sense of purpose pushed me forward, a silent determination I hadn't felt in a while.

The further we moved into the forest, the thicker the foliage got. Soon, the paths gradually grew steeper, making it slightly more difficult for me to navigate.

Celine moved ahead effortlessly, her light steps barely disturbing the leaves beneath her feet. She paused occasionally, glancing back to check on me, her eyes filled with a quiet understanding. I appreciated that about her—she never hovered, never pitied. She just... was.

I limped over a fallen branch, wincing slightly, but I was determined not to let the injury slow me down too much. "The woods have always had a way of clearing my head," I said, more to myself than to her. But Celine glanced back, offering a faint smile that spoke of her own connection to the forest.

"Do you think we'll find it easily?" I asked Celine, breaking the silence.

Celine glanced at me thoughtfully. "If the vendor's directions are correct, we should encounter the oak tree without much difficulty. Let us hope the fiend has wandered elsewhere."

I gave her a slight smile, trying to show confidence. "We'll handle whatever comes our way."

"Aye, I do hope that is the case," she replied, though I could tell she had reservations.

After a few more minutes of walking, Celine raised her hand and signaled me to stop. "We have arrived," she whispered, pointing ahead.

Through the thick brush, a massive oak tree stood tall, its sprawling branches blotting out much of the sky. At its base, I spotted a small leather satchel.

"There's the satchel," I said, relieved to actually have located it. "Now let's hope that fiend isn't around."

As I took a step forward, Celine held her arm out, stopping me. "You will remain here, Drifted. I will retrieve the satchel."

I frowned, not liking the idea of her going alone. "No way. I can at least help—"

"Your leg is still healing," she interrupted, her tone firm. "If we encounter danger, your mobility will be greatly limited. I do not have any ailments and am both quieter and more agile than you are. Stay here; cover our retreat if you seek to be useful."

Her logic was sound, but it didn't ease the knot of frustration tightening in my chest. I hated feeling so useless, being relegated to the sidelines while she ventured into potential danger. Every part of me wanted to argue, to insist that I could still fight, still be useful, even with my injury. But deep down, I knew she was right. My leg was still healing and if something happened, I wouldn't be fast enough to keep up, let alone protect her.

Reluctantly, I nodded, swallowing the bitterness in my throat. "Okay. Be careful," I muttered, the words feeling hollow in my mouth as if I was giving up more than just the argument.

With a nod, she slipped through the underbrush, moving with the grace of a shadow. I positioned myself behind a tree, keeping my eyes on her as she approached the oak. My muscles tensed, ready to spring into action if necessary.

Celine reached the tree, crouching to lift the satchel, when suddenly her head shot up, eyes wide and alert. "Drifted, conceal yourself!" she hissed urgently.

I ducked behind the tree, pressing my back against its rough bark. From my hiding spot, I strained to hear what had startled her. The sound of heavy, clumsy footsteps crashing through the forest reached my ears.

Peeking from behind the tree, I saw it —a hulking figure lumbering towards us. A Fungoid, its grotesque form barely visible in the now dim light.

Another fiend we studied greatly in school. They are simple-minded creatures driven by destruction, with bodies covered in fungal growths and burning malevolent eyes. The skin, gray and dull, looked sickly against the lush, green forest. Their brawn was unmatched, and we were always warned not to face one alone. Fungoids had no need for stealth, as monstrous strength was their greatest weapon, and they used it to devastating effect.

Getting hit by one swing from these beasts could easily shatter your ribs. I watched as its heavy footfalls echoed around the forest. Each of its steps shook the ground, and the closer it got, the stronger the smell of decaying flesh and vegetation grew.

I hunkered down next to the tree more, trying my hardest to blend in with the foliage around me. I was in no position to fight, and I was sure Celine couldn't take the creature alone. Our best chance of survival was to stay hidden.

The Fungoid sniffed the air, turning its head in my direction. My heart began to race as it lumbered toward my hiding spot, its massive feet crushing the floor. The creature was close, too close.

I held my breath, my entire body tensing as the creature's snout came dangerously close to where I hid. Its low, guttural sniffs sent chills down my spine, the sound of it so close that I could almost feel its breath through the bark of the tree. My pulse thundered in my ears, and I fought the urge to move, to run, knowing that any sudden motion would only give me away. The creature had definitely picked up my scent, its sharp, uneven breaths confirming that it knew something was lurking nearby.

But it wasn't smart—at least not smart enough to find me easily. That was my only saving grace.

I could hear the rustle of its heavy footsteps, leaves crunching beneath its weight as it circled the tree with agonizing slowness. Each second felt like an eternity, my muscles screaming at me to either fight or flee, but I was frozen in place, unsure of what would happen next. Sweat trickled down my forehead, mingling with the dirt and grime that coated my skin, as I listened to the fiend sniffing, searching for me.

The moment I feared was inching closer. The creature rounded the tree, its grotesque form gradually appearing from the corner of my vision. My heart pounded so hard I thought it might leap out of my chest. There was no escape now. I was going to be found.

Instinctively, I tightened my grip on the hilt of my sword, my knuckles turning white from the pressure. It was a futile gesture, I knew. This creature was far beyond anything I could handle with just a blade. Still, I couldn't go down without a fight. The fiend's misshapen body loomed closer, and the only thing standing between it and me was the frail hope that it wouldn't realize where I was before I had a chance to act.

Just as it rounded the tree, a sharp whistle pierced the air. The fiend's head snapped toward the sound—Celine, standing boldly in the clearing, waving her arms.

"Yes, this way, you beast!" she called out.

The creature let out a large roar and began charging toward her. The Fungoid threw a powerful punch at her, but Celine dodged out of the way effortlessly. The punch slammed against the oak tree behind her, leaving a sizable dent in its trunk.

The fiend, now enraged by its miss, began swinging its arms wildly. However, Celine was too nimble and much quicker than the large creature. She dodged fluidly, weaving her way through the attacks.

The creature's clumsy but powerful blows smashed through smaller trees, sending splinters flying and leaving a trail of destruction in its wake.

I watched in awe as Celine led the Fungoid in a wide circle around the clearing, keeping just out of its reach. Each time the creature lunged, she sidestepped, allowing its momentum to carry it past her.

The Fungoid, enraged by his inability to land a hit, let out a loud, deep bellow. Its eyes locked onto a small oak tree nearby, and with a snarl, it lumbered toward it. Without hesitation, it raised a massive fist and swung with all its might, the force of the blow snapping the top half of the tree clean off, sending splinters and branches flying. The creature barely paused, gripping the thick remaining trunk in both hands before wrenching it free from the ground, roots and soil erupting in a cloud around its feet.

With a guttural roar, the Fungoid hurled the log toward Celine with terrifying speed. She dove out of the way, but not far enough. The massive trunk clipped her right calf mid-motion, knocking her off balance and sending her crashing to the ground, her leg trapped beneath the weight of the heavy wood.

The Fungoid loomed closer, its hulking mass blocking out the forest light as it advanced on Celine. She was pinned, her usual grace now replaced by visible strain as she tried to push herself free. Her breaths came in sharp gasps, and the more she struggled, the more the log seemed to press down on her. The massive fiend, sensing her vulnerability, flexed its grotesque muscles, preparing to crush her with its next move.

Celine's eyes darted toward me; her lips pressed into a tight line. She didn't call for help, didn't cry out in fear—she was too proud for that—but the desperation in her eyes was unmistakable. I could see her straining against the weight; her body twisted awkwardly beneath the thick log. She was trapped, and the Fungoid knew it.

I knew I had to spring into action, distract the Fungoid to give Celine any chance of survival. As I stepped out from behind the tree, Celine shot me a sharp look.

"Drifted! Remain hidden and retreat to safety. You are in no condition to aid me in this battle."

Her tone was firm, but her eyes were filled with urgency. She was right—My odds of survival were low if I battled in my current state. My leg throbbed, and my body felt drained. But leaving her to die to that monstrous fiend alone wasn't an option.

"Over here, you big oaf!" I yelled, ignoring the pain as I stepped further into the clearing.

The fiend immediately turned its attention to me, its nostrils flaring as it snorted in rage. I drew my sword, gripping it tightly with one hand.

The Fungoid didn't hesitate. It charged, each thunderous step sending a tremor through the earth. I waited, muscles tensed, then leaped to the side, barely dodging its massive frame.

As I landed, my injured leg buckled under the pressure. I hit the ground hard, a cry escaping my lips as the pain shot through me like fire.

The relentless fiend adjusted its course, ready to barrel over me—but just before it could close the distance, a blur of movement flashed into view.

A Kingsguard soldier, clad in heavy armor, charged in and landed a powerful punch squarely on the fiend's face. The impact was enough to send the creature crashing to the ground with a roar that echoed through the forest.

I blinked in disbelief, recognizing the guard from earlier—the one who had vouched for Celine and me to pass. He stood tall, towering over the fallen beast, a massive man with broad shoulders and a weathered face. An eyepatch covered his left eye, adding to his rugged appearance. On his hands were spiked cestus, presumably his weapon of choice, fitting with sharp protrusions that gleamed menacingly.

He glanced down at me, offering a hand. "You alright there?" he asked, his voice deep and commanding.

I took his hand, wincing as he pulled me to my feet. "You're from the gate..." I muttered, still catching my breath.

The guard gave a small nod, a hint of a smile tugging at his lips. "Figured you two might run into trouble."

Before I could respond, the fiend stirred again, shaking off the impact. The guard shifted his stance, eyes narrowing. "Stay back," he said sharply. "I'll handle this."

The fiend let out another roar before charging, though the guard quickly met it head-on. Despite his size, the guard was quite agile, delivering a series of swift, powerful punches, each landing with a sickening crunch.

The fiend, stunned by the flurry of blows, staggered back in a daze, allowing the guard to press his advantage. His fists were a blur of motion as he hammered into the fiend's body, each punch leaving tremors in its wake. The fiend swung wildly, but the guard was always one step ahead, ducking and weaving as if he had fought these beasts a thousand times before.

A powerful blow to the fiend's ribs left it gasping, toppling over. The guard didn't let up, delivering a rapid series of strikes that sent the beast reeling. With a final, devastating punch, he crushed the side of its skull.

The fiend collapsed in a heap, its body twitching once before going still.

Breathing heavily, the guard wiped a streak of blood from his knuckles and glanced at me. "It's done. Let's help out your friend before more show up."

I nodded in response, still in awe at what had just transpired.

The guard made his way toward the log that had pinned Celine's leg. Without a word, he knelt by her side, gripping the heavy trunk with both hands. His muscles tensed as he effortlessly lifted the weight, tossing it aside with a grunt.

Celine winced as her leg was freed, gingerly testing the movement. "Thank you," she said curtly, her voice almost detached, as though the relief of being saved hadn't quite reached her tone. She offered only a brief glance in the guard's direction before standing up and quickly making her way toward me.

I reached down and grabbed my clutch just as Celine reached me, her face in a scowl and her jaw clenched tightly.

Confused, I offered her a smile. "That was a clo—"

She cut me off.

"Drifted!" she exclaimed, her voice sharp. "You fool! I told you to retreat, to stay hidden! What possessed you to join a battle you had no business being a part of?"

I opened my mouth to respond, but she cut me off. Her words came out tumbling in a rush, "Have you any idea what you have done? Your recklessness nearly cost us dearly. Your rash actions could have forced me into a precarious position. To join the fray with your leg in such a state was a bull-headed decision!"

Guilt hit me as I realized the truth of her words. "I'm sorry, Celine, I was just trying to help." I said quietly."

"Help? Your heroics did more harm than good. Battles are not won with bravado, but with the careful cooperation between allies. Remember these words, Drifted."

Without waiting for my response, she turned around and stormed off. I've never seen Celine get so worked up over anything before.

The guard, observing the argument, walked over and placed a hand on my shoulder. "Give her some time to calm down," he advised, trying to be reassuring.

As Celine stormed off, I stood there for a moment, taking in the weight of her words.

"Let's get you back to town," the guard said, snapping me out of my thoughts.

We walked in silence for a while before I decided to break the awkwardness.

"I'm Isaac," I said, "Thank you for your help back there."

He nodded, a small smile tugging at the corner of his mouth. "The name's Brute."

I couldn't help but think about how fitting of a name that was. I could tell he was someone who could handle himself in a fight. Thankfully, he was on our side.

I glanced over at him as we approached the edge of the forest. "Do you always patrol the woods?"

He chuckled deeply. "Not always. But with the recent increase in fiend activity, I've been keeping an eye out. Figured I'd check on you two after you headed in."

"Well, I'm glad you did," I admitted. "I don't think I would have lasted long without your help."

Brute chuckled again. "Just doing my duty, Isaac. Though, next time, listen to your friend. She's got a good head on her shoulders."

"Yeah, you've got that right," I replied.

As we reached the outskirts of the town, I saw Celine waiting for us; her back was turned, and her posture stiff. I quickly paced towards her, hoping to make amends.

"Celine," I called out, my voice trembling slightly.

She turned slightly, her back still facing me. "Yes, Drifted?"

I sighed, "I didn't mean to put us in danger; I was just trying to help you out. Besides, we made it back okay, no harm, no foul, right?"

Celine turned her body fully to me now, her shoulders tense, her eyes hardened. "No harm? You were a mere seconds away from death, and you think your actions caused no harm?"

I could feel her disappointment hanging heavily in the air. "I'm... that isn't what I meant," I murmured, my voice barely audible.

She turned to leave, clutching the satchel tightly. "I shall return this to the old man. This discourse will have to wait." Without another word, she walked away briskly.

"Celine, wait!" I called out, my voice breaking slightly. "At least meet me at the inn when you're done?"

She didn't turn to acknowledge me; she just kept walking until she disappeared into the crowd, out of view. I stood there, arms at my side, with a mix of guilt and helplessness.

Brute stepped up beside me, hands on his hips. "Give her some time. She'll come around."

"Yeah," I said, my shoulders feeling heavy. "I'm sure she will."

"You know what, how about you and I take a trip to the tavern. I'm sure that'll help clear your mind!" Brute replied.

I shook my head; Celine being upset with me was bringing my mood down. "I don't know, Brute, I'm not really in the mood."

He gave my shoulder a light squeeze. "That's exactly why you should go with me; dwelling on what happened isn't going to help anyone. You need a break!"

I hesitated, glancing back in the direction where Celine had disappeared. "But I-"

"No buts," Brute interrupted. "a bit of ale, some good company, lively atmosphere, it'll do you good. Trust me."

I looked at him, grateful for the distraction. "Alright," I agreed, "let's go. But I'm not drinking!"

# CHAPTER 10

As we made our way toward the tavern, the weight of my guilt lingered like a shroud, heavy and unshakable. The swarming energy of the marketplace gradually faded behind us, giving way to quieter streets. The hum of conversation grew faint, and the din of daily life ebbed into a distant murmur.

Brute walked beside me, his large frame casting a reassuring shadow. He broke the silence with some rough wisdom. "Isaac," he began, his voice gruff but steady, "take it from me—don't try too hard to make sense of women. You'll drive yourself mad."

I nodded absent-mindedly, my thoughts still entangled in worry over Celine. "It's just... I was afraid something might've happened to her," I muttered.

Brute let out a low chuckle, his broad hand resting on my shoulder as he glanced at me from the corner of his eye. "You know what I think?" he said, his tone deep and oddly comforting. "You did what you thought was right. That counts for something."

We turned down a narrow alley, where the air was noticeably cooler, carrying with it a refreshing breeze that brushed against my skin. The noise of the town faded further into the background, replaced by the soft rustling of leaves and the distant chirping of birds. I inhaled deeply, savoring the brief respite.

The alley was lined with tall, ancient trees, their branches swaying gently overhead, casting flickering shadows along the cobblestone path. The golden light of the midday sun filtered through the leaves, creating a patchwork of warmth and shadow that danced across the ground. For a fleeting moment, the peacefulness of the scene allowed my mind to quiet, to let go of the turmoil that had plagued me since the retrieval mission.

Brute clapped a heavy hand on my shoulder, nearly knocking me off balance. "You're a good man, Isaac," he said with a grin, the weight of his words unmistakable. "You've got heart, and that's more important than you think."

A small, weary smile tugged at my lips. "Thanks, Brute. I think I needed to hear that."

We continued onward in companionable silence, the soft clinking of my sword and shield the only sound breaking the quiet. Despite Brute's reassurance, Celine's distress still worried me. I couldn't shake the feeling that there was something more to her worry—something just out of reach, beyond my understanding.

By the time we arrived at the tavern, the sun was high in the sky, casting a warm glow over the lively scene. The scent of roasted meat and freshly poured ale filled the air, mingling with the hearty laughter of patrons and the clinking of mugs. It was the kind of atmosphere that normally put me at ease, but today, the weight on my shoulders was not so easily cast aside.

I let out a slow, deep breath, bracing myself for the lively social energy that awaited within. Crowds had never been my strength, and the thought of being surrounded by so many people set a unease churning in my gut. But there was no turning back now.

Brute shoved open the heavy tavern door with ease, and we stepped inside, instantly enveloped in the warm, crowded atmosphere. The tavern was alive with activity, the air filled with the heavy mix of cheerful chatter, the clinking of mugs, and the mouthwatering aroma of hearty fare. Dark wooden beams lined the ceiling, and the scent of well-aged ale clung to the air, mingling with the smell of roasting meat.

The moment we crossed the threshold, a raucous cheer erupted from a group of patrons seated near the bar. "Oi! It's Brute!" a burly man shouted, lifting his mug high in salute. The man's call was swiftly answered by an enthusiastic chorus of voices, their faces lighting up as they caught sight of him.

In an instant, Brute became the center of attention. Townsfolk gathered around, clapping him on the back, offering warm greetings and hearty laughter. "Brute! Good to see you!" "Join us for a drink, mate!" "How've you been?" Their genuine affection and respect for him was undeniable, a testament to his larger-than-life presence in the town.

Grinning broadly, Brute waved at the smiling faces. "Good to see you lot too," he called out, his deep voice easily cutting through the din. "But I'm not alone today. Got someone with me. His name's Isaac." He gestured toward me, and just like that, all eyes shifted in my direction.

The sudden attention made my heart race, but I forced a small, awkward smile and nodded at the crowd. The patrons' gazes were welcoming, their nods and friendly waves making me feel more at ease than I'd expected. "Welcome, Isaac!" one called out. "Any friend of Brute's is a friend of ours!" another added with a wide grin.

Brute guided me through the throng to an empty table near the hearth, the warmth of the fire a welcome contrast to the coolness of the outside air. He waved over the tavern keeper, signaling for a couple of drinks. "This place," he said, settling into a chair that creaked under his weight, "is more than just a tavern. It's a haven. A place where folks come to unwind, share stories, and remember they're part of something bigger."

I scanned the room, taking in the rustic charm that surrounded us. The walls were adorned with a curious collection of trinkets—weathered shields, hunting trophies, and faded maps. Each item seemed to carry a story, evidence of the countless adventurers and travelers who had passed through. The long, wooden tables bore the marks of time, their surfaces worn smooth from years of use. In the flickering candlelight, everything took on a warm, golden hue that only added to the tavern's welcoming air.

Despite the chaotic noise of conversation, laughter, and clinking mugs, there was something comforting about the sounds. It all blended into a soothing hum, like the background music of life. Somewhere in the corner, a bard strummed a soft melody on a lute, his song weaving through the tavern's energy like a calm undercurrent.

Before long, a cheerful barmaid approached with two large mugs of frothy ale, placing them in front of us with a warm smile. "Here you go, Brute. And for your friend," she said, setting the mugs down with a practiced grace.

Brute raised his mug toward me, his grin as wide as ever. "Cheers, Isaac. To new friendships—and to learning from our mistakes."

I hesitated, my fingers resting on the cool wood of the table. "I appreciate the gesture, Brute, but I told you… I don't drink," I replied, my voice sheepish despite my best efforts to sound resolute.

Brute frowned, his good-natured smile dimming just a fraction. "Ah, come on now. Why not?" he asked, his brow furrowing.

It was embarrassing to admit, especially in front of someone like Brute. I had never touched a drop of ale in my life—my mother had always warned me about how bad it was for one's health, and her words had stuck with me over the years. "It's… uh… not good for you," I mumbled, avoiding his gaze.

Brute raised a skeptical eyebrow but didn't lower his mug. "Rubbish! A single drink won't do you any harm, lad. It's not about the ale itself; it's about the moment. The act of sharing it with friends. Just one sip—for the sake of the evening?"

I glanced down at the mug, foam spilling over the rim, then back up at Brute's expectant expression. His sincerity was disarming, and I didn't want to seem ungrateful or out of place in this setting. With a resigned sigh, I picked up the mug, its weight heavier than I had expected. "Alright," I said reluctantly, "just one sip."

Brute's grin returned in full force, his eyes gleaming with approval. "That's the spirit! Cheers!"

We clinked our mugs together, the hollow sound of metal and wood briefly rising above the tavern's din. I brought the mug to my lips cautiously, expecting a harsh bite, but the ale was surprisingly smooth, its rich, hearty flavor spreading warmth through my chest as it went down. I took another sip, savoring the unexpected pleasure. "Not bad," I admitted, setting the mug down with a faint grin.

Brute threw his head back in a deep, booming laugh. "See? A little indulgence every now and then never killed anyone!"

I nodded, feeling some of the tension drain from my shoulders, the warmth of the ale loosening my body. "I better not regret this later," I muttered, more to myself than to him.

"Oh, stop your worrying," Brute said with a hearty slap to my back, causing me to nearly spill the rest of my drink. He took a long, satisfying gulp from his own mug before wiping his mouth with the back of his hand. "Now, let's enjoy the evening."

As the easy flow of the tavern came over us, I found my gaze wandering to the emblem on Brute's armor, the small crescent moon subtly etched into the center of his chest plate. It wasn't much, but I recognized it—the mark of a new initiate in the Kingsguard. My brow furrowed as I studied him, perplexed by the symbol. For a man like Brute, who carried himself like a seasoned warrior, the idea of him being new to the order seemed almost absurd.

"Brute," I began, unable to keep the curiosity from my voice, "is that a new moon on your chest?"

He followed my gaze, then chuckled as he set his mug back on the table. "A keen eye you've got there," he said with a grin. "Yes, it's true. I'm fairly new to the Kingsguard."

I raised an eyebrow in surprise. "You could've fooled me. The way you fought back there, I would've sworn you'd been doing this for years."

Brute leaned back in his chair, a thoughtful look crossing his face. His fingers drummed lightly against the rim of his mug as though he were weighing his next words. "Well," he said slowly, "it's quite the story."

His eyes flicked around the room, making sure no one was eavesdropping. Then he leaned in, his voice dropping to a conspiratorial whisper. "Don't tell anyone this," he warned, "but I'm actually from Eclipsia."

I felt my eyes widen in shock. "Wait, you're from Ecl—"

He quickly cut me off, raising a hand to silence me. "Shh! Keep your voice down," he hissed, his usual lighthearted demeanor slipping into something more serious. "It's not exactly something I want everyone knowing."

I lowered my voice, still processing the bombshell he had just dropped. "There's no way. I've never met anyone from there. We've always been told that no one is ever permitted to enter or leave that place."

Brute nodded, his expression grim. "That's what most believe. And for the most part, it's true. Eclipsia is... well, let's just say it's not a place you leave easily." He leaned back, exhaling slowly. "But I didn't exactly leave with permission."

I stared at him, trying to grasp the full weight of what he was saying. "What do you mean?" I asked, my curiosity fully piqued now.

Brute met my gaze, holding it for a long moment before finally speaking. "I escaped," he said, his voice low and steady. "Since I was a child, I trained in secret. Harder than most. The isolation, the strict control—it never sat right with me. I always knew there had to be more beyond those borders, something better. So, I found a way out."

I blinked, still trying to wrap my mind around the enormity of what he was saying. "You escaped from Eclipsia? That's... incredible. My parents and I rode past the outskirts of the city once, years ago. It was swarming with guards. They wouldn't let us get anywhere near it."

Brute gave a half-smile, leaning back in his chair. "It wasn't easy," he admitted. "The king is fiercely protective of the town, and anyone who tries to leave is branded a traitor of Moonveil. But I couldn't live that way, not when I knew there was a whole world out there waiting to be explored. I took my chances, and after a lot of running, I found myself here. The Kingsguard took me in when they saw my skills. No questions asked."

I nodded slowly, absorbing the weight of his words. His journey, his escape, it was more than just impressive—it was unbelievable. And yet, sitting here, I believed every word. "Your secret's safe with me, Brute," I said, my voice firm with sincerity. "You can trust me."

Brute smiled, the tension easing from his face. "I wouldn't have told you if I didn't think I could," he replied, his voice lighter now, a faint chuckle escaping his lips. He raised his mug again. "Now, let's get back to drinking. No more heavy talk."

We clinked our mugs together once more, the previous tension lifting as we both took a deep sip of our drinks. The evening stretched on, filled with laughter, stories, and the shared warmth of camaraderie.

I found myself growing an even deeper sense of gratitude for Brute. The way he had confided in me, shared something so personal and guarded, made me realize how much our bond had grown in such a short time. Trust was not something easily given, especially from a man like him, and knowing that he felt comfortable enough to let me in on his past only strengthened my resolve to honor that trust.

We had barely settled back into our seats when someone approached our table wearing a wide smile. "Mind if I join you two?" the man asked, gesturing toward an empty chair.

Brute grinned, his demeanor instantly lighting up. "Gareth! You don't need to ask, my friend. Pull up a chair!"

With a grateful nod, Gareth took the seat next to Brute, leaning in slightly toward me as he gestured to his companion. "You know," he said, his voice full of admiration, "your buddy here has saved my hide more times than I care to admit."

Brute shifted uncomfortably, waving off the praise with a dismissive hand. "Ah, cut it out, Gareth. It was nothing."

But Gareth wasn't having any of it. He shook his head, the grin on his face growing wider. "Nothing? You're too modest, Brute. Remember that time we ventured into the woods after that ginormous bear? You know, the one with claws the size of daggers?" Gareth's eyes twinkled as he began reliving the memory, his voice growing more animated with each word.

Brute's easy smile faded into something more serious as he listened, his gaze fixed on the table. The memory clearly held weight for him as well, though he kept his composure. Gareth, however, continued on, fully immersed in the tale.

"We were tracking that beast for hours," Gareth went on, his hands moving dramatically as if he were back in those woods. "And just when we thought we had it cornered, the damn thing came out of nowhere—jaws snapping, teeth like bloody razors!"

The tavern's lively atmosphere quieted down as more patrons

began to tune in, intrigued by the unfolding story. Brute's face grew sterner, his eyes reflecting the gravity of the encounter as Gareth spoke, though he remained silent, arms crossed over his chest.

"I barely had time to react," Gareth said, his voice dropping to a near whisper, the tension in his words hanging heavy in the air. "But Brute—he was faster than lightning. The beast lunged at me, and before I even knew what was happening, Brute was there—fist raised—and with one blow, he drove the thing back."

A murmur rippled through the crowd that had gathered around, and I found myself leaning forward, engrossed in Gareth's words. The tension in the room was palpable, and for a moment, it felt like we were all back in those woods, standing in the shadow of the monstrous bear.

"I thought we were done for," Gareth admitted, his voice laced with genuine awe. "But Brute didn't even flinch. He stepped in front of me like it was nothing, raised his fist, and met the beast head-on."

Brute kept his gaze low, staring into his mug as Gareth spoke. He gave the occasional nod but said nothing, his expression one of quiet humility as the tale unfolded.

"And with one swift move," Gareth continued, his voice rising with excitement, "Brute managed to get behind the bear and put it in a headlock. He held on, wrestling the thing until it couldn't even move. He saved me—and probably everyone else who lived near those woods that day."

Gareth finished his story with a flourish, raising his mug high in the air. "I owe my life to this man," he declared, his voice proud and filled with emotion.

The tavern erupted into cheers, the sound of clinking mugs and applause filling the room as the patrons joined in the impromptu toast to Brute's heroism. Brute, for his part, gave a small smile, the hint of color rising on his cheeks as he accepted the praise with quiet grace. I could tell He wasn't one to bask in the spotlight, but it was clear that to these people, he was more than just a Kingsguard—he was a hero.

As the cheers slowly died down and the energy of the room settled back into its usual hum, I took a moment to look around. The admiration in the eyes of those gathered, the way they looked at Brute—it wasn't the kind of respect earned through mere rank or title. It was deeper than that. These people revered him, not as an ordinary guard but as someone who had proven himself.

The rest of the evening passed in a haze of laughter, stories, and ale, each moment blurring seamlessly into the next. Brute was in his element, regaling the crowd with tales of his many adventures—each one more thrilling and exaggerated than the last. The tavern echoed with the sound of his booming voice as he recounted battles with wild beasts and harrowing escapes, every word drawing more patrons into the circle of listeners. Even I joined in at one point, recounting the night I fought off the Grimroots, surprising myself with how easily the story flowed from my lips.

For the first time in what felt like forever, I was at ease in the presence of a large group of people. The warmth of the hearth, the camaraderie of the tavern-goers, and the shared tales of heroism created an atmosphere that made it impossible to feel alone. It was as though the walls themselves were alive with the echoes of a thousand past adventures, each one contributing to the sense of belonging that hung in the air.

But as the night stretched on and the ale flowed freely, a strange heaviness settled over me. My head grew fuzzy, my words began to slur, and my movements lost their usual coordination. Brute, ever watchful, noticed my condition before I even had the chance to realize it myself.

"I think it's about time we got you out of here before you embarrass yourself," he said, his tone light but firm as he placed a hand on my shoulder.

I protested weakly, trying to wave him off. "I'm fine, Brute. Really," I slurred, though the unsteadiness in my voice betrayed me.

Brute merely chuckled, shaking his head. "Sure, you are," he said, his strong grip lifting me easily to my feet. "Let's get you moving before the room starts spinning."

I fumbled for my crutch, gripping it tightly as we made our way toward the door. The cool night air hit me like a slap in the face the moment we stepped outside, jolting me into a slightly clearer state of mind. I breathed in deeply, feeling the sharp bite of the evening breeze against my skin as the distant chatter of the town's nightlife filled the air.

"Geez, it's nighttime already," I mumbled, glancing up at the sky. The moon hung high, its pale light illuminating the cobblestone streets, while stars dotted the clear expanse above. I hadn't realized how much time had slipped by since we'd entered the tavern.

Brute laughed beside me, his breath forming visible clouds in the chilly air. "Time flies when you're having fun, huh?" he remarked with a grin.

I nodded, feeling a mix of embarrassment and contentment at the same time. "Yeah, I guess so," I replied, though the slight wobble in my step reminded me of just how much I'd indulged tonight.

We made our way through the still-lively streets, the sounds of merriment spilling out from the various taverns and inns we passed. Even at this late hour, the town buzzed with life— laughter and conversation drifting on the breeze, along with the occasional clink of mugs. It was the kind of night where everything seemed alive, yet I couldn't help but feel a strange sense of detachment as if my mind was already elsewhere.

As we neared the door of the inn where Celine and I were staying, I took a deep breath, bracing myself. "Thanks for tonight, Brute," I mumbled, my voice quieter now. "I haven't had this much fun in a long time."

Brute gave me a hearty pat on the back, his smile warm and genuine. "No problem, Isaac. It's good to see you unwind a bit," he replied before giving me a knowing look. "Though your night isn't over just yet."

He started walking away with a grin, leaving me standing at the door. It took a second for his words to sink in, and when they did, a sinking feeling settled in my chest. I had almost forgotten—Celine. She was still upset with me. The thought of facing her now, in my current state, made my stomach churn.

The warmth of the tavern, which had felt so comforting moments ago, seemed to evaporate in an instant. It was replaced by the cold, uncomfortable reality of my strained relationship. I sighed deeply, feeling the weight of the night catch up with me all at once.

With a heavy heart, I pushed open the door and stepped inside.

The inn was quieter than the streets outside, though still alive with the soft murmurs of late-night conversations and faint voices carrying through the halls. The warmth of the hearth flickered gently against the walls, casting long, dancing shadows that only deepened the stillness.

"Long night?" the innkeeper asked, her voice light and knowing, a large smile playing on her lips.

"You could say that," I replied with a faint grin.

I made my way up the stairs toward the room, each step feeling heavier than the last, the weight of the evening settling back over me. The lively buzz from the tavern had faded, leaving behind the cold reality of what awaited. As I reached the door, I paused, standing there for a long moment, gathering my thoughts, steeling myself for the conversation that I knew was coming.

Taking a deep breath, I knocked gently before opening the door.

Celine was still awake, seated in the chair by the window, her figure bathed in the pale glow of moonlight. She was staring blankly out into the night, her expression distant, her thoughts miles away. On the small table beside her rested the old man's satchel—untouched. She didn't turn at the sound of the door, though a slight shift in her posture told me she'd noticed my presence.

"Celine," I began, my voice softer than I intended, but she cut me off with a dismissive gesture of her hand.

"I arrived at the stall only to find it empty," she said, her voice steady yet cool. "The old man had gone for the day."

I nodded, not quite sure how to respond. "I see. You'll return it to him tomorrow then?"

"Yes," she replied curtly, her tone clipped. "I shall look for him in the morning."

A heavy silence followed, stretching between us, thick with unspoken tension. I could feel her disappointment lingering in the air, filling the space between us like a weight I couldn't shake. My mind raced, searching for something—anything—to say, but no words came. I shifted awkwardly, the guilt gnawing at me with each passing second.

Celine's nose wrinkled slightly as she took a sharp breath, her brow furrowing. "You reek of ale," she remarked, her tone biting, laden with quiet disdain.

I averted my gaze, feeling a bit of embarrassment build up in my chest. "Yeah," I muttered, "I was at the tavern with Brute."

Celine finally turned to face me, her violet eyes narrowing with something between irritation and disappointment. "You place your trust so easily in someone you just met, Drifted?" The accusation in her voice stung more sharply than I'd expected.

Her words lit a small spark of defensiveness within me. "You do realize it was Brute who saved us in the woods this morning, right?" I replied, my voice sharper than before. "Bad people generally don't do things like that."

Celine remained unmoved. "A single act of bravery does not reveal the true nature of a person," she said, her tone even, almost too calm. "We know so little about him, and trust is not something to be given lightly."

"He's proven it to me," I shot back, my frustration bubbling to the surface. "He put his life on the line for us. What more do you need?"

Her eyes darkened, her calm exterior slipping just enough to show a flicker of irritation. "And what if he has an ulterior motive? What if his kindness today masks a deeper deception?" Though her voice remained gentle, her words felt like a weight pressing down on me.

"You're being paranoid," I snapped, my patience wearing thin. "Not everyone is out to get us, Celine. Sometimes, people can just be good for the sake of it."

"And sometimes," she countered, "people can hide their true intentions behind the guise of being helpful. We must be cautious."

I stepped closer, the distance between us narrowing. "You don't understand," I said, the words coming out in a rush. "You weren't there in the tavern. You didn't see how much people respect him, how they trust him. He's a good man."

Celine stood, her movements deliberate, her eyes locking onto mine. "And you don't understand the importance of vigilance," she said quietly, her voice firm, though touched with a sadness that hadn't been there before. "Trust must be earned over time, not given freely based on a single act or a few friendly faces."

I felt my frustration peak, my patience fraying at the edges. "Fine," I said, throwing my hands up in exasperation. "Maybe you're right, maybe you're not. I don't care anymore; I'm done arguing about this."

Celine sighed, her posture sagging slightly as the tension drained from her shoulders. She turned back to the window, the soft glow of moonlight casting a faint shadow across her face. "As you wish, Drifted," she murmured, her voice barely above a whisper, laced with a quiet, resigned sadness that tugged at my chest.

I turned away, feeling a mix of exhaustion and frustration weighing me down. I made my way toward the bed, dropping my gear to the ground with a loud clunk, the sound echoing in the stillness of the room.

As I lay down, the bed felt cold, the warmth from the tavern now a distant memory. The silence between us was thick—heavy with unspoken words and lingering resentment, keeping sleep just barely out of reach.

# Chapter 11 Part I

I awoke to the sound of the bustling streets below, the murmur of voices, and the clatter of wagon wheels drifting up through the open window. Morning light streamed in, casting a warm, golden glow across the room, gently nudging me into the day.

As I stretched, a small smile tugged at the corners of my lips—I noticed the once-throbbing pain in my leg had all but faded to a dull memory. Curious, I tossed back the sheets and inspected the wound left by the Grimroot. To my amazement, it was fully healed, with only the faintest scar remaining as a memento from the battle. I ran my fingers over it, the skin smooth and unbroken.

My eyes scanned the room, and a pang of concern hit me when I realized Celine was nowhere to be seen. For a moment, my heart sank, thinking she might have left without a word. But then it struck me—she must have gone out early to return the satchel to the old man. Still, the thought of her absence weighed on me. We hadn't exactly ended last night on the best terms.

Rising from the bed, I hesitated for a second before testing my leg. The old crutch, once my necessary companion, now felt like a relic of a time that had finally passed. Tentatively, I put my weight on the leg, half-expecting to feel the shaky weakness. But to my surprise, it held firm. I took a few cautious steps, then more. The freedom of movement—without the constant burden of that crutch—felt exhilarating.

My gear lay in a heap on the floor where I had discarded it the night before. I bent down, strapping my sword to my hip and slinging my shield over my back. The weight of the steel comforted me. I felt as if I was ready for whatever the day had in store. With a sense of renewed purpose, I made my way downstairs to the inn's common area, eager to find Celine.

The inn was lively with the morning crowd. Patrons sat in small clusters, engaged in light conversation over breakfast, the tantalizing aroma of fresh bread and sizzling bacon filling the air. I glanced around, hoping to spot Celine among the faces, but there was no sign of her. Unease tugged at the back of my mind as I made my way to the innkeeper, hoping she might have some clue as to where Celine had gone.

"Good morning," I greeted the innkeeper, doing my best to keep the concern out of my voice. "You wouldn't happen to have seen my friend leave this morning, would you?"

The innkeeper glanced up from her work, a knowing smile creeping across her face. "Your girlfriend?" she asked with a playful wink, clearly still under the impression Celine and I were more than just traveling companions.

I had forgotten about the assumption we'd let her believe, and it felt too tedious to correct it now. "Yes, her," I replied, forcing a casual tone despite the worry tightening in my chest. "Did she happen to mention where she was going?"

The innkeeper wiped her hands on her apron, chuckling softly. "You kids are always so shy about these things," she said, her voice warm with amusement. "She left quite early; said she had some business to take care of. Seemed in a bit of a hurry, too."

I nodded, offering a smile, though it felt thin. "I see; thank you for letting me know," I said, keeping my tone polite before turning away. A sense of relief flickered through me—at least I had a lead—but the fact that Celine had left in such a rush didn't sit well with me.

As I moved toward the door, my mind racing with possibilities, a faint fragment of conversation floated to my ears from a nearby table. One voice, sharp but distant, carried a phrase that lodged itself in my mind for a moment before I could make sense of it.

"...I heard this is the closest they've been to town in ages."

My hand paused on the door handle, my brow furrowing slightly as the words echoed in my head. Who—or what—could they be talking about? Fiends? I shook the thought away. With my mind focused on locating Celine, I couldn't afford to get sidetracked by overheard gossip, no matter how intriguing. There was no time for distractions, not when I still didn't know where Celine was or why she had rushed off so early.

I pushed the door open, stepping out onto the fresh morning air, determined to find her.

As I stepped out into the street, I paused for a moment, my mind racing as I tried to piece together a plan. My first thought was that Celine would have gone to the old man's stall. She had been determined to return his satchel, and it seemed like the most logical place to start. With that thought in mind, I began weaving my way through the growing crowds, my eyes scanning the bustling streets.

But something felt off.

Though the town was still busy with its usual morning hustle, there was an unusual tension in the air. I quickly noticed that the guard's presence had increased significantly—more than I'd seen in days prior. Guards patrolled the streets in pairs, their faces set with stern, watchful expressions as their eyes darted over the crowds. It was as if they were expecting trouble.

As I moved deeper into town, I caught snippets of hushed conversations drifting through the air, carrying on the murmur of voices around me. I strained to make out their words as I passed by groups of people.

"...never seen the guards so on edge..." "...it's like they're getting bolder every day..." "...might be best to head home before things get worse..."

Something was clearly stirring in the town, and whatever it was, it didn't bode well. My thoughts immediately shifted to Celine—if the guards were on alert and the townspeople uneasy, she could be in danger. My pace quickened, urgency taking over as I maneuvered through the crowd, my eyes darting left and right in search of her.

The marketplace finally came into view, a bustling mass of people rushing from stall to stall, the usual clamor now edged with an undercurrent of nervous energy. I scanned the area, searching for the worn face of the strawberry vendor. If Celine had passed through here, he would know.

At last, I spotted him near the edge of the marketplace, his weathered hands busy packing up his stall. Red strawberries disappeared into wooden crates as he worked, his aged face lighting up with recognition the moment he saw me approach.

"Good morning, young man!" he called out, his voice warm and cheerful despite the tension in the air. His eyes sparkled as he grinned. "Back for more of my berries already?"

"Morning," I replied, trying to keep my voice steady even as worry pulled at me. "Actually, I'm looking for my friend—the one I was here with yesterday. Did she come by earlier? She was supposed to return something to you."

The vendor paused, his hands stilling as he considered my question, a thoughtful look crossing his face.

"Yes, of course," the old man replied, his eyes lighting up with recognition as he reached down beneath his stall. "She was here not too long ago. Brought me my satchel back—bless you both for that; I can't thank you enough!"

He straightened up, but a frown tugged at the corners of his mouth as he scratched his chin. "Though... I already gave her the basket of strawberries and the Selens I promised you two."

Confused, I frowned slightly without meaning to. The old man noticed immediately, his brow furrowing with concern as he leaned forward. "Is everything alright, young man?"

"I'm not sure," I admitted, the worry tightening its grip on my chest. "She hasn't come back yet, and... well, the townspeople have been acting strange this morning."

The old man's eyes widened ever so slightly, and he glanced around before leaning in closer, his voice dropping to a near whisper. "Yes, there's been talk, more than just rumors. Fiends have been spotted unusually close to town, much closer than usual. That's why I'm packing up now—my wife insisted I head home for the day. It's got the guards all stirred up."

My heart sank at his words, a cold weight settling in my stomach. Fiends? If Celine was out there, and the town was under threat... I swallowed hard, trying to keep the rising panic at bay. "Do you know which direction she headed in?" I asked, my voice tighter than I'd intended.

The vendor tapped a finger against his chin, his expression thoughtful. "It was a little while ago, but I think she went off that way," he said, pointing toward the southern gate.

I nodded, the urge to act pushing against the edges of my calm. "Okay, thank you—"

Before I could finish, a sharp scream tore through the air, cutting across the marketplace. It started distant but was quickly followed by another, this time closer. The usual hum of activity froze, replaced by a sinister, collective silence as fear rippled through the crowd.

I turned sharply, scanning the sea of heads for any sign of what was happening. My heart raced as the panic began to spread like wildfire, people darting their eyes around, searching for answers. The old man's face had gone pale, his hands trembling as he resumed packing up his stall, only now with frantic, desperate movements.

"Get home safely," I called over my shoulder as I began moving through the crowd, the sense of urgency pounding in my veins.

The streets erupted into chaos as people began rushing toward me, fleeing from whatever had caused the screams. Their faces were contorted with fear, eyes wide and desperate.

Pushing against the frantic waves of fleeing townsfolk, I forced my way through the chaos. The air was thick with fear, the screams growing louder and more frequent with every step. My heart pounded in my chest, the only thought in my mind: Celine. She was somewhere out there, and if fiends had truly entered the town, she could be in serious danger.

As I neared the edge of the marketplace, the crowd began to thin. In the distance, I could see a group of guards forming a defensive line, their expressions set with grim determination. Beyond them, I finally saw what had caused the panic.

A group of Fungoids—at least fifteen—stood just between the town's entrance and the marketplace. Their grotesque, towering forms loomed menacingly, their fungal bodies pulsing with a strange, unnatural energy. The sight of them sent a shiver down my spine. But what made my blood run cold wasn't just their presence—it was what lay before them.

A woman was sprawled on the ground, her wide, terrified eyes fixed on the monsters in front of her. She was crying, her hands shaking as she tried to crawl away, the raw fear rolling off her. The Fungoids didn't move, but their burning, unblinking eyes watched her intently, their grotesque mouths twitching as if they could already taste her terror.

"Help! Somebody, please help me!" the woman screamed, her voice cracking as she tried to stand, only to fall back down with a cry of pain. Her ankle was bruised and swollen—a clear sign she'd twisted it in her desperate attempt to escape.

My heart clenched. There was no time to hesitate. I drew my sword, determined to get her out of there, and rushed toward the guards. But before I could even close the distance, they tightened their formation, blocking my way.

"Stay back!" one of the guards barked, his voice stern. "You can't go out there. It's too dangerous."

"Of course it's dangerous; that's why she needs help!" I shot back, trying to push through their shields. I couldn't just stand by and watch.

"We know," another guard said, his face grim. "But... look at them. They're not moving. They're just... staring."

I froze for a moment, looking past the shield wall. He was right. The Fungoids, while poised and ready, weren't advancing. They were standing still, watching the woman with a malevolent calm. Their bodies were tense, but not a single one moved toward her. It was as if they were waiting for something.

"What are they doing?" I muttered, more to myself than anyone else. "Why aren't they attacking?"

The first guard shook his head. "We don't know. They've never behaved like this before. It's almost like they're waiting for a signal."

The woman's cries grew more frantic, her hands clawing at the dirt as she tried to drag herself away. The sight of her helplessness was unbearable. My grip tightened on my sword. We couldn't just stand here and watch her die.

"There has to be a way to get her out of there," I said, desperation creeping into my voice. "We can't just leave her."

"Our orders are to hold the line," the guard snapped, his face hardening. "Our priority is the safety of the town."

"She is one of the people you're supposed to be protecting!" I yelled, my frustration boiling over. "You're just going to leave her out there?"

The guards shifted uncomfortably, but their resolve didn't

falter. The woman's cries filled the air once more, her voice hoarse with terror. I couldn't wait any longer.

I couldn't let her die.

"Alright, we can't just stand here," I muttered under my breath. Before they could react, I took several steps back, then charged forward with all my strength, slamming into the line of guards. The impact was enough to break through their shields, sending a few of them stumbling.

"Get back here!" one of them shouted, but I was already past them, sprinting toward the woman.

She clung to me the moment I reached her, her body trembling violently. "Thank you, thank you," she sobbed, her fingers digging into my arm as if I were the only thing keeping her tethered to the world.

But just as I hoisted her to her feet, the Fungoids stirred.

The eerie stillness shattered in an instant. With a collective roar, they surged forward, their massive bodies shaking the ground as they charged. The sound of their guttural growls filled the air, growing louder with each thunderous step.

"We need to move!" I urged, half-carrying, half-dragging the woman toward the guards. Her weight slowed us down, her twisted ankle making her stumble with every step. Behind us, the Fungoids closed in, their grotesque forms bearing down on us with terrifying speed.

The guards ahead of us tightened their formation, bracing themselves as the ground trembled beneath the Fungoids' onslaught. "Hurry! Get behind us!" one of them shouted, his voice barely audible over the pounding footsteps.

The creatures were gaining on us. I could feel the heat of their rancid breath on my back.

With a final effort, I shoved the woman ahead of me past the line of shields. The guards immediately closed ranks around us, their weapons raised and ready as the looming threat bore down on them. I barely had time to catch my breath before the Fungoids crashed into the line of guards. The ground shook beneath the impact, the force reverberating through the air as metal met monstrous flesh in a desperate struggle.

"Thank you! Thank you so much!" the woman gasped, her voice choking with relief, tears streaming down her face.

"We've got them! Get to safety!" one of the guards shouted over the clamor, his sword flashing as he deflected a powerful blow. "Everyone, move!"

The crowd, which had initially stuck around to gawk at the battle, now realized the true danger. Panic set in as they began scattering, fleeing from the chaos that was unfolding in the marketplace.

I gripped the woman's arm, guiding her through the scrambling mass of bodies. "We can't stay here," I said, scanning the area for any sign of cover. "We need to find somewhere safer."

As I helped her limp through the fleeing crowd, the sounds of the battle behind us grew more intense. The clash of steel against the thick, fungal flesh of the fiends filled the air, punctuated by the savage roars of the Fungoids and the shouts of the guards locked in combat. Suddenly, a loud crash split the air, followed by a blood-curdling scream.

I turned sharply to see what had happened.

My heart dropped.

The Fungoids had broken through the guards' line. Their massive bodies hurled the soldiers into the air like ragdolls, scattering them across the marketplace. Panic swept through the remaining onlookers like wildfire. People screamed as they ran, mothers clutching their children as they fled in terror, tripping over one another in the desperate attempt to escape. The marketplace, once bustling with life, had descended into a scene of utter chaos.

"Help me! Somebody help!" a desperate voice cried out to my left.

I turned just in time to see one of the Fungoids snatch a man by the arm. It lifted him effortlessly into the air, its massive, grotesque body towering over him like a nightmare brought to life. The man's eyes went wide with terror, his face contorting in agony as the fiend's enormous fingers began to tighten their grip.

The man's screams grew louder, more frantic, as the sickening sound of bones cracking echoed through the air. He thrashed wildly, his free hand clawing at the Fungoid's arm in a futile attempt to break free.

"We need to move now!" I urged the woman, dragging her toward a nearby stall. I scanned the area quickly and saw a flat roof. "Climb up there! Stay low, stay hidden. I'll come back for you!" I shouted, hoisting her up onto the roof with all the strength I could muster.

She scrambled onto the roof, her hands shaking. Somehow, she managed to pull herself up, flattening her body against the surface with wide, fearful eyes. "Please… don't forget about me!" she called out, her voice trembling as I turned away.

"I won't," I promised, my mind already focused on the next task.

I spun around, drawing my sword and shield as I charged toward the man still in the Fungoid's grasp. The beast had taken notice of me, and with a frustrated roar, it dropped the man, letting him crumple to the ground like a broken doll. Its eyes fixed on me, burning with a malevolent hunger as it charged forward, its massive hands reaching out to snatch me up.

I barely managed to sidestep its first swipe, bringing my sword down hard on its arm. The blade bit into the thick, fungal flesh, but it didn't slow the creature. If anything, it only enraged it further. With a deafening bellow, it lashed out again, this time with even greater force.

I raised my shield just in time to catch the brunt of the blow, the impact rattling my bones and nearly sending me sprawling. I gritted my teeth, digging my heels into the ground to keep from falling.

Out of the corner of my eye, I saw the man I had tried to save struggling to his feet. His arm hung at an unnatural angle, clearly broken, but he was alive. I just needed to buy him more time to get away.

The Fungoid lunged at me again, its massive arm swinging wide. I ducked, barely missing the blow, and slashed at its side with my sword. Thick, dark fluid oozed from the wound, but the creature seemed completely unfazed. Its other arm swung in retaliation, crashing into my shield with brutal force. The impact sent me flying, my body hitting the ground hard as the air was knocked from my lungs.

Gasping for breath, I scrambled to my feet just in time to see the Fungoid rear back for another strike. My limbs felt heavy, and my vision blurred slightly from the impact, but I braced myself for the incoming blow.

I could hear my heart pounding in my ears, each beat echoing like a drum as the creature loomed over me, its ginormous body blotting out the sky. The ground trembled with each of its steps, shaking the earth beneath me.

The Fungoid's eyes locked onto me, and a gravelly roar tore from its mouth, sending a chill down my spine. It raised its colossal arm high, preparing to strike a final strike. The shadow of its arm cast over me, growing darker as it descended toward me with terrifying speed. My body refused to move, and for a brief, heart-stopping moment, I thought this was it.

The blow was inevitable—too fast to dodge, too powerful to block. My heart raced as time seemed to slow, the creature's massive fist barreling toward me.

Suddenly, from the corner of my eye, I caught a blur of movement. Before the creature could strike again, a group of guards rushed forward, their weapons gleaming as they drove their blades into the Fungoid's flesh.

They struck from all sides, the synchronized assault driving the creature back with a flurry of thrusts and slashes. The fiend roared, stumbling under the relentless barrage of blows.

"Get out of here, boy!" one of the guards barked at me, his voice strained with effort. "We'll handle the rest!"

I nodded and dashed towards the man with the broken arm. He was slumped against a nearby wall, his face pale and drenched in sweat. I slipped my arm around his shoulders, pulling him to his feet. "I've got you," I said, my voice steadier than I felt.

The man muttered something incoherent, his head lolling slightly as I supported his weight. He was clearly in shock, barely clinging to consciousness. We shuffled away from the carnage, each step slow and unsteady. My eyes darted frantically, searching for the woman I had helped earlier.

I spotted her still clinging to the roof of the stall, her wide eyes fixed on the chaos below. Relief flooded her face when she saw me. "You came back for me!" she cried, her voice trembling with emotion.

"Of course I did," I replied, setting the injured man down for a moment. "We need to find somewhere to lay low until all of this is under control."

With the woman supported on my left and the man on my right, we slowly made our way through the crumbling marketplace. Every few steps, my gaze swept the scene around us— it was a horrifying sight. The marketplace, once vibrant and bustling, was now a war zone. The air was thick with the sounds of screams, the clashing of metal, and the guttural roars of the fiends. Destruction was everywhere.

Broken stalls and shattered goods littered the ground, mingling with the bodies of those who hadn't been fortunate enough to escape. Guards were still valiantly fighting, their swords flashing as they tried to hold back the tide of fiends. But it was clear that they were losing ground, their lines crumbling under the relentless onslaught.

A mother, her face streaked with tears, dragged her child through the chaos, her grip tight and desperate. Nearby, a man knelt beside a lifeless body, his hands trembling as he shook the unmoving form, his silent pleas lost in the deafening noise around us. The market had become a battlefield of sorrow and despair.

The woman beside me let out a heart-wrenching sob, her body shaking as she looked around frantically. "I lost my son," she wailed, her voice thick with grief. "He was right next to me before the fiends appeared! I can't find him! I can't—"

I tightened my grip on her shoulder, trying to offer some kind of comfort. "We'll find him," I said, my voice calm despite the chaos. "We'll get through this. The guards will gain control, and we'll find your son. I promise."

We continued to move, though every step felt like wading through thick mud. I glanced back and saw that we had managed to put a decent amount of distance between ourselves and the heart of the battle. For a brief moment, hope flickered in my chest. Maybe we'd made it far enough to avoid the worst of it.

"Looks like we're far away enough from the worst of it," I said, trying to sound reassuring.

But I was wrong.

As the words left my mouth, a massive shadow passed over us, and a deafening screech cut through the air. My heart sank as I looked up, terror filling every inch of my body. Above us, a flock of Dreadbeaks descended upon the town, their enormous wings beating against the sky with a force that sent shudders through the ground.

One of them landed nearby, the earth trembling beneath its weight. Its beady eyes, cold and calculating, scanned the chaos with predatory intent. Its talons dug into the cobblestone, and I could see the sharpness of its beak, large enough to snap a man in half.

Panic surged through me. The guards were already stretched thin, barely holding back the fiends. Now, with these creatures added to the fray, it felt like all hope was lost.

The woman's sobs turned to screams as the Dreadbeak let out another piercing screech and launched its attack. It swooped down, effortlessly snatching up a fleeing man and tossing him aside like a doll, before focusing its gaze on a group of guards who scrambled to hold it back.

I tightened my hold on the injured man and woman. This wasn't just chaos—it was worse than any nightmare I could've ever imagined. Fiends attacking a town was unheard of. Something like this hadn't happened in over 1,400 years. Fiends generally stayed away from heavily populated areas, only attacking those foolish enough to wander too far away from the well-trodden paths. But now, they were here in the heart of town.

"My son... I need to find my son!" the woman cried out, her voice breaking with desperation.

Her frantic words barely registered through the mayhem surrounding us, but I heard the terror behind them.

"What if he's hurt? What if he's—"

"We don't have time! We need to move—now!" I cut her off, shouting above the din. "We need to find somewhere to hide!"

Without waiting for their response, I practically dragged the two of them forward, moving as fast as their injuries allowed. My heart pounded as another screech echoed above us. I glanced up, eyes widening in horror. A second Dreadbeak was descending upon us, its massive wings casting a shadow that blotted out the light.

It landed with a thunderous crash directly in our path, the gust of wind from its wings knocking us off balance. I struggled to remain standing, bracing myself against the force. The creature towered over us, its razor-sharp beak glistening in the light, and its black, soulless eyes locked onto us. The weight of its presence made the air around us feel heavy and suffocating.

"This is bad," I whispered to myself, shifting my stance and positioning myself between the injured pair and the monstrous bird.

The Dreadbeak's eyes gleamed with malice, and it let out another deafening squawk. It took a step forward, talons sinking into the cobblestone like a hot knife through butter, and I could feel the ground tremble beneath its weight. It was ready to strike, and there was nowhere left to run.

Out of nowhere, a voice rang out from my left. "You three!

This way, quickly! There's a group of us hiding in the tavern!"

I snapped my head in the direction of the voice and spotted a woman frantically waving her arms from the entryway of a nearby building. It was the same tavern I had visited with Brute just the day before, but I hadn't even realized we were so close. The panic of the situation had disoriented me.

But there was no way the Dreadbeak would just let us go. The man and woman were in no condition to run, and I knew I had to make a choice. If I could lead the Dreadbeak away, they might stand a chance of reaching the tavern safely.

"You two," I whispered, steeling myself as I positioned my body to block them from the creature's view. "Head for the tavern. I'll buy you as much time as I can."

The woman shook her head frantically, fear evident in her wide eyes. "We can't make it to the tavern!" she cried, her voice trembling. "We'll never get past that thing!" She clutched my arm, panic overtaking her as she glanced back at the towering Dreadbeak, its massive wings casting an ominous shadow over us.

"You have to go!" I insisted, my voice firm despite the urgency. "I can handle it—just run when you get the chance."

Her legs shook beneath her, and her grip tightened on the man beside her. "Please," she whimpered, barely able to hold back the terror in her voice. "We can't do it alone... we won't make it."

I shot her a reassuring glance, trying to summon a calm I didn't quite feel. "You'll make it," I said, stepping forward, sword raised. "Just stay low and keep moving."

Before she could respond, the Dreadbeak lunged, its beak aimed directly at me. I dodged to the side just in time, slashing my sword across its neck. The blade barely cut through its thick, coarse feathers, and I could tell I hadn't done any real damage.

The beast screeched in fury, wings flapping violently as it prepared for another attack.

I swung again, this time aiming for its wing, but the Dreadbeak was too fast. It retaliated, striking back with a snap of its beak that came dangerously close to my shoulder.

Out of the corner of my eye, I saw the woman and the man were barely moving—their progress was too slow. If I didn't do something drastic, they wouldn't make it.

With a swift movement, the Dreadbeak lashed out, and I managed to raise my shield just in time to block the blow. The force of the impact sent me staggering back, my sword slipping from my grasp and clattering to the ground.

Before I could react, the Dreadbeak took advantage of my momentary lapse, slamming its wing into me. I raised my shield to deflect the brunt of the force, but it wasn't enough. I was thrown backward, hitting the ground hard. Pain shot up my spine as I struggled to catch my breath, my eyes watering.

Desperate, I scanned the area around me, and that's when I spotted it—a spear, likely dropped by one of the fallen guards. Without a second thought, I scrambled to my feet and dashed for it just as the Dreadbeak lunged again. I barely managed to grab the spear and dive behind a nearby market stall, pushing myself under its narrow shelf as the Dreadbeak's beak came crashing down above me.

It thrust its beak again and again, each strike coming closer to my head as I tried to push myself further under the stall. The wood creaked and groaned under the pressure, and I knew it wouldn't hold much longer. My mind raced, and in a moment of clarity, I broke the spear in half, gripping the dull end with both hands.

As the Dreadbeak stabbed its beak once more, I jammed the broken spear directly into its mouth. The creature reared back, thrashing wildly, its massive body shaking the entire stall as it tried to dislodge the broken spear. The weapon had become lodged deep in its beak, preventing it from closing its jaws.

This was my chance.

I scrambled out from under the stall, retrieving my sword from where it had fallen, and sprinted toward the man and woman, who had finally made it to the entrance of the tavern. The relief in the woman's eyes was evident as I approached.

"You came back," the woman sobbed, her body trembling with fear and exhaustion.

"Inside, now!" I urged, pushing the two of them through the door with all the strength I could muster. The injured man and woman stumbled into the safety of the tavern, and I followed, slamming the heavy door shut behind us. The air was thick with tension, and every second felt like an eternity as two burly men immediately shoved a large bookcase in front of the door, barricading us in.

I leaned against the door for a moment, chest heaving as I caught my breath. My heart was still racing, and for a brief second, the sound of my own pulse drowned out the noise. My limbs ached, but I forced myself to stand tall, my mind racing with everything that had just happened.

I exhaled slowly, steadying myself before turning to take in the room. The tension hung thick in the air, almost suffocating, and it took a moment for my eyes to adjust to the dim lighting.

The tavern was packed—filled to the brim with townsfolk desperately seeking refuge from the chaos outside. People huddled in corners, their faces pale with fear. Some whispered fervent prayers under their breath, their eyes tightly shut as if trying to will the horrors away. Parents clutched their children, whispering reassurances even though their own eyes portrayed their terror. A few children cried softly, their small hands gripping their mothers' skirts, trying to find some sense of safety in a world that had suddenly turned into a nightmare.

I turned to the woman, who was still trembling, her face streaked with tears. "Are you alright?" I asked gently, trying to steady my breath as the adrenaline continued to flow through me.

She nodded, her lip quivering. "Thank you," she whispered, her voice shaky. "I don't know what we would have done without you."

The man with the broken arm slumped against the wall, sliding to the floor with a groan. His face was pale, sweat glistening on his forehead from the pain. "Aye, lad... she's right," he muttered through gritted teeth, trying to manage a weak smile. "We'd be dead without ye."

"Save your energy," I urged him, crouching beside him. His injuries were worse than I initially thought. "We need to get you some help."

Standing up, I scanned the crowd, my voice raised to cut through the murmur of fear and confusion that filled the room. "Is there anyone here who's a medic?" My eyes darted between the faces of the crowd, hoping someone had the skills we so desperately needed.

After a tense moment, a young woman stepped forward. She was trembling, her face pale, but there was a determination in her eyes. "I'm a medic," she said, her voice steady despite the fear that gripped her. Without wasting any time, she moved quickly to the injured man's side, her hands already at work.

"Thank you," I breathed. "He was grabbed by a Fungoid. I'm not sure how bad his injuries are, but his arm..."

The medic was already focused, her hands moving with precision as she gently examined the man's mangled arm. "This is serious," she muttered under her breath, her brow furrowing as she worked. "We need to immobilize his arm and stop the bleeding." Her hands moved quickly, tearing strips of fabric from her skirt to bind the wound as tightly as she could.

The woman I had saved hovered nearby, her eyes wide with concern. "Will he be okay?" she asked, her voice barely above a whisper.

The medic glanced up briefly, offering a small but reassuring nod. "He's going to be in a lot of pain," she said, her voice calm and measured, "but he should survive. We just need to keep him stable until we can get him to a proper medical center."

I exhaled, the weight of everything finally hitting me. Leaning forward, I braced my hands on my knees, trying to steady myself. My heart was still racing, but the immediate danger seemed to have passed for now.

I shot upright as panic hit me—I still didn't know where Celine was. My heart pounded in my chest as I frantically scanned the crowd, searching for the sight of her hooded figure. The tavern was full of frightened faces, but none of them belonged to her. My mind raced, flooded with images of her out there, alone, possibly in danger. Had she managed to find safety, or was she still out there, battling with the fiends?

"Stay here," I instructed the medic, the injured man, and the woman. "I need to find someone."

As I approached the barricaded door, the two men who had barricaded it earlier quickly moved to block my path, their expressions rigid.

"Where do you think you're going?" one of them demanded, his voice gruff but laced with concern. "You can't seriously be thinking of heading back out there."

I hesitated, but only for a moment. "I have to find someone," I replied, trying to push past them.

"We can't let you go out there," one of them said, his tone firm and unyielding. "It's too dangerous. What if a fiend sees you? It took everyone else a long time to convince us to let you three in here!"

I shook my head, trying to sidestep them. "I'm sorry, but I can't stay. I have to leave. I have to find my friend," I pleaded, desperation creeping into my voice.

The other man stepped forward, crossing his arms, his face serious. "Not happening, boy," he said sternly. "If you go out there, you're putting everyone in here at risk. "

His words stopped me in my tracks. My mind was screaming to get out, to find Celine, but I couldn't deny the truth in his statement. If I went out there and a fiend followed me back, I would be endangering not only myself but everyone who had taken shelter in the tavern.

I took a deep breath, forcing myself to think clearly. I looked them both in the eyes, my heart aching with indecision. "You're right," I admitted, the words leaving a bitter taste in my mouth. "I understand. I'll stay here."

They exchanged a glance, their tense posture easing slightly. They stepped aside, allowing me to back away from the door. As I walked toward the middle of the tavern, I couldn't shake the overwhelming fear I felt. I had to find another way to locate her—waiting here didn't sit right with me.

I glanced back toward the barricaded door, my thoughts heavy with worry. Wherever she was, I prayed she was safe. I couldn't lose her—not like this.

Somehow, I would find her.

# CHAPTER 12

The tavern was thick with tension, every face a portrait of fear and uncertainty. Outside, the muffled chaos continued, echoing faintly through the sturdy walls that, for now, separated us from the horrors beyond. I scanned the room regularly, observing the townsfolk huddled together, some whispering in hushed tones, others clutching loved ones close. Makeshift barricades of overturned tables and chairs had been hastily erected, offering a false sense of protection. The grim reality settled over us like a dark cloud—we were under siege by fiends. An event so rare, so unthinkable, it hadn't occurred in over a millennium.

The young medic who had tended to the man with the broken arm worked tirelessly, though her resources were few. "He's lost a fair amount of blood," she muttered with a sigh. "But this is the best I can do, given the situation." Her hands trembled slightly as she packed away her supplies, a reflection of the collective anxiety that gripped us all.

Not far from where I stood, the woman I had rescued earlier sat with her hands tightly clasped, her knuckles pale against her skin. Her eyes darted nervously from face to face, as if expecting to see her son suddenly appear. "My son... I need to find my son," she whispered, her voice a fragile echo.

I placed a hand on her shoulder, trying to convey some form of comfort, though my own heart was heavy with worry. "We'll find him. But right now, the safest place for you is here, waiting for his return."

Her eyes, wide with desperation, met mine. "Oh my! I never even got your name," she said, her voice trembling with a mix of fear and embarrassment. "How rude of me."

"Isaac," I said with a faint smile. "Don't worry about that. Just know that I'll do everything I can to bring him back to you."

"Thank you," she whispered, her voice breaking slightly. "I'm Natalia. I don't know what I would do without him."

Suddenly, a deafening crash rattled the barricaded door, causing the entire room to jump. The door shuddered under the impact, but the makeshift barricade of a bookcase and table held firm—for now. The townsfolk huddled closer, eyes wide with fear as they stared at the door, anticipating another assault. I instinctively drew my sword, bracing myself for whatever might break through.

Thankfully, nothing came. Silence stretched out, tense and heavy, though it offered little relief. The danger wasn't gone; it was only waiting. We couldn't remain trapped in this tavern forever. Sooner or later, we would run out of food, or worse, the fiends would find a way in.

I glanced toward the back of the tavern, where barrels of ale and crates of provisions were stacked. It was enough to sustain us for a few days at most, but with so many people crammed inside, it wouldn't last long. I walked over to assess our meager supplies—a few loaves of bread, some dried meat, and a couple of jugs of water. It was a small comfort, knowing we had something, but it was nowhere near enough to relieve the growing unease.

As I returned to the main room, the low hum of hushed conversations mixed with the occasional sobs of frightened children. The tension was suffocating. An older man, lines of age etched into his face, began to speak as though talking to himself.

"I've lived here all my life," he murmured, his voice distant. "Never seen anything like this. Fiends don't attack towns. Something's driven them out of the forest."

A few people nearby nodded in agreement. "Maybe something worse than the fiends moved in," a woman suggested, her voice shaking. "Something that scared them enough to push them into town."

"Or maybe they're starving," another man chimed in, his tone grim. "If their usual prey is gone, they'll hunt anything they can find."

Yet another voice spoke up, a younger man with a determined look in his eyes. "What if it's dark magic? Someone powerful enough to control the fiends and send them after us?"

The room grew louder as more people voiced their theories, each one more dreadful than the last. The panic was spreading, seeping into every corner of the tavern like a rising tide.

"What if it's a curse?" an elderly woman asked, her voice quivering. "What if we're doomed for something we did—cursed to be hunted by these monsters until there's no one left?"

A man sitting in the shadows finally spoke, his voice trembling with fear. "I heard a story once about a town overrun by fiends. They didn't just kill—they took people. Took them away to a place no one ever came back from."

At this, a child's cry pierced the air, sharp and heartbreaking. The mother of the child, a weary-looking woman, stood abruptly. "Stop it! You're all terrifying the children!" she snapped, her voice laced with anger and desperation.

The room fell into silence once again, the only sound the soft sobs of the child. The mother hugged her child tightly, her glare sweeping over the crowd. "We need to stay calm. Fear won't help us. We have to stay strong for the sake of our families."

Her words struck a chord within me. Loved ones... I thought of Celine, out there somewhere in the madness. Every moment spent in this tavern was another moment she might need me. My eyes shifted to the barricaded door, where the two men stood guard, their postures rigid and alert. I had to find a way out—at least to gather more information, if not to find Celine herself.

Turning to the barkeeper, I asked quietly, "Is there a privy here?"

The barkeep, a stout man with a large beard, nodded toward the stairs. "Aye, upstairs to the left."

I nodded in thanks and made my way up the creaking stairs. The quiet would help clear my mind and give me a chance to plan. I needed to think about how to find Celine and bring her back here safely.

The corridor upstairs was dimly lit, the air heavy with the quiet that hung over the tavern. Finding the door to the privy, I stepped inside, locking it behind me. The cold wood of the door pressed against my back as I leaned into it, trying to steady my thoughts.

*Celine was resourceful,* I reminded myself. She would have found a way to stay safe. But where had she gone after leaving the old man's stall? I pictured her darting through the streets, evading fiends with her usual grace. But what if...

No. I couldn't think like that. I had to stay focused. Positive.

Splashing some cold water onto my face from a small basin, I tried to clear my head. As I wiped my face, I noticed something in the reflection of the water. I looked up, a small skylight was on the ceiling, just big enough for me to squeeze through. A sudden idea popped up into my mind. I could wait until everyone had fallen asleep and slip out through the skylight. Risky, but it was my best shot at finding Celine.

With my mind made up, I returned downstairs, blending back into the crowd. The hours dragged on, and as night fell, exhaustion began to take its toll on the townsfolk. They settled into uneasy rest, huddling together for warmth and comfort.

Just a little longer, I told myself as I found a quiet corner and pretended to sleep. I would make my move as soon as the tavern had fully quieted.

Finally, the room was filled with the soft sounds of slumber.

I glanced toward the door, noting the two men guarding it were now slumped against the barricade, fast asleep. Their backs rested heavily against the bookshelf, their snores a steady rhythm in the otherwise tense silence.

I rose quietly from my corner, careful not to disturb anyone, and tiptoed back upstairs. Entering the privy, I shut the door behind me with a gentle click. The faint glow of moonlight seeped through the skylight, casting a silvery hue across the floor. It wasn't much light, but it was enough for me to see what I needed.

Taking a steadying breath, I climbed onto a small shelf beneath the skylight and slowly pushed it open. The cool night air rushed in, biting against my skin as I hoisted myself up, squeezing through the opening. Once outside, I carefully lowered myself onto the flat roof, ensuring my feet made no sound as they touched down.

From my vantage point, I cautiously peered over the roof's edge, scanning the ground below. The streets were eerily quiet, with only a few Fungoids scattered about, their bodies pulsing faintly in the moonlight as they rested. Fortunately, they were mostly sluggish at night—unlike during the day when they were actively hunting.

I lifted my gaze to the rooftops. The occasional Dreadbeak perched here and there, roosting like grotesque sentinels over the slumbering town. For now, they, too, seemed content to rest, their massive wings folded tightly against their bodies.

Turning my attention back to the roofscape, I spotted a sturdy drainpipe to my right, the cold metal gleaming in the moonlight. Moving swiftly and silently, I made my way toward it, each step cautious and deliberate. Reaching the drainpipe, I gave it a firm tug to test its strength. Satisfied, I swung my legs over the edge and began my descent.

The metal was cold against my hands, grating slightly as I slid down, making every effort to minimize any noise. Halfway down, I paused, pressing my back against the rough stone of the wall as I caught my breath. My ears strained to pick up any sound of movement below. All was still.

I resumed my descent, moving inch by inch until I reached the end of the pipe. Dropping the last few feet, I landed softly on the cobblestone. I crouched low, listening carefully for any sign of disturbance. Nothing but the unsettling quiet of the night.

Just ahead, a Fungoid lay sprawled in the middle of the street, its bulbous form twitching faintly with each breath. My heart pounded as I crept past it, careful to avoid making any sound that might stir the creature from its rest.

I stuck to the shadows, moving through the darkest corners and narrow alleyways. Every now and then, I paused to listen, making sure I hadn't been noticed by any lurking fiends. The town felt endless, the darkened streets stretching out in all directions like a maze designed to trap me.

I decided to start my search at the last place I knew Celine had been—the old man's stall. It wasn't too far, and if she'd left any clues, that would be the place to find them.

I noticed that there were no guards left in the streets. Perhaps they all retreated to defend key locations in the town— the town hall, the armory, or perhaps even the more noble estates. They might have been overwhelmed and scattered during the initial attack, leaving the common streets to the fiends.

As I moved closer to the marketplace, the devastation of the attack became more evident. Bodies lay strewn about—guards, townsfolk, and fiends alike—all caught in the chaos of the assault. My stomach twisted as I stepped over the fallen, trying my hardest not to vomit from the site of them.

Finally, I reached the old man's stall. It was barely standing, the roof caved in, and the wooden frame splintered beyond recognition. As I approached, something caught my eye—a single strawberry resting atop the rubble. My heart skipped a beat. Could Celine have left this for me? A sign she had passed through?

I picked up the berry, turning it over in my hand. It was unblemished, stark against the destruction surrounding it. It must have been placed there after the chaos had subsided, perhaps as a signal.

She was here. Recently.

Pocketing the strawberry, I scanned the area for any more clues. Though what I had wasn't much, it was enough to keep me going. I had a direction and a thread to follow.

As I continued through the streets, the destruction grew worse—overturned carts, shattered windows, and more lifeless bodies scattered across the cobblestone. The stench of death hung in the air, thick and oppressive. Each time I passed a body, my heart raced, fearing I might find Celine among the fallen. But each time, it was someone else, a stranger caught in the wrong place at the wrong time.

Eventually, I found myself in a narrow alley where the buildings loomed tall, their shadows stretching ominously across the empty streets. I turned a corner and froze—there, in the middle of the road, was a small basket, its contents spilled across the cobblestone. Strawberries, many of them crushed, lay scattered around the basket.

As I moved toward the basket, a sound from my left made me pause. Faint shuffling, just out of sight. Slowly, I peered around the corner.

Two Grimroots.

They were hunched over something—a body. Their gnarled limbs twitched and shifted as they moved, obscuring the figure beneath them. All I could see were a pair of boots sticking out from under their monstrous forms.

A cold chill ran down my spine. My breath caught in my throat. Was it her? Had Celine fallen victim to these creatures?

Every instinct screamed at me to charge forward, to fight. But I forced myself to stay still, to think. Rushing in blindly would get me killed, and it wouldn't help Celine if she was still out there.

The Grimroots continued their inspection of the body, their limbs twitching as they sifted through the scene, seemingly searching for something. My heart pounded in my chest; every muscle tensed with apprehension. I needed to be certain—it was too dangerous to jump to conclusions, but the thought that the body could belong to Celine worried me relentlessly.

I couldn't risk a direct confrontation with them. Not here, not now. A battle would create too much noise, likely alerting any other fiends lurking nearby. Besides, I was outnumbered. The Grimroots, with their twisted blades and unnerving speed, could cut me down before I'd even have a chance to call for help. I couldn't let my emotions override my instincts.

I had to confirm if it was her. And, if it was… no, I couldn't afford to think like that. My focus had to remain sharp. There had to be a way to observe without drawing their attention.

Glancing around, I searched for a vantage point. The alley across from me seemed like a good option. If I could make it there undetected, it would give me a better angle to see who or what the Grimroots were standing over.

I was about to move when the sound of movement behind me sent a jolt through my body. My sword was in my hand before I even thought to draw it; the blade raised defensively as I spun around to face the source of the noise.

To my shock, I found myself face-to-face with Brute. His hands were raised in surrender, his eyes wide as the tip of my blade hovered dangerously close to his neck.

"Easy there," Brute whispered in a low, steady voice, his eyes locked onto mine. "Watch where you're pointing that thing."

Relief surged through me as I quickly lowered my sword. "Brute," I whispered, the confusion clear in my voice. "What are you doing here?"

A wry smile crept onto his face as he scanned the alley. "I could ask you the same thing," he replied, his tone light but his eyes sharp.

I nodded, feeling a sense of comfort at his presence, despite the circumstances. "I'm trying to find Celine," I explained, my voice hushed. "Have you seen any sign of her?"

Brute shook his head, his brow furrowing slightly. "Your lady friend from the other day? No, I've been scouring the streets for the injured. Haven't seen her."

His gaze drifted down to my leg, and his eyes narrowed. "You're moving around pretty well for a guy who was hobbling on a crutch a day ago. It's only been, what, three days since you got injured? A wound like that should've taken weeks to heal."

I shrugged, unsure of how to explain it myself. "Guess it looked worse than it actually was," I offered weakly, forcing a small smile.

Brute studied me for a moment longer, but he didn't push the issue. "What were you looking at?" he asked, leaning past me to peek around the corner. His eyes widened as he spotted the body on the ground, the Grimroots still looming over it.

"Do you think that's—"

"I don't know," I cut him off, my voice tight. "That's what I'm trying to figure out."

Brute gave a curt nod, his expression hardening. "Alright. Well, we need to get a closer look. Let's take those two out."

I shook my head and pointed toward the alley across the street. "If we can sneak over there without them noticing, we might be able to avoid fighting altogether. No need to draw attention to ourselves."

Brute waved a hand dismissively. "Where's the fun in that? We stay quiet, sneak up behind them, and take 'em out before they know what hit 'em."

I raised an eyebrow, a hint of a smile tugging at my lips. "Not much of a stealthy guy, huh?"

Brute grinned, the gleam of excitement in his eyes unmistakable. "Never been my style. I'll take the one on the right. Follow my lead."

Together, we moved carefully, our bodies low to the ground as we crept through the shadows. The Grimroots remained fixated on the body, oblivious to our approach. With each step, my heartbeat quickened, the tension in the air nearly suffocating. A few feet away, Brute and I paused, exchanging a quick glance to ensure we were both ready.

Brute moved first, his large frame deceptively nimble as he crept up behind the Grimroot on the right. In one swift, silent motion, his hands clamped down on the creature's head. A sickening crack followed as he twisted its neck. The sound was faint, barely noticeable, and the creature collapsed to the ground in a heap.

I followed suit, mirroring his movements as I approached the Grimroot on the left. My grip tightened on the hilt of my sword, the cool metal comforting against my palm. In one decisive thrust, I plunged the blade through its chest, aiming directly for its heart. The creature stiffened, a grotesque gurgling sound escaping its twisted form before it slumped lifelessly to the ground.

For a moment, Brute and I stood there, catching our breath, eyes scanning the area for any signs of additional threats. The street remained still, the oppressive quiet of the night settling around us once more.

I turned my attention to the body the Grimroots had been

hovering over. The boots, still visible, belonged to a young woman. As I moved closer, my heart pounded in my chest, fearing the worst. But when I saw her face relief washed over me—this wasn't Celine. She wasn't here. But that relief was quickly replaced by guilt. Another life had been lost, even if it wasn't hers.

Brute knelt beside me, his eyes sweeping over the scene. "Not her, right?" he asked, his voice low.

I shook my head. "No... it's not her." My gaze shifted to the ground, where a small basket of strawberries lay near the woman's body. I pointed toward it, my voice tinged with both hope and unease. "But that must be the basket she was given. She must've passed through here."

Brute's eyes narrowed in thought, then he gestured toward something else. "Look at that," he muttered, nodding toward a small object a few feet from the basket. "A shoe."

I hadn't noticed it before. It was small, a child's shoe, half-buried in the dirt just ahead of the fallen basket. My stomach twisted with uncertainty.

"What do you think it means?" I asked, my voice hushed.

Brute frowned; his brows furrowed in thought. "Could be nothing," he murmured. "Or it could be something. Either way, we should keep moving."

I nodded in agreement, but before we could move, the faint sound of crying reached my ears. The voice was small, frightened—it sounded like a child. Brute and I exchanged glances, our expressions tense before we sprinted toward the source of the cries.

The sound grew louder as we approached a small courtyard, and there, to my shock, I saw Celine. Her face was streaked with dirt and sweat, her eyes wide with fear as she carried a small boy on her back. Behind her, a pair of Grimroots were closing in, their scythe-like arms swinging through the air, eager to strike.

"Celine!" I shouted, my voice echoing through the courtyard as I broke into a full sprint toward her.

She turned to the sound of my voice, her eyes locking with mine, a flash of recognition and desperation crossing her face.

"Drifted!" Celine's voice rang out, sharp and urgent. Without warning, she removed the young boy from her back and hurled him toward me. My heart leaped into my throat as I dropped to the ground, sliding across the cobblestones just in time to catch him in my arms before he collided with the hard surface. The boy trembled against my chest, his tiny frame shaking as I cradled him close.

A shrill screech pierced the air, sending a shiver down my spine. I looked up just in time to see a Dreadbeak swooping down from above, its massive talons outstretched. Before any of us could react, the fiend's claws closed around Celine's shoulders, lifting her off the ground with terrifying ease.

"Celine!" I screamed, the sound tearing from my throat, echoing helplessly across the courtyard.

Without thinking, I handed the boy off to Brute and sprinted after the creature. My sword flashed in the moonlight as I charged forward, intent on reaching her—on doing something, anything to stop the nightmare unfolding before me.

But as I ran, movement to my side caught my eye. The two Grimroots that had been chasing Celine pivoted their attention to me.

I didn't slow down. With a growl of determination, I pivoted mid-stride and slashed at the first Grimroot. My blade cut through its bark-like flesh with a crack, and it toppled to the ground with a shudder. The second lunged toward me, but I sidestepped it, bringing my sword down in a vicious arc, severing its arm and cleaving through its torso in one clean motion. The creature collapsed in a heap of splintered limbs.

There was no time to pause. I kept running, my lungs burning as I pushed forward, my eyes locked on Celine. But I was too late.

The Dreadbeak let out a screech and, with one final flap of its wings, ascended far beyond my reach. I swung my sword in desperation, the air slicing around me, but the creature soared into the night sky, carrying Celine further and further from me with every beat of its wings.

Our eyes met for the briefest of moments, her gaze filled with something I had never seen in her before—fear. A raw, visceral terror that made my heart stop. In that instant, everything around us disappeared. It was just her and me, caught in the unspoken truth of our helplessness.

"Hold on!" I shouted, my voice cracking under the weight of my despair. "I swear, I'll find you! Wherever you are, I'll come for you!"

The words felt hollow, swallowed by the vastness of the dark sky, but I forced myself to believe them. I had to make her believe them too.

Celine's face, pale and stricken with terror, seared itself into my mind as the Dreadbeak's talons dug into her arms, carrying her higher and higher into the inky darkness above. Her wide, fear-filled eyes met mine for a split second—a silent plea, one that made my heart clench painfully. Her mouth opened as if to call out to me, but the wind and the creature's screeches drowned out whatever words she might have spoken.

The Dreadbeak's massive wings beat rhythmically, its shadow blotting out the faint light of the moon as it ascended, dragging her further and further away. My chest tightened, my breath coming in shallow gasps as I watched her shrink against the vastness of the sky. My vision blurred with tears, stinging my eyes, but I refused to look away. I couldn't. I had to watch—no matter how much it hurt—until she was swallowed by the night, her silhouette fading into the endless expanse of stars.

Helplessness pulled at me as she disappeared from sight, and the world around me seemed to collapse into silence, leaving only the memory of her terrified face imprinted on my mind.

"I promise!" I screamed one last time, my voice hoarse and trembling.

But deep down, I knew the truth. The promise I made felt fragile, almost meaningless in the face of the reality before me. The chances of finding Celine alive were dwindling with every beat of the creature's wings, every second that passed. She was as good as gone.

Powerless and broken, I fell to my knees, my breath ragged and labored. I watched as the Dreadbeak, with its powerful wings, carried her higher and higher until the night swallowed them both. The emptiness that followed was suffocating, a void where hope once lingered.

# CHAPTER 13

I tore through the streets, heart pounding as Celine's voice still echoed in my mind, haunting me with every step. I had to reach her. Nothing else mattered—nothing else could matter. Her name filled my lungs as I pushed forward, ignoring the growing ache in my legs and the panic rising in my chest.

"Isaac, stop!" Brute's voice boomed behind me, but I refused to slow down. His words felt distant, swallowed by the rush of wind and the desperation pounding in my veins. My eyes locked on the dark wall of the forest ahead, that vast expanse that had swallowed Celine whole. Each branch and root snagged at my boots, threatening to trip me, but I pressed on faster, harder.

Brute's heavy footsteps thundered closer, his breath coming in hot bursts behind me. In seconds, a massive hand gripped my shoulder, wrenching me back with brutal force.

"Are you out of your mind?!" Brute growled, spinning me to face him. His face was shadowed with frustration and fear, his grip tight enough to bruise. "Charging into that forest now, of all nights, will get you killed! You might as well dig your grave now."

"I can't just stand here doing nothing!" I shouted back, trying to tear free from his iron hold.

"Doing nothing is better than charging straight into death!" Brute's eyes burned as he gave me a hard shake, rattling my resolve. "Running into the forest in the dead of night? You're not saving anyone like this—you're throwing your life away."

"I don't care!" My voice cracked with desperation. "I promised her, Brute! I promised her I'd find her; she needs me!"

I tried to shove him away, but he didn't move, his massive frame a stone wall against my fury. "Celine needs me—"

Before I could finish, Brute's hand whipped out, slapping me hard across the face. The shock of the blow hit me before the pain. I stumbled back, clutching my burning cheek.

"What the hell is wrong with you?" I spat, the taste of blood in my mouth. My vision blurred with anger, my body shaking with the urge to keep running.

Brute stepped closer, his voice a low rumble. "Look around us, boy!" His eyes flashed dangerously, but there was something else in them—concern, anger, maybe fear. "All the noise we made back there? It's waking the other fiends. They'll be on us before you even take another step."

I wanted to argue, to push back against the truth in his words, but I couldn't. I looked around—really looked this time—and realized he was right. The air was thick with the presence of the creatures stirring, the shadows alive with danger.

"This is what Celine warned you about," Brute growled, his voice dropping to an intense whisper. "She knew. She knew what happens when you let your emotions drive you—when you act without thinking. You think running into that forest makes you some kind of hero? No. It'll get you killed, Isaac, and then who will be left to save her?"

His words struck deep, slicing through my rage like a knife. The ground beneath me felt like it was crumbling, and I punched a nearby tree in frustration, my knuckles throbbing with the impact.

"Damn it!" I shouted, my voice cracking. The weight of my failure crashed over me, suffocating my chest. He was right—I was acting recklessly. But the thought of doing nothing, of letting her slip away... it was unbearable.

"I... you didn't see her face, Brute," I said, my voice barely a whisper now. "She was terrified."

Brute's hard expression softened slightly, but his grip remained firm. "I know, Isaac. I know it's tearing you apart. But listen to me—this isn't over. We'll find her. But if you go in blind and get yourself killed, you'll never get that chance."

I looked up at him, my breath coming in short gasps. "There's no chance of finding her," I muttered bitterly, the words tasting like poison. "No one survives after being taken by a fiend like that. We both know that."

Brute leaned closer, his face inches from mine, his eyes locked on mine with a fierceness that made me pause. "You have to trust me. As long as she's out there, there's a chance. We can find her, Isaac, but you need to stay alive if we're going to bring her back."

"How can you be so sure?" I whispered, my voice thick with doubt.

"I've seen people come back from worse," Brute replied, his tone quiet but filled with conviction. "You have to trust me on this. We'll get her back. But first, we need to get this little one to safety."

I glanced at Brute's side, where the young boy—Celine's last desperate hope—clung to his leg, his wide eyes filled with fear. I had forgotten, in my frenzy, the weight of that responsibility.

"Okay," I said, my voice breaking. "I'll trust you."

Brute nodded, releasing his grip on my shoulders. "Good. Now, let's get moving before those fiends wake up for real."

I glanced toward the forest one last time, feeling the pull to run, to keep going. But Brute was right—I couldn't save her if I died tonight.

"The tavern from yesterday," I said, standing straighter, determination hardening my voice. "There's a group holed up there; it's safe enough for the boy."

Brute's eyes glinted with approval. "Sounds like a plan. Let's move."

Navigating the streets back to the tavern was like walking a tightrope over a pit of fiends. The town had transformed once more, danger lurking in every corner, every shadow thick with the possibility of death. Each sound—the creak of a distant door, the rustle of wind through broken windows—set my nerves on edge. We moved swiftly but cautiously, sticking to the narrow alleys, our breaths shallow as we hugged the walls.

At one point, a Fungoid shuffled past the mouth of the alley we were in. Brute and I pressed ourselves tight against the stone, barely breathing as it lumbered by, its steps slow and unhurried, like it was hunting something unseen. We waited, hearts pounding, until it was finally out of sight.

Further ahead, a pair of Dreadbeaks circled above, their screeches slicing through the night air. Every time those monstrous birds crossed the moon, I felt a chill run down my spine, knowing how easily they could swoop down and turn us into their prey.

Brute led the way, the boy clinging to his back, his tiny hands gripping Brute's shirt as if letting go meant being swept away by the darkness. The boy's face was buried against Brute's broad shoulders, and I could hear the faint sound of him whimpering softly. His fear was palpable, and every part of me wanted to get him to safety as fast as possible.

Finally, the silhouette of the tavern came into view, its sturdy walls and barricaded windows offering a glimpse of sanctuary amidst the chaos. We approached cautiously, making sure not to draw any unwanted attention. The last thing we needed was to lead any fiends right to the people huddled inside.

"We're here," I whispered, my chest tightening with both relief and apprehension. But as I glanced at the barricaded door, a realization hit me. "But… I don't know how we're going to get back inside. I snuck out through the—"

Before I could finish, Brute stepped forward without a word and, with a single push of his massive arm, forced the door open. The barricaded furniture inside groaned as it gave way under his strength, and the door swung inward with a heavy creak.

"Let's get in," Brute said, motioning for us to hurry.

I blinked, dumbfounded, then nodded and followed him inside, the weight of the night pulling at my steps.

The dim glow of candlelight illuminated the room, casting long shadows over the frightened faces of the townsfolk who had taken refuge there. Their tense expressions mirrored the fear that had gripped the town all night, but when their eyes landed on Brute, I could see the fear start to ebb away, replaced by relief.

"Brute! Oh, thank the moon, you're here!" an elderly man called out, his voice trembling with hope.

"Praise be, Brute has arrived!" a woman echoed, her voice cracking with emotion.

It was as if the entire room had exhaled all at once, their collective anxiety melting into gratitude. Brute, ever humble, nodded in acknowledgment but quickly raised his hands, signaling for quiet. He was used to this—used to people looking at him like he was their savior.

Before he could speak, a figure pushed through the crowd. Natalia. Her eyes were wide, frantic, as they locked onto the young boy. She rushed forward, her face crumpling with emotion.

"Nikolas!" she cried, her voice breaking as she fell to her knees in front of him. Tears were streaming down her face, hands shaking as she reached for her son. "Nikolas, my baby!"

Brute carefully lowered the boy to the ground, and the moment Nikolas touched the floor, Natalia wrapped him in her arms, sobbing uncontrollably as she held him close, her body trembling with the weight of relief.

"I thought I'd lost you," she whispered through her tears, pressing kisses to the top of his head. "I thought I'd never see you again."

Nikolas clung to his mother, his small body shaking as if only now, in her arms, he could allow himself to feel the terror of the night. Natalia looked up at Brute and me, her eyes glistening with tears, her gratitude palpable.

"I don't know how to thank you," she said, her voice trembling. "You kept your word; you saved my boy."

I blinked in surprise, the realization settling in. This boy—Nikolas—was the one Celine had rescued earlier, the one she had fought so hard to protect. He was Natalia's son. The connection made my heart ache, a sudden swell of relief mixing with the exhaustion that weighed heavily on my shoulders.

A tired, weak smile tugged at the corners of my mouth as I processed the unexpected link between the boy and the woman before me. "I couldn't have done it without Brute," I said, glancing over at him. "And Celine, she—" I caught myself, the words slipping out before I could stop them. My throat tightened as I thought about her, carried away into the night. "...Brute made sure we stayed safe."

Brute waved a hand, his eyes softening as he looked down at Natalia and her son. "Just doing what needed to be done," he muttered, his voice gruff but kind. He turned slightly, glancing around the room, ensuring the boy was now truly safe.

Natalia wiped the tears from her face, still clutching Nikolas to her chest as though she would never let him go again. "You both... you're heroes," she whispered, her voice breaking again.

But there was no room for heroics in my heart—not now, not after what had happened to Celine. My mind kept drifting back to the sight of her being carried away into the night. Even in the warmth of the tavern, I couldn't shake the cold grip of fear that held onto me. Celine was still out there, and I had no idea how to save her.

As Natalia and the others offered their thanks, my mind was elsewhere, already plotting the next step. Brute had been right to stop me from rushing into the forest, but that didn't change the fact that time was slipping away.

As I stood there, I could hear the whispers of a few townspeople behind me, their hushed voices tinged with curiosity. They were murmuring about how I had managed to slip outside the tavern when the door had been barricaded shut. I chose to ignore them. My mind was heavy and clouded, not feeling well enough to entertain their questions.

The noise of the tavern—the soft hum of conversation, the crackle of the hearth—began to fade into the background as I distanced myself from the crowd. My feet carried me to a quiet corner, away from the flickering lights and prying eyes. I slid down to the floor, resting my back against the cool wooden wall, and let out a long, shaky breath. The weight of Celine's disappearance pressed on my chest, each moment of her abduction playing over and over in my mind.

The memory of her being ripped away echoed through my thoughts, every detail still vivid. I could still see the fear in her eyes and hear the way she had called out to me. The helplessness I felt was thick, threatening to break whatever composure I had left.

The tavern chatter dulled to a distant murmur. I needed space. Silence. I closed my eyes, exhaustion seeping into my bones, though I knew I wouldn't sleep. My thoughts wouldn't let me.

A few minutes later, I sensed someone beside me. I opened my eyes to find Brute lowering himself to the ground, sitting next to me. His presence was steady as always, a quiet reassurance.

"First thing in the morning," Brute started, his voice low and deliberate, "we're going to leave."

I turned to look at him, my brow furrowing. "Brute, what's the point? Celine—"

He cut me off, his tone firm. "Didn't I tell you to trust me?"

He sighed, casting his gaze across the room at the weary townsfolk huddled together for safety. "I would stay behind and make sure these people stayed safe, but reinforcements from Selunaris are arriving tomorrow. The rest of the Kingsguard will be here to take control of the town and drive the fiends out. I trust them to handle it." He turned back to me, his expression hard but not unkind. "My place now is with you—to help find Celine and bring her back."

I nodded, the tension in my chest loosening just a little. "Thank you, Brute. I don't know what I'd do without you."

Brute met my gaze, his own softening just a fraction. "Get some rest, Isaac. Tomorrow, we leave at first light."

"Where?" I whispered, the weight of exhaustion starting to pull at me. "Where are we going?"

His next words sent a chill down my spine. "Eclipsia."

I stared at him, disbelief flooding through me. "Eclipsia? That's impossible. How will we get through the northern gate? It's always heavily guarded."

Brute leaned in closer, his voice barely more than a whisper. "No one's guarding the northern gate now. With the town under attack, the defenses have shifted. This is our only chance to slip out unnoticed."

Confusion swirled in my mind. "But why Eclipsia? How does that—"

Brute raised a hand, silencing me with a subtle gesture. "I can't explain everything right now," he said, his eyes flickering toward the crowded room. "Too many ears here. Just trust me. We'll talk more once we're on the road."

I stared at him, trying to process this new piece of the puzzle.

Brute was the only person I'd ever met from Eclipsia, and that alone made it a mystery to me. It was a place of whispers and rumors, a town cloaked in secrets. Even passing by it as a child, I remember feeling a strange unease. To be honest, I was scared.

What could be there that would help us get Celine back? Why Eclipsia?

A shiver ran down my spine. I trusted Brute, but the thought of going to Eclipsia filled me with undeniable unease. Something about it felt... wrong. Dark, even.

Brute must have sensed my hesitation. "Get some rest now," he interrupted. "We've got a long journey ahead of us. You'll need all your strength."

Reluctantly, I nodded and shifted to make myself comfortable on the tavern floor. The dull murmur of the room became background noise as I closed my eyes, trying to calm the chaos in my mind. What was Brute's plan? I didn't have the energy to dwell on it. Despite the storm of thoughts swirling inside me, exhaustion finally pulled me into a restless sleep.

When I awoke, the first light of dawn was filtering through the small cracks in the window shutters. The tavern was quieter now, though the occasional soft murmur of the townspeople drifted through the air. Some were still sleeping, while others spoke in low voices, their words filled with the tension of uncertainty.

Brute was already awake, standing near the barricaded door, peering out through a gap in the makeshift cover over the windows. His silhouette against the dim morning light was both imposing and reassuring.

Rubbing the sleep from my eyes, I pushed myself to my feet and made my way over to him. He turned to greet me with a slight smile. "Morning," he said, his voice low but steady. "Ready to get moving?"

I nodded, though my chest tightened at the thought. "Yeah, I guess. As ready as I'm ever going to be."

But as my mind cleared, a new worry took root. "Wait," I started, glancing out the window, "how exactly are we supposed to get out of town? The fiends are still out there."

Brute chuckled softly like I had asked something ridiculous. "Oh, that's easy," he said with a grin. "We're going to run."

I blinked at him. Was he serious? "Run?" I repeated incredulously. "Just... for the woods? Like that?"

Brute nodded, his grin widening. "Exactly. It's simple. I'll run ahead and clear the path for you. You just have to follow behind and keep moving. Easy."

I frowned, my skepticism growing by the second. "That sounds... half-baked. What about the Dreadbeaks? They're still out there, flying around. How do we avoid them?"

Brute scratched his chin thoughtfully as if the idea hadn't been fully considered. "The Dreadbeaks are a problem, sure. But we've got options. We'll stick close to the buildings and use them for cover as we make our way to the edge of town. Once we hit the trees, the forest cover should help us avoid them."

"And what if they spot us before we reach the woods?" I pressed, the knot of worry in my gut tightening.

"If that happens," Brute said, "we improvise." He gave a slight shrug, patting a pouch at his side, the contents clinking softly. "I've got a few tricks up my sleeve. Don't worry, Isaac, I'll do my best to keep them off you."

I let out a long breath, trying to steady my nerves. "Alright," I muttered, still unsure. "Let's do this."

Brute grinned and clapped me on the shoulder, his grip solid and reassuring. "That's the spirit! Stick close to me, and don't look back."

With one last glance at the townspeople, who watched us with a mixture of hope and fear, we slipped out of the tavern and into the pale morning light. The streets were eerily quiet, the remnants of last night's chaos still scattered across the ground. Rubble, overturned carts, and freakish silence hung in the air like a fog, but before I could gather my thoughts, Brute's voice cut through the stillness.

"Let's go!" he barked, launching into a sprint with startling speed.

Caught off guard, I stumbled for a moment, my feet barely catching the ground beneath me as I forced my legs into motion. Brute was already barreling through the narrow alleys and deserted streets ahead, his pace relentless. I did my best to keep up, my heart hammering in my chest.

From the shadows, Fungoids began to emerge, grotesque and twisted, their malformed bodies shifting as they caught sight of us. One lunged at me from a side street, its gnarled hand swiping inches from my face. I stumbled back, narrowly avoiding its grasp.

"Keep moving!" Brute shouted, his voice booming as he turned and delivered a bone-shattering punch to the creature, sending it sprawling into the dirt.

Even though I'd seen his strength before, watching him send a Fungoid crashing to the ground with a single hit left me stunned. I barely had time to register the thought before I was running again, my legs burning with the effort to keep up.

The town felt like a maze—strewn with debris, broken carts, and the remnants of lives left behind in the frantic scramble for safety. Brute cleared the path ahead, his fists and brute force carving a way through the chaos. I followed, dodging and weaving, my breath growing more ragged with each step.

Another Fungoid appeared from behind a collapsed wall, stepping directly in Brute's path. Without hesitation, he grabbed the creature by the neck and slammed it into the ground with a force that shook the street. "Stay close!" he barked over his shoulder.

I nodded, too breathless to respond; my vision locked on Brute's broad back as he bulldozed through everything in our way. My mind was racing, my focus narrowing as the weight of every near miss, every narrow escape hung over me like a cloud. We couldn't afford a single mistake.

We rounded a corner and froze—perched on a nearby rooftop were a group of Dreadbeaks, their hollowed, beady eyes trained on us. They screeched, their cries sharp and shrill in the morning air, and I felt a jolt of panic rise in my chest.

Brute didn't flinch. With a swift motion, he pulled a vial from his pouch and hurled it toward the building where the creatures roosted. It exploded in a burst of red smoke, and the air suddenly filled with the pungent smell of peppermint and other spices.

The Dreadbeaks recoiled instantly, their flight paths erratic as they screeched in confusion, desperate to escape the overwhelming scent. I glanced at Brute, caught off guard by the unexpected reaction, but there was no time for questions.

"Run!" he yelled, and we sprinted forward, dodging beneath low-hanging awnings and vaulting over the scattered debris in our path. The Dreadbeaks circled overhead, but the smoke held them at bay for now, giving us just enough cover to push forward.

The edge of town was in sight—the dark silhouette of the forest looming ahead, just a few more blocks away. My legs screamed in protest, my lungs burning, but I couldn't stop now. We were so close.

Suddenly, a Fungoid lunged out from an alley, its claws wrapping around Brute and dragging him back with a guttural snarl. He struggled, his muscles straining against the creature's grip, but it held fast.

Without thinking, I drew my sword and dove forward, sliding

across the ground. With one swift motion, I sliced through the Fungoid's Achilles tendons, sending it crashing to the ground with a pained roar. Brute wasted no time—he broke free and delivered a final, devastating punch to its face, silencing it for good.

Breathing hard, he looked over at me, a grin spreading across his face. "Nice timing," he said, nodding his thanks. "Now, let's keep moving!"

Finally, we reached the last stretch of street. The forest loomed ahead, the dense line of trees seeming both impossibly close and unbearably far. Brute paused, glancing up at the sky. The Dreadbeaks were circling again, their shadows cutting across the ground like ominous ghosts.

"Keep moving!!" Brute shouted, stepping in front of me. As I darted past him, I saw him pull another vial from his pouch. With a quick flick of his wrist, he hurled it into the air. The vial exploded overhead, a cloud of thick smoke bursting out, filling the sky with a pungent haze.

The Dreadbeaks shrieked and scattered, their flight disrupted once again by the smell. We didn't waste a second—we sprinted across the final stretch of open ground and plunged into the safety of the forest.

The moment the trees closed in around us, I collapsed against the nearest trunk, my body shaking with exhaustion. My legs felt like they were on fire, and my chest heaved with ragged breaths. Brute stood beside me, his gaze fixed on the canopy above, ever watchful.

"Come on," he said quietly, his voice low but insistent. "We need to keep moving. The forest gives us some protection, but we can't let our guard down."

I nodded, still struggling to catch my breath. "Lead the way," I managed, the weight of our escape finally settling in.

Brute took the lead, his steps sure as he moved through the dense forest with ease. I followed close behind, my breath still uneven as I tried to settle my racing heart. The forest canopy overhead blocked much of the early morning light, casting long shadows across our path. Each step took us deeper into the unknown, and the further we went, the more the weight of our journey ahead pressed down on me.

My thoughts began to drift as we walked in silence. I knew these roads well enough. My years of traveling with my parents had made me familiar with the land. In Moonveil, each town sat roughly 220 miles from the next, connected by well-trodden paths that made for easier travel. The distances were daunting, but predictable.

I found myself doing mental calculations, trying to focus on something practical to keep my nerves steady. "If we walk eight hours a day, we could cover about 25 miles each day," I said, more to myself than to Brute. "That means... it would take us roughly nine days to reach Eclipsia."

Brute glanced back at me, a grin tugging at his lips. "Sounds about right," he said.

"That's too long," I replied, shaking my head. The thought of Celine suffering for nine more days felt unbearable.

Brute's grin widened, his eyes glinting with determination. "Which is why we'll push harder. We'll travel ten, maybe twelve hours a day. We'll shave a couple of days off that time."

A smile crept onto my face, a flicker of gratitude swelling in my chest. I appreciated his determination, his willingness to go the extra mile for Celine and me. "Thank you, Brute. I mean it."

Brute nodded, his expression growing serious again. "We'll make it, Isaac. We'll get to her."

His confidence rekindled the fire inside me. The thought of finding Celine alive, though still daunting, filled me with purpose. But there was still one nagging question that I couldn't shake. "Brute," I began cautiously, "can you explain why we're going to Eclipsia? How is it supposed to help us find Celine?"

Brute turned quickly, his eyes narrowing as he scanned the trees around us. "Shush, boy!" he hissed, his voice low and urgent. "We don't know who might be listening."

I instinctively clamped my mouth shut, realizing the gravity of our situation. The forest was silent, but in that silence lay danger. Brute glanced around again before leaning closer, his voice barely above a whisper. "We'll talk when we're further off the road, deeper into the forest. It's not safe here."

I blinked in confusion. "Off the road?" I whispered back.

Brute nodded. "Aye. The guards might still be out here, patrolling. The only reason we slipped through the northern gate was because they were all preoccupied with the town. If we stick to the main path, we're bound to run into trouble sooner or later."

"How far off are we talking?" I asked.

"Four miles should be enough to keep us hidden," he replied, his tone matter-of-fact.

I swallowed hard. The idea of straying so far from the safety of the path made me uneasy. I wasn't a stranger to wandering off the beaten trail to find some quiet, but four miles? That was farther than I'd ever gone, and the further one went from the path, the more dangerous the forest became. The fiends that lurked out here were not ones to be trifled with. I'd learned as much back in class—stories of fiends larger and more vicious than anything I'd ever come across. Though I'd never seen them myself, the tales had always stuck with me. Even seasoned guards spoke of them with caution, recounting encounters where whole patrols barely escaped with their lives.

We moved deeper into the woods, the trees growing thicker around us, their branches closing in like skeletal hands reaching for us. Every sound seemed amplified—the snap of a twig, the rustle of leaves. Brute moved confidently, his steps light despite his size, and I did my best to match his pace, though every muscle in my body screamed with fatigue.

After what felt like hours, Brute finally deemed it safe enough to stop. We found a small clearing, and I sank to the ground, my legs trembling from the effort. Brute sat beside me on a fallen log, his eyes scanning the forest for any signs of movement.

Satisfied that we were alone, he turned to me. "There are things in Eclipsia that defy explanation, Isaac," he began, his voice low. "Things I can't fully put into words. You'll have to see them with your own eyes."

His words piqued my curiosity, though they did little to ease my growing apprehension. "With my own eyes? What are you talking about?"

Brute's gaze softened as if he were about to reveal something profound. "Isaac, all your life, you've been told that Moonveil is the last bastion of civilization, right?"

I nodded. "That's what everyone says."

"Well," Brute said, crossing his arms, "it's not entirely true."

I stared at him, my brow furrowing in confusion. "What do you mean? Are there more places out there? Beyond Moonveil?"

Brute nodded. "Aye, there are places—hidden places— structures that have been forgotten for centuries. Places that hold secrets far beyond what you've ever imagined."

I could feel the confusion written on my face, but Brute continued speaking. "There's an old rumor, Isaac, one that's whispered through the streets of Eclipsia even now. It's said that anyone taken by fiends isn't killed outright—they're taken to a place, far from here, where they're held captive."

A chill ran down my spine as his words sank in. "You mean... Celine could be alive? Held somewhere?"

Brute nodded. "I believe that's where she is. And I know

someone in Eclipsia who can help guide us there."

The weight of his words settled heavily on my shoulders. My mind raced with questions. "But why hasn't anyone spoken about this before? If this place exists, why the secrecy?"

Brute shook his head. "I don't have all the answers. That's why we're going to Eclipsia—to find out the truth, to get to the bottom of all of this."

I frowned, still trying to wrap my head around everything he was saying. "And you really think we'll find what we need there?"

"As sure as I can be," Brute replied, his voice steady. "It's risky, but it's the best shot we've got."

Despite the uncertainty, Brute's confidence steadied me. I nodded, feeling a sense of determination swelling within me. "Then let's do it." As we sat in the clearing, a strange mix of fear and hope stirred within me. The unknown loomed large before us, but the possibility of finding Celine, of bringing her back, gave me the strength I needed. Whatever secrets lay in Eclipsia, I was ready to face them.

Together, Brute and I would uncover the truths that had been buried for so long. And with any luck, we would bring Celine home.

# CHAPTER 14

As the first light of dawn stretched through the canopy, a chill hung in the air—sharp, crisp, and unmistakably fall. The forest around us, once lush with summer's green, had begun to surrender to the changing season. Leaves of amber and gold littered the path, crunching beneath our boots as we pressed on toward Eclipsia.

"Feels like fall's coming," I remarked, breaking the silence that had settled between us. "The air's getting cooler."

Brute nodded, his eyes never leaving the shifting branches above us. "Yeah, we'll need to be ready for whatever the weather throws at us as we travel." His voice was steady, but his gaze seemed distant as if weighing the challenges that lay ahead.

The cool air was invigorating, but it also carried a certain urgency. Every gust of wind, every fallen leaf, seemed to remind me that time was slipping away. We were closing in on Eclipsia, less than a day out now. With each step, my determination grew—fueled by the hope that we were getting closer to finding Celine.

As we walked in silence, Brute turned his head slightly, his tone more casual than usual. "So, Isaac, what's the deal with you and Celine? She your girlfriend?"

The question caught me off guard, heat rushing to my face. I stumbled over my words, unsure how to answer. "Uh... well... we're friends, I think."

Brute glanced at me with a teasing smirk. "You think?"

"No, I mean—" I hesitated, trying to gather my thoughts. "We're close, I guess."

He raised an eyebrow, clearly amused. "Close, huh? She's a

good-looking girl, that Celine. From what I've seen, you two make a good pair."

I felt my face flush even more. "I don't know what you're talking about."

Brute chuckled, his laugh deep and knowing. "Come on, Isaac. You can't fool me. There's something there, isn't there?"

I wasn't sure how to answer. Was there something between us? Celine was hard to read, distant even. She cared about me—I knew that much—but was it just because of the journey, the destiny she always spoke of? Maybe I was just a means to an end for her. A necessary piece in whatever larger plan she envisioned.

The thought made me uncomfortable. Celine wasn't the romantic type; she hardly displayed any emotion beyond determination. She was always focused on our path north, always serious about the mission. And now, with everything happening, maybe it wasn't the time to complicate things.

"I..." I paused, trying to find the right words. "We're just friends, that's all."

Brute shot me a skeptical look, a grin tugging at the corner of his mouth. "Well, if you're not interested, maybe I'll give it a shot once we get her back. Cute girls like her don't come around too often."

A sudden pang of jealousy flared up inside me, catching me off guard. I must've made a face because Brute burst out laughing.

"Relax, I'm messing with you." He clapped a hand on my shoulder. "But seriously, Isaac, if you don't make a move soon, someone else might."

I forced a smile, trying to laugh it off. "Right, yeah... I'll keep that in mind."

Brute handed me a piece of bread, still grinning. "Here, take this. It's the last of the food we've got before we reach Eclipsia."

"Thanks," I said, my stomach grumbling in appreciation as I took the bread. We'd been lucky enough to stretch our supplies—some bread, water, dried meat, and whatever small game we managed to catch. It had been enough to keep us going, though I knew it wouldn't last much longer.

The deeper we ventured, the more the forest seemed to close in on us. The path narrowed, becoming harder to navigate with each step. Twisted roots tangled underfoot, and the ground grew soft and marshy, each step sinking with a squelching sound. The air grew thicker too, carrying the smell of decaying leaves and stagnant water. It felt as though the forest itself was warning us of what lay ahead.

As we rounded a bend, the trees began to thin, their roots sinking deep into the dark, murky waters that stretched out before us like a looming shadow. The forest gave way to a wet and marshy land, its waters rippling with unseen currents. A thick, stagnant mist hovered just above the surface, clinging to the air with a heavy, almost suffocating dampness.

I glanced over at Brute, curiosity tugging at the back of my mind. "Brute... what is this place?"

Brute adjusted his pouch and scanned the expanse ahead, his expression serious. "This," he began, gesturing toward the waters, "is one of the many swamps scattered across Moonveil. You'll only find them deep in the forest. Most people live their whole lives without ever setting foot in one."

I frowned, a distant memory surfacing—Professor Rennard had spoken about these areas in one of his many lectures. Swamps, he explained, were borderlands, the fringes where the known paths of Moonveil gave way to the untamed wilderness. Few ever ventured into them, and even fewer returned with stories to tell.

"I've never seen anything like it," I admitted, my eyes tracing the roots disappearing into the water.

Brute nodded knowingly. "That's because most travelers stick to the safer routes. The forest is full of places like this—where land and water bleed into each other. Beautiful, sure, but dangerous all the same."

I squinted at the murky waters, trying to see through the haze. The air felt like it clung to my skin, and a sense of unease crept into my chest. "Are we safe here?" I asked, the question sounding foolish even to my own ears.

Brute chuckled softly, his eyes scanning the horizon. "Safe? Probably not." He shot me a glance. "Stick close. Watch your step."

I nodded, trying to swallow the lump in my throat. Every step I took felt as though the ground might give way beneath me. The swamp was alive with sound—distant, croaking calls and the faint rippling of something moving through the water. There was no telling what lay hidden beneath the surface.

"There's something... off about this place," I muttered, more to myself than to Brute.

"Swamps do that," Brute said, not bothering to look back. His voice was low as if even he didn't want to disturb the silence too much. "Keep your senses sharp. You never know what might be lurking."

We pressed on, the path growing narrower and more treacherous. I followed Brute's lead, every step slow and deliberate, each footfall sinking slightly into the soft, wet earth beneath us. The ground squelched beneath our boots, no doubt a show of how easily the swamp could swallow us whole if we weren't careful.

Suddenly, Brute raised his hand, halting our progress. I froze in place, my breath catching in my throat. Ahead, I could make out sluggish forms moving through the water—twisted, grotesque shapes that slithered and writhed just beneath the surface.

"Stay low," Brute whispered, barely audible. His eyes never left the water. "We're not alone."

I peered ahead and caught glimpses of the creatures moving through the murk. Whatever they were, they were massive—slimy skin glistening in the faint light, bodies shifting with unnatural movement as they trudged through the swamp-like shadows in the deep.

"What ar—" I began to ask, but Brute swiftly gestured for silence, his expression deadly serious. Leaning in, he whispered, "Blighttongues."

My heart stilled as memories of more lectures flooded my mind. Blighttongues were notorious fiends—blind, but they hunted with uncanny precision, sensing vibrations through the swamp's murky waters and the air itself. I'd never encountered one before, but the stories were enough to keep anyone awake at night.

In the dim light, I could just make out their forms. Their mottled skin was a sickly blend of green and brown, speckled with patches of fungus and algae that oozed mucus. Their long, serpentine bodies writhed with unsettling grace, every inch covered in warty protrusions and trailing bits of decaying plant matter. Short, muscular limbs ended in webbed claws that allowed them to move effortlessly through the swamp and leap great distances when needed.

But it was their tongues that struck the deepest chord of fear within me. Long, forked, and terrifyingly agile, their tongues could strike faster than any snake. Worse still, their saliva was known to be highly corrosive—capable of melting through flesh in seconds. The mere thought sent a shiver down my spine.

I locked eyes with one of the creatures; its milky, useless eyes were staring blankly ahead. Blighttongues didn't need sight—those elongated tongues flicked through the air, feeling for vibrations, seeking any sign of movement or sound.

Suddenly, a bird flew overhead, its wings flapping noisily in the still air. In a flash, one of the Blighttongues lashed out with its tongue, the wet, sticky appendage wrapping around the bird mid-flight. I watched in horror as the bird's skin began to bubble and hiss, melting away within moments. Its cries were abruptly silenced as the fiend pulled it into its gaping mouth and swallowed it whole, the process over in mere seconds.

I glanced at Brute, my body slick with sweat. He returned my gaze, his expression grim but focused. He gave me a small nod, signaling for me to stay silent and follow his lead.

We began to inch our way around the cluster of Blighttongues, each step slow and deliberate, our movements measured to avoid making any noise. Every rustle of the swamp, every whisper of the wind seemed deafening in the tense silence. My heartbeat was loud in my ears, the pressure of the moment unbearable as we crept forward.

Just as we were nearing the edge of the cluster, I stepped on a brittle branch hidden beneath the muck. The sharp crack echoed through the swamp like a gunshot. My blood turned to ice as I froze in place, and my breath caught in my throat.

The Blighttongues' heads snapped towards the sound, tongues flicking out as they tried to pinpoint the source of the disturbance. They began to move, wading through the water with unnerving speed.

Brute shot me a look, his eyes wide with urgency. He gestured for me to move, and we picked up the pace, slipping through the underbrush in a desperate attempt to escape. But the Blighttongues were closing in, drawn to the vibrations of our movements. I could hear their heavy bodies cutting through the swamp water, growing closer with each passing second.

In my haste, I tripped over a twisted root, the sound of my stumble far too loud in the stillness. The Blighttongues surged toward the noise, their tongues lashing out. One of them flicked its tongue at me, fast as lightning. Thankfully, the tongue collided with the shield on my back, bouncing off it with a loud thud.

The impact reverberated through my body, the force nearly knocking me off balance. The sound of the tongue hitting the shield was like a thunderclap in the quiet swamp, sending ripples through the water and stirring the air around us. I could feel the corrosive saliva hissing against the shield, sizzling as it dripped off.

The Blighttongues hissed as they converged, drawn by the noise. Brute glanced over his shoulder, his eyes flashing with urgency. "Keep moving!" he growled, low and tense.

My heart pounded in my chest as I drew my sword, my hands trembling with both fear and adrenaline. Another Blighttongue lashed its tongue at me, its speed blinding. I barely had time to react, raising my sword just as the slick, forked appendage wrapped around the blade. Without hesitation, I swung hard, slicing through the tongue. The severed piece fell to the ground, writhing violently as the Blighttongue let out a guttural screech that echoed across the swamp.

The creature's screech sent unease through me, knowing it would only draw more of them. And it did. The swamp came alive with the hissing and slithering of Blighttongues closing in, their long tongues flicking toward the source of the commotion.

Brute's eyes widened. He knew the same thing I did: staying quiet was no longer an option. "Run!" he shouted.

We bolted, tearing through the swamp as fast as the dense underbrush and uneven ground would allow. The Blighttongues were in a frenzy now, their tongues snapping and lashing out like whips, each strike capable of melting flesh and bone. I ducked and weaved, dodging the strikes as they hissed past, narrowly missing me by inches.

The fiends were fast, drawn by the vibrations of our feet pounding through the muck. Their hisses grew louder and closer as if they were right on top of us. My legs burned from the effort of sprinting through the mire, but I couldn't stop. One wrong move, one moment of hesitation, and I knew I'd be done for.

"Keep moving!" Brute roared, his voice barely audible over the cacophony of snapping tongues and rustling foliage. "Don't let them catch you!"

I ducked beneath a low-hanging branch just as another Blighttongue's tongue cracked through the air, its acidic spray hissing as it hit the tree, sizzling through the bark like molten metal. The heat from the reaction made the hairs on the back of my neck stand on end.

Brute was ahead of me, glancing back every few steps, assessing the situation. "We need higher ground!" he shouted. "Something to give us an advantage!"

I scanned the darkened swamp, my breath ragged and chest heaving. Through the twisted trees and thick vegetation, I spotted a small rise where the ground seemed to level out. The swamp thinned slightly there—maybe, just maybe, we could catch a break.

"There!" I pointed ahead, my voice desperate but firm. "We can make it!"

Brute nodded, and we veered toward the rise, pushing ourselves harder, our feet squelching through the marshy ground. The Blighttongues were relentless, but the uneven terrain slowed them down just enough to give us a small window. My lungs burned with every breath, my body aching from the frantic dash, but I refused to slow down.

Finally, we reached higher ground, scrambling up onto the slight plateau. We turned to face the oncoming fiends, weapons at the ready. The Blighttongues hesitated at the edge of the rise, their blind eyes searching in vain, their tongues flicking out into the air, tasting for vibrations but unable to pinpoint us with the same accuracy they'd had in the swamp.

"We're not out of danger yet," Brute panted, his voice hoarse from the exertion, "but we've bought ourselves a moment."

I nodded, my breath coming in ragged gasps as I scanned the area. The rise we stood on wasn't much of a sanctuary—it led to a terrace carved into the hillside, a flat, narrow ledge shaped by years of erosion. Above us was a steep, unclimbable slope, and the drop behind us was perilously steep. We were trapped—cornered with no way up and nowhere to run.

"We're stuck," I muttered, tightening my grip on my sword.

Brute's eyes narrowed as he glanced around. "Maybe," he replied, his voice laced with determination. "But we'll make our stand here. Whatever happens, we won't go down without a fight."

I nodded, but the weight of our situation pressed down on me. I glanced up at the sky, already darkening as the sun sank below the horizon. Night was coming. I could feel the air growing colder, the shadows around us lengthening. The fiends below had the advantage of numbers, but the darkness would be their ally. If we didn't move soon, they'd tear us apart.

The hours dragged on, each minute making it clearer just how trapped we were. The croak of the fiends echoed through the trees, filling the forest in a dangerous melody. Brute shifted beside me, restless.

"You should try and get some rest," Brute said, "we can come up with a plan tomorrow morning."

I shook my head, refusing Brute's suggestion. "I can't rest," I muttered, my voice barely above a whisper. "Not when Celine's still out there somewhere. We don't have the luxury of waiting until morning."

I couldn't help but think of Celine. Where was she? Was she trapped somewhere like we were, or worse? The thought of her out there alone, maybe hurt—or worse—stirred a pang of anxiety inside me. My thoughts drifted to Lunaria, to Aunt Silvia and Uncle Alfarr, to the twins, Marcellus and Marciana. The people I loved. They were the entire reason I agreed to follow Celine on this journey anyway.

I couldn't let them down. I couldn't let her down.

Brute sighed heavily beside me, leaning back against a rock. "I get it, kid, but if we run ourselves into the ground now, we won't be any good to anyone. You need to be sharp if we're going to survive this."

I shifted uncomfortably, staring out into the dark forest. My eyes scanned the treeline, searching for any sign of hope in the oppressive darkness. But there was nothing, just the low growls of the fiends stalking below. A sense of urgency pressed down on me, thickening the air with the weight of decisions that had yet to be made.

That's when my gaze landed on the slope, the brittle, dry brush stretching down its length. It wasn't much, but maybe… just maybe, it could buy us some time.

My mind raced, piecing together a plan born out of desperation. The dampness at the top of the rise wouldn't catch easily, but the dry foliage further down—if we could ignite it, it might create enough of a barrier to keep the fiends at bay. I turned to Brute, a spark of determination cutting through the haze of exhaustion.

"Brute, I've got an idea! Step back!" I called out.

Without waiting for a response, I struck my sword hard against a nearby rock, the clash sending a cascade of sparks flying into the brittle brush below. The dry foliage ignited almost immediately, a small flame flickering to life before spreading quickly along the path of dried reeds and branches. We watched as the fire crept down the rise, the flames flickering and crackling in the silence.

The Blighttongues, their blind forms swaying as they homed in on the vibrations of the crackling fire, slithered closer, their tongues flicking out to investigate. But as the fire reached them, they recoiled in confusion, their milky eyes unable to comprehend the growing danger. The flames spread rapidly, fueled by the dried vegetation, creating a wall of heat and light that the Blighttongues couldn't penetrate.

The creatures hissed and thrashed as the fire neared, their slimy skin drying and cracking under the intense heat. Some of the Blighttongues, overwhelmed by the flames, began to writhe in agony, their bodies stiffening as the fire consumed them. Others, sensing the danger too late, flailed wildly before retreating back into the swamp's murky waters, their screeches echoing through the air.

"That was close," I breathed, my heart still pounding.

Brute clapped me on the back, his face a mixture of pride and relief. "Good thinking, boy. That bought us some time. But we shouldn't hang around. Let's move before they regroup."

With the fire behind us still crackling and hissing, we carefully slid down the side of the rise that had already been burnt out, our boots crunching against the charred ground. The hissing of the Blighttongues faded into the distance as we pressed onward, the dim glow of the dying flames casting long shadows on the trees behind us.

The swamp was eerily quiet now, the only sounds coming from our own careful footsteps and the occasional drip of moisture from the canopy above. The air remained thick with humidity and heavy with the acrid scent of charred vegetation, and our movements were more cautious than ever. Every snap of a twig or rustle of leaves made my heart skip a beat, my ears straining for any hint of danger lurking in the shadows.

"We need to find solid ground," Brute muttered, his voice barely audible as he scanned the path ahead.

I nodded, glancing over my shoulder every few steps to make sure we weren't being followed. "Do you think we're close to Eclipsia?" I asked, my voice hushed with a mixture of hope and exhaustion.

Brute gave a nod, his brow furrowed. "It shouldn't be too much longer now. This swamp is disorienting, but if we keep moving north, we'll come upon it soon enough."

Fatigue clawed at the edges of my strength, but the thought of reaching Eclipsia—and the hope that Celine might still be within our grasp—kept me moving. Every few minutes, Brute and I would toss stones far ahead of us, testing the ground for any signs of lurking fiends. Each time a stone landed with a dull thud and no response, my heart lifted slightly. The swamp, for now, seemed still.

Finally, after what felt like an endless trek, the landscape began to change. The murky waters beneath our feet gave way to firmer ground, and the dense, twisted foliage of the swamp began to thin out. Small patches of solid earth appeared before us, and with it, the oppressive humidity began to lift, replaced by a cooler, fresher breeze.

"Look," I said, my voice filled with relief as I pointed ahead. "We're almost out of this nightmare."

Brute followed my gaze and grinned. "Yeah, let's move."

We quickened our pace, eager to leave the swamp behind. As

our feet touched the firmer ground, I couldn't help but feel relieved. I glanced back at the swamp; the dark trees and sluggish waters were now a distant memory. We had made it through.

"Praise the moon," I muttered, taking a deep breath of the fresh air. The smell of the forest filled my lungs, replacing the putrid, stagnant odor of the swamp.

Brute let out a relieved sigh, placing his hands on his hips. "Only a couple more hours at best before we reach Eclipsia."

The path ahead seemed clearer now. The ground was firm, the trees stood tall, and the rustling of leaves, accompanied by the occasional chirp of birds, filled the air. For a short while, I even started to feel more at ease.

CHAPTER 15

The day had started off quiet, almost deceptively so. After the chaos of the previous days, the stillness of the forest felt like a welcome respite. We'd been walking for hours, the tension from the swamp still hanging in the air, though neither of us spoke about it. For a brief moment, I allowed myself to believe we might actually make it through without another encounter.

But deep down, I knew better. The woods had a way of lulling you into a false sense of security, only to strike when you least expected it.

I caught a glimpse of Brute walking slightly ahead of me, his posture tense. He'd been acting differently, his usual relaxed confidence replaced by something closer to paranoia.

After a while, he stopped abruptly, his head snapping from side to side.

"Isaac, don't move. We're surrounded."

*Not again*, I thought to myself, the image of the Blighttongues was still fresh in my mind. Was a break too much to ask for?

I froze in place. "Surrounded by what?" I whispered, instinctively drawing my sword.

At first, I saw nothing out of the ordinary. The forest was quiet, peaceful even, but the way Brute's expression darkened sent chills down my spine. His usually composed face had tightened, his jaw clenched with an intensity I hadn't seen before. His eyes were sharp, like those of a predator locked onto its prey.

His muscles tensed; his fists clenched so tightly that his knuckles were white beneath his spiked cestus. Brute was always cool and collected, so seeing him like this set off alarms in my head.

"Wolves," he said quietly, his voice a low growl. "I can hear them moving in the underbrush. Get ready."

I strained my ears, closing my eyes to focus, but I couldn't hear a thing. The forest seemed peaceful, but Brute's instincts had never failed us before. I raised my shield, preparing myself for the inevitable.

Moments later, I saw them—four wolves emerging from the bushes and trees, their growls low and menacing. They began to circle us, their eyes gleaming as they sized us up.

"Stay close to me, boy," Brute muttered, his tone grim. "These wolves won't be easy to scare off."

The wolves were well-coordinated, their movements synchronized as they circled closer. One lunged forward, testing our defenses. I swung my sword, but the wolf dodged easily, its eyes glowing with intelligence and menace.

Brute didn't hesitate. His fist shot out, connecting with another wolf that had tried to flank us. The force of his punch sent the creature sprawling, but it quickly regained its footing, snarling in anger. Brute moved like a force of nature, dodging and striking back with lethal precision. He drove a powerful kick into the side of one wolf, sending it yelping away, then delivered a crushing elbow to another as it leaped at him. I swung my sword again, aiming at a wolf that darted too close. It dodged effortlessly, mocking my slower reflexes with its graceful agility. Another wolf lunged at Brute from behind, but he spun just in time, landing a powerful backhand that sent it skidding across the ground.

Despite our efforts, the wolves kept coming. Their attacks were relentless, but I began to notice something strange—they were all focused on Brute. None of them seemed interested in me. I swung my sword again, missing as another wolf dodged out of reach. It was almost as if I wasn't there.

"Why aren't they attacking me?" I muttered under my breath.

Brute didn't hear me, too preoccupied with fending off the

pack. He dodged another lunge, his fist smashing into a wolf's muzzle. The creature yelped and retreated, only for another to take its place.

I kept swinging, but my strikes seemed futile, the wolves always staying just out of range. It didn't make sense. Why were they ignoring me?

Suddenly, one wolf darted in close and nipped at my hand, forcing me to drop my sword. The metallic clang echoed through the forest as I stumbled backward, my eyes locking with the wolf's. For a brief moment, we just stared at each other. Its growl wasn't threatening, though. There was something else there, something I couldn't quite grasp.

The wolf's amber eyes were filled with an intensity that seemed almost... aware, but of what? It felt like it was trying to communicate something, a message I couldn't understand.

Behind me, I could hear Brute grunting, fighting off the others. I turned just in time to see him catch a wolf mid-leap, slamming it to the ground with a force that left it dazed. The wolf near me rushed to help its comrade as I stood there, still reeling from the strange moment I had just experienced.

Before Brute could deliver a fatal blow to the stunned wolf, another lunged at him from the side, forcing him to turn and defend. The wolf scrambled to its feet, shaking off the impact.

Brute's eyes blazed with fury. "Come on! Is that all you've got?" he bellowed, his voice a low growl. "Fight me!"

But the wolves had a different plan. One by one, they began to retreat. The wolf that had locked eyes with me gave one last lingering look before disappearing into the underbrush with the rest of its pack.

Brute was livid, shouting into the forest. "Cowards! Come back and fight me!"

I watched the wolves retreat, still trying to process the strange encounter. "Brute, what just happened?" I asked, my voice shaky.

Brute, still seething, grunted. "Damn wolves. They must've realized we weren't easy targets."

"No, not that," I said, shaking my head. "Why did they ignore me?"

Brute frowned, confusion briefly flickering across his face. "They probably saw me as the bigger threat. Wolves are pack animals—they recognized me as the leader. They thought if they got rid of me, you'd be easy prey."

"Maybe," I muttered, though doubt lingered in my mind. "Let's just keep moving. Eclipsia is close, right?"

Brute nodded, his voice firm. "Yeah. We're almost there. Just a little further now."

As we continued our journey toward Eclipsia, the strange encounter with the wolves lingered in my mind. There was something unsettling about the way that wolf had looked at me, a feeling I couldn't shake. But for now, reaching our destination was the priority.

Despite the exhaustion weighing down my muscles, Brute and I pressed forward.

Hours passed in silence, and before I knew it, the sun dipped below the horizon, covering the forest in shades of dusky purple.

"We're close now," Brute murmured, his voice low and gravelly. "Let's stop here and wait for nightfall."

Relieved for a moment's rest, I dropped to the ground beside him, the cool earth grounding me. We waited in silence as the final traces of daylight disappeared, the shadows deepening into black. When the sky finally darkened, we set off again, the trees thinning to reveal a worn path leading to the outskirts of the town. Towering stone walls loomed ahead, their imposing height casting long shadows. The faint clatter of armor and the distant hum of conversation drifted toward us, the ever-present patrols guarding Eclipsia's walls.

Brute gestured toward the town, his voice a mere whisper. "We'll need to be quiet. As I'm sure you know, they don't just let anyone walk in there."

I nodded, my heart already beating faster. We'd left the wolves and Blighttongues behind, but now we faced a different kind of danger: infiltrating one of the most heavily guarded towns in Moonveil.

"What's the plan?" I asked, keeping my voice as soft as possible.

Brute scratched his chin, eyes narrowing as he assessed the layout ahead. "We'll need to find a way past the guards. This place is locked down tighter than anything you've ever seen."

We crept forward, staying low as we approached the city's southern perimeter. From our cover among the trees, I could make out Eclipsia's southern gate. It was heavily reinforced with thick iron bands, towers flanking either side where archers stood at attention, their sharp eyes scanning the area. A sturdy barricade of crossed beams covered the gate itself, sealing it off from intruders.

Brute motioned for me to follow as we moved quietly along the city's edge, sticking close to the shadows cast by the towering walls. Every step felt like a risk, and the guards' movements were unpredictable as they patrolled the area. After what felt like an eternity of crouching and crawling, Brute led us to a dense thicket.

"We'll wait here for a moment," he whispered. "Need to time it just right."

The silence in the underbrush was suffocating, broken only by the faint rustle of leaves and the distant murmur of the guards.

I crouched beside Brute, trying to control my breathing. Suddenly, two guards came into view, their lanterns casting flickering light that crept dangerously close to our hiding spot.

"Did you hear that?" one guard muttered, pausing and squinting into the darkness.

My heart leaped into my throat. I pressed myself deeper into the shadows, my fingers curling into the dirt. Beside me, Brute's hand flexed, ready to strike if it came to that.

The other guard shook his head. "Probably just a rabbit or something."

But the first guard wasn't convinced. He took a few cautious steps in our direction, the flame of his lantern bobbing closer. I held my breath, every muscle in my body screaming to stay still as he inched forward. Just when I thought we'd been found, a shout echoed from further down the wall.

"Oi! We need some help over here!"

The guard hesitated, glancing between us and the source of the call. After a tense moment, he cursed under his breath and jogged back to join his companion. They disappeared into the night, their footsteps fading into the distance.

Brute exhaled slowly, and I realized I'd been holding my breath too. "That was too close," I whispered.

"Too close," Brute agreed, his voice low. "Let's move. Now."

We crept out of the thicket, sticking to the shadows and moving as quietly as possible. Every now and then, the light of a swinging lantern would come uncomfortably close, but we managed to stay hidden. At one point, a guard passed so near that I could see the glint of his sword in the moonlight, but he kept walking, oblivious to our presence.

Finally, we reached a section of the wall covered in dense, overgrown ivy. Brute pushed aside some of the undergrowth and revealed two dark navy cloaks.

"What are these for?" I asked, grabbing one.

Brute grinned, throwing one over his shoulders. "It's what everyone in there wears. We'll blend in better."

I raised an eyebrow. "You just left these here?"

"I stashed them when I... left. Looks like they're going to come in handy getting back in."

I threw the cloak over my head, the fabric heavy against my shoulders, feeling the weight of secrecy that seemed to cling to it. "Now what?"

"Now we keep moving," Brute said, pulling up the hood of his cloak. "Follow me and stay close."

We wrapped ourselves in the cloaks, the thick fabric muffling our movements as we continued toward the walls. The guards' patrols were still steady, their eyes sharp, but we kept to the periphery, slipping between the shadows.

The closer we got, the more imposing the city walls felt, looming over us like an ominous warning. It was clear that sneaking in wouldn't be easy, but with Brute's knowledge and our disguise, it seemed possible—at least for now.

As we crept along the perimeter, the murmur of voices grew louder. Two guards were stationed overhead on the wall, their conversation becoming more distinct with each step.

"You think those rumors are true?" one guard asked, his voice carrying through the still night air.

"About the fiends? I wouldn't be surprised. Noctiluna was attacked not too long ago," the other replied, a hint of unease in his tone.

Brute and I pressed ourselves against the stone wall, blending into the shadows as the guards' boots clinked on the cobblestones above us. The cold stone bit into my back as I tried to make myself as invisible as possible.

Suddenly, a loud shout pierced the air, coming from the

direction of the main gate.

"Fiends! A pack of fiends is approaching the town!"

The guards sprang into action, their footsteps pounding against the stone as they rushed toward the source of the commotion.

Brute's eyes gleamed in the low light as he turned to me. "This is our chance. Let's move."

We darted forward, staying low, the guards' hurried movements providing the perfect distraction. Eventually, Brute halted, gesturing for me to crouch beside him. We had reached a more secluded area, where the noise from the guards had faded into the distance. He pushed aside a thick curtain of overgrown vegetation, revealing a large, weathered sewer pipe embedded in the wall, its entrance hidden beneath layers of vegetation.

"This is it," Brute whispered, his voice barely audible above the rustling leaves. "This is how I escaped Eclipsia all those years ago."

I peered into the dark, uninviting tunnel. The air inside was thick and damp, a musty smell rising from its depths. "Where does it lead?" I asked, my voice tight with a mix of curiosity and apprehension.

Brute stepped into the pipe, his large frame disappearing into the shadows. "It leads to an old and secluded section near the edge of town. When I escaped, the area was already mostly forgotten about, we should be able to slip in unnoticed."

Swallowing my unease, I took a deep breath and followed Brute into the sewer. The cool air inside was a stark contrast to the night outside, and the town's distant clamor faded to a dull hum behind us. The pipe was narrow, the stone walls slick with moisture, and each step echoed eerily in the confined space. The darkness pressed in from all sides, but Brute moved with purpose, guiding me through the twisting passage as if he had memorized every turn.

After what felt like an eternity, we emerged into a small, dimly lit chamber. The faint drip of water echoed from somewhere above, and the walls were coated in a sheen of moisture. Brute paused, listening carefully, his hand hovering over a set of crumbling stone steps that led upwards.

He turned to me, his voice low but firm. "Listen, keep your hood up and your head down. Don't speak to anyone, and if someone tries to engage you, keep walking. Whatever you do, don't make eye contact."

I nodded, adjusting the hood of my cloak to cast a shadow over most of my face. "Got it," I muttered, though my voice was tighter than I intended. My heart raced as we approached the steps. Eclipsia—this place had always been more myth than reality to me, a town spoken of in hushed whispers, cloaked in secrecy and fear. As a child, I'd been warned to stay away from its borders, the tales of its dangers enough to chill my spine even on the warmest days. Now, here I was, about to step into that very place I had only ever heard stories about. The unknown pressed against me, suffocating. Every instinct screamed at me to turn back.

Brute seemed unfazed, but I couldn't shake the feeling of worry in my gut. The air itself seemed heavier, as though it knew we were intruders. My palms were slick with sweat, and I clenched my fists, trying to steady myself, but the gravity of this moment was overwhelming.

Brute gestured for me to follow him up the steps, and with a deep breath, I forced my legs to move. We moved cautiously, each footfall on the ancient stone feeling precarious. My pulse thrummed in my ears as we climbed, and I swallowed hard, trying to ignore the lump in my throat.

At the top, Brute knelt and carefully lifted a rusted metal

grate, the hinges groaning faintly in the still air. Beyond the grate lay a narrow, empty alleyway, the faint glow of moonlight filtering through the gaps between buildings.

"We're in," Brute whispered, his voice carrying the weight of years of experience. He reached out and helped me through the grate. "Stay close and follow my lead."

The alleyway was eerily silent, the faint shuffle of feet in the distance the only indication of life in the town. The walls around us felt imposing, the looming structures adding to the sense of claustrophobia.

My breath hitched. This was it—Eclipsia, the town that had haunted me— no, everyone in Moonveil. And now, I was about to walk straight into its heart.

Brute turned to me one last time, his voice barely above a breath. "Remember, head down, and don't look at anyone. We can't afford any mistakes here."

I nodded once again and followed Brute out of the alleyway, the weight of his warnings pressing down on me. As we walked deeper into Eclipsia, the eerie atmosphere of the town wrapped around me like a cold shroud. Even under the cover of night, there was an unmistakable strangeness about this place— something that made my skin crawl with every step.

The architecture only added to the unease. The buildings towered over us; their dark stone facades twisted with ornate carvings that seemed almost unnatural. Jagged spires reached toward the sky, their sharp edges cutting into the night like blades. Many of the structures were rundown, their walls cracked and weathered, while others stood eerily pristine, their barred windows casting shadows across the cobbled streets. The air itself felt oppressive, as if the town were cloaked in a heavy sense of unease.

Despite the late hour, the streets were far from deserted. Hooded figures moved in and out of the shadows, their navy-blue cloaks identical to the ones Brute and I wore. Their faces remained hidden beneath their hoods; their heads lowered as they shuffled through the narrow streets. There was something unsettling about the way they moved—silent, methodical, as though they were sleepwalking through some unknown nightmare. Every so often, I could hear faint murmurs from the passersby, their voices low and fragmented, like whispers carried on a ghostly wind.

The street lamps, placed sporadically along the road, barely provided enough light to pierce the darkness. Their dim glow created long creeping shadows that seemed to move and shift, playing tricks on my mind. The more I looked around, the more I felt like we were being watched, though from where or by whom, I couldn't tell.

Brute walked ahead of me, his pace slow and deliberate, blending into the crowd of hooded figures. He shuffled his feet as though he, too, was weighed down by the same unseen force that blanketed the town. I did my best to mimic his movements, keeping my head down and my steps light, every sense on high alert. The occasional creak of a door or the distant echo of footsteps sent my heart racing, but I forced myself to keep moving, to blend in like Brute had instructed.

Suddenly, a piercing scream shattered the oppressive silence. I nearly jerked my head up, instinctively wanting to look, but Brute's earlier warning rang in my mind. I forced my eyes back to the ground. The scream was raw, filled with desperation, like someone teetering on the edge of madness. It came from somewhere close by, followed by a low commotion in the distance.

Despite the terrifying sound, no one around us reacted. The hooded figures continued their silent shuffle as if they hadn't heard it, their calm only adding to my growing unease.

"What was that?" I whispered, my voice trembling despite my attempt to sound steady.

"Nothing to concern yourself with," Brute muttered under his breath, his voice taut with tension. "Just keep moving."

Another scream rang out, cutting through the night. I couldn't help myself this time—my head snapped up just enough to catch a glimpse. A woman stood in the distance, her wide, terrified eyes locked onto a guard. "You don't know! None of you know what's out there! They're coming for us!" she shrieked, her voice wild with fear.

The guard tried to push her away, but she clawed at his armor, her hands shaking as though trying to make him understand some unseen terror. The crowd of cloaked figures still barely reacted, as if this scene were a part of the town's twisted routine.

The guard's patience ran out, and with a vicious shove, he sent the woman sprawling to the ground. "Get away from me, you filthy wench!" he spat, his voice laced with disdain.

Brute nudged me sharply, pulling me out of my trance. "Keep moving," he hissed, his tone brooking no argument.

I tore my gaze away and lowered my head, forcing my feet to move forward. The woman's cries continued behind us, her voice growing weaker as we distanced ourselves from her. But the sound lingered in my mind, the raw terror in her voice unsettling me more than anything I had seen so far.

We continued through the dimly lit streets, the oppressive weight of the town bearing down on me with every step. My focus remained on the ground, but the sensation of being watched refused to fade. My nerves were on edge, every sound amplified in the tense silence. Then, without warning, someone slammed into me, breaking the rhythm of our cautious movement.

Startled, I looked up. My eyes met those of a woman standing just inches from me. Her face was gaunt and hollow, her skin stretched tight over sharp bones. Her eyes were wild, filled with a frantic energy that made me shudder. Before I could react, she grabbed my shoulder, her grip vice-like despite her frail appearance. Her breath was hot and rapid against my face as she began to speak, her words pouring out in a feverish rush.

"Your eyes... they're pure. How can you not see? How can you still be blind?"

I froze, fear rooting me to the spot as her words tumbled over each other, her voice filled with an urgency I couldn't comprehend. Her nails dug into my skin, her grip tightening as she continued her cryptic rambling. "You must see! You must know! They're coming for you!"

My throat tightened, my voice caught somewhere between fear and confusion. I tried to pull away, but her hold was relentless, her wild eyes locked onto mine as if trying to transfer her madness into me.

Before I could fully process what was happening, Brute was at my side, his face hard with determination. He grabbed my arm and yanked me away from the woman's grasp, his strength pulling me free in an instant.

The woman's eyes widened in shock, her mouth opening and closing as if searching for the right words. But Brute didn't give her the chance. He pushed me forward, forcing me to keep moving, his presence a solid wall between me and the frantic woman.

I glanced back, unable to resist, and saw her crumple to the ground, her body trembling as she sobbed into her hands. "He hasn't seen! He hasn't seen!" she wailed, her voice echoing through the empty streets, the sound hollow and despairing.

I stumbled forward, the weight of her words clinging to me

like a dark cloud. What hadn't I seen? What did she mean? The fear and confusion churned inside me, but there was no time to dwell on it. Brute's pace quickened, and I had no choice but to follow.

I heard the commotion behind me as guards approached the woman, their shouts echoing off the narrow walls. I didn't dare turn my head, knowing that one wrong move would draw attention to us.

"Get up, you madwoman!" one of the guards barked, his voice sharp and impatient.

She continued to wail; her voice filled the air, piercing my ears. "The boy... the boy is pure! His eyes haven't been sullied!"

Brute's grip on my shoulder tightened as we moved faster through the crowd. "Don't look back," he muttered, his voice low and tense. "Keep your head down; just keep moving."

We quickened our pace, melting into the shuffling crowd of hooded figures. The streets of Eclipsia felt like a suffocating maze of narrow alleys and shadowy corners, each more foreboding than the last. It was as though the very air in this town carried the weight of fear and secrecy.

As a child, I had always imagined Eclipsia to be a place of intrigue and mystery—a place where dark secrets lurked, waiting to be uncovered. But the reality of it was far more unsettling. There was no thrill in the air, only a heavy tension that pressed in from every direction.

Eventually, Brute led us into a small, secluded courtyard. The area was eerily quiet, the only sound the faint rustle of wind through the overgrown vines that clung to the ancient walls. Brute motioned for me to crouch behind a large, crumbling fountain at the center of the courtyard. He leaned in close, his voice barely a whisper.

"We need to get into that building," he said, pointing to a large structure at the far end of the courtyard. Its dark stone walls rose ominously against the night sky, two carved gargoyles perched atop it, their stone faces twisted into snarls. "That's where we'll find what we're looking for."

The building looked heavily fortified, but oddly, only two guards stood watch outside. They seemed relaxed, almost complacent, as if no one ever dared to challenge the order of things here in Eclipsia. The people here shuffled through their lives in a daze, too cowed or too conditioned to even think of defying the guards. The guards must have known this well, leaving the area mostly unattended.

From our hiding spot, I could just make out the guards' conversation. "I'm gonna take a leak," one of them said lazily, veering off into the shadows at the edge of the courtyard.

Brute's eyes narrowed. "Wait here," he instructed, his voice firm. "Stay low, and if you hear me call out, be ready."

I gave him a curt nod and watched as he melted into the shadows. He crept up behind the guard who had wandered off, his massive frame barely making a sound. With one swift motion, Brute struck the guard at the back of his head. The man crumpled silently, and Brute caught him before lowering his limp body to the cobblestone floor.

From his new hiding spot behind a pillar, Brute let out a soft whistle, just enough to draw the attention of the second guard. The remaining guard perked up, gripping his sword and stepping forward cautiously. "Who's there?" he called, his voice tinged with suspicion.

The guard moved closer to the pillar, his eyes scanning the darkness. The instant he was within range, Brute lunged from the shadows, delivering a crushing blow to the man's jaw. The guard collapsed in a heap, his sword clattering to the ground. Brute quickly dragged him into the shadows, hiding his body from view.

Brute let out another soft whistle, signaling that it was clear. I stood and hurried over to him, not wanting to get left behind in this creepy atmosphere.

We moved cautiously towards the looming building; each step more calculated than the last. The air seemed thicker here, and the sense of being watched clung to me like a shadow. I glanced back towards the entrance of the courtyard, but the hooded figures continued their aimless shuffle, oblivious to the violence that had just unfolded.

At the base of the building, I couldn't help but crane my neck to take in its towering structure. The gargoyles above seemed to sneer down at us, their hollow eyes watching our every move.

Just as Brute reached for the door, a faint noise from inside made us both freeze. We exchanged a tense glance, pressing ourselves flat against the cold stone walls on either side of the entrance.

The door creaked open slowly, and a guard stepped out, muttering angrily under his breath. "Where did those idiots go?" he grumbled. "If they've slacked off again, I'll have their heads."

The guard took a few more steps forward, scanning the courtyard with growing frustration. "Can't do anything right, those fools," he continued, his voice fading as he stalked toward the main gate.

Brute's eyes locked with mine, silently telling me to hold still. We remained motionless, barely daring to breathe as the guard's footsteps echoed in the quiet night. Finally, after what felt like hours, he disappeared into the distance, his curses trailing behind him.

We waited a beat longer, just to be sure, before Brute nodded at me and approached the door once again. His large hand gripped the handle, and to our surprise, the door swung open without resistance.

"This is it," Brute whispered, his voice filled with a mix of anticipation and tension. "We're almost there."

I swallowed hard as we stepped inside, the darkness of the building swallowing us whole. The air was cold and damp, and the silence was suffocating, as if the walls themselves held their breath in anticipation of what was to come.

# CHAPTER 16

As we stepped into the building, the door creaked shut behind us, its echo quickly swallowed by the silence of the room. I was immediately struck by the sheer size of the place. The ceiling soared high above, disappearing into shadows so deep they seemed to stretch endlessly into the void. The dim lighting revealed only fragments of the interior, casting long, distorted shadows across the stone pillars that lined the hall like ancient sentinels, their surfaces worn with time, etched with carvings that hinted at forgotten histories.

The air was damp and thick with a stench so pungent that it hit me like a wall. A sharp, acrid odor of decay clung to everything, mingling with the metallic tang of rust and something far more foul. The floor beneath us, made of large, cracked stone slabs, felt uneven beneath my boots, and the faint sound of dripping water echoed through the cavernous space.

Despite its size, the floor we were on was eerily empty. No guards. No staff. Just silence.

I caught a glimpse of iron bars lining the walls like ribs in a skeletal cage, and the realization hit me like a punch to the gut— this was some sort of prison. As we moved deeper into the hall, my eyes were drawn to the cells. Dark, foreboding, and filled with shadows.

Curiosity got the better of me as I leaned in to peer into the nearest cell. A hooded figure sat hunched in the corner, rocking slowly back and forth, their face buried deep in their hands. The low, unintelligible whispers that escaped their lips made my skin crawl—an endless stream of fragmented words, as if they were trapped in some nightmarish loop. My heart pounded harder, a bead of cold sweat forming on the back of my neck. I wanted to move on, to look away, but something in the air—something about the way those whispers filled the silence—held me in place. I could feel my breath quickening as I forced myself to step forward.

In the next cell, the scene was worse. A woman stood facing the wall, her back to the bars, utterly still. Her arms hung limp at her sides, and there was something about her—the way she stood so utterly defeated—that twisted my stomach. She wasn't moving. She wasn't even breathing. She was just... there. As if her spirit had already left, leaving behind only a shell.

Each prisoner seemed more broken than the last, lost in a world of madness, their sanity eroded by whatever horrors they'd endured. Some muttered in a language only they could understand; others were deathly still, hollow-eyed, and detached from reality.

A chill crawled up my spine, settling heavily in my chest. "What is this place?" I whispered to Brute, my voice trembling.

"This," Brute said, his tone dark, "is called the Asylum."

"The Asylum?" I repeated.

Brute nodded grimly. "Aye. It's been here longer than I can remember. People don't talk about it much—too many questions lead to problems. But everyone in Eclipsia knows to stay far away."

I swallowed hard. My unease deepened with each step. "But why? What is this place for?"

Brute glanced back at me, his eyes shadowed with something close to pity. "You'll understand soon enough. But it's something you have to see for yourself." His voice was low, almost reverent, as if speaking any louder would awaken something in the darkness around us.

We continued down the hall, the smell intensifying with each step. It wasn't just the mustiness of old stone or the scent of rot; it was something far more sinister. We passed several closed doors, all reinforced with thick iron beams. From behind some of them came faint rustlings, muffled groans, and the occasional sharp cry, as if the walls themselves were haunted by the memories of those trapped within.

Brute led us down a narrow corridor, and the walls seemed to close in around us, oppressive and suffocating. The stench was nearly unbearable now, clawing at the back of my throat, making my stomach churn. I gagged, pulling my sleeve over my nose in a futile attempt to block out the foul odor.

At the end of the corridor loomed a set of steps, each one slick with moisture and worn down by the passage of countless feet. The air grew heavier as we climbed, the sound of metal rattling softly above us like chains in a forgotten dungeon.

"What is that smell?" I asked, my voice thin with discomfort.

Brute paused, turning to me with a look that made my blood run cold. "Soon, Isaac. You'll see the true nature of this place. And it's not something you'll forget easily."

We ascended the steps, each one harder than the last as the smell grew thick enough to choke on. My eyes watered from the stench, and I fought the urge to turn back. The anticipation gnawed at me, each heartbeat echoing in my ears as we reached the top of the staircase.

There, at the end of our path, stood a massive iron-bound door. Cold and ancient, its surface was etched with symbols I didn't recognize, their lines crude and violent. Brute stopped just shy of the door, placing a hand on it as if testing its weight. The air around us was stifling, almost unbearable in its stillness. This was no doubt the source of the stench.

"Isaac," Brute said softly, his voice more serious than I had ever heard it. "What you're about to see—it's going to change you. You won't understand it, and there's no way to prepare for what's beyond this door."

His face, usually so hard and unreadable, softened for a moment, the weight of his words sinking in. He looked at me, and I could see the burden he carried reflected in his eyes.

"Are you ready for this?"

I nodded, though the knot of fear in my stomach had tightened into something closer to panic. Whatever lay behind that door was going to be more than just disturbing. It was going to be a revelation, one that would unravel everything I thought I knew.

"I would've loved for you never to see this, Isaac," Brute muttered, his voice thick with regret. "But this is the only place I could think of that'll get us closer to finding Celine."

Hearing Celine's name made my heart tighten. I nodded, doing my best to steady my nerves. The heaviness of the Asylum weighed on me like a lead blanket, and the pungent stench clouded my senses, making it hard to breathe. Brute gave my shoulder a firm squeeze, a gesture of reassurance, though it did little to ease the suffocating anxiety building inside me.

He turned back to the door, placing a hand on the cold iron handle. With a slow, deliberate push, the door groaned as it swung open, the creak echoing ominously in the silent prison. As the gap widened, a fresh wave of rot and decay hit me with full force, making me gag and retch, my stomach twisting painfully. I pressed the sleeve of my cloak over my nose, but it barely masked the stench.

Beyond the door, the room lay cloaked in near darkness, only faint strands of moonlight slipping through a small, grime-covered window high up on the wall. The light did little to chase away the overwhelming shadows that clung to every corner, amplifying the sense of unease that hung in the air.

Brute moved ahead, and I followed closely, though each step felt heavier, as if the very floor was trying to pull me into its depths. My eyes adjusted slowly to the dim light, and as more of the room became clear, a chill crept down my spine.

The room was lined with cages—too many to count—and the walls were cluttered with strange, tattered sheets. Some of the cages stood empty, their bars rusted and bent, but others... I couldn't bring myself to imagine what lay beneath the draped cloth.

In the center of the room sat a long, scarred wooden table cluttered with an array of surgical instruments. They gleamed faintly in the pale moonlight, their sharp edges catching the light with a wicked glint. Scalpels, forceps, and tools I didn't even have names for were strewn haphazardly across the table, some of them stained with what looked like dried blood—though the thought of it being anything else was somehow worse. Shackles dangled from the edges, their chains clinking softly as if disturbed by a breath of wind that didn't exist.

"Brute," I croaked, my voice trembling. "Where... where are we?"

He didn't answer. His face was set, jaw clenched tight as he led me deeper into the room, his movements deliberate and grim. We weaved through the maze of cages and equipment, the sound of our boots on the cold stone floor the only thing breaking the deathly silence.

Finally, we stopped in front of one of the covered cages. Brute hesitated, his hand gripping the sheet that covered the bars. He took a breath, glanced at me, and then pulled the sheet away in one swift motion.

I took an instinctive step back, my heart lurching in my chest as I gasped, my body recoiling in horror at the sight before me.

Inside the cage was... a person, though they barely resembled one anymore. They were huddled in the far corner, their limbs drawn up to their chest, their body wasted and gaunt. Their skin was pale, almost translucent, but marred by strange, dark lesions that spread across their arms and neck like a grotesque web. Their eyes—glassy and lifeless—stared blankly ahead as if they were looking at something far beyond the confines of the cage, something only they could see.

The person—if they could still be called that—sat in filth, their body trembling, though whether from fear or madness, I couldn't tell. They muttered to themselves, soft, incoherent words spilling from their lips, a broken stream of thought that had no anchor in reality.

"Brute..." I whispered, my throat dry, "What the hell is this place?"

Again, he didn't answer. His expression was hard, distant, as though he was deliberately shutting himself off from the horror in front of us. Without a word, he turned and moved toward another cage, this one covered like the first. I watched, frozen in place as he grasped the sheet and pulled it back with the same grim resolve.

To my disbelief, it wasn't a person at all. This time, it was a fiend—a Grimroot. The creature, which I'd once thought of as purely monstrous, stood in a pitiful state. Its bark-like skin was cracked and bleeding, sap oozing from the wounds like blood. Once terrifying and fierce, the Grimroot now looked broken, its eyes dull and lifeless. It also sat in its own filth, unmoving, as though all the fight had been drained from it. Oblivious to our presence, it merely rocked back and forth, a hollow shadow of the menace it once was.

This time, I couldn't hold back the bile rising in my throat. I turned away, gagging as my stomach rebelled against the horror of what I was seeing. I wanted to run—to leave this cursed place behind—but my legs wouldn't move. The image of the prisoners, twisted and broken, seared into my mind.

"Brute…" I choked out, my voice barely more than a whisper. "What the hell are they doing to these creatures?"

Brute continued his grim task, moving from cage to cage, pulling back the sheets that covered them without answering me. Each time, I was met with another horror. Fungoids and Grimroots alike, all trapped, all suffering. Some were missing limbs, their stumps festering and raw. Others had been mutilated beyond recognition, their bodies twisted and broken. Yet all of them were in the same dazed state, as if their minds had been shattered along with their bodies.

I couldn't take it anymore. My voice rose, filled with frustration and horror. "Brute! Answer me!"

He sighed, finally pausing to look at me. His face, usually stoic, was clouded with a mixture of resignation and disgust. "I don't know for sure," he admitted, his voice low. "When I was younger, I was forced to work here, but they never told us everything. From what I could gather, they're experimenting on these fiends, trying to understand them—maybe even control them. But whatever they're doing, it's not working. It's only causing suffering."

I stared at him, the weight of his words pressing down on me like a leaden cloak. Even though they were fiends—creatures that had brought destruction and death to so many—I couldn't shake the feeling of revulsion. The idea that people could inflict such cruelty, even on monsters, was more than I could comprehend.

"But why?" I asked, my voice barely more than a whisper. "Why would they do this?"

Brute ran a hand through his hair, his expression hardening. "My guess? They're trying to protect themselves. Trying to find a way to fight back against the fiends or gain control over them. But..." He paused, glancing around at the pitiful creatures in the cages. "It's clear they've lost their way. This place... it's become a nightmare."

He turned away, making his way toward another large door on the far side of the room. "Alright," he muttered, his voice heavy with weariness. "Now that you've seen it, let's keep moving."

Brute reached for the door, but it was locked. Without missing a beat, he pulled out a set of lockpicking tools from his pouch, kneeling down to work on the lock. "Give me a second."

As Brute focused on the door, I stood there, rooted in place by the cage. My mind was spinning, the stench of the room mingling with the horror of what I had seen. The atmosphere was suffocating, a thick fog of fear and decay that seemed to seep into my bones. My thoughts swirled with questions—about the experiments, about the people of Eclipsia, and about what Celine could possibly have to do with this place.

And then I heard it.

A faint whisper, soft but insistent, coming from behind me. I turned slowly; my gaze drawn to the Grimroot that sat hunched in its cage. Its eyes—once dull and lifeless—were now locked onto mine, a flicker of awareness lighting them from within.

The Grimroot's eyes locked onto mine with unnerving intensity. Fear coiled tightly in my chest, but I couldn't tear myself away from its gaze. Its lips twitched, moving ever so slightly as if trying to form words. I hesitated, keeping my distance, unsure if I was imagining things.

Its raspy, uneven breaths were the only sound in the stifling silence. I leaned in, straining to catch whatever it was trying to say. Then, barely more than a whisper, the faintest trace of a word: "Help…"

I froze. Did it really just ask me for help? A fiend? My heart pounded in my ears, and I felt dizzy, torn between disbelief and the undeniable desperation in its eyes. The Grimroot's gaze remained locked onto mine, pleading.

Swallowing hard, I took another cautious step closer. "Did you just… ask for help?" I whispered, my voice barely audible, half expecting the room to mock me with silence. I felt dumb trying to speak to the fiend, but something urged me to try.

The Grimroot's cracked lips moved again, struggling to form words. I leaned in further, my fear momentarily eclipsed by the need to understand. "He…" it began, the word trailing off as if it couldn't find the strength to continue.

But before it could finish, something shifted. The creature's eyes, once filled with desperation, now flared with a wild, furious intensity. In an instant, it lunged at the bars, slamming against the cage with a force that rattled the iron. I jumped back, stumbling, my body hitting the cold stone floor with a thud.

"What are you doing?" Brute's voice cut through the panic, low and sharp. He glanced back at me, his eyes narrowed in warning. "Get up. I got the door open."

Scrambling to my feet, I hurried toward him, the Grimroot still thrashing violently in its cage. The earlier plea for help was lost in its sudden rage. I spared one last look at the creature, a cold unease settling deep in my stomach. I had no idea what had just happened, but something about that moment would not leave me.

The iron door creaked shut behind us, sealing us away from the horrors of the room. The air was marginally fresher, with a faint breeze filtering through the narrow, dimly lit corridor, but the stench of decay still clung to my lungs. Brute moved ahead, his steps steady as if the weight of this place didn't bother him. I, on the other hand, felt the walls closing in with every step.

"What was that about?" Brute asked, his tone stern but with a hint of curiosity.

I glanced at him, trying to steady my breath. "What was what about?" I muttered, feigning ignorance.

"Back there, with the Grimroot," he pressed, his eyes narrowing. "What set it off?"

I shook my head, my thoughts spinning. "Nothing. I just got too close, I guess," I lied, forcing my voice to remain steady. I wasn't ready to tell Brute what I thought I heard. I wasn't even sure if I believed it myself. The Grimroot's raspy plea echoed in my mind—"Help..."—but I shoved it aside, unwilling to linger on something so disturbing.

Brute gave me a cautious glance, but he didn't push for more. "We need to stay focused. This place is dangerous, and we can't afford any mistakes."

I nodded and fell into step beside him, my mind still reeling from everything I had seen. "Where are we headed now?"

Brute peeked around a corner, making sure no one was nearby before he answered. "We need to get to the roof. From there, I believe we can get some information on where Celine might be."

The narrow corridor ahead felt like it was closing in around us, each step through the darkened halls adding weight to the oppressive atmosphere. The flickering torches along the walls cast distorted shadows, making everything seem more menacing than it already was.

"Brute?" I called out softly.

"Yeah?"

"You were part of all this... when you were younger?"

He didn't look at me as he spoke, his voice heavy with bitterness. "Not by choice. I spent a lot of time in the woods, learned about the fiends. The people here found out and forced me to work for them. But I never agreed with what they were doing. I saw things I'll never forget, things that still haunt me."

We rounded another corner, the corridor opening into a larger chamber lined with more cages and tables. The sight made my stomach churn.

Brute continued speaking as we walked. "You remind me of a little brother, Isaac. I wouldn't have returned to this forsaken place for anyone else. But I can see how much Celine means to you, and I'm here to make sure we find her."

A small, unexpected smile tugged at my lips. The thought of Brute seeing me as a younger brother brought a warmth I hadn't felt in years. Growing up as an only child had been lonely, and after losing my parents, I'd felt adrift—like there was no one left to look out for me. Brute's words filled a void I hadn't even realized was there.

"Thanks, Brute," I said quietly.

Brute glanced back. "We'll find her, Isaac. Together."

We continued through the chilling interior of the building, the temperature dropping as we climbed another narrow staircase. Halfway up, Brute stopped suddenly, his body tensing.

"What is it?" I whispered, barely able to see him in the dim light.

"There's something up ahead," Brute murmured, crouching lower. "Stay close."

We moved slowly, careful to avoid making any noise on the uneven stone floor. At the top of the stairs, we entered a small, cramped room with a single trapdoor above us.

"This is it," Brute whispered. "The roof is just through there."

Just as he reached for the trapdoor, a faint noise stopped us in our tracks. It came from a darkened corner of the room, a soft, pitiful sound that sent a shiver up my spine.

"Did you hear that?" I asked, eyes scanning the shadows.

Brute nodded, his face grim. "Stay behind me."

We edged closer to the source of the noise, and as we neared the far corner, I made out a small, frail figure huddled in the darkness. It was another fiend—but different. Smaller, weaker, and in far worse condition than any we'd seen so far.

"What's it doing here?" I asked, my voice barely above a whisper.

Brute crouched beside it. "Looks like it's been abandoned. Left here to die."

The fiend looked up at us, and for a moment, I thought I saw fear in its dull, clouded eyes. It let out a faint, pitiful whimper.

"We can't just leave it like this," I said, my voice trembling.

Brute nodded. "We won't. But you don't need to see this."

"What are you going to do?" I asked, though I already knew the answer.

"The kindest thing we can do is end its suffering," Brute said quietly.

I turned away, closing my eyes as I heard the dull thud of Brute carrying out the mercy kill. The fiend's whimpering stopped abruptly, replaced by a heavy silence that hung in the air like a shroud. Relief and sorrow warred within me as I took in what had just happened. Even fiends didn't deserve this kind of torment.

Brute rose from the floor, his expression hard. "Come on," he said gently. "We're almost to the roof."

He led the way to the trapdoor, climbing the ladder quickly. When he reached the top, he paused before knocking on the door: *knock... knock... knock, knock, knock*. The sound echoed softly in the air, a pattern that seemed to hold some significance to Brute.

Moments later, I heard the creak of the trapdoor opening, and fresh air rushed in, filling the room with a much-needed breeze. For the first time since entering the building, I felt the suffocating weight of the Asylum lift, if only slightly.

# Chapter 17

Brute hoisted himself through the trapdoor first, swiftly scanning the rooftop before giving me a subtle nod. I followed, pulling myself up onto the cold stone roof. The trapdoor shut with a soft thud behind me, and Brute immediately moved to secure it from the outside, his hands steady and practiced.

Before I could fully take in the surroundings or even catch my breath, my attention snapped to a hooded, shadowy figure standing just a few paces away. Instinctively, my hand reached for my weapon, my body tensing.

"Who's that?" I whispered urgently, eyes locked on the figure's silhouette.

"It's alright," Brute replied, raising a hand to calm me. "He's a friend."

The figure stepped forward, moving slowly into the pale moonlight. As his features came into view, I could see he was tall and slender, with an air of quiet authority. His face, though stern, carried a kindness in the lines etched by age. His graying hair framed sharp, observant eyes that scanned our surroundings.

"Brute," the man said in a deep, steady voice, "It's been too long. I'm surprised you still remember the knock."

"Aldhard," Brute replied, a rare note of relief in his voice. "Far too long. We hit some trouble on the way, but we made it."

Aldhard's gaze shifted briefly to me, his sharp eyes appraising before settling back on Brute. "It's good to see you, Brute. And I see you brought company."

Brute gestured toward me. "This is Isaac," he introduced.

"He's with me."

Aldhard extended his hand toward me, his grip firm but not forceful. I hesitated for a second before taking it. "Isaac," Aldhard said, his voice calm but weighted with something unspoken. "Pleasure to meet you, though I'm guessing you're not here for pleasantries."

I gave a nod, unsure how to respond. His presence commanded attention in a way that made me uneasy.

Aldhard turned back to Brute, a slight frown creasing his features. "Brute, you've escaped this cursed town. Why come back? You had the chance to build a better life away from all this."

Brute let out a heavy sigh, his eyes flickering toward me before meeting Aldhard's again. "We're looking for someone. Her name is Celine. She was taken, and we've reason to believe it's connected to the rumors of people being abducted by fiends. I thought you might know more."

As Brute spoke, I took a moment to absorb the surroundings. The rooftop was far larger than I expected, its stone surface cold underfoot. Scattered about were tables and strange instruments whose purpose I couldn't immediately decipher. The silence up here felt unnatural, as though the night itself held its breath.

Among the shadows, I noticed large, iron cages—some empty, others holding twisted creatures. Two of the cages contained a Dreadbeak, their mouths sealed shut and their wings tightly bound to its body. I locked eyes with one. They were dull and lifeless, sharing the same vacant stare as the fiends we'd seen in the Asylum below.

Aldhard sighed deeply, the sound heavy with uncertainty. "Brute, I'm not sure if I can help you this time," he muttered, his voice strained with the weight of reluctance. His hand ran through his graying hair as if trying to release the tension building in his mind.

Brute didn't flinch, his eyes narrowing as he stepped closer. "You know more than you're letting on, Aldhard," Brute pressed, his tone low but firm. "You've always known more than the rest of us. Don't start playing coy now."

Brute and I followed Aldhard as he moved toward a table cluttered with papers and scrolls, his expression growing darker with each step. The dim light from the moon made his face seem even more weathered, as though the weight of the information he carried had aged him prematurely.

"This is dangerous, Brute. You know the kind of trouble you're getting into by coming back here," Aldhard said quietly, his tone heavy with warning.

"I didn't have a choice," Brute replied, his voice resolute. "This boy here is important to me, and Celine is important to him. I'll do whatever it takes to help him find her."

Aldhard's eyes lingered on Brute, his hesitation clear. I could feel the tension between them, the unspoken history that passed through their gaze.

"We need your help, Aldhard," Brute continued, breaking the silence. "Any information you have—any leads—could make all the difference."

Aldhard's gaze shifted from Brute to the city beyond, his brow furrowed. "There have been whispers, yes. Dark rumors of places where the fiends take their victims. It's said to be a dark, mountainous area far from Moonveil. But... there's more." He paused, his voice growing quieter as if even saying the words caused unease.

"I've heard snippets of speech—fragments, really—barely coherent," he continued, his tone dropping. "People... or perhaps something else... living there. Not just surviving, but prospering. They're not captives. They're... thriving in some twisted sense." He turned back to us, his eyes dark. "It doesn't make sense, but the whispers suggest there's more than just death awaiting those taken by the fiends. There's a life beyond, but it's not the kind of life we'd ever want to imagine."

His words hit me like a blow to the chest. Life... beyond Moonveil? It felt like the ground was falling away beneath me. I stared at Aldhard, struggling to wrap my mind around the revelation. I had been raised, like everyone else, to believe that Moonveil was the last haven of humanity—the only place left where people lived. That was the truth we'd all grown up knowing, the very foundation of everything I understood about the world.

But now… now Aldhard was telling me there was something else. Somewhere else. I felt my pulse quicken, my breath shallow. If there was life outside Moonveil, if people were thriving, then... what had we been told all these years?

Curiosity overpowered the fear swirling in my gut, and before I could stop myself, I spoke up. "How haven't I heard of this place? I grew up here, and no one's ever mentioned it. Not even in passing."

Aldhard turned to face me, leaning against the desk. "That is by design, Isaac. Every hooded figure you've seen here in Eclipsia—every person you passed in the streets—they've all been close to that place. Some have been there and returned, though not of their own free will. Some managed to escape, while others were found wandering aimlessly in the woods, left there by their captors. But why? That, I don't know."

He paused, letting his words hang in the air like a weight. "These people... they're the ones you know as being afflicted by Hysteria. You've seen it yourself: the shuffling, the lifeless eyes, the incoherent ramblings. It's all connected to that place."

I felt a cold shiver run through me as Aldhard's words sunk in. The people I'd always been told were suffering from madness or some unexplainable illness—were they victims of something far worse than anyone had ever admitted?

"Once they're found, these people are brought to Eclipsia," Aldhard continued. "They're segregated from the rest of society, kept under tight watch to prevent mass frenzy. Those in power believe that if the general populace knew about this place, it would lead to chaos. So, the stories are suppressed, and the survivors are kept here, out of sight and out of mind."

His voice grew softer, tinged with sorrow. "I've seen it all too many times. Families torn apart, people becoming shadows of who they once were, haunted by something they can't fully remember or explain. Yet, the king and his advisors keep the truth buried, afraid of the panic it would unleash."

My anger flared, burning away the shock and fear that had momentarily paralyzed me. "But that's monstrous!" I exclaimed. "People deserve to know the truth! To know what happened to their loved ones!"

Aldhard nodded grimly. "You're right. But those in power see it differently. They think they're protecting the greater good, even if it means sacrificing a few to save the many. Imagine what would happen if the common folk knew there were places out there where people were taken, never to return—places beyond the known borders of Moonveil. It would break the fragile peace. People would question everything: the king's authority, the safety of their homes, the very foundation of our world."

His voice grew more somber. "Fear of the unknown is a powerful weapon. The rulers of this land would rather keep people in the dark than risk losing control. If the truth were exposed, chaos would follow. Social and political structures would crumble. And so, the stories remain buried."

A cold, hollow feeling settled in my chest. It made sense, as much as it sickened me. But it didn't make it right.

"If all of this is true," I began, locking eyes with Aldhard, "then why are you here? You seem pretty sane yourself."

"I was unlucky," Aldhard began, his voice steady but tinged with pain. "While it's true that most of Eclipsia's residents are brought here after being deemed no longer of sound mind, there are a few of us who were born here. You see, many guards find it easier to take advantage of the citizens in their current state. It's a dark reality, one that's obviously seldom spoken of, but it happens. I'm one of those who was born here under such conditions."

His words hit me like a punch to the gut. The full implication of what he was saying was sickening. I opened my mouth to speak, but all I could manage was, "That's...horrible. I'm sorry, Aldhard."

Aldhard gave a small, sad smile, but it didn't reach his eyes. Brute, standing beside him, placed a comforting hand on Aldhard's shoulder.

"So, not only are we up against the fiends," Brute said gravely, "we're also up against the very people who are supposed to protect us."

Aldhard nodded, his expression grim. "Yes, and the path you two are on is rife with danger. I can't say what will happen once you leave Moonveil, but if it's discovered that you managed to return from that place, there will be many who will want to silence you."

A heavy silence followed, the weight of Aldhard's words settling on me like a cloak. I clenched my fists, as anger and resolve flooded through me. "Then it's settled," I said firmly. "We'll find Celine and expose the truth. We'll show everyone what's really going on in Moonveil."

Brute raised a fist in agreement, his eyes filled with determination. "That's the spirit, Isaac! We've come too far to turn back now."

Aldhard straightened up, his demeanor shifting to one of focus. "Very well," he said. "I'll help you in any way I can."

He moved behind the desk and sat down in an old chair, pulling open a drawer. From within, he took out a large, detailed map and spread it across the table. Brute and I leaned in closer to examine it.

The map was of Moonveil, with all its cities—Selunaris, Lunaria, Noctiluna, Crescentia, Eclipsia, and Nyxaris—clearly marked. The region was surrounded by dense, sprawling forests, just as I'd always known. But then, as I scanned further, my eyes caught something strange: a mark far to the east, beyond the edge of the map's territory.

"What's this?" I asked, pointing at the distant mark, my curiosity piqued.

Aldhard folded his arms, his eyes narrowing slightly. "That," he said, "is where I believe you'll find Celine. Based on the accounts and stories I've gathered from citizens across Eclipsia, I've been able to piece together this rough map. It's the best lead we have."

My mind raced, struggling to process what I was hearing. For my entire life, I had believed that Moonveil was the entire world. The idea that there could be something beyond—another place, perhaps even another civilization—was staggering.

"How do you know this?" I asked, skepticism creeping into my voice. "How can you be sure this place even exists?"

Aldhard sighed, leaning back in his chair. "I can't confirm it with absolute certainty. The stories I've gathered are fragmented and inconsistent. Everyone here suffers from Hysteria, so by nature, their accounts are unreliable. There's no guarantee this place exists. But it's the best conclusion I've drawn."

I stared at the mark on the map, my thoughts swirling. Traveling beyond Moonveil, into unknown lands filled with unimaginable dangers—it was overwhelming. But at the same time, the possibility of bringing Celine back was all I could focus on.

Brute broke the silence, noticing the doubt flickering in my eyes. "We've come this far, Isaac. There's no turning back. If this is the only lead we have, we'll just have to trust it."

His words steadied me, and I felt my resolve returning. "You're right. No other choice," I said, letting Brute's confidence give me strength.

"Alright, then," I asked, glancing between Brute and Aldhard, "what exactly is this place called?"

Aldhard's face darkened slightly as he answered. "I've dubbed it, the Madlands."

The name lingered in the air like a dark omen, and I could feel its weight.

"Madlands…" I muttered, swallowing the unease that rose like bile in my throat. "Sounds... inviting."

Aldhard gave a slight, almost knowing nod. "There's more you should know," he said, his voice calm but laced with gravity. "Based on what I've gathered, the Madlands lie about 2000 miles west of here."

The number hit me like a physical blow. "2000 miles?" I repeated, my voice barely above a whisper. The sheer distance alone made the task feel insurmountable. "That would take months. We don't have that kind of time. Not to mention the terrain or the fiends we'd have to fight along the way. The journey could be impossible."

Brute crossed his arms, nodding grimly. "And who knows what might happen to Celine in that time? We've already spent days getting this far. If it takes months… We might be too late."

His words dredged up the fears I had been desperately trying to suppress. Images of Celine—alone, scared, possibly suffering—flashed in my mind, and I was instantly hit with the feeling of despair. "We can't afford to wait that long," I said, my voice tight with desperation. "We need to find a faster way."

Aldhard's eyes gleamed with something I hadn't seen before—a spark of mischief. "Fortunately," he said, rising from his seat, "there is a faster way."

He gestured for us to follow him. Brute and I exchanged puzzled glances before trailing behind. Aldhard led us toward a large, shadowed cage near the edge of the roof. As we got closer, I felt my skin prickle with unease. Inside the cage, the outline of a Dreadbeak loomed in the moonlight.

"You'll be traveling to the Madlands using this," Aldhard said, his voice calm, as though suggesting something entirely mundane.

I stared at him, blinking, then glanced at Brute. "What do you mean?" I asked, utterly baffled.

Aldhard chuckled lightly. "Through some… experimentation, I've managed to train two Dreadbeaks. They can understand and respond to human commands. Not perfectly, but enough."

I struggled to process his words. "You're telling us that a fiend—a Dreadbeak, of all things—will listen to us?"

"Precisely," Aldhard replied, his tone matter-of-fact.

Brute's brow furrowed, the disbelief evident on his face. "But they're fiends. How can we trust them?"

Aldhard shrugged as though the answer was obvious. "Trust isn't the issue here. It's about establishing dominance. If you show them who's in control, they'll respond. They're more intelligent than most realize."

A flicker of hope ignited within me despite the absurdity of the situation. The thought of cutting down our travel time made my heart race. "And they're... ready to go?" I asked, stepping closer to the cage, where the Dreadbeak shifted slightly, its eyes gleaming in the darkness.

"As ready as they'll ever be," Aldhard said, unlocking the cage. "But remember, never undo the binds around their beaks."

"Don't they need to eat?" I asked, eyeing the tight chains wrapped around the Dreadbeak's deadly beak.

Aldhard chuckled again. "They can endure hunger for far longer than you might think. Their resilience is… impressive. But it's safer this way. Trust me, you don't want to see what happens if one of these creatures decides it's hungry."

I nodded, swallowing hard. "Got it. What else?"

Aldhard gestured to the Dreadbeak inside the cage, whose wings were tightly bound to its body. "Be aware of their body language. They'll sense fear. Stay confident, be firm, and they'll respect you."

I glanced at Brute, whose expression had shifted from disbelief to steely determination. "Well," he said, rolling his shoulders. "It's worth a shot. We don't exactly have time to waste."

"Then let's get started," I said, the nerves settling in as I stepped closer. "Teach us what we need to know."

Aldhard unlatched the cage and gestured for us to approach. The Dreadbeak inside shifted uneasily, its beak snapping against the binds as it turned its glowing eyes toward us. "The first lesson," Aldhard said with a slight grin, "is to show them you're not afraid."

*Easier said than* done, I thought. I took a deep breath, feeling the weight of what was about to happen. I was about to ride a fiend—possibly one of the deadliest creatures I had ever encountered—into the unknown.

Brute gave me a firm nod. "We can do this, Isaac. We have

to."

"Right," I said, my heart hammering in my chest. "Let's give it a try."

As I approached the cage, a strange mix of excitement and nervousness buzzed through my veins. My pulse quickened, and I could feel the sweat on my palms despite the cool air around us. The Dreadbeak's massive form loomed before me, its piercing black eyes tracking my every movement. I swallowed hard, feeling the dry lump in my throat, as Aldhard stood beside me, offering quiet words of encouragement.

With a deep breath, I cautiously mounted the creature. Its feathers were surprisingly slick beneath my hands, almost like polished stone, and its body shivered beneath my touch. The muscles rippled and tensed as it adjusted to my weight. I could feel the bird's raw power coiled beneath me. My legs wrapped tightly around its massive frame, and I could feel the rhythmic rise and fall of its breathing—steady but undeniably dangerous. For a brief moment, fear shot through me as I wondered if it would buck me off before I even had a chance to hold on properly.

Brute, grunting beside me as he clambered onto his own Dreadbeak, wasn't faring as well. The sharp scent of sweat and leather filled the air as his creature let out a low, warning screech, its talons scraping the ground in protest. The feathers beneath him bristled with tension, and the Dreadbeak beneath him bucked violently, its powerful wings twitching as if trying to throw him off. "Whoa! Easy there!" he yelled, his voice laced with panic, clutching tightly to the reins. His legs slipped precariously on the sleek feathers, nearly losing his balance.

I couldn't help but laugh at the sight—Brute, the tough and fearless warrior, struggling to stay on the back of the creature like a novice. The sound of my laughter was strange in the tense atmosphere, but for a moment, it lightened the weight in my chest.

"Just hold on and give it some direction!" Aldhard's voice was calm and authoritative. "They'll get used to you, but only if you show them who's in control."

I took a deep breath, focusing on the creature beneath me. Its talons clicked softly against the stone roof as I gripped the reins more confidently. "Alright, let's go," I said firmly. To my surprise, the Dreadbeak responded, stepping forward in a smooth, controlled motion. I guided it around the rooftop, its powerful strides giving me a thrill I hadn't expected.

Brute, on the other hand, was still struggling to maintain his balance. "Hold still, you oversized featherball!" he yelled as his Dreadbeak gave another defiant shake, nearly unseating him again.

I couldn't hold back a chuckle. "Just relax! It's all about showing it who's boss!"

"Easy for you to say," Brute shot back, his voice a mix of frustration and amusement. "You got the tame one!"

Despite his struggle, there was a hint of a grin forming on his face. Aldhard watched with a knowing smile. "Remember, confidence is key. If you show hesitation, they'll sense it. Take charge, Brute."

Taking a cue from Aldhard, I urged my Dreadbeak forward again. "Let's pick up the pace!" I called out, tugging slightly on the reins. The creature responded immediately, speeding up, and I felt the wind rush past as we circled the rooftop with increasing speed.

"Hey!" Brute shouted, watching as I whizzed by. "No fair, I want mine to go faster too!"

"Then make it listen!" I called over my shoulder, grinning as I watched him wrestle with his own stubborn mount.

Brute took a deep breath, his grip tightening as he straightened in the saddle. With a commanding shout, he pulled hard on the reins. "Alright, you overgrown bird! Let's go!"

At first, the Dreadbeak resisted, but then, as if sensing Brute's newfound determination, it fell in line. Slowly but surely, it began to move more smoothly, and soon, Brute was riding alongside me, his expression a mix of triumph and disbelief.

"There you go!" I called out, laughing as we both sped around the rooftop. "See? It's not so bad!"

"Yeah, well, remind me not to try taming one of these again," Brute muttered, though the smile on his face betrayed his enjoyment. "But I'll admit, it's kinda fun."

Aldhard watched us with a grin. "You've both got the hang of it. Remember this moment. When you're soaring high above the trees, you'll need to hold on to that confidence."

We guided our Dreadbeaks back toward the center of the roof, their heavy talons clattering softly against the stone. Brute, still flushed from the excitement, shook his head with disbelief. "Not bad for a couple of rookies, huh?"

I couldn't help but smile. "Yeah, who knew riding a fiend could be... enjoyable?"

Aldhard's expression grew more serious as he stepped closer, motioning for us to gather around the table again. "You've got the basics down," he said, "but the real challenge lies ahead. The journey to the Madlands won't be easy. We need to discuss the route."

"How long will it take us to get there?" I asked, leaning forward with anticipation.

Aldhard stroked his beard thoughtfully. "Based on their speed, you're looking at five to six days. These creatures can cover vast distances quickly, much faster than you could on foot."

Brute's eyes widened in surprise. "Five to six days? That's it?"

Aldhard nodded. "That's right. They can fly for long stretches without needing rest. But don't let your guard down. The skies are no safer than the ground."

I glanced at Brute, feeling relieved. "That's a lot quicker than I expected."

Brute's excitement was contagious. "Think of the sights we'll see along the way! Mountains, forests—who knows, maybe we'll discover creatures no one's ever laid eyes on before."

"Or run into more fiends," I added, feeling a bit more cautious. The excitement was there, but so was the ever-present danger.

Brute shrugged, undeterred. "Eh, we'll deal with whatever comes our way. Fiends, whatever—nothing we can't handle, right?"

I couldn't help but grin at his confidence. It was contagious, even though I knew the dangers ahead. "Let's just hope we don't run into anything worse than a Dreadbeak."

Aldhard's smile faded, replaced by a grim expression. "While I admire your determination, there's something you both need to understand," he began, his tone weighted with warning. "The Madlands are deeply connected to Hysteria. I've spent years researching the illness, but I still can't say for sure what causes it or how to cure it. What I do know is that if you catch it out there, there will be no saving you."

His words sent a chill through me. The idea of heading into a place that could strip away my sanity made my stomach turn. What if we lost ourselves the way so many others had? What if we became like the mindless husks roaming Eclipsia, lost forever? The weight of the mission felt heavier, the stakes rising with every step we took.

Before I could let those thoughts consume me, Brute's voice

cut in, strong and reassuring. "Don't worry, Isaac," he said, as if sensing my unease. "We'll come back in one piece—Celine included."

"And what if Celine's already been afflicted by Hysteria?" Aldhard asked, his voice pressing with grim practicality.

"We'll deal with it when the time comes," I said, steadying my voice. "We're not leaving her behind, no matter what."

Aldhard's expression softened, and he gave a slow nod. "I believe you. But I had to make sure you understood the risk. If anyone can bring her back, it's you two."

Brute flashed his usual grin, flexing his arm theatrically. "Of course we can! We've got this."

Aldhard's stern demeanor cracked into a small smile. "Good. Now, we need to get serious about flying. You don't have much time."

Before we could move, a loud, insistent banging echoed from the trapdoor we'd entered through, the sound startling the Dreadbeaks. The birds bucked slightly, rattling their bindings as their wings flapped in alarm.

I whipped my head toward the noise. "What's that?"

Aldhard's face tightened. "Guards," he muttered. "It seems they've figured out where you are."

The muffled shouts of guards followed the banging, demanding that Aldhard open the door. Each thud reverberated with growing urgency, the trapdoor straining under the force of their efforts.

"They won't hold back much longer," Brute said, his eyes darting toward the trapdoor. "What's the plan?"

Without missing a beat, Aldhard grabbed the reins of both Dreadbeaks, guiding us toward the edge of the roof. "You need to leave, now. Mount the Dreadbeaks—I'll deal with the guards."

"But—" I started to protest, but Aldhard silenced me with a sharp glance.

He turned swiftly toward Brute, handing him a worn leather bag I hadn't noticed before. "Take this," Aldhard instructed firmly, his tone leaving no room for hesitation. "Inside is the map I showed you earlier, along with supplies for your journey. You'll need them."

Brute took the bag without question, his expression hardening as he slung it over his shoulder. I could hear the faint clinking of metal and the crinkling of parchment as he adjusted the strap.

"No time for arguments. Go now!" Aldhard ordered, his voice leaving no room for debate. He swiftly cut the ropes binding the Dreadbeaks' wings.

"But we don't even know how to fly them yet!" I argued, my voice rising with panic.

"You'll figure it out as you go," Aldhard shot back. "The key is absolute confidence. If you command them with strength, they'll follow your lead."

I glanced over the edge of the roof, feeling a sickening lurch in my stomach as I took in the drop. My Dreadbeak shifted beneath me, sensing my hesitation. I forced myself to breathe, trying to steady my nerves.

*Confidence, Isaac.* You need to believe you can do this.

Aldhard moved toward the trapdoor, readying himself to remove the blockage and confront the guards. "I'll hold them off. Head straight for the Madlands and don't look back."

"Thank you, Aldhard," Brute said, his voice tight with emotion. "I swear, I'll come back for you and your mother."

"Stay safe," Aldhard replied, nodding firmly before turning his attention to the door.

I took a deep breath, gripping the reins tightly. "Fly," I

commanded, my voice dropping slightly but determined.

The Dreadbeak responded, its massive wings beating against the air with a heavy whoosh, lifting us slightly off the ground. Brute's Dreadbeak followed suit, its wings stirring the wind as it took to the sky.

My heart hammered in my chest as the ground fell away beneath me. The Dreadbeak struggled to gain altitude, its wings straining as I held on for dear life. My legs squeezed tightly around its body, trying to stabilize myself as the bird fought to level out.

"Steady!" I called out, the words escaping my lips almost instinctively. To my relief, the Dreadbeak responded, its movements smoothing as I began to fall in sync with its rhythm. With every powerful flap of its wings, I felt a rush of air, a sense of freedom tempered by fear.

Brute, hovering beside me, was starting to find his own rhythm. "This is insane!" he yelled, but there was a thrill in his voice.

"Aldhard!" I shouted over the wind. "Will you be okay?"

He nodded, his voice carrying across the rooftop. "Don't worry about me. They need me to keep their experiments running—they won't harm me."

"Why not leave with us?" I pressed, feeling a pang of guilt for leaving him behind. "You don't have to stay here!"

Aldhard smiled sadly, shaking his head. "I can't. My mother's still here, and she wouldn't last long without me. This is where I need to be."

I swallowed hard, my throat tight with the sudden rush of emotions. Guilt, frustration, and helplessness tangled in my chest. I couldn't help but feel like I was abandoning him to a fate he didn't deserve. The man who had risked everything to help us was choosing to stay behind, trapped in a city we were desperate to escape. And there was nothing I could do about it.

I gave a reluctant nod, turning my attention back to the sky. "Thank you," I called out, my voice filled with gratitude.

Brute hovered beside me, his Dreadbeak gliding smoothly now. "Time to go," he said, his voice more serious than usual. "Let's get out of here."

With one final look back at Aldhard, we turned our Dreadbeaks toward the horizon. The city of Eclipsia, along with its guards and shadows, faded behind us as the wind whipped around us, carrying us toward the unknown dangers of the Madlands.

The days that followed blurred into a relentless march of survival and focus. From the moment we left Eclipsia behind, Brute and I were propelled into a routine of constant motion. Each day, the Dreadbeaks carried us further from Moonveil and closer to the shadowed realm of the Madlands.

The first few hours of flight were challenging, to say the least. Controlling the Dreadbeaks while navigating the strange currents of the open skies took every ounce of concentration. The creatures were powerful, but they had minds of their own. Yet, slowly, the rhythm of their wings became second nature to us. Each beat of their powerful limbs was a reminder of how far we had come, both physically and mentally, on this perilous journey.

As the days passed, the landscape beneath us shifted. At first, the lush green plains of Moonveil spread out like a comforting blanket, but that soon gave way to rocky outcroppings and the stark desolation marking the outskirts of the Madlands. The air grew colder, the skies darker. Each evening, we scouted for a hidden spot to land. We would tether the Dreadbeaks, binding their wings to ensure they stayed grounded, though they had grown surprisingly compliant. There was a kind of mutual understanding forming between us and the beasts, a fragile trust.

Once grounded, Brute and I split our duties without needing to speak. One of us would set up a rudimentary camp while the other ventured out to hunt or gather what little food could be found. The Dreadbeaks watched us, their beady eyes following every movement as though they, too, were part of this strange, makeshift team. They stayed close as if they sensed the dangers looming in the Madlands and knew we were their best hope of survival.

At night, as the fire flickered weakly against the cold air, Brute and I would talk. Our conversations often drifted to Celine and the uncertain future that awaited us in the heart of the Madlands. Every so often, I would catch myself thinking of her, her face hovering at the edge of my dreams, a beacon pulling me forward.

There was a time, earlier in our journey when I wasn't so sure these Dreadbeaks were on our side. We had been flying for hours, trying to cover as much distance as possible, when suddenly, both of them refused to listen to our commands. Brute and I shouted, tugged at the reins, and tried everything we could think of, but the creatures wouldn't respond. Instead, they dipped low, skimming the treetops and landing without our permission.

Frustration boiled over between Brute and me as we scrambled off their backs, confused and more than a little angry. "What the hell was that about?" Brute had grumbled, pacing back and forth. I had no answer for him, only the same worrying confusion.

But before we could even try to get them back in the air, I heard it—a distant sound growing louder. I looked up just in time to see a massive flock of Dreadbeaks flying overhead. My heart stopped. If we had stayed in the air just moments longer, we would've flown straight into them. A chill ran down my spine at the thought.

The two Dreadbeaks we'd been riding stood firm, their eyes locked on the sky as if watching over us. It was then I realized— they had landed us on purpose. They knew the danger before we did. It wasn't disobedience; it was protection. They had saved us.

There was another night when a storm caught us off guard, forcing an early landing in a rocky alcove. The winds howled through the jagged landscape, and the Dreadbeaks huddled close to us for warmth. It surprised me how the creatures, once fierce and untamable, now sought our protection just as much as we relied on their strength. Maybe the bond we were forming was more than just a practical necessity.

Most of the flight toward the Madlands had been exactly what I expected—endless views of sprawling forests, their canopies dense and dark, stretching as far as the eye could see. Occasionally, patches of misty swamps interrupted the greenery, their murky waters reflecting the dull sky. It was a landscape both beautiful and desolate, filled with pockets of wilderness that had gone untouched for years. At times, I'd spot streams cutting through the woods like silver veins, or small clearings where wildlife roamed freely. But beyond that, it was just miles upon miles of the same—forests, fields, and swamps, blending together into one long blur beneath us. The steady rhythm of the flight had lulled me into a strange sense of calm.

Now, as we soared through the gray sky, something new caught my eye—a jagged range of mountains appeared on the horizon. Their dark, imposing peaks tore through the clouds, stretching endlessly in both directions.

"Isaac, look!" Brute's voice broke through my thoughts. He pointed towards the mountains. "That has to be it. The heart of the Madlands."

I followed his gaze.

The mountains seemed alive, their rocky faces carved with gaping, shadowy caves. From this distance, I couldn't make out much, but those dark mouths promised shelter—or perhaps, something far worse.

"We should land and hike from here," Brute suggested, his voice laced with caution. "Whatever's up there, we're better off staying unseen. It'll be easier to hide if we're on foot."

Nodding in agreement, we guided the Dreadbeaks into a gradual descent. We touched down on a flat, rocky expanse at the base of the mountains. The air here felt different—heavier, as if even the atmosphere knew we were crossing into dangerous territory. As soon as my feet hit the ground, I began securing the Dreadbeaks, my fingers moving quickly despite the growing unease in my stomach. The birds shifted nervously, their eyes darting across the landscape with a sense of unease that only heightened my own.

I hurriedly packed my gear, my mind already racing ahead to the trek that awaited us. The mountains loomed ominously above; their jagged peaks veined with the shadows of countless caves. Lost in thought, I was startled by a sharp, cracking sound that echoed through the rocky valley. Whipping around, I saw Brute standing over one of the Dreadbeaks, its neck twisted at an unnatural angle.

"Brute!" I yelled, the shock in my voice reverberating off the stone walls. "What the hell are you doing?"

Brute looked at me, his expression disturbingly calm, even mocking. "Isaac, these are fiends. Don't tell me you actually grew attached to them."

"They helped us get here!" I shot back, anger flooding through me. "We relied on them!"

Brute's face hardened as he shook his head. "We're at our destination now. We can't afford to be sentimental, Isaac. Leaving them alive is a liability. What if they escape? Or worse, what if someone else uses them to track us? We're in the Madlands. Trust is a luxury we don't have."

I stood there, dumbfounded, watching as Brute strode toward the remaining Dreadbeak, which was already flapping its wings in panic, sensing its imminent fate. "We're months out from Moonveil," I stammered, struggling to wrap my head around his ruthless logic. "How are we supposed to get back now?"

Brute didn't stop, his voice cold as he replied, "We have the map. We'll figure it out. But right now, survival is our only goal. Any mistake could cost us everything."

I glanced down at the lifeless creature at my feet. We'd formed a bond with these Dreadbeaks during the journey, relying on them not just for transportation but for a strange, tenuous sense of companionship. But as much as I hated to admit it, Brute was right. In this unforgiving land, anything left alive that could turn against us was a threat.

Another sickening crack echoed through the mountain walls as Brute finished the job. I closed my eyes briefly, the weight of guilt pressing heavily on my chest. "Remember why we're here," Brute said, his tone firm but not unkind. "We're here for Celine. Stay focused on that."

Reluctantly, I nodded, trying to bury the sadness that I felt. Survival was all that mattered now.

"Let's move," Brute said, already turning toward the mountains. "We've still got a long way to go."

I cast one last look at the two dead Dreadbeaks, their once powerful bodies now limp and cold. It felt wrong, but necessary. With a deep breath, I turned and followed Brute into the shadows of the mountains.

As we climbed deeper into the jagged terrain, the landscape became more imposing with each step. The path was narrow and winding, a natural corridor carved between the towering rock formations. The cliffs around us loomed high, their silver-gray surfaces gleaming dully in the fading light. Massive boulders and jagged outcrops lined our way, creating an almost claustrophobic maze of stone.

The higher we climbed, the sharper the air became. My breath fogged in the crisp air, and I pulled my cloak tighter against the biting cold. Occasionally, the haunting cry of a buzzard echoed above, but otherwise, the silence was deafening. The only constant was the steady crunch of our boots on the loose gravel beneath our feet.

Brute walked beside me, his pace determined. His eyes were fixed ahead, seemingly unaffected by the oppressive atmosphere that clung to the mountains like a shroud. The rock faces on either side of us were dotted with deep crevices and dark caves, their interiors lost to shadow. I couldn't shake the feeling that unseen eyes were watching us from those hollow spaces.

As we pressed on, the path grew steeper; the mountains towered over us. The peaks were shrouded in a blanket of low-hanging clouds, and the light faded into a dull, grayish haze. It felt as though we were crossing into another world, one where the rules of survival were harsher and the line between life and death far thinner.

"This place gives me the creeps," I muttered, breaking the silence that had settled between us.

"I bet," Brute agreed, glancing down at the map Aldhard had given us. "Keep your wits about you."

After trudging along the rocky trail for a few more minutes, we reached a plateau that opened up a breathtaking view, a sharp contrast to the desolate landscape we had been traveling through. From here, the Madlands sprawled in all directions, an endless expanse of twisted terrain. But something caught my eye far below—a town nestled in the valley, its rough, stone buildings stretching out in a haphazard grid. Tiny figures moved about the streets, suggesting a decent population.

"Is that... a town?" I asked aloud, unsure if my eyes were playing tricks on me.

Brute narrowed his gaze. "Looks like it. And a big one at that."

"How are people living here? I thought the Madlands was supposed to be a wasteland filled with fiends. How could anyone survive in a place like this?" I asked Brute, confused.

Brute shook his head slowly, but there was something in his tone—a subtle hint of knowledge he wasn't sharing. "Looks like Aldhard was right. Some kind of civilization is thriving here. The world's full of surprises, it seems."

His calm demeanor annoyed me. I could barely wrap my head around what I was seeing, yet Brute seemed hardly phased. I pushed the feeling aside, figuring he was just better at keeping his emotions in check.

I scanned the town again, still struggling to reconcile the sight before me with everything I'd been told about the Madlands. Who built these structures? Were they survivors, stranded here for generations, or something else entirely? It didn't make sense. The town below felt impossibly out of place in this supposed hostile landscape.

As I continued to take it in, my eyes caught sight of something striking at the far end of the town. A massive rock face rose up, and carved into it was a large opening, almost like the entrance to a cave. The stone surrounding the entrance was adorned with gleaming jewels and gold, their faint glimmer catching the dying light of the day. Embedded into the side of the mountain was a large stained-glass mural depicting what appeared to be two wolves.

"Look at that!" I said, pointing toward the shimmering rock face. "What is that?"

Brute followed my gaze, his eyes narrowing as he took in the scene. "If we're going to find any clues about Celine, that's where we should start. Something important is going on there."

"You're right," I agreed, already feeling the pull to investigate.

"Let's get closer. Maybe we can figure out what's going on."

Brute nodded, but his expression remained cautious. "We need to keep a low profile. We don't know who—or what—lives here. Let's not draw attention until we know more."

We began our careful descent toward the town, sticking close to the shadows of the rocky outcrops, using the uneven terrain to shield ourselves. The closer we got, the more my sense of disorientation grew. Everything I thought I knew about the Madlands was unraveling before my eyes.

As we approached, the details of the town became clearer. The buildings, though roughly constructed from stone, were surprisingly sturdy, blending seamlessly into the surrounding environment. This wasn't some temporary encampment—it was a permanent settlement.

As we approached the heart of the town, I felt a drop in my stomach. We were about to cross paths with one of the Madlands' inhabitants for the first time. My pulse quickened, a mix of curiosity and dread bubbling up inside me.

Brute moved ahead without hesitation, but I lingered a step behind, my nerves getting the better of me. As we neared the first person, I couldn't help but steal a glance, trying to prepare myself for whatever I might see.

At first glance, the figure appeared human enough, but as we drew nearer, something about them felt... off. Their ears weren't normal; they were furry, perched atop their heads like those of some strange, animalistic hybrid. It was unsettling. Had the Madlands altered them? Was this some kind of mutation?

And their eyes—deep scarlet, glowing faintly in the dim light. It was as if I were staring into a pair of blood-red orbs, quietly observing me from beneath the hood of their cloak. They didn't make direct eye contact, but the intensity of their gaze sent a chill through me. Their attire was equally strange— a hooded cloak made from natural materials, lined with fur, and adorned with intricate designs that seemed to tell a forgotten story.

The rest of their clothing followed suit—a tunic and trousers made of leather and woven fibers, with high boots that were worn but sturdy. A belt, fastened with charms and trinkets carved from bone and wood, hung loosely around their waist. Every detail felt deliberate, as if each piece of their outfit carried some hidden meaning I could only guess at.

The tattoos were the final piece of the puzzle that unnerved me. They bore intricate markings on their face—patterns snaking under their eyes. They appeared to be ceremonial and meaningful, though their exact purpose was a mystery.

It wasn't just this one person either—everyone we passed had the same strange look. The hooded cloaks, the leather tunics, the belts adorned with charms; it was as if the entire town adhered to some unwritten dress code. Their tattoos were all slightly different from one another. I noticed a variety of colors and patterns—some around their eyes, others tracing across their lips or stretching over their foreheads. It felt as if the tattoos told stories of their own, ones I couldn't decipher, but they were undeniably important to the people here. Every person wore them with an air of quiet reverence, and it only added to the otherworldly aura that surrounded this place.

As we moved deeper into the town, the unsettling feeling only grew stronger. It was larger than I had initially realized, bustling with life in a way that seemed at odds with everything I had originally thought about this forsaken land. How had no one in Moonveil spoken of this place? How had it stayed hidden for so long?

"Brute, how do you think they survive here?" I asked.

"Maybe they've found a way to coexist with the land," Brute replied nonchalantly, his eyes scanning the strange town. "Or maybe they have their own way of dealing with the dangers."

His calm, almost disinterested attitude was beginning to bother me. How could he be so composed when everything about this place felt so wrong? But I swallowed my frustration, not wanting to stir any conflict between us.

As we finally reached the outskirts of the town, the air hung heavy with the scent of damp rock and earth. The people moved with purpose, their furry ears twitching now and then as they passed us. There was an unsettling feeling of being out of place, of being watched.

"Let's head towards that rock face," Brute suggested, nodding toward the large opening we had spotted from the plateau. "If there's anywhere to find answers, it's probably there."

I nodded, trying to ignore the uneasy feeling in my gut. We moved cautiously, sticking to the edges of buildings as much as possible, and I kept my hood low to conceal my face. The closer we got to the center of town, the more oppressive the atmosphere became. I could feel the weight of their stares—eyes filled with suspicion and something darker, something I couldn't quite place.

"They don't look too friendly," I whispered to Brute, noticing how the townspeople watched us with hard, scrutinizing glares. Every time someone's eyes landed on us, it felt as though the temperature dropped a few degrees.

"Just stay calm," Brute replied, his tone steady. "We don't want to provoke anyone."

Just as Brute spoke, a man bumped into me, his shoulder colliding hard with mine. I stumbled, catching myself before I fell, and instinctively shouted, "Hey!"

The man turned to face me; his expression twisted with disgust. His sharp features were only amplified by the furry ears atop his head, twitching with irritation. "Watch where you're going, boy," he sneered before turning away. Anger flared in me, my fists clenched, ready to respond, but Brute grabbed my arm, his grip firm. "Let it go, Isaac," he warned, his voice low. "We can't afford to draw attention to ourselves."

I glanced around and saw that many of the townspeople had stopped to watch the exchange. Their eyes, now filled with open hostility, bored into me, making the hairs on the back of my neck stand on end. More of those strange, furry ears twitched in unison as if silently communicating something I wasn't privy to.

Taking a deep breath, I forced myself to swallow the rising anger and nodded. Brute was right. We couldn't risk a confrontation, not when we were this close to finding Celine. "Fine," I muttered, my voice tight with barely suppressed frustration. "But what's with these people? Why are they looking at us like we're criminals?"

Brute's expression remained neutral as his eyes flicked around, taking in our surroundings. "I don't know. But whatever's going on here, we need to stay focused."

He began walking again, and I followed, trying to shake off the uneasy feeling that clung to me. There was something wrong about this place, something deeper than just the hostility we were receiving. The way the townspeople moved, the look in their eyes—it was as though they had secrets hidden beneath their skin.

As we neared the rock face, I couldn't help but marvel at its grandeur. The intricately carved stone gleamed with embedded jewels, and the entrance loomed large, framed by two imposing figures that I could only assume were guards. They stood like statues at the base of a long set of stone steps, each step worn smooth by time.

We approached cautiously, the weight of the town's stares

pressing into our backs. I took a deep breath, preparing myself for whatever lay ahead. Brute turned to me, his expression unreadable. "Let me handle this," he said quietly.

I nodded, trusting him to do the talking. As we reached the top of the stairs, one of the guards stepped forward, his eyes glowing with a fierce red intensity. He was tall and lean but radiated strength. A long, white dagger hung at his side; its hilt carved from what looked like bone.

"State your business," the guard demanded, his voice echoing off the stone walls.

Brute stepped forward confidently. "We're looking for someone. We believe she's here. We need to speak with those in charge."

The guard's gaze narrowed, suspicion clear in his eyes. "Many come with stories of urgent matters. Why should we believe yours?"

Brute held the guard's stare, unflinching. "We don't have time for delays. Please, allow us to pass."

The guard's eyes flicked toward me, and his expression twisted with disdain. "And you expect me to let someone like him inside?" His tone was dripping with contempt as his gaze lingered on me, his words striking like a physical blow.

Confusion flooded me. What did he mean by "someone like him"? I glanced at Brute, hoping for some sort of explanation, but his face remained calm, though there was a tension in his posture I hadn't noticed before.

Brute took another step forward, his patience wearing thin. "He's with me. If you have a problem with him, I'm sure your superiors would see it differently."

The guard's grip on his dagger tightened, but before he could respond, a voice echoed from deep within the cavern—clear, firm, and commanding. A woman's voice. "Let them through."

The guard hesitated, his eyes flickering between Brute and

me. With a reluctant sigh, he stepped aside. "Fine. But don't forget — I'll be keeping a close watch on the both of you. Him especially."

As we passed, the guard's gaze lingered on me with an unmistakable look of disdain. His lips curled slightly, as if the mere sight of me was a source of irritation. I couldn't shake the unease that settled in my chest. Why was everyone here so hostile towards us? Or should I say, me? The townspeople's suspicious glances, the guard's scornful stare — it all added up to a sense of unwelcome, of not belonging.

I glanced at Brute, who seemed entirely unfazed by the reactions we were receiving. How did he manage to stay so calm, so collected, amidst the cold stares and disdain? Didn't he feel the weight of their judgment like I did? The disparity between our reactions only deepened my confusion about this place.

What was it about me that drew such negative attention? The thought ate away at me, amplifying my frustration. Was it my demeanor? My appearance? Or was something more insidious at play?

We walked deeper into the cavern, the walls narrowing slightly as the shadows grew thicker around us. This was supposed to be a quest to find Celine, yet it felt like something more. It felt almost as if we were walking straight into a web of danger.

Brute, still ahead of me, seemed to sense my unease. He always had that uncanny ability to read the emotions of others. He turned slightly, giving me a reassuring nod. "Stay close," he murmured. "We'll get through this."

I nodded, trying to draw strength from his confidence, but the questions and doubts still swirled in my mind. Who were these people with their scarlet eyes and peculiar ears? Why did they regard me with such contempt?

Lost in my thoughts, I hadn't noticed Brute stop walking until I bumped into him, nearly stumbling. When I looked up, I was momentarily disoriented—and then stunned by the sight before me.

We had entered an enormous cavern, its ceiling towering high above us. This was no mere cave—it was a place of power, of royalty. Intricate carvings adorned the walls, depicting battles and ancient symbols. Precious gems and metals were inlaid into the stone, catching the dim light and casting it in mesmerizing patterns across the room.

Guards stood at attention along the sides, identical to the ones at the entrance, their postures rigid and alert. Their sharp eyes followed our every movement, and I couldn't help but feel exposed under their scrutiny.

At the far end of the cavern, seated on an ornate throne carved directly from the rock, was a woman. She had the same strange ears as the townspeople; yet here in this setting, they appeared regal and almost majestic. Her scarlet eyes glowed faintly in the dim light, but unlike the hostile stares we'd encountered before, her gaze was filled with a mixture of amusement and curiosity.

She was draped in elaborate robes of deep violet and gold, her silver hair flowing like a cascade of moonlight over her shoulders. Her beauty was striking, almost ethereal—delicate features that carried a sense of authority and command. Despite the calmness of her expression, there was something sharp, almost dangerous, about the way she observed us.

Brute suddenly dropped to one knee, his head bowed low. "Your Majesty," he said, his voice steady and respectful.

I stood there, frozen in place, my mind racing. *Majesty?* What was going on? Who was this woman?

Before I could fully process the situation, the woman's voice rang out—sharp and commanding. "Drop to your knee, boy!"

Her tone held such weight, such authority, that I found myself instinctively obeying, dropping to one knee before I even realized what I was doing. The speed of my response startled me, leaving me feeling disoriented and vulnerable.

A tense silence followed, broken only by the faint sound of dripping water somewhere in the cavern. I kept my head bowed, my heart pounding as confusion swirled through me.

Then, the woman spoke again, her voice carrying a note of satisfaction. "You did well, Remus."

*Remus?* The name caught me off guard. Who was she talking about? The name was unfamiliar, but before I could puzzle over it, a voice beside me sent a chill through my spine—a voice I knew all too well.

"Yes, Your Majesty," Brute responded, his voice calm and even.

I blinked, barely keeping my surprise in check. Remus? That's Brute's name? How had I not known that before?

"It was easier than I had anticipated, Your Majesty," Brute replied smoothly, his voice calm and measured. "The boy easily put all of his trust in me."

The words sank in slowly, like poison spreading through my veins. They were talking about me; this much was certain. But why was Brute, or Remus, speaking like this? My mind raced, trying to make sense of it all. Who was this woman, and how long had they been plotting together? Nothing made sense.

The woman let out a soft, melodious chuckle that sent a shiver down my spine. "I told thee it would not be difficult, Remus. The hearts of the trusting are easily swayed."

I turned to look at Brute—no, Remus, as he inclined his head in agreement. "Indeed, Your Majesty. He followed me without question, just as you predicted."

The realization hit me like a blow to the gut. They were talking about me. Brute had been deceiving me this whole time. The man I had come to rely on, who I thought was my friend, had been leading me into a trap. The betrayal hit me harder than any physical blow ever could.

"Well then," the woman continued, her voice cold and commanding, "there's no time to waste. Deal with the boy. Place him in the hold for me to handle later."

Remus—Brute—stood up, his movements deliberate. "As you wish, Your Majesty."

I watched him rise, the truth slowly solidifying in my mind. "Brute, what's going—"

I didn't see it coming. His fist slammed into my jaw, sending me sprawling across the cold stone floor. Pain shot through my face, and my thoughts scattered like leaves in a storm. Dazed, I tried to push myself up, but the world spun wildly around me. My vision blurred, and I could barely make out Brute's figure standing over me, his expression cold and distant.

"What the hell is wrong with you?" I shouted, holding my aching jaw.

Brute—or whoever he really was—didn't answer right away. Instead, he calmly opened his pouch, slipping on his spiked cestuses.

"Seems they were right about you," he said, his voice tinged with something like regret. "Any normal human would've had their jaw shattered by that hit."

Normal human? What was he talking about?

"What are you saying?" I demanded, forcing myself to stand despite the throbbing in my face. "Brute! What's happening?"

He looked at me with something like pity in his eyes. "You really don't understand, do you, Isaac? Even now, you think we were friends."

The woman rose from her throne, her eyes filled with disdain. "Enough talk, Remus," she commanded. "Do as I said. I have other matters to attend to."

I watched helplessly as she disappeared into the shadows of another passage. Brute turned back to me, his expression hardening. Before I could even react, he lunged at me again.

I barely managed to dodge his first strike, but the second blow grazed my ribs, sending a jolt of pain through my body. Staggering back, I tried to create some distance, but he was relentless. Each punch came faster than the last, and each time I evaded one, another followed.

"Brute, stop!" I shouted, my voice cracking with desperation. But he wasn't listening.

He landed another punch to my jaw, sending me crashing to the floor again. My head spun, and before I could fully recover, his hand was around my throat, choking the life out of me.

Time seemed to slow as Brute's grip tightened around my throat, the air in my lungs growing thinner with every second. My chest burned, my mind growing foggier by the moment. I could feel tears welling up in my eyes—not from the pain, but from the sickening realization that I might have to defend myself against him, against someone I had trusted. Against someone I considered a brother.

Panic surged through me as I clawed helplessly at his arm, trying to pry his iron grip loose. Darkness crept in at the edges of my vision, and the world around me blurred, distant, and cold. I wasn't ready for this. I wasn't ready to strike at someone I cared about.

But I had no choice. If I didn't act now, it would all be over.

Frantically, I reached for my sword. My fingers found the hilt, and with a last, desperate effort, I slashed upward. The blade met flesh, cutting through fabric and skin, slicing across Brute's face.

Brute roared in pain, releasing me as he staggered back, clutching his wounded eye. Gasping for breath, I collapsed onto the stone, tasting blood in my mouth. Through my blurred vision, I saw him reel, blood pouring from the deep cut across his eye.

As he removed his hand, his eyepatch fell, revealing something that was hidden before—a tattoo encircling his now-ruined eye. It was an intricate, sharp, and jagged pattern, resembling the fangs of a beast—just like the ones I'd seen on the townspeople.

So, it was true. Brute—Remus—was tied to this place. He wasn't the man I thought I knew.

Brute's remaining eye glared at me, filled with fury and something else—grudging respect. "You actually managed to land a hit on me," he growled, his voice tinged with admiration. "But it won't save you."

He lunged again, faster this time. I barely had time to bring my sword up to block his assault. His blows rained down with terrifying force, pushing me further and further back. Each strike was heavier than the last, and I struggled to keep up.

With one final, powerful hit, he knocked the sword from my grasp. It clattered to the ground, far out of reach.

All I had left was my shield. I raised it just in time to block another savage punch, but the force of it reverberated through my arm, making my bones ache. Brute's attacks came harder and faster, hammering against my shield until I was driven back against the wall.

"You can't keep this up forever," Brute snarled, his voice dripping with cruel satisfaction. Each punch splintered the wood of my shield until, with a final strike, it shattered into pieces.

I was defenseless. My body shook with exhaustion, and I had nothing left to give. Brute stood over me, his face twisted into a grim smile.

"I expected more from you, Isaac," he said quietly.

His fist drew back for the final blow. My mind screamed for my body to move, to do something—anything—but I was too weak, too tired. The fist came closer, filling my vision.

And then, everything went dark.

# Chapter 19

A fog of confusion still clung to me as I gradually came to, my mind sluggish and my body heavy with pain. My head throbbed, and the cold stone beneath me felt like a fleeting comfort against the raw ache in my jaw. Blinking away the blur clouding my vision, I tried to make sense of where I was. Iron bars surrounded me. I was in a cage.

A faint, flickering torch on the far wall cast weak light into the room, barely illuminating the shadows that pressed in from every side. I could hear the slow, rhythmic drip of water echoing in the distance, and the air was thick with the damp, stagnant scent of rot. I forced myself to take in my surroundings. The cave's ceiling loomed above, rough stone formations hanging like jagged teeth, and strange symbols were etched into the walls. The carvings sent a shiver down my spine, their meanings alien but undeniably sinister. My thoughts raced to the dark jars and containers stacked on nearby shelves, their contents hidden from view. I dreaded imagining what might be inside them.

I scanned the cage around me, quickly realizing my sword was missing. Of course. Remus—Brute—had likely taken it when I dropped it during the fight. Pain flared through my side as I shifted slightly, reminding me of the beating I had taken. My body screamed in protest with every movement and bruises decorated my ribs and arms.

Wincing, I lifted my shirt to assess the damage: dark, angry welts spread across my torso, still fresh. At least that meant I hadn't been unconscious for long.

The urgency of my situation started to sink in. I needed to get out of here—and fast. Celine was still out there, and these people, whoever they were, wouldn't hesitate to finish what Remus had started if I stayed trapped much longer.

As my eyes adjusted further to the dim light, I realized I wasn't alone. Cages lined the walls of the room, each one filled with slumped figures. These weren't the people of the Madlands—the lack of tattoos and animal-like features made that clear. They were from Moonveil. Just like me. The realization made my stomach hurt. What had these people endured to end up here?

I was snapped out of my thoughts when movement caught my eye. In the cage beside mine, an older man stirred, his wild, matted hair framing a face twisted with madness. His eyes darted around the room before settling on me. Suddenly, he lunged at the bars, gripping them with skeletal hands.

"Unseen truths! Eyes untainted by lies!" he shrieked, his voice ragged with desperation. "You must see, you must see it all!"

I recoiled, his words a torrent of delirious ravings. His ramblings were frighteningly familiar, echoing the same hysteria I had witnessed back in Eclipsia and Lunaria. His eyes were wide with mania, his voice hoarse from what seemed like endless screaming.

"The truth is hidden! Cloaked in shadows! Don't believe their lies!" he wailed, his words growing more frenzied by the second.

Footsteps echoed down a set of stairs I hadn't noticed before. From the far corner of the room, two figures emerged, both cloaked in the same garb as the guards at the entrance to the cave. Their red eyes glowed with malice, and I felt a chill creep over me.

"Silence, human filth!" one of them barked, striding over to the man's cage and delivering a vicious kick to the bars. The old man flinched but didn't stop, his ramblings now more frantic.

Without a word, the guards unlocked the door to his cage and dragged him out. His frail body offered no resistance as they tossed him to the floor like a rag doll.

"Think you're above the rest of us, old man?" sneered one of the guards, delivering a brutal kick to the man's side. "You're nothing. Just another worthless human."

The man groaned, curling into himself as the beating continued. Each blow was accompanied by cruel laughter, the sound of fists striking flesh mixing with the old man's pained whimpers.

"Stop it!" I couldn't hold back any longer, my voice cutting through the chaos. "Leave him alone!"

The room fell silent. The guards turned toward me, their eyes locking onto mine. One of them, a tall figure with a vicious smile, approached my cage slowly, his hand gripping one of the bars.

"Did you just address us?" he asked, his voice low and dangerous. His eyes gleamed in the dim light, filled with cruel delight.

My heart raced, but I refused to back down. "You heard me," I replied, forcing my voice to remain steady. "There's no honor in beating a defenseless man."

The guard chuckled, the sound chilling and hollow. "Honor? In this place?" he mused. "You must be truly deluded to think such a thing still exists here." He leaned in closer, his voice lowering to a venomous whisper. "Here, we are your masters. You are less than nothing—prey for us to break as we see fit."

The second guard joined him, both of them staring down at me with malicious intent. "Perhaps he wishes to experience the same lesson as his unfortunate companion."

I could feel the tension building, but I stood my ground. "I'd rather die with honor than live as your coward."

The guards exchanged glances before their smiles widened.

"As you wish," one of them said, his hand reaching for the latch on my cage.

The moment they unlocked the cage, the first blow struck my gut like a sledgehammer, driving the air from my lungs. I doubled over, gasping, but they didn't stop. A fist collided with my jaw, and stars burst behind my eyes. Staggering back, I was trapped—nowhere to run, no escape. The iron bars pressed into my back as they hammered me with punches and kicks from every direction.

Each strike felt like a blaze of pain, my ribs aching with every blow. I tried to shield my face, but their relentless assault made it impossible. My body felt like it was being ripped apart, every muscle screaming under the punishment. The metallic taste of blood filled my mouth as a kick sent me sprawling to the ground, gasping for breath.

"Filthy human," one of the guards spat, his boot driving into my side. "You think you can defy us? You're nothing here."

I collapsed, struggling to breathe. Another kick landed square on my back, sending shockwaves of agony down my spine. Their laughter echoed around me, mingling with the sickening thud of their fists and boots. My vision blurred, and every fiber of my being wanted to scream, but I held it back. I wouldn't give them the satisfaction.

"Enough!" A new voice cut through the brutality, cold and commanding.

I lifted my head, barely able to see through the haze of pain. A figure approached, her small frame a stark contrast to the towering guards. Yet, the moment she spoke, they fell silent, their respect—no, their fear—of her palpable. She was dressed like them, but her aura screamed authority.

"Chief," they murmured in unison, bowing their heads.

I was taken aback. This woman, slight in build with her jet-black hair pulled into a long, intricate braid, held sway over them? Despite her delicate appearance, her striking red eyes glowed with an intensity that sent a chill through me. The furry ears atop her head twitched slightly, adding to her unnerving presence.

She surveyed the scene with icy disdain, her gaze lingering on me before turning to the guards. "Have you forgotten your orders?" Her voice, though calm, carried an edge sharp enough to cut stone. "The queen instructed you to guard this one, not beat him senseless. You overstep your bounds."

The guards shifted uncomfortably, shame creeping into their expressions. "We were simply—" one began, but she silenced him with a withering glare.

"You were indulging yourselves at the cost of your duty," she snapped, her voice sharp. "You serve the queen. You are bound to carry out her orders to the letter, or you shall answer directly to me."

The guard who had spoken opened his mouth again, but before he could finish, the female guard moved. She grabbed his hand and, with a harsh crunch, crushed it in her grip. His scream filled the cavern, raw and desperate. The other guard took a step back, his face pale, eyes wide with fear.

She let go of the mangled hand, watching dispassionately as the guard crumpled to the ground, cradling his injury. "Return to your posts," she ordered coldly, "and remember your place. Do not make me repeat myself."

They scrambled to obey, the injured guard barely able to stand as he clutched his shattered hand to his chest. The two of them hurried out, their footsteps echoing in the now silent cavern.

"Thank...you," I croaked, my voice barely above a whisper.

She turned to me, her eyes filled with contempt. Without a

word, she spat on the ground at my feet before locking my cage again. She then turned sharply and followed the others up the stairs.

I lay there for a moment, my body throbbing with pain, my ribs protesting with every shallow breath. Slowly, painfully, I managed to sit up, resting my back against the cold iron bars of the cage. I could taste blood on my lips, and each movement sent fresh ripples of agony through my limbs.

A hollow chuckle escaped my lips, though it was quickly stifled by the sharp pain in my chest. "They hate us," I muttered to myself, wincing as I shifted. "Hate me. Hate all of us."

These people—no, these creatures—were different. They weren't human, or at least they didn't consider themselves as such. From the moment I had arrived, their disdain for me had been palpable. Their sneers, the way they spoke with such venom—this was more than mere contempt. It was loathing. Pure, unbridled hatred for who I was.

These people—if they even could be called that—weren't like us. The guards, the queen, Brute, and everyone I had encountered so far didn't see themselves as our equals. I was in their domain now, a world where their rules reigned, and they showed no mercy to those who didn't belong.

Where was I? They looked human enough, save for the ears and the faint red glow in their eyes, but it was clear they wanted to set themselves apart from us. The malice in their voices, the way they looked at me like I was less than nothing, was more than simple contempt—it was pure hatred. They loathed me, loathed all of us in these cages simply because we were human.

But why? What had we ever done to deserve such treatment? It didn't make sense, but I was beginning to understand that it didn't have to. They hated us not for our actions, but for our very existence. To them, I was something to be discarded after serving my purpose. Whatever that purpose may be.

Then something clicked—the female guard's words echoed in my mind. *I was meant to be guarded, not beaten.* But she hadn't said the same for the old man they had attacked earlier. Why was I different? Why had she intervened? What did the queen want with me? Whatever it was, it couldn't be good.

I had no answers, only more questions. And to top it all off, I was no closer to finding Celine. My heart twisted in my chest as I thought of her. I scanned the cages around me, desperate to see her face, but all I saw were strangers. Each face I passed was gaunt, bruised, and hopeless. Celine wasn't here—not anywhere I could see.

Relief and dread swept over me simultaneously. Maybe she had escaped capture, but if she were here, I had no doubt she'd be in worse shape than I was now. She wouldn't have stayed silent. Celine had never been one to hold her tongue, and in a place like this, that could get her killed. My pain seemed insignificant compared to the thought of her suffering. I had to get out of here—for her sake as much as mine.

The oppressive darkness of the cavern seemed to press in around me as I lay back against the cold, unyielding stone floor. Despite the pain coursing through my body, exhaustion overtook me, and I drifted into an uneasy sleep.

In my dreams, the cavern vanished, replaced by a dense forest shrouded in twilight. The trees stood tall and skeletal, their twisted branches creating an almost suffocating canopy above. A low mist hugged the forest floor, and the air was thick with the smell of damp earth and decay. Despite the creepy atmosphere, there was something familiar about this place.

Ahead, a figure moved through the trees—Celine. Her silhouette was barely visible through the mist, but her presence was undeniable. She turned to face me, and even from a distance,

I could see the urgency in her eyes. I tried to call out, but my voice was gone, swallowed by the silence of the forest. Her eyes pleaded with me, desperate, as if she was trying to warn me of something.

I ran towards her, but as I did, the forest began to twist and shift around me. The mist thickened, swallowing Celine, and I suddenly found myself surrounded by a pack of wolves. Their eyes gleamed in the darkness, fixed on me with uneasy glares. They circled me, silent, their movements graceful yet menacing.

I braced myself for their attack, but when they opened their mouths to snarl, no sound came out. It was as if the world had been stripped of all noise, leaving only the visual threat of their snapping jaws.

Suddenly, one lunged at me, and just as its fangs were about to sink into my flesh, I woke with a jolt. Gasping for breath, I found myself back in the cold, harsh reality of the cave. The unsettling weight of the dream lingered in my chest, even as I tried to shake it off.

Footsteps echoed from the stairway leading into the cavern. I looked up to see the female guard from earlier descending once again. This time, she carried something with her—my sword and what appeared to be a bundle of fur. The blade gleamed faintly in the dim light as she approached my cage.

I sat up as quickly as I could and balled my hands up into a fist. I was weak and beaten, but I wouldn't go down without a fight.

She knelt beside the bars, her eyes no longer cold and detached but softer, almost curious. "You are the one they refer to as 'Drifted,' are you not?" Her voice was surprisingly gentle, catching me off guard.

*Drifted?* The word echoed in my mind. That's how Celine

referred to me, but how did this guard know? And why was she using it now?

I nodded cautiously, unsure of what to make of her sudden change in demeanor. I expected the cruelty that had become commonplace here, but instead, she surprised me. Her expression softened even more, showing something I hadn't seen before—kindness.

"I apologize for the mistreatment you've endured," she said, her voice calm and measured. "Such actions were not meant for one like you, or anyone else down here."

I blinked, trying to process what was happening. Was this a trick? A game? Why the sudden shift from hostility to...this? My mind struggled to keep up.

Before I could question her further, she pulled out a small vial from a pouch at her side and held it out toward me. "Take this," she said. "It will help your wounds heal faster."

I hesitated, staring at the vial in her hand. Nothing about this made sense. Only moments ago, she had spat on the ground in disgust. Now, she was offering me something to heal? My confusion deepened, but so did my curiosity.

I glanced up at the guard, searching for any sign of malice or deceit, but her expression remained surprisingly soft. Could she truly be trying to help me?

"What is it?" I asked, hesitant as I eyed the strange liquid inside the vial.

"It is a remedy passed down through our people for generations," she replied in a calm, steady voice. "It will ease your pain."

I hesitated, still suspicious. But something in her tone— perhaps the quiet authority with which she spoke—made me want to believe her. Besides, I wasn't in any condition to refuse help. The beating I took had left me battered and desperate. With a trembling hand, I accepted the vial, staring at the strange, dark green liquid. It was thick and unappealing, the muddy color doing little to comfort me. One last glance at her revealed nothing more—her face unreadable, calm.

Taking a deep breath, I tipped the vial to my lips and took a cautious sip. The taste hit me immediately—bitter, sharp, and unpleasant, but I forced myself to swallow it. Almost instantly, a warmth began to spread through my body, a tingling sensation running along my skin. My muscles, once locked in painful tension, started to relax. The throbbing in my ribs, my jaw, and every bruise dulled to a faint ache.

It felt like magic—like a rush of energy knitting my wounds together from within. The pain that had gripped my body loosened its hold. I could breathe easier, my chest no longer burning with each shallow inhale. The relief, sudden and almost miraculous, was a shock in itself.

I lowered the empty vial, wiping the last of the liquid from my lips. I was speechless for a moment, my body still tingling as the warmth settled. The pain had been replaced with a strange calmness, like I had been reset. The exhaustion was still there, lingering at the edges, but the sharp agony was gone.

The guard's eyes remained on me, watching intently as if studying my reaction. "Better?" she asked, her voice carrying the same gentle calm.

I nodded slowly, still trying to comprehend what had just happened. "What... what is this?" My voice came out stronger, no longer a weak rasp.

She tilted her head slightly, considering her words. "It's an elixir. Our kind has used it for as long as I can remember. It heals, but not without a cost."

"A cost?" I repeated, my sense of relief quickly tempered by concern. "What kind of cost?"

Her gaze flickered briefly as if deciding whether to share more. "The healing it offers comes at a price. It forces your body to repair itself at an unnatural pace, and in doing so, it burns through your life force. Each time you use it, you lose a piece of your future."

I stared at her, feeling the weight of her words settle in my chest. The warmth from the elixir now seemed tainted with something darker. "How much of my life did I just lose?"

She shook her head. "It's impossible to say. It varies for everyone, depending on their strength, their will. But know this—every use brings you closer to your end."

A chill ran down my spine as the reality of her words sank in. I had needed the elixir, but the thought of trading pieces of my future to survive left a bitter taste in my mouth. Still, I knew I hadn't had much choice. The pain had been too much, and I might not have survived without it.

"It was necessary," I said, though it was as much to convince myself as to seek her confirmation.

The guard nodded solemnly. "Yes. And be grateful for the strength it's given you—for what lies ahead."

I shifted the conversation, my mind now racing to the many unanswered questions I had. "Who are you? What's going on here? And what are your people?"

She shook her head, cutting off my questions. "There's no time for that now." She glanced over her shoulder as if sensing she was running out of time. "The one you seek... she's here. In the queen's hold."

My heart skipped a beat. "Celine?" I asked, my voice barely a whisper.

The guard nodded, confirming what I had suspected. "Yes."

A surge of adrenaline coursed through me. Celine was here. After all the doubts and all the uncertainty, she was within reach. "Where is she? How do I get to her?"

The guard hurriedly reached into her cloak, pulling out a small, weathered key. "Listen closely," she said, her tone urgent. "Follow the path to the left when you leave this chamber. It will take you through the lower tunnels. Stay low, avoid the guards. They are not like me, and they will not hesitate to kill you."

She moved swiftly, unlocking my cage. The door creaked open, and I stumbled out, my legs still shaky but recovering. Before I could thank her, she pressed my sword and a cloak into my hands. The weight of the blade was reassuring, grounding me amidst the chaos.

"The sword is obvious," she continued, "but the cloak—wear it. It will help conceal your scent."

I blinked, confused. Conceal my scent? Did they track people by smell? I didn't question her, though. There was no time for doubt. I donned the cloak, feeling its heavy fabric settle over me. Whatever strange powers these people possessed, I needed every advantage I could get.

"Why are you helping me?" I asked, unable to hold back my curiosity.

She paused for a moment, her gaze meeting mine. There was something in her eyes, a depth of emotion she wasn't willing to share. "I've done what I can. Now, it's up to you."

Without another word, she turned and disappeared back up the stairs. I stared after her, uncertain of what to make of it all. But there was no time to linger. I wrapped the cloak tightly around myself and gripped my sword. The path ahead was clear—I had to move fast.

Ascending the stairs, I emerged into a narrow corridor dimly lit by flickering torches. The air was damp, carrying a faint musty odor that clung to the stone walls. It was eerily quiet, the silence broken only by the soft crackle of flames. Dark tapestries adorned the walls, their faded colors telling tales of a world I didn't understand—symbols and figures that seemed almost alive in the torchlight.

I moved cautiously, each step feeling heavier as I followed the guard's directions. *Stay low, avoid the guards.* The words echoed in my mind, a warning I couldn't afford to forget. My breath was shallow, my heart pounding in my chest as I pressed myself against the cold stone, trying to stay as invisible as possible.

The path twisted ahead, veering into darker stretches where the light barely reached. My pulse quickened as I passed a series of iron-barred cells. The faint sound of whispers reached my ears—desperate, unintelligible murmurs. My throat tightened. I couldn't tell if they were real voices or figments of my anxiety.

As I crept through the tunnel, I paused at the slightest echo of footsteps, ducking behind a thick pillar as two armored figures marched past. Their footfalls were heavy, their armor clinking ominously in the stillness. My body was tense, every muscle coiled, ready to spring if they noticed me. But they didn't. I let out a shaky breath, the tension in my chest easing slightly.

I rounded a corner and spotted a heavy wooden door, intricately carved, just like the one where the queen had sat. My pulse quickened. This must have been it—the final barrier between me and Celine.

With my hand resting on the door, I forced myself to focus. I needed to be ready for anything on the other side. Every muscle in my body tensed as I ran through different scenarios—combat, an ambush, or something worse. I gripped the hilt of my sword, drawing strength from it.

"Enter, boy!" A voice echoed from the other side, sharp and commanding.

CHAPTER 20

As I stepped into the chamber, the heavy door closed behind me, seemingly of its own will. The walls, carved with symbols and adorned with glistening stones, shimmered in the dim light, almost like they were alive, breathing with the pulse of the queen's power. It was disorienting, as though the space itself wanted to unsettle me.

The queen sat in the center of the vast room, her posture regal and unmoving upon a stone throne that seemed to be carved out of the very mountain itself. Above her loomed the same massive stained-glass window I saw from outside the cave. It depicted two wolves—one as white as snow, the other as dark as night—locked in a silent stare. The window cast a multicolored glow over the queen, bathing her in an ethereal light that only heightened her air of authority.

But my eyes were drawn not to the queen, but to the figure slumped at her side—Celine. She was chained, her head bowed, unconscious. Heavy iron shackles bound her wrists, and my heart clenched at the sight of her so vulnerable, so unlike the fierce, resilient woman I knew. The anger that surged through me was immediate and hot, like a flame igniting in my chest.

"Celine!" I shouted, my voice cracking, echoing through the chamber.

I took a step forward, but before I could move further, the queen's voice sliced through the air like a blade.

"Silence!" she commanded, her tone sharp and imperious. "How dare you raise your voice in my presence, boy?"

Her words hit me like a slap, cold and biting. I stopped, my senses screaming, but I refused to let her intimidate me. Not now. My eyes stayed locked on Celine, my pulse hammering in my ears.

Swallowing hard, I steadied myself. "What have you done to her?" I demanded, my voice shaking with both anger and fear. "Why is she like this? Answer me!"

The queen's expression twisted into one of disdain, her lips curling slightly as she regarded me like one would an insect. "You dare question me?" she hissed, her eyes narrowing. "You think you have the right to address me with such impudence?"

I balled my hands into fists, the anger threatening to boil over. "I'm not here to bow to you or anyone else," I shot back. "I'm here for Celine. What have you done to her?"

The queen's eyes flared with a cold fire, and she rose slowly from her throne, her movements precise, calculated. "You insignificant human!" she began, her voice laced with venom. "You come here, into my domain, making demands? You, who are not even worthy to stand in my shadow?"

With each word, the temperature in the room seemed to drop. As she stepped down from her throne, she untied her long, silver hair, pulling it back into a tight, controlled bun. Her regal robes fell away, revealing a sleek, battle-hardened figure beneath. The outfit she wore clung to her slim, muscular form, made from a dark, leather-like material that appeared both flexible and durable. Intricate patterns, sharp and jagged, were woven into the hide, similar to the designs etched into the walls and weapons of this place.

Every detail of her attire screamed authority and power. It was clear now: she wasn't just a ruler; she was a warrior.

"I will waste no more breath on your foolishness," she said, her voice low and dangerous. "You would do well to ready your sword. You've come here seeking a fight, and a fight you shall have."

For a moment, I hesitated. The weight of my sword felt heavier than ever, my fingers trembling slightly as they hovered over the hilt. Could I really take on someone like her? My mind raced, doubt clawing at the edges of my resolve. But my eyes drifted to Celine again; her body slumped in chains, and I felt a renewed feeling of determination. I had come too far to back down now.

The queen's cold gaze never dropped as she drew closer, her movements smooth and unhurried, as though she already knew the outcome of this confrontation. "You are nothing," she continued, "but a lost child fumbling in the dark. Your bravery means nothing here."

I swallowed the fear building inside me and gripped the hilt of my sword, the leather of the handle pressing against my palm. My legs shook slightly beneath me, but I managed to stand firm, lifting my sword and pointing it at her. "I don't care what you think," I said, my voice low but resolute. "I'm not leaving without her."

The queen's grin widened, a slow, mocking smile that seemed to see straight through me. Her eyes flicked to the tip of my sword, and a low, cold laugh escaped her lips. "Your courage," she said, her tone dripping with disdain, "is tragically misplaced. You stand before me, trembling, yet you dare draw a blade. You truly don't understand your place in this world." She paused, her gaze sharpening. "But no matter. I shall teach you."

I barely had time to blink before she moved. One second, she stood still, observing me like a predator, and the next, she was right in front of me, closing the gap with a speed that seemed impossible. My heart lurched in my chest—how could someone move like that? There was no weapon in her hand, no blade to strike with, yet the force behind her movement made my blood run cold.

I raised my sword instinctively, but it was too late. She delivered an open-handed strike aimed squarely at my chest, and though I twisted at the last second, the rush of air as her hand missed me by inches sent a chill down my body. I stumbled back, desperately trying to regain my footing, but she was already moving again, her fists and feet a blur of motion.

Her fist came at me, fast and unrelenting. I ducked just in time, but the momentum of her strike grazed my shoulder, sending sharp pain radiating through my arm. I gritted my teeth and tried to counter with an upward slash, but she was too quick, too fluid. She danced away from the attack with the grace of someone who had fought a thousand battles, and my blade cut through nothing but air.

Her foot lashed out before I could react, catching me just above the knee and sending me stumbling. I could feel the strength draining from my legs, but I forced myself to stay upright. Her strikes came from every direction—fists, elbows, knees, and kicks—each one delivered with pinpoint accuracy. There was no pattern to her movements, no rhythm that I could follow. She was a storm of attacks, forcing me to twist, duck, and block, but no matter how hard I tried, I couldn't keep up.

I swung again, this time aiming for her midsection, but she effortlessly sidestepped the blow. My sword passed harmlessly by, and in an instant, her leg swept out, striking me just above the wrist. My grip on the sword faltered, pain shooting through my arm as the force of the kick almost knocked the weapon from my hand.

I tightened my hold, refusing to let go, even as her next strike came—an open palm slap aimed at my jaw. I jerked my head back just in time, her fingers grazing my chin. But before I could react, she spun on her heel, her leg whipping out in a graceful arc. I barely managed to block the kick with my arm, but the impact sent me reeling back, struggling to maintain my balance.

She was relentless. Every time I thought I had a moment to recover, she was already on me, her strikes coming faster and harder. I could feel my strength waning, my movements growing slower with each passing second. My sword, once an extension of myself, now felt heavy and unwieldy, like a burden I could barely carry. The queen's attacks were unforgiving, and I was quickly running out of options.

She delivered another lightning-fast strike, this time aiming for my ribs. I twisted to avoid it, but her fist grazed my side, sending a jolt of pain through my body. I staggered, my breathing ragged and uneven. I couldn't keep up with her, and she knew it. She was toying with me, waiting for the moment when I would collapse from exhaustion.

I swung once more, aiming for her shoulder, but she deflected it with ease with her bare hand. My eyes widened; how was this possible?

My eyes darted to her hand just as she shot out another punch. That's when I noticed— her nails weren't just long; they were sharp, almost like claws. She didn't deflect my blade with flesh; those claws must have been as hard as steel. I had no time to process reality before her hand shot out again, gripping my sword arm with an iron-like strength. Her claws dug into my flesh, twisting my arm at an unnatural angle.

With a savage pull, she yanked me forward, her knee slamming into my ribs with bone-shattering force. I gasped, the air leaving my lungs in a painful rush as I crumpled to the ground, coughing and trying to regain my breath. Every fiber of my body screamed in agony, but I forced myself to stand, knowing that if I stayed down, I was done for.

As I scrambled to my feet, she was already upon me, her fist colliding with my side. Pain radiated through my torso like wildfire. I swung my sword blindly, desperately, hoping to force her back even for a second. The blade cut through the air with a sharp hiss, but she was gone, darting around me with the grace and speed of an animal toying with its prey.

I tried to follow her movements, but she was too fast. Her hand jabbed toward my throat, and I barely managed to block the strike with the flat of my sword, the impact reverberating through my arm. Before I could recover, her other hand snapped out, striking my wrist with brutal precision. Pain exploded, and my grip faltered. My sword fell from my hand, clattering to the stone floor. In an instant, her knee slammed into my stomach once more.

I doubled over, gasping for air, the metallic taste of blood coating my tongue. But she gave me no time to recover. She grabbed me by the collar, yanking me upright as her fist crashed into my jaw with devastating force. My vision blurred as my head snapped back, the world spinning around me as I staggered, barely managing to stay on my feet.

The queen circled me like a wolf closing in on its meal, her eyes cold and predatory. Every move I made, every desperate attempt to fight back, was anticipated and countered effortlessly. I was outclassed in every way. She was faster, stronger, and far more skilled. A force of nature, an unstoppable storm. Sweat poured down my face, stinging my eyes as I struggled to focus.

But I couldn't give up. Not with Celine so close. I had come too far. I had to find a way—any way—to break through her defenses. If I could just land a single blow, something to turn the tide.

"You're faltering," the queen said, her voice filled with mockery. "Is this truly all you have to offer? The Drifted, they call you, yet here you are, shaking and broken. This is the one spoken of with such reverence?"

I tried to steady my breath, but each inhale was like fire in my lungs. "You... you can't stop me," I managed, though my voice was weak, barely more than a whisper. "I'll save her."

The queen's laugh was cold and cruel, echoing off the chamber walls. "Save her? You can barely stand, and yet you cling to these empty hopes. Do you really think you can challenge me? A mere human against a power beyond your understanding?"

Her words cut deep, each one reminding me of how outmatched I was. But I couldn't let her see me break. "I'll... find a way," I muttered, though even I could hear the hollowness in my voice.

"Bravado means nothing here," she sneered, her claws flashing as she lashed out, this time aiming for my chest. I reacted, shifting my body just enough to let her claws sink deep into my left shoulder. The pain was excruciating, searing through me like molten fire. But it was exactly what I needed.

As her claws dug into my flesh, I gritted my teeth against the pain and grabbed hold of her wrist with my free hand. Her eyes widened slightly in surprise, but I didn't give her a chance to react. With all the strength I could muster, I yanked her forward, using her momentum against her. Quickly, I drove my head forward, slamming it into her nose with all the force I could.

The queen staggered back, blood spraying as her hand flew up to clutch her nose in disbelief. For a brief moment, I saw something flicker across her regal features—surprise. But it quickly melted into pure, unbridled rage. Her eyes, once cold and calculating, now blazed with scarlet fury, lighting up the chamber with an otherworldly glow. Her once-pristine silver hair unraveled, falling wildly around her face.

"How dare you!" she roared, her voice booming through the

room like a violent storm. "A mere human, an insignificant, insolent subspecies, dares to lay a hand on me?" Her words dripped with venom, each one punctuated by her burning hatred. "You think yourself worthy of such defiance? You will pay for this insolence!"

I barely managed to keep my composure, the shock of the queen's reaction still rippling through me. But it wasn't just her words that shook me—it was what she said next.

"I will take immense pleasure in watching you suffer," she snarled, her voice lowering to a cruel whisper. "Just as your mother pleaded for her wretched life all those years ago."

My heart stopped. My mother? What did she mean? How could she know about my mother, let alone her death? Was she there? Was she responsible? Her words struck me like a blade to the chest, rattling me to my core. Anger surged through me, stronger than anything I'd felt before. If this queen had anything to do with my mother's fate, I needed answers. And I needed them now.

But before I could react, the queen's fury reached a fever pitch. She crouched down, and her body began to shift and contort in ways that defied human understanding. My breath caught in my throat as I watched her transformation unfold.

Her teeth elongated, transforming into vicious fangs that gleamed in the dim light. Her snout pushed forward, turning her once-human face into that of a monstrous beast. A tide of shimmering silver fur erupted across her skin, growing rapidly as her limbs expanded and stretched. Her regal garments tore and fell away, revealing a hulking figure covered in thick, silvery fur. Her hands—no longer hands, but powerful, clawed paws—grew in size as she dropped to all fours, her posture shifting from a queen to a predator.

It was a grotesque and awe-inspiring sight, watching her shift into a massive wolf. Her scarlet eyes, more intense now, locked onto me with a primal hunger that sent shivers down my spine. The transformation was complete, and standing before me was a towering wolf, a beast far more terrifying than the queen's human form could ever be.

For a moment, I stood frozen, my mind struggling to process the creature in front of me. The queen—now a wolf—was massive, her silver fur shimmering eerily under the faint light filtering through the chamber. Her eyes blazed with an animalistic fury, her low growl reverberating through the stone walls.

*Move, Isaac, move!* My instincts screamed at me, but my feet felt rooted to the ground. The wolf crouched, readying itself to strike. I could see the muscles in her powerful legs tense, preparing to lunge. My heart raced, every beat pounding in my ears as the world seemed to slow around me.

And then, she leaped.

The air was filled with the terrifying sound of her claws slicing through the space where I had just stood. I ducked, just barely evading the beast's lethal jaws. The force of her leap sent her crashing past me, her claws scraping the stone floor. I hit the ground hard, rolling to the side as the wolf circled back, her glowing red eyes never leaving mine.

I scrambled backward, desperately trying to create space between us, but I quickly found myself trapped. My back hit something solid, and I glanced over my shoulder to see the queen's stone throne towering above me. Just within arm's reach, Celine remained slumped in chains, unconscious and vulnerable.

I had to protect her. I couldn't fail now.

The wolf advanced, its low growl sending tremors through the ground. Each step brought the beast closer, its frame blocking out everything else in the chamber. There was nowhere left to run.

With a snarl, the wolf lunged at me once more. I barely had time to react, raising my left arm in a desperate attempt to block the attack. The wolf's jaws closed around my forearm, its fangs sinking deep into my flesh. A sharp, searing pain shot through my body as the beast's claws raked across my arm, shaking it violently.

Blood splattered everywhere, painting the stone floor beneath me in dark, crimson pools. Each savage tear of the wolf's teeth sent droplets flying—across the floor and even over the cold, unyielding throne behind me. The spray coated everything within reach, the violence of the attack seeping into every corner of the chamber. My vision blurred as the creature's relentless jaws tore into me, the wet sound of ripping flesh blending with the dull thuds of my own blood hitting the ground.

Strangely, at that moment, the pain began to feel distant, almost muted. Perhaps it was the shock, or perhaps my mind couldn't fully comprehend the terror of the situation. Either way, I found myself staring at the wolf, disbelieving, as its jaws tightened around my arm, teeth tearing through muscle and sinew.

In my head, a single thought echoed over and over: *I can't believe this is how it ends.*

I closed my eyes, bracing for the inevitable. The gnashing of teeth, the hot breath of the beast—it all became a blurred, distant reality. I prepared for the final blow, the moment when the world would fade away.

Suddenly, a loud rumbling noise echoed to my left, followed by a deep, ferocious snarl that cut through the haze of my fear. The pressure on my arm loosened, and with a low, pitiful whimper, the wolf began to retreat. My breath came in shallow, labored gasps as I slowly opened my eyes, not fully believing what was happening.

I forced myself to turn my head slowly to the left, every muscle screaming in protest. My vision swam, but through the blur, I could make out the outline of something massive, something powerful.

To my shock, another wolf—much larger than the one that had been tearing into me—stood next to me. Its fur was a striking orange-brown, and it exuded an overwhelming presence, one that demanded compliance. It stood between me and the queen, its eyes fixed solely on her, its ears pinned back in aggression. The queen, still in her wolf form, backed away slowly, her body language completely different now—subdued, almost fearful.

I could barely process the scene unfolding before me. The larger wolf ignored me entirely, its eyes burning as it stared at the queen. Step by step, it advanced, its body taut with tension, ready to strike.

The smaller wolf—the queen—let out a desperate growl, her ears flat against her skull. With a sudden burst of motion, she lunged at the larger wolf. But the attack was futile. The larger wolf responded with terrifying ease, swinging its massive head and sending the queen crashing into a stone wall. The impact reverberated through the chamber, the tapestries fluttering in the wake of the collision.

I stared in stunned silence as the queen's form began to change, her wolfish features receding. Fur melted away, her snout shrank, and soon enough, the monstrous wolf was gone, replaced by the human queen, crumpled on the floor. She lay there gasping, her once regal composure shattered.

The large orange-brown wolf watched her for a moment before slowly turning to me. It padded over to where my sword had fallen, its piercing eyes never leaving me.

The wolf barked, a sharp, insistent sound that pulled me out of my daze. I blinked, unsure of what it was trying to communicate. The wolf barked again, this time glancing between me and the sword. I finally understood—it wanted me to retrieve it.

With great effort, I forced myself to move. Pain flared through my body, but I pushed it aside, focusing on the task at hand. I crawled toward the sword, my good hand grasping the hilt. The wolf kept its gaze locked on the queen, letting out a low, threatening growl as I rose to my feet, sword in hand.

The moment I stood, the wolf barked again, tilting its head toward the queen, who was now coughing and struggling to regain her bearings. The message was clear: finish this.

Confusion still swirled in my mind. Why was this wolf helping me? What did it want? But there was no time to question it. The queen was vulnerable, and the wolf was giving me a chance. My legs trembled as I approached her, my sword drawn, the weight of everything that had happened pressing down on me.

The queen glared at me, even now, lying helpless at my feet. Her eyes were filled with contempt, and her lips twisted into a mocking sneer.

"So," she rasped, "you think this makes you more than a filthy human? Do you believe your actions here will make you my equal? Pathetic." She spat the word, her voice dripping with scorn. "You are nothing compared to me."

I tightened my grip on my sword, forcing down the anger rising in my chest. "Who are you?" I demanded, my voice hoarse. "Why do you, and everyone else here, hate me so much? What have I ever done to you?"

The queen let out a weak, bitter laugh. "You poor, ignorant boy. You truly know nothing, do you?" She coughed, blood trickling from the corner of her mouth, yet she still managed to chuckle. "You're nothing but a pawn, led around by those stronger and smarter than you. And yet, here you are, demanding answers."

My jaw clenched as I stared down at her. "What was your plan for me? Why did Brute—Remus—bring me here? What was all of this for?"

Her response was a chilling, mirthless laugh. "Plan? You think you're so important, there was a grand design for you? No, you were nothing but a tool. Remus brought you here because I commanded it. There's no deeper meaning beyond that, nothing for you to unravel."

The queen tried to stand, but her body gave out, and she slumped back down, gasping. "I should've killed you the moment you set foot in my town. But no, I wanted to see you squirm. And here you are, barking questions like a righteous hero. You're no hero. You're a pathetic little boy—worthless, just as your mother was. You humans will never be more than stains on this world."

Her words cut deep, especially at the mention of my mother.

"What do you know about my mother?" I shouted, my voice shaking with anger.

The queen's laugh came again, brittle and venomous. "Your mother, Alara? A foolish, trifling woman who thought she could exist among us. She was weak, a pitiful creature who begged for her life like a coward."

Every insult was a dagger to my chest. "She was nothing more than a desperate whore! Her death was a mercy, one she didn't deserve."

My rage flared, a hot, burning sensation rising in my chest. I gripped my sword tighter, my knuckles white with fury.

"You should've seen her face," the queen continued, relishing every word. "She begged, wept for her life—just like you will—"

I couldn't take it anymore. With a roar, I swung my sword, silencing her mid-sentence as the blade slashed through her throat. Her eyes went wide in shock, her voice dying in a gurgle as she choked on her own blood. She staggered, hands clawing at her neck, but it was over. The queen collapsed, the life draining from her body as she crumpled to the floor.

I stood there, frozen, staring at her lifeless form. My hand was still clenched around the sword, and a cold chill crept over me as I realized what I'd done. The anger that had driven me moments ago evaporated, leaving behind only a hollow emptiness. I'd killed her—not a fiend, but a living being.

This wasn't how it was supposed to end. I had come here to save Celine, not to murder someone in cold blood. The queen's taunting face, the blood pooling around her, it all blurred together in my mind. I had wanted her to pay for what she said about my mother, but now that it was done, all I felt was guilt.

But then, there was the rage—the fire that had consumed me the moment she spat those words about my mother. The way she twisted the knife, brought up her death as if it were some insignificant thing. How could I just stand there and let that go? My mother. Her memory. The life she was robbed of.

And Celine... I had to save her, had to get her back. The queen had taken her from me, taunted me with her captivity, and treated me like I was nothing but a tool to be discarded. Her insults still stung—calling me weak, saying I was worthless, comparing me to my mother as if we both didn't matter.

A nudge at my side snapped me out of my spiraling thoughts. The large wolf had approached me, its head gently pushing against my arm as if sensing my turmoil. I turned to look at it, meeting its steady gaze. There was something in those eyes— understanding, maybe even comfort.

I glanced back at the queen's body, then at the wolf. The

shock still buzzed in my veins, but the wolf's presence grounded me. I couldn't lose myself in this moment, not now. There was still so much I didn't understand. And Celine—she was still chained beside the queen's throne.

Except, when I turned back toward where Celine had been, my heart skipped a beat. She was gone. Only broken chains lay where she had been bound.

Panic clawed at my chest as I scanned the room frantically. "Celine?" I called, my voice shaky, desperate. But there was no response. Only the echo of my own voice bouncing off the walls.

I felt sick. How had she vanished? What had happened while I was distracted by the queen?

The wolf nudged me again, more insistently this time. I turned to face it, and then something caught my attention. The wolf's eyes—they weren't just any eyes. They were deep, striking purple. Nostalgic. Hauntingly so.

My breath caught in my throat. Those eyes—they were Celine's.

My mind raced, trying to make sense of what I was seeing. Could this wolf... be Celine? How could she have transformed? Was this some dark magic of the queen's, or had something else happened?

The wolf—Celine—held my gaze, the recognition clear in her eyes. The panic that had been gripping me faded, replaced by a whirlwind of emotions—relief, confusion, fear. It was overwhelming, but there was no mistaking it. Celine was right here.

I swallowed hard, feeling foolish for what I was about to say. "Celine?" I asked, my voice barely more than a whisper.

She nudged me again as if to confirm my suspicions. Even though everything felt surreal, the sight of her gave me something to hold on to.

Suddenly, the doors to the chamber burst open with a deafening crash. I spun around to see guards flooding into the room, their eyes wide with shock as they took in the scene before them. One shouted, "The queen is dead! They've killed the queen!"

Tension crackled in the air. We were far from safe. The guards, initially human, began to shift, their bodies contorting and expanding into large, snarling wolves. Their growls filled the room, bloodlust burning in their eyes.

Before I could react, Celine moved. She grabbed me by the cloak and effortlessly tossed me onto her back. I barely had time to grip her fur before she let out a powerful, resonant howl that shook the chamber's very walls.

The guards froze, their growls faltering as they recoiled in fear. Celine's howl had sent a ripple of dominance through the room, forcing them to take a step back. It was only a brief moment, but it was all she needed.

Without hesitation, Celine turned and leaped forward, propelling us toward the massive stained-glass window above the queen's throne. I barely had time to brace myself as we crashed through the glass, shards exploding around us.

The wind howled as we soared through the shattered window, weightless for a brief, heart-stopping moment. Then gravity took hold, and we began to plummet. My heart raced as I clung tightly to Celine's fur, trusting her as we fell toward the town below.

I sit here now, the crackling of the fire offering the only warmth in this cave as the night closes in from all sides. It's quiet, save for the occasional pop of burning wood and the whisper of the wind outside. The stars are hidden tonight by thick clouds, but I don't need their light to reflect on these memories. The events of those days are etched into my mind—clearer than the flickering embers before me.

It hadn't been long after we crashed through that window that we found ourselves outside the town's walls. The distant sounds of pursuit had gradually faded into the background, swallowed by the trees. The town itself had long disappeared into the shadowy landscape. But none of that mattered. What mattered was that we had made it out—though I should say, she had.

I still don't know how far we ran, how many miles we'd crossed—my mind had been spinning, consumed by the chaos that erupted back in the queen's chamber. But somewhere along the way, after traversing rocky paths and crossing streams that cut through the land, Celine collapsed. It wasn't abrupt, but it felt like the weight of everything had caught up to her all at once. One moment, she was the tireless, powerful wolf carrying me through the wilderness; the next, she was simply...herself.

She lay there, still and silent, her transformation back into human form complete. My heart lurched in panic. "Celine?" I knelt beside her, my hands shaking her gently. She didn't stir.

"Celine, wake up!" I pleaded, my voice more desperate this time.

But there was nothing.

It wasn't until I reached for her that I noticed—she felt different, more fragile. The familiarity of her slender limbs and face returned to me, bringing with it a rush of understanding. The cloak she always wore, the one she pulled up even on the warmest days… she had been hiding this. Her ears—the same ones I'd seen on the townspeople in the Madlands. The same ears that had belonged to those who chased us out of the town where she was held captive.

But now there was something more, something different about her. I quickly glanced away, feeling the night air grow even colder. Whatever magic had transformed her, whatever allowed her to shift between human and wolf, had left her vulnerable. And here I stood, bathed in the moonlight, struggling not to dwell on what it all meant.

I gently draped my cloak over her, shielding her from the chill that crept deeper with each passing moment. I stood there, unsure of what to do next. The wind howled through the mountain passes, its biting cold cutting through my clothes. It carried with it distant calls—creatures I couldn't see, but I knew they were out there, searching. We wouldn't survive long exposed like this.

There wasn't much time. I had to find shelter, somewhere safe for us both. Celine remained unconscious, her breathing shallow but steady. She was still with me, but as the days slipped by without her waking, a sense of dread grew inside me. Every step I took was heavier than the last, and every distant sound kept my nerves on edge. Wolves, sometimes footsteps, echoed through the trees, and I would press us against the jagged rocks, praying we wouldn't be discovered.

I carried her through the mountain passes, my muscles screaming with the strain, but I didn't stop. I couldn't. I wouldn't leave her behind—not after everything we had been through. Exhaustion clung to me like a weight I couldn't shake, but still,

I pushed forward. Each night, I'd check her breath, feeling the gentle rise and fall of her chest, just to make sure she was still with me. It was the only thing that kept me moving. As long as Celine was alive, I couldn't give up.

Eventually, I stumbled upon this cave, hidden away from prying eyes. It wasn't much, but it provided shelter. I managed to start a small fire, the flames flickering softly, offering just enough warmth to fight off the cold. And now, here we are—alone, with only the crackle of the fire and the wind outside for company.

I glance over at her now, lying beside the fire, my cloak still draped over her fragile form. Her face is peaceful in the dim light, giving me a rare moment of relief. It's strange, this stillness—after everything we've been through, the chaos, the fear—now, for the first time in what feels like forever, there's calm. A brief chance to breathe. But even in this quiet, the weight of it all presses down on me, heavy and relentless. I don't know what comes next, whether we'll ever truly escape what's chasing us. But right now, at least, we have this. We have each other.

My arm throbbed, serving as a reminder of the queen's savage attack. I'd bandaged it as best I could after the battle, wrapping it tightly to stop the bleeding, but the deep gashes had yet to heal, and the pain pulsed with every beat of my heart. I flexed my fingers experimentally—still stiff, but at least I could move them.

I reach for another handful of wood, intending to stoke the fire, when a soft sound makes me freeze. It's faint but unmistakable—Celine's voice, breaking through the stillness like a whisper from a distant dream.

"Drifted…"

The wood slips from my hand as I turn toward her, my heart pounding in disbelief. She's awake—after all this time, she's finally awake. Her deep purple eyes are open, staring at the cave's ceiling with a faraway look, as if she's been someplace else, someplace I couldn't follow.

"I understand now… why we must head north," she murmurs, her voice soft but filled with a clarity that hadn't been there before.

Her gaze drifts toward mine, and I see it—recognition, the flicker of the old Celine, her resolve shining through once more.

"We must go see my father."


END OF BOOK ONE

# AUTHOR NOTE

Dear Reader,

Thank you for joining me on this journey through Drifted. Writing this book has been an incredible experience—equal parts challenging and rewarding. What started as a seed of an idea grew into a story that's now in your hands, and I couldn't be more grateful that you've taken the time to read it.

The process of writing Drifted was far from smooth. There were late nights, rewrites, and moments when I questioned whether I could bring this world to life the way I envisioned. But every step of the way, I kept imagining someone like you—someone who loves stories, who gets lost in them like I do. That thought kept me going.

If you enjoyed Lupine, I'd be honored if you left a review on Amazon. Reviews are so much more than just feedback, they are a lifeline for authors like me. They help other readers discover the book, and they let me know what captured you. I read every single one, and I cherish the thought that my story might have left an impression on someone else.

Whether you choose to leave a review or not, I want you to know how much it means to me that you've spent time in the crazy world I crafted.

Thank you from the bottom of my heart, and I hope you'll join me for the next chapter of this journey in the sequel.

With gratitude,
Renton Wolfe.

# ABOUT THE AUTHOR

Renton Wolfe, a new and passionate voice in fantasy fiction, was born in Bronx, New York, and raised in Columbus, Ohio. Balancing the demands of work and family, Renton found solace and inspiration in quiet moments, using every spare second to craft his debut novel, Drifted.
What began as a personal passion project soon grew into a full-fledged journey of storytelling, fueled by a love for immersive worlds and complex characters. His dedication to bringing this story to life is a testament to the belief that, no matter how busy life gets, there's always room to pursue your passion.

Follow and keep in touch with me and Isaac's journey on the socials below:
X/Twitter: @rentonwolfe
Tiktok: @rentonwolfe
Instagram: @rentonwolfe

9 798999 183620 3